Praise for *The Book of Someday*

"Absolutely mesmerizing! Dianne Dixon's *The Book of Someday* is packed with vivid storytelling and palpable emotion. This novel made me think of all the 'somedays' in my own life—the ones I dreamed about as a child, and the ones I've yet to add to my list."

—Sarah Jio, *New York Times* bestselling author of *Blackberry Winter*

"In *The Book of Someday*, Dianne Dixon creates a spellbinding landscape, dictated by the haunted memories of a brilliant little girl. Dixon's writing is both lush and restrained; she has a great gift for creating complex, absorbing characters. This is an exciting new writer, capable of creating a well-paced, emotional page-turner of the best kind."

—Katie Crouch, *New York Times* bestselling author of *Girls in Trucks* and *The Magnolia League*

"I truly enjoyed this...Dianne's writing flows through the pages, choosing perfect words to tie the emotions together."

—Annie Philbrick, Bank Square Books, Mystic, CT

"Dianne Dixon's characters are secretive and flawed but warm and loving, and have much to teach us. Highly recommended."

—Karen Briggs, Great Northern Books & Hobbies, Oscoda, MI

"A mesmerizing book that will keep you up all night."

—Beth Carpenter, The Country Bookshop, Southern Pines, NC

The
Book of Someday

A NOVEL

Dianne Dixon

Published by Sourcebooks Landmark, an imprint of Sourcebooks, Inc.
P.O. Box 4410, Naperville, Illinois 60567-4410
(630) 961-3900
Fax: (630) 961-2168
www.sourcebooks.com

Library of Congress Cataloging-in-Publication Data

Dixon, Dianne.
   The book of someday / Dianne Dixon.
      pages cm
      (hardcover : alk. paper) 1. Dreams—Fiction. 2. Self-realization—Fiction. 3. Secrets—Fiction. 4. Psychological fiction. I. Title.
   PS3604.I943B66 2013
   813'.6—dc23
                            2013017019

Printed and bound in the United States of America.
MA 10 9 8 7 6 5 4 3 2 1

For Hank & Denise.
With love.

Traveller there is no road,
the way is made by walking.

—Antonio Machado

Prologue...Olivia

HER FATHER. SHOUTING HER NAME. "OLIVIA!" HIS FOOTSTEPS falling loud and heavy on the wood of the floor.

Olivia. The soles of her feet pressed hard against the same wood floor. Feeling the vibration of his every step. As he's circling, gaining momentum, coming closer to the place where she's hiding. Fierce jolts rippling through her. Edged on one side with terror, on the other with hope.

The air in the living room, the air throughout the house, is cold. Stale with the wintry funk of blankets in need of a good washing. Sour with the odor of boiled cabbage. Musty with the papery scent of books. Books piled onto windowsills, sagging on shelves, stacked in cluttered doorways.

It is because Olivia is only nine years old, thin and small for her age, that she is fitting so neatly into this cramped space. Stuffed in like a cork in a bottle. Knees drawn up, arms wrapped tight around them, spine jammed flat against a few inches of living room wall. One elbow pushing into the cracked leather of an old armchair, the other pinned against the side of a wooden cabinet. The cabinet door—open. Pulled flush against the front of the armchair to create the fourth wall of her hiding place. Suffocatingly close. Fogged with her breath.

Again. Her father's roaring shout: "Olivia!" This time not quite as near. And with a different quality. Something wild, slightly unhinged. And in the tender place at Olivia's core, where fear is wedged against hope, there is the sensation of fire and snakes. And knives.

The chill from the wall at Olivia's back is agonizing, shaking her with cold. She lowers her head—letting her hair fall across her arms and shoulders. Her hair, honey-blond, has never been cut. It's extraordinarily long and thick. As it settles around her, Olivia feels its weight but no warmth. She whispers a single, angry word: "Stupid!" Last night she put a quilted bathrobe, and mittens, and her fleece-lined slippers at the foot of her bed. Then this morning, only minutes ago at first light, when she was running out of her room, she forgot them. She has come away unprotected, wearing only her nightgown.

Olivia's shivering is making her teeth chatter. She's worried about the noise. She bites down—trying to quiet it. And for a split second...absolute stillness. Then a flash of light. A thundering BANG. Searing pain. Her father's fingers twisting deep into her hair. Knotting it into a handle, lifting her off the ground. Olivia is coming away from the floor with her knees to her chest, her arms still tightly wrapped around them.

She is momentarily airborne. Then she's landing on her back, on the sofa. With the wind knocked out of her. Just for an instant something strange: as if time has stopped. Her father. Making a tiny hushed sound that sounds like, "Sorry." The look in her father is bordering on terror. Then it's gone. The look—and the terror. And he's screaming: "What the hell? What the bloody hell?"

Calista. With her ink-black eyes and soap-white face. Rushing into the room, wailing: "How could you do such a hurtful thing?

Knowing we'd be getting out of bed with the house quiet like death, and you nowhere to be found. Your poor father calling for you, and you not answering. Like you'd been taken or something!"

Olivia. Being dragged to her feet. By her father, gasping, gulping. As pale as paste except for the skin right above his cheekbones, which is blotchy red. "What the hell's wrong with you? What in God's name did you think you were doing?" The darkness in his eyes obliterating Olivia's hope, leaving only her fear. She's trying to make herself hold still but can't. She's shaking too hard. With the fear. And the cold. She's barely able to breathe as she's telling him: "I wanted to know…would you miss me if I was gone?"

But it's not her father who's swooping toward her, it's Calista. Calista in her rumpled gray nightgown, wafting the smell of sleep-musk and sweat, saying: "Have you lost your mind? What kind of child even thinks of tormenting her parents with such a wicked prank?"

There is the sting of a slap on Olivia's face as she answers: "You're not my parent."

"And for that," Calista mutters, "I thank the Lord."

Olivia only half-hears what Calista has said. Olivia's focus is on her father, even though she's trembling with the cold. Even though her eyes are watering from it. And she can barely see him. Even though she's in terrible pain because he lifted her up by her hair and let her full weight dangle from her scalp, she cannot move away.

Olivia, too young to comprehend the concept of impossibility, remains at her father's side. Trembling in her faded nightgown, gazing up at him. Longing for him to kneel and put his arms around her: to hold her close, the way a father in a storybook would. If the little girl he loved had been lost and now he had found her.

⁓

When her father turned and walked out—ashen and silent, his anger spent, his expression blank, hands hanging loose at his sides—Olivia came back upstairs. Cold. Sick with sadness.

She went to the end of her bed. Gathered up the quilted bathrobe, the mittens, and her fleece-lined slippers. And with her teeth chattering and her fingers blue, she put them away and wrapped herself in the blanket from her bed. Later, after she heard the thump and whoosh of the heat being turned on, she went into her closet to get dressed.

She is near her bedroom window now. Watching dawn give way to morning. She's at the little pine table that serves as her school desk. Her books are in tidy stacks at one end and her pencils in orderly rows at the other. She's wearing a beige sweater, brown corduroy pants, striped socks, and navy-blue sneakers. She is meticulously clean and neat. With the exception of the place at the crown of her head where her father's fingers were dug in to lift her from the floor. There, her hair is wildly snarled. And she has no way to deal with it. Olivia's hair hangs from her head to her hips in a massive, weighted curtain. Only the reach and strength of an adult can maneuver a brush from one end to the other.

Olivia is wondering what her punishment will be. Wondering whether or not she is going to be hit—and if she is, with what, and how hard. Her mouth is flooding with the taste of salt. Tears crowding every inch of her. Fat and hot. She's afraid to let them go. Terrified of all the ways they could hurt her if they were to show themselves on the outside. Where other people could see them.

Olivia shifts her attention to the window—and her telescope. The view it provides is of rolling hills. Dormant vineyards, winter-bare.

And a long, dusty road with a modest country house at the far end. A house that used to look exactly like Olivia's, battered and brown, and has now been transformed. By a picket fence and banks of roses. By walls painted white, and a bright-red front door. By a family named Granger: a pretty mother, an amiable father, and two young children.

Olivia has never spoken to any of the Grangers. Never come close enough to touch their picket fence. Or hear the sound of their voices. Yet she hungers for them—yearns to be inside a house like theirs.

Through the telescope Olivia is seeing the school bus stopping outside the Grangers' gate. Where their mailbox is. The mailbox that has their name painted on it in bold black letters. And Mrs. Granger with her radiant prettiness, long shearling coat, and rainbow-colored muffler is running her fingers through her children's hair. Giving each of them a kiss as they're scrambling onto the bus.

Then the bus pulls away. And Olivia is grieving. Watching Mrs. Granger go back into her house.

When both the school bus and Mrs. Granger have disappeared Olivia closes her eyes and dreams. She dreams Mrs. Granger is still at the side of the road and that it is she, Olivia, who's being lovingly sent off to school. She's wearing a backpack, her shoulders warm with the sun. The air smells like perfume, like roses. And she's hearing the friendly squeak and rattle of the bus as it's stopping—for her. The sensation is glorious. Like dancing with butterflies. Mrs. Granger is raising her hand. On the other side of the dream, Olivia, with her eyes still closed, is raising her own hand and slipping her fingers into her hair. For the span of a heartbeat she is experiencing a mother's caress. The sweetness of it, almost unbearable.

And in the midst of the sweetness—excruciating pain. Olivia's fingers snagging against the tangles, pushing at the sore places on her scalp. Shattering the dream. Letting in the harsh reality that Calista has marched into the room, muttering: "Stop whatever nonsense you're up to. And for goodness sake, open your eyes!"

Calista. Wearing a baggy, ankle-length woolen skirt, a flannel shirt, and a pair of blue clogs, scuffed at the toes. Placing an apple onto the pine table. Putting it on top of one of Olivia's books, a thin volume in a dust jacket made out of white wrapping paper.

Olivia is frantic to keep the book away from Calista, to stop her from opening it and reading it. And killing the things that are inside it by simply laying her flat, black gaze on them.

But Calista doesn't realize the book is different from any of the others on the tabletop. She's pointing to the apple, telling Olivia: "Your father didn't think you deserved any breakfast. You have me to thank for this."

Olivia wants to believe Calista is lying. She wants it to be her father who sent the apple, although she knows he has offered no opinion on the subject of her breakfast. She knows he's left the house and has done what he always does when he's upset. He has vanished.

Now Calista is pulling a wooden-handled brush through Olivia's hair. Inflicting hurt with each grim, determined stroke. And Olivia is thinking about the women in her history books, the women of the Old West. She's thinking they must have had this same grim determination in their strokes when they were beating rugs. Or intruders.

Calista is gathering Olivia's hair into a thick braid. "I envy you this. I've never seen hair so long and magnificent."

"I hate it," Olivia tells her.

Calista brusquely fastens the braid with a rubber band. "I think it pleases your father—for your hair not to be cut."

"How do you know?" Olivia has turned so that she can look directly at Calista. Something she rarely does; she's intrigued, curious. Her father seldom speaks, unless he's instructing Olivia in her schoolwork. She's eager for any scrap of information. "What did he say?"

"It's not so much what he's said, it's more like—" Calista pauses; a slight catch in her breath, the same one that's in Olivia's when she thinks about her father. "He's a complicated man. He's brilliant, a genius. Geniuses don't see the same world other people do. Ordinary people like you and me."

"My father says I have an excellent mind." Olivia doesn't want to be grouped with Calista in any way.

"Well, you should use that 'excellent mind' of yours to do something other than play ugly tricks on the one person who's sacrificed everything for you. Your father has devoted his life to raising you, schooling you, all on his own. He's been a saint. Something that certainly can't be said about your mother—"

A loud roaring. In Olivia's ears. Like the bellow of a caged lion. The ferocity of it is stinging her eyes. Putting a low moan in the back of her throat.

"—your mother abandoned you, ran away, when you were still a baby in diapers. Because she was blond and beautiful and all she thought about was her own pleasure." Calista is gripping Olivia's chin, not letting her look away. "That heartless prank you pulled this morning tells me you're headed down the same selfish road as your mother—more concerned with what you want than what you owe."

Olivia expects this is where her punishment will come. A hit with the back of the wooden hairbrush. Or maybe a slap from Calista's wide, bricklike hand.

To Olivia's surprise, Calista steps away and has an unfamiliar gentleness in her voice as she says: "I'm not telling you these things to be cruel. I'm trying to teach you a lesson. You're a difficult child and you need to grow up to be a good woman."

Calista sits at the edge of Olivia's bed, saying: "I've been trying to show you how to mend your ways, every day, for the two years I've lived in this house, the entire time I've been your father's wife. I think it's one of the reasons he married me. Being alone with you was too much for him; he needed a woman's help." Calista is smoothing the folds at the waistband of her baggy skirt and sighing. "But soon I won't be able to look after you as much. You'll need to be on your own. I'm going to have a baby, Olivia. A child that's mine." Calista's tone is incredibly soft, as if she's speaking only to herself. "There isn't anything as precious as a baby of your own, if you're a good woman. To a woman with a true mother's heart there is nothing more important than cherishing her child."

Olivia is again experiencing the sensation of fire and snakes. And knives.

In the afternoon, Olivia is standing in front of a shelf near her bed. The shelf contains an assortment of little-girl treasures that, over the course of her childhood, Olivia has discovered in her father's attic. The most beloved of these objects is a small, beautifully delicate copper-wire cross. Olivia keeps it hidden, tucked away behind two other items from the attic. A portable record player and a stack of old record albums.

Olivia has put the soundtrack of a Broadway show onto the record player's turntable. She waits for the music to begin. Then lowers herself out of sight. Into the sliver of space between her bed and the wall. There is no lock on her door: this is the only place she can find privacy. She has brought along a pencil and the book in the white dust jacket—and she's opening the book to its first page. On that page, written in the perfect cursive taught to her by her father, is the book's title:

"The Book of Someday"

The pages beneath the title page have been filled with what is essentially an evolving map of Olivia's heart. Every sentence a dream being born, a vow waiting to be kept. Among them are notations such as:

> *Someday I will have a birthday party with people and singing.*
> *Someday I will go to ballet lessons and wear pink ballet shoes.*
>   *I will have a friend and we'll hold hands and she'll think I'm nice.*
> *Someday after the century changes, when it's in the 2000s and I'm all grown up, I won't stay in the hills out by Santa Ynez, California any more. I'll go to a place that is somewhere else. I will live in a house with a red door and roses.*
> *Someday I will be pretty and not have long, heavy hair that aches my head.*
> *Someday when I'm a mommy I'll never run away because I'm selfish and bad. I'll stay and I'll say I love you. I'll say it all the time, and give hugs. And I won't hit, especially*

not with a wooden hairbrush because of the hurt not ever
stopping, even after the bruises go.
Someday I will attend a real school.
Someday I will be brave and tell Mrs. Granger how much I
love her. Maybe she will let me come and live with her and
she will smile at me and let me have a dog. One that's little,
and is white with a curly tail.

Olivia is abruptly looking up from her book. The song coming from the record player is describing a concept she has never
thought of before. A "someday" that needs to be added to her list.

Someday I'll go to town in a golden gown and have my
fortune told.

Olivia's pencil is flying across the page—spelling out this new
promise. And there is unbridled bliss.

When the day has faded, and night has come, there is unbridled
terror.

Olivia is waking from a horrific dream. Screaming and at the
same time burying her face in her pillow. Trying to stop the sound
so he won't hear. But her father is already on the other side of her
doorway. In the darkness. She can feel him there with the look in
his eyes that is soft, like sadness, and then harsh, like the sharp edge
of a stone.

Her father knows about her nightmare. Olivia has told him
exactly what she sees when she dreams it and that it has been with

her for as long as she can remember. She doesn't understand why, but she senses the knowledge of these details is what brings that strange look to her father's eyes. That look of sorrow, and of stone.

Once her father is gone from the doorway, Olivia crawls into the frigid space between her bed and the wall. Desperate to stay awake. To keep the nightmare at bay.

The dream is ghastly in its silence and its simplicity. A void. And a woman. Floating in an eerie kind of sleep. Draped in a shimmering garment that flows from her shoulders to her knees like a column of starlight. Wearing pale-colored, high-heeled shoes fastened with a strap at the instep, each strap anchored by a single pearl button. Her arms outstretched. A silver band encircling her head. In the band, a plumed white feather. Her hair is short. Chestnut brown. Her face is in shadow. Only her lips are visible. Fiery red and slowly parting. Making way for a noise. A shrieking howl. Which, when it comes, will be the sound of unadulterated horror.

Olivia's fear of her nightmare is colossal. Her only defense is to gaze toward the window—waiting anxiously for the protection that morning will bring.

This will become a habit with Olivia—her passion for morning. As an adult, she will greet each new dawn by walking briskly toward the rising sun. And on one of these walks, almost twenty years from now, Olivia will again encounter the fiery-lipped woman in the pearl-button shoes. But she will no longer be an apparition haunting the night. She will be a reality. Existing in the cold, clear light of day.

Livvi

Los Angeles, California ~ 2012

HONEY-COLORED CURLS." HE'S LEANING TOWARD HER, RUFFLING her hair. "Very pretty. But awfully short. Do you ever think about letting it grow?"

Livvi's answer is emphatic. "No. I can't stand long hair."

He gives her a surprised look.

She realizes how overly adamant she must have sounded. And she's embarrassed, ducking her head, softly saying: "It's ancient history."

"Okay, no more hair questions." He's grinning at her now, with a charming, easygoing humor.

The two of them are in a butler's pantry, sitting at the end of a marble-topped counter, in a mansion. In the hills above Los Angeles.

And he's telling her: "Remember that thing I was talking about when we came in here? I was serious. I really do want to know everything about you. From the time you were a little kid right up to the minute we met." He's saying this while slipping a spoonful of caviar into Livvi's mouth.

For a split second, she's in a state of shock.

She's never had caviar before. The taste of it, the feel of it on her tongue, the sensuality of the salt and the satin, is indescribable.

He's leaning back in his chair. Relaxed. Smiling.

This is the most beguiling man Livvi has ever seen, and he's making it clear that he finds her attractive. She is breathless. Amazed.

He's absolutely compelling. Stunningly handsome. In his early forties. Beautifully muscled. Several inches over six feet tall. With hair so dark it's almost black. And eyes that are steel gray. His body language has an effortless, predatory elegance. He moves the way a tiger moves, completely at ease with what, and who, he is.

Livvi knows he's flirting with her. It's something she's not accustomed to—it's making her slightly self-conscious.

"Why aren't you saying anything?" he's asking.

Livvi blushes. "I don't go out a lot. I'm not good at flirting."

He's chuckling as if she's told him a joke.

Her smile is hesitant. "Why are you laughing?"

"Because you're a gorgeous woman who shows up unescorted at a black-tie fundraiser, and—"

"Oh, but I'm not unescorted. I came with a friend—he's my literary agent. I'm a writer."

"You're a writer wearing stilettos and a little gold dress that fits you like a very attractive second skin."

"It's new. I bought it in kind of a hurry."

Livvi is scooting back in her chair, hoping to move her hemline lower on her thigh. She would never have chosen a dress this short or heels this tall, but the sales clerk was so sophisticated, so self-assured: Livvi hadn't felt qualified to contradict her.

"And in light of your killer outfit," he's saying, "tell me again how you don't know anything about flirting?"

Livvi responds with a wry smile, a quick shrug. "I think it's one of those things you have to learn early on. I never learned. I'm twenty-six and it's too late."

He narrows his eyes, shoots her a questioning look.

She's worried she's said the wrong thing and he's changed his opinion of her, and now he thinks she's silly.

Livvi is shy around people she doesn't know. A little tentative. Because she never learned "playground rules" and sometimes has trouble figuring out what everyone else's normal is.

She suspects he's probably waiting for her to say something—yet she's keeping her gaze fixed on the floor. On the gleaming, intricately laid black-and-white tiles. She's thinking that maybe she shouldn't have come in here with him. She should've pulled back when he suddenly appeared at her side with a sly grin, slipping his arm through hers and whispering: "Follow me. I know where they keep the good caviar." But he hadn't given her the chance to pull back. He'd literally, physically, swept her off her feet. Swept her through the crowd and away from the party. The sparkle in his eyes making it seem safe and innocently adolescent.

Spontaneity is new to Livvi. And in its presence she'd been caught completely off guard, overtaken by an eager, childlike excitement. But now. Now that she's alone with a man she doesn't know. In this empty, tucked-away room. She's feeling insecure and slightly embarrassed.

"Should I bother to tell you how beautiful your eyes are? How they're the color of French coffee and Belgian chocolate?" he's asking. "Or would I lose points for too many food references?"

His question has been delivered with a delightful lightness. It's making Livvi laugh and momentarily forget how nervous she is.

He's laughing with her—holding his hands out in a gesture of comic pleading. "I'm giving you some of my best stuff here and I'm getting nothing back. Come on. Cut me some slack. Give me *something.*" His expression is open, full of fun.

Livvi's smiling. Liking him. As she asks: "What kind of something?"

He thinks for a minute, then says: "Your favorite guilty pleasure. In summertime."

She glances away, suddenly feeling shy again. "Peach ice cream," she tells him. "Where I live has a little courtyard garden, and I like being there in the evening, watching the sun set and eating peach ice cream—right out of the carton."

After a lingering pause, he says: "And in the winter?"

There's something in his voice, something about the way he asked the question, that's making it easy for Livvi to get past her usual reticence. "In the winter, the very first time it rains, I like to stay home, by myself. I light a fire in the fireplace. And then I get this incredibly soft white woolen throw that I keep on my bed, and I take it into the living room and cuddle up in it—in a chair near the fireplace. And I read a book—one that I've been dying to read, but have been saving for winter—for that first rainy day."

"I like that," he says. He pauses for a beat, gives her a slow smile. "But I'm still waiting to hear your life story. Come on, keep talking to me. I want to know you." He's looking at her with an expression of rapt attention.

Livvi is captivated. For a heartbeat. Then she realizes that what he's actually saying is: *"Tell me where you grew up. Where you went to school. What life was like when you were a little girl."* The thought of it is tying her stomach in knots.

She rarely talks about her childhood. She's wondering if it would be all right to tell him a white lie about having grown up beside a vineyard. In a rose-covered house.

But he's already letting her off the hook, saying: "Never mind about giving me your personal history. I'll do it for you."

He has moved his chair so close to hers that she can feel the heat from his body and smell his scent, cool and clean like a night breeze. He's opening her hand, tracing the lines on her palm, his fingertips firm and steady on her skin.

His touch is sending a tingle through Livvi.

"Just for the record," he's telling her, "I'm not a pro at this, I own a public relations agency. The palm reading I learned from my gypsy godmother. And by the way I can't start until I know your name."

"Livvi." The tingle he has caused is making her voice the slightest bit unsteady.

"Livvi?"

"It used to be Olivia. I like Livvi better."

"And I like Olivia." He brings her hand close to his lips. "I'm Andrew." His breath is moving softly across Livvi's fingers as he's murmuring: "I want you to say it."

"What?"

"My name."

"Andrew." Livvi's eyes dart away from his; she knows she's blushing again.

When she looks back at him she sees amusement and playful indulgence.

"It's all here in your hand," Andrew is saying. "The story of who you are." He pauses, studying Livvi's palm. "You're the youngest of three. Your parents were poets, who worshipped you. After graduating from a big-name college—where you were on a full scholarship and still managed to be the hottest thing on campus—you had a brief, sex-fuelled marriage to a good-looking parolee you met while buying a used car and then you went on to become who you are today, the designer of an award-winning line of can openers."

He lets go of her hand—with a mischievous smile. "So. How close did I come?"

There's wistfulness in Livvi's voice as she says: "Not very close."

"You were only right about one thing," she tells him. "I did go to college on a scholarship. But I was home-schooled right up until the first day of my freshman year, and I wasn't the coolest thing on campus—I was more like an Amish hermit dropped into the middle of a rave. Most of the time I was hiding out in the library."

Andrew looks at Livvi for a long beat, then says: "I was wrong about the adoring parents too. Wasn't I?"

Livvi nods.

"How about the brothers and sisters?"

Andrew's inquiries are probing at vulnerable places in Livvi. Her throat is tight, crowded with old, unexplored sorrow while she's explaining: "I almost had a half brother once...but he was stillborn."

For a short while, both Andrew and Livvi are silent. The only sound is the steady dripping of a faucet, into a limestone sink, near the door.

The mood of playfulness has disappeared.

Livvi is certain she has made a fool of herself.

"I should go," she's whispering.

"Wrong. That's exactly what you shouldn't do."

Andrew is looking directly into Livvi's eyes. His gaze is so assured, so seductively commanding, it's setting off a visceral reaction in Livvi. A sensuous desire to belong to him. The craving to be, most willingly, owned by him.

Which is why Livvi is offering no resistance as Andrew, with tender care, is sliding her out of her chair. Bringing her to her feet. And pulling her close. Leaving not a millimeter of space between them.

Andrew is tilting her face upward, preparing to kiss her. And Livvi's hands are coming to rest on the smooth coolness of his shirtfront.

She is closing her eyes. While Andrew's lips are settling against hers in a way that is possessive. And deliberate. And full of desire.

It's a kiss so complete. So deep. It is haunting. Mesmerizing.

Under its spell Livvi's breathing is beginning to slow and take on the steady rhythm of the water dripping into the stone sink. It's the same hushed, deliberate rhythm in which her heart has begun to beat.

And in that broken place—the place where Livvi is starving to be wanted and to be loved—there is an exquisite moment of soaring, perfect peace.

And then.

Out of nowhere.

Livvi's heart is banging. Skipping, pounding, like a runaway jackhammer.

Andrew has left her.

Abruptly. Unceremoniously. The way a man might leave a cup of airport coffee after he's heard his flight being called.

Andrew is already halfway across the room, his concentration riveted on the phone he's pulling from his pocket. He's opening the door and saying something, but the noise from the party on the other side is drowning it out.

The door is swinging shut—and the only sound in the room is the splash of water falling into the stone sink.

Livvi is mute. Stunned. With hurt. And humiliation.

For several minutes she's motionless.

While her mind is whirling.

She's trying to sort out what has just happened. Trying to make sense of it. But the noise of the dripping water—its steady, relentless echo—is making it impossible.

It's when Livvi goes to the other side of the room, to shut the faucet off, that she sees the windowsill above the sink. The sill is coated in a fine layer of dust. And for the first time since Andrew's departure, a sound comes out of Livvi. A sharp, startled laugh: a gut-sick realization. Tonight's humiliation isn't new. She has experienced it before…

…In a dusty basement room. Where she is about to lose her virginity. To one of her college professors. A man who has said "Trust me. I'll be gentle." An old man. With hair that smells like cigarettes and hands as cold as ice. The minute their clothes come off, he's grabbing them and leaving Livvi—without saying a word—leaving her alone. On the floor. Naked and humiliated. She's watching him hurry to his desk and turn his back on her, taking the time to fold their clothes into two separate stacks arranged in ascending order of smallness. Jeans on the bottom. Socks on the top. The bones of his spine poking up like a string of burrs under his skin. His butt-cheeks, sallow and creased. Hanging. Swaying a little. Like a pair of empty pockets.

And Livvi, standing alone in this gleaming butler's pantry, is remembering that that peculiar man was able to have her, there, on the dusty floor of his basement office, simply because he'd asked. And no one else had. And she assumed no one would.

The memory of this has Livvi frozen in place. Astounded. Wondering where to go from here.

"After all the years of aimless needing and hoping she knew exactly what she was going to do. She would never again wait to be chosen. From this point forward she'd be the one doing the choosing, and she'd settle for nothing less than precisely what she wanted." Livvi pauses. And closes the book from which she has been reading aloud.

The applause is instantaneous.

She's thrilled, and a little overwhelmed. This is one of the most important stops on the book tour promoting her debut novel—the moment feels surreal.

Livvi is in upstate New York, thousands of miles away from California, and the city of Pasadena, and the little guest cottage she rents there. She's behind a microphone on the second floor of a truly gorgeous bookstore. A place with high ceilings, wood-paneled walls, and silk-shaded lamps.

She is in a cathedral of books, suspended in a strange sort of splintered reality. The forty people seated in front of her are seeing Livvi Gray, a new critically acclaimed voice in literary fiction, a self-confident woman in an ivory silk shirt and well-tailored black pants. And the person looking back at those forty people is the same bewildered individual who, two months ago, in a yellow-gold dress, was seduced and discarded. In a butler's pantry.

It always worries Livvi a little to know that many of the men and women who come to her book signings assume she's special because she's written a novel and gotten it published, when all she really did was pour her pain onto paper. Then get lucky enough to have someone put it between the covers of a book.

She's experiencing the same shyness, the same concern about measuring up to people's expectations, that has been with her at every bookstore appearance she's made so far.

All over the room, people are raising their hands, ready to ask questions. The serene old lady in the third row. The pair of impec-cably dressed blond men nestled together, their shoulders lightly touching. The fresh-faced group of teenage girls leaning against the back wall. The pretty woman sitting near the front of the room, her left hand ringed in diamonds.

And for an instant, the sight of these people is dropping Livvi into a flash of remembered panic…

...She's surrounded by strangers. Staring. Curious. A rare trip to town. And she has stumbled, fallen. In new sandals. Onto a summer sidewalk. Blistering hot. An open doorway. A blast of music and air-conditioned air: yeasty, whiskey-sweet. Dirt-covered work boots. And cowboy boots. Hurrying out of the doorway. "Little girl...you all right?" She's trying to say she's hurt, needs help, but she can't catch her breath. The boots. Backing away. Making room. For the angry tap of scuffed blue clogs. "Don't pay her any mind. She just wants attention." Lying on the sidewalk: the feeling of tumbling into a bottomless hole. Calista's lips brushing her ear. "No wonder you're never taken out in public. You can't even walk down the street without making a spectacle of yourself..."

This old, ingrained panic—its embarrassment—is, for the briefest flick of time, keeping Livvi speechless. Tonight's book-signing event has been so lovely, so perfect. Now she's nervous that she'll stumble, do something clumsy, and spoil it.

Several more people in the room are indicating they have questions—Livvi is worrying that she has let too much time pass without responding. But whatever awkwardness was created by her momentary silence seems to have passed.

A middle-aged woman, pale and plump as a marshmallow, is rising from her chair, beaming at Livvi. "I want you to know I stayed up all night last night reading your novel. What an incredibly moving story!"

Someone else is calling out: "I loved it, I really loved it!"

Livvi's nervousness is lessening. She's taking a slow, deep breath.

While a thick-necked man in a leather jacket is saying: "A woman who has no idea how to get what she wants...to me that feels like a period piece. How did you make the decision to set the story in 2011 instead of, let's say, 1911?"

"It wasn't a conscious decision," Livvi tells him. "I guess I just wrote what I know about, the here and now."

Then Livvi sees the glimmer of disappointment. The man was hoping for something deeper, more dynamic. And for the space of a breath she feels, on some tiny level, that she's failed, because she hasn't met his expectations.

The pretty woman with the diamonds is informing Livvi: "You write beautifully, but your main character's backstory is a little unbelievable. Having her grow up in almost total isolation is something I simply don't think would happen. Why wouldn't she find a way to get out and make friends—find somebody she could get a reality check from? Excuse me for putting it like this, but she comes off as either mentally ill or completely retarded."

This isn't the first time this question has been asked, and Livvi still hasn't found the right way to deal with it. The simplest thing would be to admit that the facts in her book are actually the facts of her life, but she can't—in the same way some veterans can't talk about the horrors of war and some Holocaust survivors couldn't talk about the tortures they endured.

Livvi's history has left her haunted, disoriented. And she isn't sure how to find her way out of that.

But the thick-necked man is already turning around in his chair, explaining to the diamond-draped woman: "The kid in the book wasn't retarded. From the time she was a baby, she was raised pretty much as a prisoner. The only thing she understood was being a hostage."

And the other woman, the plump, marshmallowly one, is adding: "She knew there was a larger world, but she'd been robbed of the power to get out and make contact with it."

One of the teenagers in the back is calling out: "It's like what happened to that girl in Utah, Elizabeth Smart. She wandered all over the place with the people that kidnapped her—not ever trying to escape, or ask for help."

"That's right." The old woman in the third row is leaning forward, eager to have her say. "Elizabeth Smart grew up in a loving family. She'd only been away from them for a short time and was manipulated into submission. The girl in the book never knew anything but cruelty and captivity. The only information she had was that she was unlovable, unwantable...and completely unprotected."

"You're right," Livvi says. "That was the girl's reality—that she was completely unlovable. And unprotected. Other than in books, and in her own imagination, she had no idea if kindness or compassion were things that really existed."

Livvi glances at the woman in diamonds—the woman purses her lips and seems unconvinced.

A young mother with a baby in her lap raises her hand. "What I don't understand was why the stepmother character was so awful to the little girl. It was like she had a vendetta against her."

The man in the leather jacket looks toward Livvi. "It was some kind of weird jealousy...like in that scene on the sidewalk in front of the bar...the stepmother was pissed off because the girl was the center of attention, surrounded by a bunch of men. Am I right?"

"Maybe. Or maybe she was just plain evil," Livvi says. Her voice is very quiet as she adds: "There's a lot about the stepmother that's still a mystery to me."

The woman in the diamonds rolls her eyes. "It's crazy that the girl would accept that she was totally unlovable...and totally on her own...just because the stepmother said so."

The old woman in the third row is indignant. "The child's father hardly ever spoke to her. The stepmother's opinions were the only ones she ever heard. How can you expect a little girl to know things she's never been taught?"

The woman in diamonds shrugs. "Sorry. I just don't buy it."

It isn't yours to buy, Livvi is thinking. *It was mine to live. And my life being so far from your reality that you can dismiss it with a shrug? You'll never know how much that hurts. How much it makes me envy you.*

A hand has gone up in the back of the room: Livvi turns her attention to one of the teenage girls, who's asking: "Where did you get the title, *The Book of Someday*?"

"It's been in my head a long time," Livvi tells her. "It seemed like a perfect fit for the character in my book—somebody who doesn't realize, until it's almost too late, that she can go out and—"

Livvi is being interrupted by a female voice: "And when you find the thing you want, all you have to do is claim it and not let other people derail you—that's the key to a really fulfilled life, right?" It's a mousey young woman wearing large, blue-framed glasses who has said this. Behind the blue frames, her eyes are brimming with neediness.

Livvi, instinctively wanting to give the woman what she needs, responds with an instantaneous "Yes." But as soon as the *yes* has been uttered, Livvi is thinking about taking it back—worried that she's setting the woman up for disappointment.

Livvi's impulse is to explain that she, Livvi, doesn't have the easy quick-fix answer to happiness and that the one lie she told in *The Book of Someday* (its only real fiction) was the unshakably upbeat ending. The manuscript's original ending was much truer to what Livvi knows. It was far more ambiguous.

But it's too late. The young woman has already hurried away with a group of people rushing downstairs to the display area, in search of Livvi's book. And someone has put a hand on Livvi's shoulder, saying: "I'm in awe. You were a star tonight—radiant."

It's David. Livvi's literary agent—her best friend.

David who, three years ago, had been a stranger seated beside her on a flight from Los Angeles to New York. When Livvi was on her way to the funeral of the first person to encourage her talent as a writer: the chairman of her college English department. Someone who, when Livvi graduated, sensed how unready she was to face the world and arranged a job for her in the university's research library. A woman of ageless elegance named Gwyneth Holly who had retired and moved east—and died a short time later.

Gwyneth Holly had been what David became on that flight to New York, a hero in Livvi's life.

It was David who had gathered up the scattered pages of Livvi's manuscript and read them after she'd fallen asleep, after they'd slipped off her lap onto the floor of the plane.

David with his quiet smile and watercolor-blue eyes.

David, the intelligent, soft-spoken man who, as they were landing, had gently woken Livvi to tell her she'd written a remarkable book and that he intended to see it was published.

Livvi adores David.

She's also a little intimidated by him. He belongs to a life very different from hers. He comes from people of privilege. Who, in summer, roam the beaches of New England. In loose cotton shirts and sun-bleached shorts. And in winter, command the streets of Manhattan. Armored in Armani and black limousines.

Now David is leaning close to Livvi, telling her: "Later, after you've finished signing the books all those eager readers are rushing downstairs to buy, I want to take you to dinner, to celebrate."

Livvi is thrilled. And excited. And grateful.

"We'll go someplace special, Livvi, someplace that…"

David is continuing to speak, but Livvi is having trouble hearing his voice. It suddenly seems garbled and distant. Her focus is being moved away from David and shifted—entirely—to what she's seeing over his shoulder.

A man. At the top of the stairway.

His eyes are locked on Livvi's. He's loudly calling her name. A name no one has called her in years. "Olivia!"

Micah
New York City ~ 2012

I THINK MY NAME'S BEING CALLED. I'LL EMAIL YOU THE STUFF about the new exhibit later." Micah drops her mobile phone into her purse. It's an expensive phone and an equally expensive purse.

The nurse who's just coming out from behind the reception desk, a tiny Filipina woman in hot pink scrubs, is saying: "Meeka? Is Meeka here?"

"It's Micah…like 'Mike' with an 'ah' at the end of it." Micah is rising from her chair, conscious of the subtle shift that's taking place—the attention of the other patients in the waiting room moving from the pages of their magazines and coming to rest on her.

Micah is accustomed to this; she likes it, people looking at her. She knows they look because she's six-foot-one, and because her legs are long and her breasts are full. Because she has sea-green eyes, hair the color of black cherries, and skin like fresh cream. And because her lips, and ears, and nose are every bit as breathtaking as the rest of her.

The nurse is now ushering Micah into a corridor, leading her past a wall where there are several large, framed photographs. One of them, a Venetian canal scene, dominates the others. It's an image that's completely devoid of life. No people, no dogs, no birds, not even a potted plant—nothing but a gondola, a bridge, and the façade of a timeworn palazzo overlooking the water. The photo, taken from an extremely forced perspective, has a cutting-edge style that borders on the bizarre.

While she's passing the photograph Micah is giving it a quick, critical glance. The nurse notices and says: "Big-name photographer. Very expensive picture—very famous."

"Yeah. I know," Micah tells her. "I'm the one who took it."

"Wow." The nurse is impressed. And then she asks: "Is it true you never have people in any of your pictures?"

Micah nods.

"Why?" There's interested eagerness in the nurse's voice.

"Because I erase them," Micah explains. The statement is made quietly—almost reluctantly.

After a quick check of her weight and blood pressure, Micah has been brought to the doctor's office, not into an examining room. All the complicated stuff, the tests and scans, were completed days ago—no more need for fluorescent lighting and paper gowns. It's time for the Persian carpets and diploma-lined walls.

Micah is in a stylish low-backed chair upholstered in tobacco-brown suede, and the doctor is seated behind an imposing Park Avenue desk. He's studying the contents of a file folder and hasn't spoken, or looked up, since giving Micah a brief nod when she first arrived. This is confusing her—she rarely enters a room without creating a microsecond of intense concentration. A moment in which her exquisite face and body capture everyone's attention.

Her confusion is now rapidly being replaced by irritation. Micah doesn't like people wasting her time, and this doctor has left her sitting for several minutes with nothing to do but map the bald spot on the top of his head.

She lets out an annoyed cough and glares at him.

The doctor continues slowly flipping through the documents in the folder.

Without looking up, he says: "I see that it's been quite a while—back in 2004, eight years ago—since you had your last medical check-up, Ms.—" He stops and riffles through the paperwork, scanning for her name.

"Lesser." There is a deliberate edge in Micah's tone. She wants him to know he's getting on her nerves.

"Lesser. Right." He remains impassive, intent on the data in her medical reports.

Micah is making no attempt to conceal her irritation as she tells him: "How about we skip the doctor-patient chat and go straight to you signing whatever piece of paper it is that says I qualify for the big fat insurance policy I'm about to take out. I have things to do."

The doctor remains focused on the paperwork. "It says here you're forty-one. Unmarried. No children."

"Not that it's any of your concern, but this has nothing to do with my personal life. My new business partner and I are both increasing our life insurance—it's a standard corporate practice." Micah looks from the doctor to the Mont Blanc pen that's lying a few inches away from her file. When he makes no move to reach for it, Micah grabs the pen and slaps it down on top of the open folder. "I don't know what you think you're doing, but this is a monumental waste of time. You don't need to sit there memorizing my medical history; trust me, we're never going to see each other again. I don't go to doctors—I'm too busy. So just mail me the damn papers. Or ship them to the insurance company. Do whatever it is you're supposed to do and send me the bill."

Micah has already left the tobacco-colored suede chair. Heading out of the office. Not noticing that the doctor has looked up—and is finally giving her his full attention.

She's almost at the door when she realizes that he has begun to speak. In a flat, detached monotone.

This is when she knows she will need to hold on to the doorframe.

To keep from falling down.

While he's delivering this murderous blow.

"In all likelihood you have an aggressive breast cancer, Ms. Lesser. It appears you may have had it for a significant amount of time."

Micah is afraid to inhale—as if the air is rapidly filling with thorns. The doctor's drone is coming at her in disjointed bits and pieces. "Oncologist." "Biopsy." "Possible complete removal of—" "Surgery." "Chemo." "Radiation."

When Micah is finally able to let go of the doorframe, when she has the strength to turn and look at him, the doctor is consulting a calendar on his computer, mumbling: "…set up an appointment for the day after tomorrow, but no later than the end of the week…"

There's sudden, uncontrollable fury. And Micah's response is a rasping scream. "No!"

"No? To what…?" The doctor seems genuinely at a loss.

"To hacking my breasts off, you son of a bitch."

There is terror—everywhere—in Micah.

The doctor is coolly telling her: "I don't think you're taking quite the right attitude, Ms. Lesser."

And Micah says: "What attitude would you take if we were talking about doing away with your dick?"

He pauses for a moment. Then clears his computer screen. "Is there someone we can call? A family member? Someone you're close to?"

A cynical, bewildered voice in Micah's head is wondering, *Who do other people, regular people, call at a time like this? Their commuter-train husbands? Their crappy mothers, their bullshit fathers? Maybe the chatty best friend they go to the mall with? Somebody who just fucking loves the shit out of them?*

The doctor has closed the file folder, and is pushing it aside. "Ms. Lesser, is there anyone we can call?"

"No. There's no one."

Micah's response is coming from a place of undiluted emptiness. She can hear very little of what the doctor is explaining to her—because, for a fleeting moment, she isn't in his office. For some reason she's in a place that doesn't exist anymore. Hasn't existed for a long time. A late-summer garden surrounded by an expanse of soft green grass, and a sea of coral-colored lilies. She's being held in a heartfelt embrace—listening to a voice that's light and lilting, like music, saying, *"Believe that I love you...won't you please?"*

And then Micah is back with the doctor, in his office—hearing him ask where she's going—and unable to give him an answer.

She is leaving the room, moving toward the corridor. Stumbling toward the elevator. Believing this dreadful thing that has happened to her is retribution, her punishment. For the evil she has done. The terrible trespass she once committed in a moment of unforgivable weakness.

"So how was your month in New York?"

Micah's assistant Jillian is asking this as she's bringing Micah her morning coffee. She and Micah are in the bedroom of Micah's row house in south Boston—a room that's both unyielding and fanciful. Two of its walls are surfaced in rough, exposed brick; the other two are swirled in plaster as light and smooth as the frosting on a wedding cake. The planked floor is dark mahogany. The tall windows are hung with billowing lengths of crimson Chinese silk. The bed is wide and plush, draped in layers of orange-hued cashmere and snowy Egyptian cotton.

Micah is in the center of the bed. Sitting cross-legged, leaning over her laptop. She's wearing a black camisole and loose, satin pajama pants. Her hair is in disarray and her fingers are flying over the computer keys, pursuing a frantic Internet search. She's startlingly pale and seems diminished, as if she has been struck by a force so violent it has left her less tall, less present; somehow, less real.

Jillian has put Micah's coffee on the table beside the bed. And now she's saying: "Other than taking a lot of pictures and getting the new gallery space finished...how was your month in New York?"

Micah can hear that Jillian doesn't intend to let this question go. She glances up, keeping her tone neutral. "New York is New York." Micah isn't in the mood to talk. She wants to get back to her web search and finish it while she still has the courage. The simple act of entering the query information has begun to make her tremble.

Jillian is gathering up Micah's scattered clothes from the floor. Keeping her eyes on Micah. "So. No problems in New York?"

Micah takes a careful breath. "What makes you think there might have been problems?"

"There were phone messages this morning. A whole lot of

them." Jillian is street-smart. Cagey-tough. A born and bred Boston southie. The rasp in her voice has steel in it. The sound of that steel is putting acid into Micah's stomach as Jillian is explaining: "The messages are from a doctor's office. They said it's important not to lose any time and that you really need to call them back."

Jillian walks to the side of Micah's bed and gives Micah a determined stare. "Why would they be saying that?"

Micah doesn't respond; she isn't ready. The situation is too complicated. There are scores that need to be settled before she can know what to do about her cancer. Before she can decide whether she deserves to live. Or to die.

"Miss Lesser, I need you to tell me what's going on." Jillian's statement isn't a request—it's a demand.

In spite of that, Micah shakes her head. The answer is no.

"Look," Jillian tells her. "This is the thing…me and you both know you get off on making your own rules—going over the top. Seeing what you want and taking it. You're pretty much roaring hell-on-wheels. I'm not asking you to do anything about that. I know you can't. It's just who you are. All I'm saying is…I care about you."

For the briefest fragment of time, Micah is again in that long-ago, late-summer garden surrounded by coral-colored lilies—experiencing the feel of that heartfelt embrace.

While Jillian is insisting: "Miss Lesser, you're gonna tell me what the doctor wants with you. 'Cause I'm owed that and you know it."

Micah does know it. And knowing it has made her look away, look down. And in looking down, she has seen the black camisole. The lovely curve of its neckline along the top of her breasts. Her eyes are suddenly hot with the threat of tears.

After the threat has passed, when Micah turns back toward Jillian, the look they exchange holds a defiant kind of respect and admiration. But very little, if any, tenderness.

Jillian continues to stubbornly stand beside Micah's bed. "I'm not leaving till we get this done, Miss Lesser."

Hearing the words "Miss Lesser" in the context of this conversation is putting Micah on edge, highlighting the awkwardness that exists between herself and Jillian. Jillian is Micah's most trusted employee; she has either seen or spoken to Micah every day for five years, and is quite possibly the closest thing to a friend that Micah has. Yet Jillian has never called Micah anything but "Miss Lesser," and Micah has never made any attempt to change that. She has never taken the time to say, "Call me Micah." Now, it seems too late. Too difficult.

"I'm waiting for you to give me what I'm owed," Jillian is insisting. "I'm waiting for you to tell me what's going on with you, Miss Lesser."

Micah braces herself. And then in a manner that's calm to the point of being cold, she says: "Breast cancer."

Jillian is equally calm: "You gonna die?"

"I don't know. I haven't decided yet."

"What're you gonna need? What can I do for you?" No sweetness from Jillian, no sentimentality—simply rock-solid loyalty.

It's by sheer force of will that Micah is managing to sound unemotional as she tells Jillian: "I'll need you to keep an eye on things for a while. At the gallery here in Boston. And the one in New York. You know how to handle all the day-to-day stuff."

"Okay," Jillian says. Then she asks: "Does your new partner, the guy who's gonna run the New York gallery, does he know about the cancer?"

"No. I don't want anyone to know."

"That's fair." Jillian shifts her weight from one foot to the other but doesn't move from the side of the bed. "So what happens now?"

Micah has returned to the laptop: the results of her search. She feels as if she's going to pass out. There—on the screen—are the first small clues. The beginning of the trail that will eventually lead her to people she's terribly afraid of. People to whom she needs to make restitution. And the people from whom she needs to hear the truth about who she really is.

There is a rising sense of apprehension in Micah as she's telling Jillian: "I'll be going on the road. To settle some debts."

"When are you leaving?"

"Not for a while," Micah says. She suspects that locating the people she needs to find will require a lot of time and effort.

"Once you go, how long you gonna stay gone?" Jillian asks.

"I'm not sure…as long as it takes."

"Well, if you're gonna be gone for a long time, there's something you and me need to discuss—just in case. Something that's got nothing to do with business, or the galleries." The steel has disappeared from Jillian's voice; she's suddenly nervous. "Miss Lesser, if something unexpected happens, and you're not here, you better tell me what you want to do about the woman—"

The Woman. The most important person in Micah's life. The one who once looked so spectacularly beautiful in a silver dress and pearl-button shoes. At the mention of her, Micah has flinched. As if she's been stung by a scorpion.

An inordinate amount of time passes before Micah responds, in a whisper. "Leave her alone. Let her stay where she is. For as long as possible."

It is a devastated whisper. Full of regret.

AnnaLee

Glen Cove, Long Island ~ 1986

YOU NOT GOING TO REGRET? YOU SURE?"

The tone of this question, delivered in Mrs. Wang's clipped English, is both sincere and ambivalent. The excited reverence with which Mrs. Wang is holding the blue-and-white porcelain vase is making it evident that she wants a swift, profitable close to this transaction. While the way she's looking at AnnaLee suggests a sort of reluctant empathy.

In reply to Mrs. Wang's inquiry about regrets, AnnaLee gives only a quick shake of her head. She's overwhelmed. By loss. By the vacant place on the mantle. Where up until a few seconds ago, the porcelain vase had always been.

"I know this hard for you." Mrs. Wang is cradling the vase in a way that's apologetic and slightly awkward.

She's standing behind AnnaLee, their images reflected in the beveled mirror above the fireplace. Diminutive, delicate Mrs. Wang who at age sixty retains only a trace of the magnificence that once made her the raven-haired toast of Shanghai. And tall American-born AnnaLee, who has hair the color of wheat and a quiet prettiness that, at age thirty-three, is in full bloom.

AnnaLee is thinking how very different they are, she and Mrs. Wang. But when AnnaLee looks more closely, when her eyes and

Mrs. Wang's meet, she's startled to see how much they share—the staggering amount of disappointments, and sorrow, that is in each of them.

"We all on same journey, only riding different horses." Mrs. Wang's voice is gentle with compassion.

It fills AnnaLee with longing. For her mother. For the comfort of being, even for a little while, someone's child again.

In that same moment Mrs. Wang is discreetly glancing back toward the mantle—looking at a second blue-and-white porcelain, a perfect match to the one she has in her hands. "More money if you sell both," she's saying. "Much more valuable to people coming in my shop, to collectors, if they can have pair, not just single one."

There's an ache in AnnaLee as she asks: "How much more?"

"I could give you more than double. Three maybe four times as much. Very desirable as pair. Very valuable."

AnnaLee reaches for the vase, then pulls back and softly says: "These porcelains were my mother's wedding present from my father. He carved this mantle himself so she could have the perfect place to display them."

Mrs. Wang nods curtly and says: "This a very fine home. Full of story. Full of history. It should be kept just so."

And AnnaLee is thinking, *You have no idea what a rare place this is, Mrs. Wang. My parents built it when they were newlyweds, it's where they planted their roots and conceived their only child. It's where I was born. Where I was loved so well when I was growing up. Where, now, I'm raising a baby of my own. This is the home my parents entrusted to me when they passed away. It's a sacred space. And I've begun to loot it. Because I don't know what else to do. And every time I sell you even the smallest piece of it, Mrs. Wang, I'm selling off a part of my soul.*

Every detail of this stately house in Glen Cove, on Long Island, is a treasure to AnnaLee. The wide staircase and the rolling lawns. The gracious fireplace and the slender French doors opening onto the moss-covered terrace. There isn't an inch of her birthplace that she would willingly trade or change.

And now as she's watching Mrs. Wang counting out the money for the porcelain vase—piling wrinkled, neatly stacked bills onto a table near the front door—the sight of it is making AnnaLee sick.

"Your husband should be ashamed." Mrs. Wang's voice is harsh and annoyed. "I don't care it is now brave new world. I don't care there are equal rights. To me…no honor in a man who look at a woman for his support."

AnnaLee's face is burning with embarrassment.

There have been a number of these transactions in recent months; she and Mrs. Wang have never discussed the reason for them. It hasn't occurred to AnnaLee, until now, that Mrs. Wang is fully aware of why AnnaLee has begun to sell off irreplaceable pieces of her history and inheritance.

AnnaLee's embarrassment is coming not only from the bluntness of what Mrs. Wang has said but also from the fact that, in a way, AnnaLee agrees with it. As much as she loves her husband, in some small chamber of her heart AnnaLee is furiously angry with him. *I hate Jack's quietness,* she's thinking, *and the way he runs from any kind of confrontation—how he lets those things keep him from building a decent career.*

But to AnnaLee's surprise it's not her anger, it's her most tender feelings toward her husband that answer Mrs. Wang. "Jack is a good man," she says, "a good father. He loves me, and our baby, very much."

Mrs. Wang stays quiet until she has put the porcelain vase into an excelsior-lined box and closed the lid. Then she tells AnnaLee:

"Soon maybe your husband make more money. In meantime I can take painting too. Give you top dollar."

The painting, a landscape by an artist called Roger Medearis, is worth a good amount of money. In a single, sudden motion, AnnaLee takes it from the wall and gives it to Mrs. Wang. She does it with blinding speed, before she has any time for second thoughts.

When Mrs. Wang has left and AnnaLee is alone, there's no weeping, no tears. But there is a lingering melancholy.

In addition to the vacant place on the mantle, where the blue-and-white porcelain vase had always been, there is now a new vacancy. The blank space marking AnnaLee's most recent loss. The large rectangle in which the buttercup-colored paint is noticeably darker than the surrounding wall. A place that is painfully empty.

Several hours later, AnnaLee has remembered a gilt-framed canvas with dimensions almost identical to those of the Medearis, the painting she sold to Mrs. Wang.

AnnaLee is certain that this gilt-framed picture will make the perfect cover for the emptiness on the living room wall. And now she's hurrying to find it. It's upstairs, in a closet. A simple painting done in the 1920s, by an anonymous artist; something AnnaLee bought years ago, on an impulse, at a tag sale. The haunting portrait of a dark-haired woman in a shimmering silver gown and pearl-button shoes. A woman who—AnnaLee has always thought—looks like something out of a dream.

Livvi

Northern Dutchess County, New York ~ 2012

A NDREW!"

For a second Livvi isn't sure if he's real—actually at the top of the bookstore stairs—or if he is a dream.

All at once he's coming closer, calling out again. "Olivia!"

Livvi seems to be the only thing Andrew is able to see. He isn't acknowledging David, isn't noticing that David is standing only a few inches away. Andrew is simply sweeping Livvi into his arms. And kissing her. With the same intensity he'd kissed her before—at the party, in Los Angeles. Settling his lips confidently against hers in a way that's possessive, and deliberate, and full of desire.

Livvi is continuing to constantly replay this moment, the sight of Andrew at the top of the stairs and his kiss, even though it happened hours ago. In the bookstore, in upstate New York. And now she's hundreds of miles away, in the St. Regis Hotel in Manhattan.

She is in an extravagant bed. Under a canopy of silky fabric flowing from a crown-shaped fixture in the ceiling. Surrounded by walls the color of sugared sand and furnishings upholstered in biscuit-brown, the dappled color of seashells.

And she's experiencing passion that's almost beyond comprehension. She is having sex with Andrew for the first time and tumbling into the cashmere-gloved grip of an irresistible narcotic.

The taste of it, the smell of it—is intoxicating. Exhilarating. The heart of it—is wild. And fiercely physical.

Andrew is, as a lover, what he is as a man. Powerful. And confident. He has a voice that's clear and low—effortlessly commanding. And a body beautiful beyond description. He's a deeply sensuous male with a devilishly boyish grin. He's a rogue. A charmer. Master at being both playmate and seducer.

And in his steel-gray eyes there is a fascinating, complicated mix of information. Intelligence, and infinite caring. And just beneath the caring, a hint of something darker. Something unpredictable. A little bit dangerous.

But the only things Livvi can see are the marvels and thrills of being in Andrew's presence.

From the moment they left the bookstore there hasn't been a single minute when Andrew's hands haven't been roving Livvi's body. Or a microsecond when her lips haven't been hungry for his.

Andrew and Livvi have come together in a magnetic, fevered heat. A physical chemistry that's spellbinding.

And for Livvi, this attraction, this connection, feels miraculous. For her, this is far more than sex. It's the miracle of being welcomed, celebrated, and safe—the priceless gift given to someone who's been lost and has finally come home.

Her eyes are shining with happiness as they're searching Andrew's, and she's asking: "How did you find me? How did you know to look for me in that bookstore?" This is an experience Livvi has never had. Someone has missed her and come looking for her. She is eager to hear the story of how, and why, it happened.

Andrew seems to be aware that she's anxious to have this information; and yet he's saying nothing. Instead he is turning Livvi onto her stomach, sliding his hands along the length of her back, slowly bringing them to rest on the curve of her waist, and telling her: "If I was a sculptor I'd spend the rest of my life trying to do you justice."

Livvi raises her head and looks over her shoulder at him. She can't wait. She needs this information. "What were you doing at the bookstore? How did you know how to find me?" She wants to hear everything, wants to savor each detail.

Andrew is stroking his cheek across the back of her neck—his breath leisurely skimming her skin—feeling like a tease, like torture. She rolls over and sits up, gathering the sheet, wrapping it around herself, and begging: "Tell me, please!"

There's amusement in Andrew's tone. "It's pretty simple, really. I was in the area, over in Rhinebeck, visiting a friend. I saw a local paper next to the cash register when we were leaving a diner…and there was your picture, the information about your book signing—"

"—and then you came for me," Livvi marvels.

"Then I came for you," Andrew tells her.

With those words—*I came for you*—Andrew has gone, like a bolt of lightning, straight to the lonely core of Livvi's soul. He has burned himself into her and claimed her.

She can scarcely breathe as he's saying, "I was supposed to be on a flight back to Los Angeles yesterday," and she's replying, "But you came looking for me instead."

"Yes, Olivia," he smiles. "That seems to be how it turned out."

Suddenly, in the midst of Livvi's joy, there's a faint prickle of unease. The feeling of being edged toward a place she doesn't want to go back to.

"I don't like that name, Olivia," she says. "No one calls me by it anymore."

Andrew is trailing kisses across Livvi's belly. With each kiss, he's murmuring, "Olivia." "Olivia." "Olivia." When he brings his mouth close to Livvi's, he's whispering: "Olivia is a glorious name. I'll never stop saying it."

While Andrew is nestling her into the cloud-soft pillows, a microscopic sadness is flickering through Livvi. The battle of Olivia has been lost.

But as Andrew is enticing her. Stroking her. Lowering his weight onto her—entering her. It seems like such a small defeat.

Insignificant. Compared to what she is being given.

Andrew—moving deeper and deeper into Livvi—is touching her in ways, and in places, that are sending a series of magnificent shudders through her body. A spectacular, visceral current of sensation.

Powerful pulses. From an exquisitely pleasurable earthquake.

Rippling uncontrolled rushes of pure, carnal, release.

This is Livvi's first orgasm.

And it's Andrew who is here—inside her.

Livvi's night at the St. Regis in New York is followed by a morning flight home to California. The reassuring weight of Andrew's shoulder, which has been resting against Livvi's since takeoff, suddenly isn't there anymore. The plane has just touched down in Los Angeles. Andrew has leaned away to check his phone.

This has sparked a memory, a twinge in Livvi. "Why did you leave without saying a word?" she's asking. "Why did you walk out on me?"

Andrew looks baffled. "What are you talking about?"

"I'm talking about when we met. The first time I saw you. When you took me away to the butler's pantry and the caviar."

Andrew rests his head against his seat back. His tone is conversational, relaxed. "Something came up…a text I needed to take care of. You had to know I wasn't gone for good."

"But I didn't know." Livvi is worrying—just a little—that their new connection might turn out to be as tenuous, and as easily broken, as it was on that first night.

But Andrew is giving her a sweet grin, assuring her: "This is crazy. You know I told you to wait, I said it right when I was going through the door."

"Then why didn't I hear you?" Livvi asks.

"The noise from the party must've been drowning me out."

Livvi is in the window seat: Andrew, sitting beside her. He has loosened his seat belt, and hers—and is swinging the armrest up.

He's turning toward Livvi. Leaning across her, shielding her from view—and kissing her. His kiss is slow and deep. All-encompassing. Erasing everything but the ferocious attraction they have for each other.

And just as it did on that first night, Livvi's hand is coming to rest on the cool smoothness of Andrew's shirtfront. Beneath the coolness, she can feel the heat of his skin—the heat of his desire.

Andrew is caressing the outline of Livvi's leg, just above her knee. His fingertips are resting on the fabric of her skirt, traveling steadily upward in lazy, insinuating circles. The movement is so subtle, and blatantly sexual, that it's sending shock waves through Livvi—arching her spine, parting her lips, and leaving her eyes only barely open.

Andrew's breath is warm and urgent on Livvi's cheek. While his hand is purposefully gliding over the rise of her hip.

The teasing circles being made by Andrew's fingertips are now lingering at the waistband of Livvi's skirt. Exploring the side button and the zipper. Tempting her. Exciting her. Making her shift and squirm. Building a lust in her that is beyond her control. A need that's making Livvi frantic—for Andrew to peel her skirt away, and give her the feel of his skin on hers.

He is setting a fire in every fiber in Livvi's body.

With the deliberate, leisurely movements of his hand Andrew is generating a wantonness in Livvi. A blind, animal urge to have him strip her, and take her. Here. Now. In the middle of this crowded plane.

Andrew's voice is low, intensely intimate, as he's telling Livvi: "That night in the butler's pantry, you were a stranger. Now you're the woman who has given me the most incredible twenty-four hours of my life."

While he's saying this, his hand is continuing to move in those seductive, sensuous circles. The fever it's creating—the need for him, the rampant desire in Livvi—is becoming unbearable. She's on the brink of lifting out of her seat—moaning, and crying out.

And in this same instant Andrew is slipping his hand beneath the fabric of Livvi's blouse, and the satin of her bra. Andrew is stroking her breast. In a quick, masterful way that is bringing her an ecstatic relief.

It is as if in the days and weeks following their return from New York, Andrew has put Livvi at the center of his universe.

He is opening the world to her. Introducing Livvi to a flow of miracles and wonders—wonders that exist solely because Andrew exists.

A little more than two months into her relationship with Andrew,

Livvi is rising into air that is crystal-clear—floating toward a glow of rose-colored light. From time to time, just above her head, there are bright bursts of flame and an exhilarating rumble of noise. A roar. As if she's being lifted away from the earth on the wings of a dragon.

Livvi is looking up, gazing into the vault of a towering dome patterned in crayon yellow and neon green, and shimmering like silk.

She is in New Mexico. With Andrew's arms wrapped around her waist. Ascending into the dawn sky in a hot-air balloon. Believing that for as long as she lives, there will never again be a moment as breathtaking as this one.

And then on that same day, just before midnight, Andrew is giving Livvi the astonishing thrill of rushing along an empty desert road in a black Porsche convertible, with the top down, under an ocean of glittering stars.

Andrew has one hand on the wheel of the speeding car and the other firmly on Livvi's back. She's standing tall—braced against the glove compartment, clutching the rim of the windshield. The night wind is racing across her face. Whipping through her hair. Whirling the fabric of her dress. Sailing it up and away from her legs, like the flying skirts of a dervish.

And now Andrew's hand is moving from her back and sliding under the lace edge of her underwear. His touch, on this hot night, is remarkably cool. Light and inviting. Its upward slide deft and swift.

Then when Andrew has found the velvety harbor that is his goal,

he becomes watchful. Careful. Every movement being timed, perfectly, to Livvi's pace.

Livvi glances down and catches the briefest glimpse of Andrew's
expression. A look of supreme satisfaction. As if he is taking great
pleasure in the pleasure he's so expertly giving.

With one hand firmly on the steering wheel of the speeding car
and the other nimbly guiding Livvi, Andrew is driving her toward a
rapturous euphoria. A place where Livvi is wild and free. He's creating a shout in her. That's spontaneous. Uncivilized. A shout of ecstasy.

In the motel room, later, when both of them are sleepy and sated
with sex, Andrew is spooned against Livvi's back.

As she's lying on her side, with her knees bent, she's remembering that she used to lie curled in this same position when she was
a frightened little girl who believed in fairy tales. When she used
to slide her arm under the crook of her knees and pretend she was
being carried to safety by one of the knights in her storybooks.
Someone tall and strong. A man with the power to tame dragons—
and create magic.

And while Andrew is sleepily kissing the back of her neck, Livvi
is asking him: "Out there, in the dark. How fast did we go?"

"You don't want to know…"

His voice has trailed off; he's yawning.

Livvi, too, is drifting into sleep.

"If you hadn't talked me into it," she murmurs, "I'd never have
done it. I was scared."

"I like how wild it made you." Andrew's murmur is husky, full
of innuendo.

The sound of it rouses Livvi; her eyes flutter open, briefly. Then she wills herself back into sleep. Into a reverie where she's again hurtling toward the thrill of the open road and the burn of the night wind.

And Livvi is beginning to smile.

The discovery that she has an appetite for wildness, for freedom, is coming as a surprisingly delightful revelation.

In each new place, with each new pleasure that Andrew brings, Livvi is continuing to encounter revelations and surprises.

She's also encountering unexpected information. About Andrew. About who he was, and who he is.

The initial surprise comes after they've been together for a little over three months. When Livvi and Andrew are on a trip to Canada, to Vancouver Island, where they're celebrating Livvi's birthday. She and Andrew are on a rented sailboat, at sunset. The air is brisk and chilly, and the smell of the sea is salty clean. Both Livvi and Andrew are in jeans and cable-knit sweaters. Livvi's birthday present from Andrew is the diamond bracelet on her wrist—and for Livvi, almost as dazzling as the gift is the wonderfully playful way in which Andrew presented it.

"I love how you gave this to me," she's telling him.

It isn't clear whether or not Andrew is hearing what Livvi's saying; he's struggling to adjust a sail that has come loose.

While she's watching him bring the sail under control, she's letting her thoughts wander, letting them take her back to the way the day began...*She's waking up to a boisterous rendition of "Happy Birthday" being sung by a trio of male voices. At first she's confused, startled. Then all at once she's laughing. Because it's Andrew and a pair of room service waiters who are serenading her. One of the waiters is standing beside a breakfast cart laden with chocolate croissants and cold champagne; the other is presenting her with an enormous stuffed animal. A Paddington Bear in a whimsical red hat and matching boots and a blue pea coat.*

Andrew has delivered another miracle, another wonder. He has made all of Livvi's childhood birthday dreams come true in this one, singularly lovely moment.

She's thrilled. Holding on to the bear. Crying and laughing. While Andrew is kissing her and explaining that she hasn't officially gotten her present yet—she needs to read the tag dangling from one of the bear's coat buttons.

The first part of the information on the tag is the preprinted message that comes with all Paddingtons, "Please look after this bear." But handwritten below that message, in Andrew's flowing script, is a note that says, "And kindly check his pockets for Birthday Valuables."

In the bear's pocket Livvi is discovering a diamond bracelet, twinkling like a circle of stars. A gift far beyond her imagination, or expectation. A gift that's moving her to tears as she's telling Andrew, "I haven't ever had anything this beautiful. Not in my entire life…"

And now, all these hours later, as the sun is setting, and Andrew is bringing the sailboat in toward the shore, Livvi's telling him: "It's like you know how to make magic. Like you have command of a whole other world."

Livvi is stretched out on the deck, looking up at Andrew, marveling at him. "You even know how to sail a boat. Amazing."

"Yeah," he laughs. "It puts me right up there with Popeye and Cap'n Crunch."

Livvi absentmindedly pulls their open picnic basket toward her.

It was Andrew who packed it. Andrew who chose the French champagne. The assortment of artisan cheeses. The Graber olives. The fresh-baked baguette with the perfectly crisped crust. The hothouse melon and the finely marbled prosciutto. The little apple tarts, each one flawless and glistening, like a jewel.

Livvi has never seen or eaten food like this. And she has never before been out on the ocean. Never experienced the splendor of rolling waves, or the exciting rattle and snap of sails that are towering and periwinkle blue. She has never drifted homeward, lazy and content, beneath evening clouds rimmed in gold by the setting sun.

Sailing on this boat has been like going to heaven—and it is Andrew who has taken Livvi there.

They are entering the harbor now. The Empress, the grand waterfront hotel where they're staying, is coming into view. And Livvi is lost in thought, not really expecting an answer as she asks: "Have you ever, ever, been in such a spectacular place…?"

"Actually I have," Andrew says. "I was here about twenty years ago. On my honeymoon."

And just like that, it's as if the deck of the boat is dropping into the sea.

Livvi is thunderstruck. "You were married?"

Andrew is apologetic. "I didn't mean to upset you." He quickly sets out the fenders and maneuvers the boat into the slip at the dock. "It was no big deal. Honestly. She was my college sweetheart. The whole thing lasted less than six months."

"What was she like? Where did she go?" Livvi's mind is swimming with questions.

Andrew's attention is on mooring the boat. "She was funny and cute. And I don't know where she went. It was nothing. Two kids who ran off to have a good time and woke up married. It happened a lifetime ago."

Now he's kneeling beside Livvi, taking her face in his hands, assuring her: "That girl is somebody I don't even think about anymore. And I doubt she ever thinks about me."

Livvi is looking into his eyes. Those compelling, steel-gray eyes that amaze her and make her weak, every time she sees them. And in this moment their gaze is fully and solely on her.

As Andrew is saying: "It was a blip on the radar. It was nothing."

Four weeks after their return from Canada, Livvi is with Andrew on a business trip to Chicago. One of his public relations clients, a radically creative clothing designer, is showing a new collection.

Livvi and Andrew are at the side of the runway, in front-row seats. Andrew with his legs stretched out and casually crossed at the ankles. Livvi sitting up straight, leaning forward—enthralled by the extravaganza unfolding around her.

The exhibit hall is cavernous. There are speakers everywhere, the size of jet engines. The pulsing techno-beat of the music feels as if it's being pumped through Livvi's veins. Rainbow ribbons of light are arcing and dancing all around her, making it seem like the entire room is a spinning wheel of color.

And on the runway—from one end of it to the other—are designs that are audacious and exotic. Clothes so exciting they're making Livvi gasp.

Without taking her eyes off the spectacular show parading down the runway, she's leaning close to Andrew—preparing to tell him how much she loves him and how wonderful it is to have him in her life. At this same instant, the spotlight is focusing on a gorgeous, dark-haired young model who's strutting past Livvi with an exaggerated, high-stepping gait. And Andrew is murmuring: "Jesus… that girl looks exactly like Katherine."

Something in Andrew's tone makes Livvi's heart jump.

And miss a beat.

When the show is over, when Livvi and Andrew are on the sidewalk in a pouring rain, Andrew is hailing a cab. While Livvi is mentally, and emotionally, still inside the exhibit hall…*where a girl is marching along the runway with eyes that are empty and glittering, like they're made of glass, and Andrew is murmuring, "Jesus…she looks exactly like Katherine."*

Then Livvi is suddenly back in the rain-soaked present and the world is in a clear, hyper-sharp focus. She is feeling, beneath the soles of her shoes, each dimple and bump in the sidewalk. She's hearing, separate and distinct, every drop of rain. Every sound on the street. Every car horn. Every click of the changing traffic lights.

And she's scared.

She's gripping Andrew's upraised arm, yanking it down. Causing the cab he was hailing to swerve away and move back into traffic.

Over the noise of the car horns and the rain, Livvi is shouting: "Who's Katherine?"

And Andrew is shouting back. "She was somebody I loved. And she's gone."

His face is wet with rain. His voice ragged with emotion.

"Tell me about her. I want to know," Livvi says.

"I can't. It's too hard."

"I don't want there to be things about you I don't know, Andrew. It scares me too much. It makes me feel too alone."

And in the face of Livvi's distress, Andrew seems to melt—taking Livvi in his arms, bringing her close. "It wasn't a love affair," he tells her. "It was something different…but it wasn't anything for you to be afraid of. I swear."

"Then—*please*—tell me."

"It's hard for me to talk about. But I will. Someday. I promise."

Now Andrew has stepped away from Livvi and is holding her at arm's length. "I need you to listen to me, to believe me. You have nothing to be afraid of. I'm not going to hurt you."

Andrew's eyes are not leaving Livvi's. His voice is quiet, hushed with emotion. "I love you."

Andrew has never before said *I love you* to Livvi.

Hearing it has left her dazed.

Andrew seems as if he doesn't know what to say next. He's wiping at his eyes. Livvi can't tell if it's the rain, or tears, that he's trying to be rid of.

He's reaching for her, pulling her back toward him. Gripping her so tightly that even through the buffer of his raincoat and jacket she can feel that he's cold—and trembling like a child. In the same way Olivia used to tremble, in the bleak cold of Santa Ynez. Needing someone, anyone, to put their arms around her and hold her close.

From the minute of his arrival in the bookstore in upstate New York, Andrew has lavished Livvi with gifts—with delight and pleasure and untold joy. And in this moment, her only thought, her only desire, is to give him the gift of comfort and consolation. The priceless gift that Olivia never received.

◦◦◦

After several weeks of uninterrupted happiness, Livvi is waking up in a hotel room early on an Easter Sunday morning. She's in San Francisco, where she has been invited to do a book signing.

She's smiling—sleepily reaching for Andrew.

Discovering that he's gone from their bed.

Andrew isn't an early riser—he rarely opens his eyes before eight, and the sun has just come up. There's no note. No text message. No indication at all of where he went. Or when he left. Or why.

And immediately there's a pinch of nervousness in Livvi.

She glances at the luggage rack near the window.

His suitcase is still there.

On a nearby tabletop is the Easter basket he surprised her with last night. A lavishly engraved, light-as-air, silver bowl containing an abundance of Swiss chocolates and a hand-painted music box, with a lid that looks like a patch of flower-strewn grass. In the center of the lid is a pair of formally dressed rabbits who, at the press of a button, do silly pirouettes to a goofy rendition of "Tiptoe through the Tulips."

The presence of the Easter basket and Andrew's suitcase are easing Livvi's anxiety, but only to the smallest degree.

This feeling of dread that Livvi is experiencing is out of her control. Automatic. A dance learned long ago at her father's knee. The waltzing uncertainty of loving a man she doesn't fully understand.

Livvi has picked up her phone and is about to press Andrew's number. Then she's letting the phone drop. Because the door is being opened. In silent, stealthy increments.

Someone is sneaking into the room. One light footstep after another.

When Andrew notices Livvi, sees that she's awake and watching him, he seems rattled. As if he's been out doing something a little dicey—and was hoping that she'd still be asleep.

He takes his time closing the door.

"Where have you been?" Livvi asks.

There's a hint of hesitation before he says: "I went to a sunrise Mass. I always go to Mass on Easter, and on Christmas."

"Mass? I never knew you were a Catholic."

"Well." His attitude is boyish, sheepish. "Now you know."

For the space of a pulse beat Livvi's uncertainty continues. Undiminished.

And then.

Then she's receiving a kiss that's sweet with the taste of communion wine. A lingering kiss—being delivered with the purity of a sacrament.

In addition to the trips and the hotel rooms, there are the days and nights Livvi and Andrew spend together in the Pasadena guesthouse that is Livvi's home. A little treasure she's able to afford only because her landlady, a flamboyant former television writer, gives Livvi a reduced rent in return for Livvi's services as a part-time personal assistant.

The guesthouse has a lovely, old-world sensibility. There's a gracefully tiered fountain in a little outside courtyard. The courtyard's perimeter is blanketed in bougainvillea blossoms that are the color of red chili peppers and as delicate as rice paper. Inside the little three-room house are vases of fresh-cut flowers, walls finished in cream-colored plaster, arched windows kept open to the breeze and fronted by fine, wrought-iron grillwork, and floors covered in rose-colored Saltillo tile. Livvi's furniture is simple. And her bed is high and welcoming, dressed in clean, unbleached cotton.

Livvi has been in this serene space for thirty-six months. Andrew is the only man who has slept with her under its roof.

This is Livvi's cloister. The hiding place where she has insulated herself from the shadows of the past.

Now a missile has been sent whispering through the night. The attack has come in the form of a midnight phone call—and it has shattered her sense of safety.

While Livvi is putting her cell phone back onto the bedside table she's wary, glancing at Andrew, to see if he's still asleep. He is. The call must have been too brief to wake him. It is one of several that have occurred in the last few weeks. This time, unlike the others, Livvi picked up on the first ring. The entire exchange lasted only a few seconds.

There was Livvi's groggy "Hello" as she was turning on the lamp.

The whispery voice saying: "Olivia. Is that you?"

Then Livvi pressing the Off button—dropping the phone as if she'd touched fire.

Livvi is shifting her attention back toward the bedside table— afraid the phone will ring again.

When it doesn't, she cautiously turns out the light. And slides down under the comforter—holding her breath. She is wide awake. And she stays awake. For hours. Agitated and sick.

Livvi had truly believed she was safe from the ghosts of her past, but they are making it clear that they're more agile, and have a much longer reach, than she ever imagined.

Sleep, when it finally comes, is riddled with disturbing images.

Among them is the vision of the woman in the silver dress and pearl-button shoes—the woman whose fiery-red lips are making way for a shrieking howl.

And at the first sight of her, Livvi is fighting for consciousness.

She wakes up shaking—and crying.

Andrew is instantly bringing her near. Nestling her against his chest. Lacing his fingers into hers like a drowsy parent comforting a frightened child.

Livvi—infinitely grateful for his sheltering presence—isn't noticing that in Andrew's grip her fingers are being spread unnaturally wide. She isn't noticing that the fit is just the tiniest bit uncomfortable.

Micah

A Small Town in Kansas ~ 2012

THE CAB IS TURNING THE CORNER, BRINGING THE PLACE INTO view. Micah isn't comfortable with what she's looking at. The worn steps. The neglected lawn. A cracked driveway littered with old newspapers, all of them rounded, in various stages of decay, like a trail of decomposing turtle shells.

The smudged leather on the back of the seat is faintly sticky. The taxi smells of gasoline and of the driver's rancid breath. While the cab is pulling to a stop, Micah is looking toward the door handle. Eager to be gone. But also apprehensive about what's waiting for her on the other side of the passenger window.

"Are you sure this is it?" she asks. There's tension is in her throat and in her chest.

The street is completely silent. Not even the bark of a dog.

The driver turns his head, sunlight glittering across the gray stubble on his cheeks. Micah is listening to the click of false teeth and watching a fine spray of saliva sail from his mouth as he's telling her: "You said Pine Street. One-eight-nine. This here's one-eight-nine."

Micah gets out and hands the driver twenty dollars to cover the fourteen-dollar fare. Then the cab pulls away—and she's alone. In the middle of a street that's as wide and flat and plain as the wind-whipped Kansas landscape that surrounds it.

Being in this vast, open space has Micah on edge; she's not fond of freshly tilled fields and sunshine. She prefers forests and the dark of night—places friendly to things that need to be concealed.

The noiseless emptiness of the street is bordering on eerie. Micah's instinct is to abandon her plan. This search for answers and absolution suddenly seems much too frightening. But before she can unzip her purse to find her phone, to get another cab and escape, the weather-beaten door at 189 has been opened. By a man who's calling to her. And saying: "You're a little early, aren't you?"

Micah can't comprehend what she's seeing. She can't believe how much he's changed. If she'd passed him on the sidewalk she wouldn't have recognized him. It's obvious that he's only in his early forties, but he's skeleton thin and has a scruffy beard. His hair, the magnificent hair that was as black as a midnight ocean, is gray. And he's leaning on a cane, looking incredibly frail, as if he could be toppled by a passing breeze.

What in the world has happened to him? To Jason. Her Jason. The Jason who was always so lithe and alive.

"Well, don't you want to come in?" he asks.

Micah, not knowing how to respond, tells him a lie: "Yes. I want to come in."

While she's walking up the driveway, and onto the porch, and into the house, Micah is wildly uncertain.

She has searched Jason out and traveled here assuming he would be essentially the same man she left seventeen years ago. On that sun-dappled day in September, in Cambridge, not far from the Harvard campus; when she had walked away from him, down the steps of the brownstone where a Justice of the Peace was waiting to perform their wedding. This is the Jason that Micah has come here wanting to see. The young man, the handsome, appealing man.

He's the one who could have given her the reassurance—and the forgiveness—she needs.

But the Jason in Micah's memory isn't in any way the man who has ushered her into his house, who is standing in front of her now. And it's tearing her apart.

His living room is small and square-shaped, surprisingly tidy. The thrift-shop furniture, a sofa and two chairs, is spotless: slip-covered in sky-blue bed sheets held in place by neat rows of chrome-colored safety pins. He's gesturing for Micah to take a seat on the sofa. After she does, he slowly, tentatively, as if trying to keep pain at bay, lowers himself into one of the chairs. He's struggling to hold his head up, drawing ragged breaths, exhausted by the effort of simply sitting down.

Nothing about this moment or this place seems to make any sense. Micah can't think of what to say, how to begin. She can't sort out her tangled emotions. Her shame—for having treated Jason so badly on that September day in Cambridge. Her pity—for the wreck that he's become. Her selfish disappointment—for having flown all the way to Kansas, wanting the beautiful Jason she knew so well, and ending up with an invalid she doesn't even recognize.

Micah has had countless men. Countless lovers and affairs. She's spent her life in a carnival of male attention and sexual adventures. But in that delicious, ever-changing parade of men, there has only been one Micah has never forgotten, never stopped loving. Only one who has been important. Only Jason. Always. And only. Jason.

His expectant expression is letting Micah know he's waiting for her to speak first. "I'm not sure where to begin," she says.

"Well, I figure you probably have some questions you need to ask." His cane has fallen onto the floor; he's leaning forward, fishing for it with a hand that's colorless and unsteady. "Want to know the joke of this?" he laughs. "When I was a kid my mother's favorite charity was multiple sclerosis. Because it was such a bitch of a disease and she felt so sorry for the poor bastards who got it."

Micah can't bear to see how depleted and feeble he is. She's glancing around the room, doing her best not to look at him, wishing it were yesterday and that she'd never gotten on the plane. All she can think to say is: "How long have you been living here?"

"I figured you'd have that information already."

"Why?"

Micah shifts her gaze to meet his. And he smiles in a strange, surprised sort of way.

And she asks: "Why are you looking at me like that?"

"I don't know," he chuckles. "I was just thinking...you're mighty pretty."

Mighty pretty. That homey, Midwestern style of saying things. Micah hasn't heard a phrase like that for a long, long while. For some reason, hearing it now is bringing her close to tears. The heat of those waiting tears—and the kindness she's noticing in his eyes—is melting something in Micah. Something that's been frozen with fear ever since the final day of her trip to New York.

Without intending to, she's telling him: "I have cancer. It's bad and they want to do surgery. I'll probably lose my breasts—"

Micah stops. For an instant everything has gone blank.

Then she tells him: "If I don't say yes to treatment right away, I'll probably die. But I'm thinking maybe, because of the evil I've done, dying is what would be fair. I'm thinking maybe I shouldn't fight the cancer...that it's my punishment and I should just let it happen. To finally make amends."

He shakes his head, staring off into mid-distance, processing what he's just heard. "Sounds to me like right now you're not thinking straight."

After a while, he looks back at Micah. He seems perplexed and asks: "What could you ever have done that would deserve letting yourself die for it?"

His gaze is open, direct; and in it Micah is catching a glimpse of unvarnished truth. This is a good and honest man whose concern for her is genuine. There's not one shred of judgment or revulsion in what he has said. And Micah, craving the release that comes with confession, tells him something she has never told another living soul. She names, precisely, the evil that she has done.

It leaves him stunned.

For several minutes neither of them speaks, neither of them moves. The stillness is so complete that Micah can hear the beating of her own heart and the pulsing of blood in her veins.

When the phone rings, it shatters the silence like a scream. When Micah answers it, everything she thinks is real is being made unreal.

Such a profound mistake—with such simple roots.

A rushed text message: 189 Pane Street inadvertently typed as 189 Pine Street.

A disabled man in his forties, an MS patient, expecting a noon visit from his new caseworker; a woman he's never met.

Micah's arrival on Pine Street at eleven forty-five.

While Jason—the man Micah has come to see—is three miles away. Waiting for her on Pane Street.

In the background of the photo that Micah has just been handed there's what appears to be a church picnic, or perhaps a neighborhood block party. In the foreground is a moderately pretty woman with an unremarkable haircut and a slightly lopsided smile. On either side of the woman—leaning against her affectionately—are a pair of extraordinarily handsome teenage boys.

Micah is taking a last look at the photo then handing it back to Jason, while he's saying: "Wendy. Scott. And Coulter. Those three are my world."

The expression in Jason's eyes suggests that he's a truly happy man. "It's amazing how good our life is right now. Wendy's just opened a cupcake business, she's a terrific baker. And the boys are doing great. Growing like weeds. Scott's a sophomore...unbelievable soccer player. Coulter, our basketball star, starts high school next year. God, I wish you weren't leaving this afternoon. I'd love for you to come by and meet everybody. Have dinner with us, or maybe..."

Micah isn't really focusing on what Jason is suggesting. For most of the hour that she's been with him in this coffee shop, on Pane Street, she's had trouble keeping track of the conversation. She has been too upset and confused. Now she's beginning to understand why.

In spite of how fit and healthy he is, Jason has turned out to be more of a shock, more of a disappointment, than the frail, frayed man she'd encountered on Pine Street. It's dawning on Micah that that man, because he was crippled and suffering, was, in a strange way, what she had expected Jason to be—what on some perverse level she'd needed him to be.

This actual Jason is thriving and completely content. And it's almost as if Micah has been blown apart by that.

"I'm considering a run for city council," he's saying. "I think I can make a difference, do some good." Then he pauses and asks: "Does that sound too corny? What do you think?"

Micah's head is spinning...*I don't know what to think. I came here expecting you to say how hard it was to survive without me all these years. I was planning to ask you to forgive me. For walking out on you and breaking something sacred—something that never should've been broken. I thought the hurt from that would be permanent. It never even occurred to me that it could be temporary—that it could heal, and go away. Jason, you used to say I'd marked you, made you mine. I thought that mark was indelible. I honestly don't understand...how could what you had with me be replaced by things as trivial as cupcakes and soccer games?*

Micah is startled to see that Jason is settling the bill, getting ready to leave. He's planting a brotherly peck on her cheek and scooting out of his chair. "Wish I could stay longer but I've got to pick my boys up. Coulter has a game this afternoon."

When Jason is a few feet from the table, he pauses and looks back at Micah. Taking in every detail. The way an art lover would admire a recently rediscovered Rembrandt.

Then Jason is strolling away, sending Micah a jaunty wave, a lighthearted good-bye. Completely free of nostalgia. Or reluctance.

And the pain is devastating.

It wasn't that Micah came here wanting to rob Jason of whatever bliss he has found. It's that she had needed the reassurance of knowing he'd missed her, and felt his life was diminished, just a fraction, because she hadn't been in it.

While she's watching him walk away, Micah is experiencing a jealous sort of mourning. She's not wishing Jason any harm. She's simply wishing he could have proved to her that she was important. That she had been loved. That she had mattered.

On the way to the airport Micah is at first numb. Then disappointed. And finally, in an unexpected way, relieved.

She discovers the relief when her driver, a black man with a shaved head and flawlessly manicured fingernails, glances up at the rearview mirror and says: "Your time in Kansas—business or pleasure?"

Micah is recalling fleeting images of the haggard MS patient in the blue, slip-covered chair: and Jason, happy and smiling in the crowded coffee shop. "I was here on business," she says.

"You get everything done you came to do?"

Micah, looking out at the horizon, is talking more to herself than to the driver, when she replies: "I came here to see a man I used to know…to say things I thought were important."

"Did you get the chance to say those things to him?"

"Not really," Micah murmurs. "They turned out to be irrelevant."

The driver puts his full concentration on the road. He does it with a kind of courtliness, as if trying to give Micah some privacy.

And Micah, continuing to gaze toward the flat line of the horizon, is realizing that the only item of importance she communicated during her trip to Kansas was the secret she confided to the stranger on Pine Street.

The admission made in that splinter of time just before Jason's phone call came, asking why she wasn't on Pane Street.

The single sentence that explained what her evil was—the heart-sick confession in which Micah said: "I killed someone."

AnnaLee
Glen Cove, Long Island ~ 1986

HEARTSICK.

This isn't the emotion a woman should experience while she's watching her husband coming across the terrace of their home carrying a single, long-stemmed white rose—a rose obviously intended as a gift for her.

But heartsick is exactly what AnnaLee is feeling.

It's a little before three in the afternoon on a Wednesday and here Jack is with a flower in his hand and a vague, endearingly shy smile on his face when he should be at the office, adding to his billable hours. Focused on climbing the ladder at the law firm and on making money. Money he and AnnaLee desperately need in order to keep a roof over their heads.

AnnaLee, in faded overalls and an old straw hat, has been scrubbing the accumulated muck out of the reflecting pool at the edge of the garden. Now as she's stripping off the wet, heavy gloves she's been wearing, she's noticing that Jack is dropping the white rose onto the arm of a weathered Adirondack chair, and veering away from her.

He's striding toward the other end of the terrace, saying: "Bella! There's my beautiful Bella!" Bella is the pet name they call their child. It started as Tinkerbelle, became Belle, then somehow evolved into Bella. It had its beginnings on the day of their baby's birth—when an awed AnnaLee had said that their little girl looked like a tiny, magical fairy.

Now Jack is lifting Bella from the quilt that's spread out on the lawn, the spot where Bella has been napping and playing for most of the afternoon. He's swooping her through the air, delighting in her laughter, and telling her: "I wish I were you, Bella. I wish I could fly! I wish—"

AnnaLee cuts him off—saying "You're home early"—hating the nagging tone in her voice. And at the same time remembering the hurt of having to sell her mother's wedding present, the blue-and-white porcelain vase, to Mrs. Wang.

Jack keeps his conversation directed at Bella, finishing his thought as if he hadn't been interrupted. "I wish I could do what you do every day, Bella…I wish I could spend my time out in the sunshine with your incomparable, wonderful mother."

He then delivers Bella into AnnaLee's arms, and tells AnnaLee: "I love you." He does it with an attitude that suggests apology and unhappiness.

It makes AnnaLee weary. He's constantly leaning on her, needing her to be his compass and his strength. And in spite of the love she has for Jack, sometimes the weight of him is too much. Which is why AnnaLee is closing her eyes and pressing her cheek against Bella's, escaping into the comforting feel and scent of her little girl's skin, seeking the warmth of sunshine and the smell of summer grass.

Jack is passing his finger over the reddening welt on AnnaLee's forearm that runs from her elbow to her wrist, and he's asking: "Where did this come from?"

"Thorns," AnnaLee says. "From earlier—when I was trimming the roses."

"It could get infected. We should go upstairs and clean it."

Jack's touch on her arm is extraordinarily compassionate.

And AnnaLee murmurs: "Eleven."

"Eleven...?" Jack says.

"It's been eleven years. Since the emergency room. In Brooklyn." AnnaLee is momentarily lost in thought. "I can't believe how young we both were."

"We're not so old now, are we?"

"I think maybe we are. I think maybe I am." AnnaLee shifts Bella so that her hold on the baby is more secure. Then she asks Jack: "Do you ever think about that night?" There's a hint of brittleness in her tone, something slightly combative.

Before Jack can answer, she says: "I think about it...about how it felt just after the truck hit me. When my face was on the pavement and I could see my leg, bent at that odd angle. Mangled. Cut-up like chunks of meat. Like something on a butcher's table."

AnnaLee's eyes haven't moved from Jack's face; she's trying to get him to engage with her—she wants him to let her know that he's hearing what she's saying. But the way he's looking at her— the way he's standing there, wordlessly, helplessly—is showing AnnaLee something she already knows.

It isn't in Jack's power to give her what she needs.

All AnnaLee has is the sound of her own voice, as she's telling him: "I know the accident was a long time ago and that every-thing's fine now. I'm alive. I can walk. But I'm not talking about now—I'm thinking about that night. About me. Who I was. I was a really good dancer...in rehearsal for *Giselle*...the ballerina who was going to dance the lead."

AnnaLee understands that she's resurrecting an old and unsolv-able riddle. It's an exercise in futility. And she can't stop herself.

Because part of her is still refusing to come to terms with what happened that night. With its randomness—and permanence.

"There was coffee in the rehearsal hall," she's explaining to Jack. "And I was running across the street for espresso. I hardly ever drank espresso. Why did I want it right then, at that particular moment? And why, when there was barely any traffic on the street and there were lights everywhere…streetlights…store lights…why didn't the truck driver see me? Why?"

AnnaLee is begging Jack to help her make sense of it.

But all he says is: "It was an accident, Lee. Accidents happen."

She glances down at her wedding ring, murmuring: "Accidents happen…then they cause other accidents."

Jack sighs. The apology—the unhappiness—that was in him earlier has returned.

"Do you know what made me fall in love with you that night?" AnnaLee asks.

He shakes his head, telling her no.

"Your compassion," she says. "Your incredible sweetness."

Jack's tone is nostalgic. "I was just a second-year surgical resident who wanted to be my best for you. You were the most beautiful thing I'd ever seen."

"You still have it, you know. That incredible sweetness."

AnnaLee rests her head on Jack's shoulder. Loving him intensely for who he is. And wishing, with all her heart, that he were different—in so many ways.

On the surface, Jack is AnnaLee's idea of perfection: fair skin and sandy hair and hazel-green eyes. But it's what's below the surface—his mystifying, disjointed frailties—that wear away at her. Daily. Like a drizzling, acid rain.

The damage that has been done by his weaknesses is what

AnnaLee is thinking about as she's telling Jack: "After all these years, I still can't understand how you could've turned our lives upside down the way you did."

Jack is moving apart from her, putting his hands in his pockets, drawing a long slow breath that's warning AnnaLee he doesn't want to go down this particular road. But he is listening to her. With his head bowed. As if he's slightly embarrassed. And doesn't have the right to stop her from giving voice to what she's about to say.

"You were a brilliant trauma surgeon, Jack." AnnaLee pauses, then says: "And you just threw it away…just came home one day and announced you couldn't stand the blood and the pain anymore, and that you'd enrolled in law school. Jack, you hadn't even mentioned you'd decided to apply to law school."

There's a catch in AnnaLee's voice—the sound of disappointment and disbelief. She's holding Bella close, rocking her gently, asking Jack: "How could you have put us into such staggering debt?"

Jack shifts his weight, leans against the trunk of a nearby tree, and says nothing.

His passivity, his silences, are infuriating. AnnaLee is fighting the urge to shout at him as she says: "What you've done to us isn't fair. You graduated from law school with honors, got recruited by a top firm. Everything was fine. And then out of nowhere you start coming home earlier and earlier. Because now instead of hating being a doctor you hate being a lawyer. Because—" AnnaLee pauses. "Wait. Let me think of the words you used…your exact words were 'I'm as derailed by the moral ambiguity of the courtroom as I was by the carnage in the emergency room.'"

She's staring at Jack, defying him to look away. "That's what you said. It was like you didn't have a clue you were talking about real life, about our life. You sounded like some overeducated character in a bad soap opera."

"I'm sorry. I'll try to do better." There's desperation in Jack's voice. "Tell me you believe me, Lee. Tell me you believe me."

AnnaLee isn't answering, and she can see it's hurting him.

As soon as she's able to subdue her own hurt, she soothes his, saying: "Yes, Jack. I believe you."

I know you'll try, she's thinking. *I know you want to be different... want to be a hero and a rescuer. But you don't have the heart for it, Jack. You're defenseless against brutality and ugliness. The truth is you're at your best when you're away from the world. In a cocoon of books and ideas... lost in contemplation.*

AnnaLee is aware that if these traits belonged to a poet or a saint, she would probably see them as virtues. But in her husband, because of the precarious life he's given her, she sees them as betrayal, as pathetic and weak.

A breeze is sending flower petals skipping across the terrace, and across the tops of AnnaLee's shoes. She's feeling a chill and wants to go inside, to get a sweater for Bella.

But Jack is inspecting a limb on the tree he has been leaning against. He's making a point of sounding decisive and capable, like a man who knows how to take charge and fix things: "This branch needs to be cut, it's hanging too low. Somebody could walk into it and get hurt. I'll trim it next week."

AnnaLee—knowing he'll forget to do the work on the tree, and too weary to argue—simply nods.

"I understand what a lucky man I am," Jack is telling her. "I have the most wonderful wife in the world, and the most wonderful child." He's smiling as he's looking at AnnaLee, and then at Bella, and then at the house. "Whatever bumps in the road we've had, whatever bumps we have ahead, we've got each other, and we've got this beautiful place to come home to."

Jack's mention of the house is like vinegar splashing into an open cut. *The only thing keeping us in this house is me,* AnnaLee is thinking. *I'm the one making the repairs, doing the gardening. I'm the one who brought us here, who keeps us here. Every time you don't work enough hours to pay the bills, it's me who has to endure the losses—and make those humiliating calls to Mrs. Wang. Don't talk about how much you enjoy this house, Jack. You haven't earned the right.*

AnnaLee is convinced it would destroy Jack if she were ever to lose control and tell him what she's thinking at moments like this. Which is why all she says is: "It's cold out here."

Jack is standing beside her now. Concerned and contrite. "Let's go inside—I'll clean that cut on your arm. You shouldn't have been pruning the roses. I could've taken care of it. I'm almost always home early—"

Her frustration is out of her mouth before she can stop it. "Where you should be is in your office. That way we could afford a gardener."

It has been a long, tiring day and AnnaLee has run out of patience.

She's pushing past Jack now, with Bella still in her arms, stumbling slightly, landing hard on her left foot, letting out a small whimper. And Jack is quickly taking Bella, to make it easier for AnnaLee to walk.

She often experiences bouts of debilitating pain in her left ankle. And she's acutely aware that if it hadn't been for Jack, for his extraordinary skill as a surgeon eleven years ago, after her accident, she would never have been able to walk at all.

And as she's approaching the bottom of the terrace steps AnnaLee is doing her best to keep the edge out of her voice—she's trying to make amends. "Tell me about your day. How was it?"

There's a long pause. Silence from Jack. As if he knows he's being patronized.

AnnaLee has started up the short flight of terrace stairs, and her ankle is wobbling. She's losing her footing. Instantly, Jack's hand is under her elbow—steadying her, supporting her.

With Bella cradled against his chest, Jack is matching his stride to AnnaLee's. He's keeping his steps measured and slow, helping her to maintain her balance.

Then as they're moving toward the French doors that lead to the living room Jack takes a quick, tense breath and tells AnnaLee: "Brian called. From Belgium—to say hello."

The mention of Brian's name immediately makes AnnaLee apprehensive. "What did he want?"

"I sent him some pictures from Bella's party. He wanted us to know how great they were. He can't believe she's had her first birthday already."

AnnaLee slows the pace until she and Jack are at a standstill. "Bella's birthday was months and months ago, that can't be the reason he called."

Jack clears his throat—looking out at the garden and not at AnnaLee. "He wants to know what we decided…about this summer."

AnnaLee is recalling a ghoulish snake tattoo and a silver nose ring. Purple hair, kohl-rimmed eyes, thick-soled Army boots. And the angry shriek of heavy metal music.

She's quickly taking Bella away from Jack, saying: "Tell him the answer is no."

"For God's sake, AnnaLee, he's not asking for the world. It'll only be a couple of months."

"I don't care." AnnaLee is troubled, for reasons she can't fully explain.

"It seems ridiculous," she tells Jack. "He has plenty of money. Why does he want his daughter to stay here for the summer? He can afford to send her anywhere. Europe. Summer camp. Anything she wants."

"She's alone and lonely." There's a stubborn tone in Jack's voice—this is a conversation they've had before. "She needs a home, even if it's only for a little while."

While Jack is wrapping his arms around her—embracing her and Bella—AnnaLee is thinking about the sadly forlorn expression she has seen flit those kohl-rimmed eyes.

Jack is resting his cheek against AnnaLee's, asking for her understanding. "Brian is my brother, he needs my help. It's just for the summer...a couple of months. All we're talking about is one, little teenage girl. And the only thing she has is money. We have so much more than that, Lee. How can we not share it?"

The familiar warmth of Jack's embrace is bringing AnnaLee both comfort and apprehension. It is the sensation of being lifted up and, in the same instant, being drowned.

After a while. After AnnaLee has let Jack lead her into the house. After Bella is tucked into bed. And President Reagan has begun a speech on television and twilight has come. The single, long-stemmed white rose remains forgotten on the terrace. Being buffeted by a cold wind that will soon strip it bare.

Livvi
Pasadena, California ~ 2012

AYBREAK. THE WIND IS THUMPING A HEAVY TREE BRANCH against the side of the house. Rattling the wrought-iron gate in the courtyard. Shaking the air with an ominous boom—like an explosion from a cannon.

Livvi has been startled awake by that echoing boom. And as she's scrambling out of her warm soft bed she is, for a fraction of time, in the cold grip of her barren room in Santa Ynez. Frantic to determine what has been broken—and to find a way to make it whole again. Seized by the stomach-churning fear that if she fails she'll be punished.

And the fear stops her in her tracks.

This consuming sense of dread is as fixed in Livvi as the color of her eyes or the shape of her face. Its roots are old and deep. Even now, as she's waking up in her own home, safe and protected, part of her is still in a place where the night-quiet is being shattered by her father's screams: screams so agonized that their echoes are leaving her huddled in her childhood bed, shaking with fear.

For several long moments Livvi is a little girl again…*she's waiting out the screams. Afraid of the eerie stillness that will follow them. Terrified of what will erupt in the wake of that stillness. Pandemonium that will sound like a rampage of demons.*

She is fearing the morning. When she'll go downstairs and see what awful thing is being illuminated in the light of the new day.

Will it be fist-prints pounded into the cracked plaster of the walls? Or a trail of blood splattered across a broken window? Or entire rooms filled with upended furniture?

Whatever it is, she knows her father will be somewhere nearby, standing mute. With his clothes in disarray. Sweat-soaked. As if he's been hurling boulders. She'll see the devastated look on his face. And that his knuckles are raw. Or that his hands are clumsily wrapped in blood-soaked bandages. And in the confusion of a child's logic, and because she doesn't have anyone to tell her any different, she'll be convinced she's responsible for her father's pain. Because she hasn't been able to figure out—at the age of five, or six, or nine—how to calm his madness.

Each new explosion in that house in Santa Ynez reinforced Livvi's sense of anxiety—until eventually the feeling became permanent. It's why now, as Livvi's thoughts have returned to the present, and she is moving toward the archway that leads from her bedroom into the living room, she's doing it with a sense of dread.

When Livvi enters the living room, she sees the front door is open. And that someone is in the house. A redhead. Perched on the arm of the sofa, backlit by the soft, pink light of earliest morning. She's wearing platform heels and a skintight, acid-green mini-dress.

And she's saying: "Baby, do you have any idea what the hell just happened in your driveway?" Her voice is a peculiar combination of gravel and honey—part roller-derby queen, part high-rent seductress. Her body suggests she could be in her late thirties but her face hints that she's somewhere closer to fifty. The cynicism in her gaze says she's churned through a lot of bad dates and hard knocks.

She is Livvi's landlady. Sierra. Owner of the main house to which Livvi's little guesthouse belongs. Livvi, in a sleep-rumpled T-shirt and pajama bottoms, isn't surprised to see Sierra—at dawn—in high heels and sequins. Sierra is no doubt at the tail-end of a long night of partying.

She has a key in her hand. Waving it above her head. Wafting the scent of bourbon and Chanel No. 5. Telling Livvi: "I didn't want to wake you by ringing the doorbell, so I used my handy-dandy passkey."

After delivering this announcement, Sierra makes herself at home on Livvi's sofa. She's slipping her shoes off and reaching into her dress to loosen her strapless bra, while saying: "Hey, I asked you a question and I didn't get an answer. Do you or do you not know what just happened in your damn driveway?"

"No," Livvi stammers. "I'm sorry, I just woke up. I…"

"What're you apologizing for? Calm the heck down, sugarplum." Sierra is now easing her bra out through the armhole of her dress. When she finishes, she drops the bra into her lap and says: "It's five-twenty in the morning, and I'm barging into your house asking you stuff I already know you don't know—that's called being an asshole. Doesn't it ever occur to you to tell people like me to go fuck themselves?"

Livvi blushes and shakes her head.

"Sugarplum, that's something I've always found interesting about you…you never seem to know when you have the right to be pissed off." Sierra gives Livvi a long, steady look, then adds: "I'm guessing that somewhere along the line…early on…you got smacked hard by an asshole who was world-class. Somebody who told you that everything was your fault, that you were the problem."

Sierra waits for a response. When she doesn't get one, she says: "Knowing when to tell assholes to fuck off is an important skill, kiddo. Come up to the house when you have some time, I'll give you a couple of lessons. But for the moment"—Sierra is leaving the sofa, going to the door and opening it wide—"you got other things to think about."

Livvi now has a clear view of the driveway—and of what caused the cannon-like boom that startled her out of bed. The massive, arrow-shaped, cast-iron weather vane, the crown on the guesthouse roof for the last eighty years, has been torn loose by the wind. And has plummeted through the top of Livvi's little car. The thick shaft of the weather vane's arrow has sliced into the car's interior and buried its vicious-looking tip right in the middle of the driver's seat.

Livvi is fighting a wave of nausea. The car is only a few months old, bought after her ancient, second-hand Civic died by the side of the road and was towed to a scrap yard. A major part of the advance on her book went to cover the down payment. She has no idea how she's going to pay for the damage the weather vane has just done.

Sierra is slipping her arm around Livvi and chuckling. "Hope you don't need to go anywhere for a while, sugarplum."

Livvi can hear the buzz of her alarm clock coming from the bedroom—and her nausea is being replaced by panic. "Oh, god. I have a breakfast meeting in Culver City at seven forty-five."

Sierra is stretching and yawning, getting ready to leave. "From Pasadena to Culver City? In rush-hour traffic? You'd need to be on the freeway by six-fifteen. Car rental places don't even open till seven."

Livvi groans and sinks down onto the doorstep, her hand over her mouth.

Sierra's smile is as easy as her shrug. "No worries. Crawl back into the sack. Get some sleep. Everything'll be fine."

"No, it won't," Livvi says.

And she's thinking, *I'm not like you. I've got no cushion, no buffers.*

I live with my back two inches away from the edge of a cliff and there's nothing between me and the drop. I don't even have the littlest piece of a safety net. I never have. And listening to you right now makes me want to tell you to go screw yourself.

But even before Livvi has fully processed the thought, her anger is already fading—and instead of telling Sierra to screw herself, she's explaining: "I can't reschedule the meeting. It's one of those once in a lifetime things…a European producer is interested in optioning the movie rights to my book. He's leaving this afternoon and I don't know when he'll be back." Livvi is looking at her crumpled car. "The option money probably wouldn't have been a lot, but whatever it might've been, I really needed it."

Sierra is searching for something in her purse, paying only minimal attention to Livvi, explaining: "I'd lend you my ride, but the Jag's in the shop."

Now she's tossing a cell phone in Livvi's direction. "Here. Problem solved. You don't even have to get up and go looking for your phone."

While Livvi is leaning forward to catch Sierra's phone, Sierra is muttering: "Use it to call that hot guy who's been sleeping with you for almost seven months—tell him you need a little help."

Andrew. Of course. Andrew. It hadn't even occurred to Livvi to call him.

Her immediate response to seeing her crushed car had been the sensation of being Olivia trapped in the frigid space between her bed and the wall. Alone in the dark. Trying to keep the nightmare at bay. Desperately needing someone to come and help her. Clearly understanding no one would.

But now, Livvi is suddenly realizing, all of that has changed—she isn't alone anymore. She has Andrew.

There's a sense of excitement—of lightness—as she's entering his number into the phone. But when the call goes unanswered, when she leaves a message and several minutes pass without a response, the lightness fades. And Livvi begins to wonder why, at five in the morning, Andrew, a man who's never more than a few feet from his phone, is unable to answer it.

The look on Sierra's face makes it clear to Livvi that Sierra's wondering the same thing.

And Livvi is trying to come up with an explanation. "Andrew said he was exhausted last night. That's why he didn't stay here—he needed a solid eight hours in his own bed. He's probably out cold and isn't hearing the phone. So…" Livvi falters into silence. She's embarrassed.

Along with the cynicism in Sierra's eyes, Livvi is now seeing a hint of pity.

Sierra has gone to the main house, to sleep. Livvi is in the guest-house kitchen distractedly wiping spilled coffee grounds from the countertop, dropping them into the sink, and thinking that she needs to call David. She checks the antique clock on the shelf above the stove. It's five-fifteen. Eight-fifteen in New York. Livvi won't be disturbing David if she phones him now; he's always up by seven-thirty.

David answers her call on the second ring. He sounds foggy, vague, as if he's been roused out of sleep and is barely conscious. But the first thing he says is: "Are you okay? Is something wrong?"

"Oh god, I woke you! I thought you were always up by seven-thirty, I'm so sorry—"

David interrupts, his voice soft but now fully awake. "I'm in LA, Livvi. In Beverly Hills at the Peninsula Hotel. I got in late last night—a spur-of-the-moment trip. I'm here for my cousin's graduation. You had no way of knowing that."

The morning's disasters have drained Livvi. The compassion in David's tone is making her feel like she's going to cry.

"What's happening?" he's asking. "Something's wrong. I could hear it the minute I picked up the phone."

Livvi is leaning over the sink, dizzy with disappointment. "My car is smashed, I can't make the seven forty-five meeting you set up for me with that European producer. I need to let him know, but I don't have his cell number and—"

"Remind me where the meeting is again."

"Culver City."

She hears a rustling and a soft thump as if David is getting out of bed while he's saying: "I'll pick you up in an hour."

Livvi's knees are threatening to buckle. She's weak with gratitude. But before she can thank David, she's hearing a snippet of muffled conversation—a woman's sleepy voice murmuring, "Want me to wait for breakfast till you get back?" and David replying, "That's okay, I'll catch up with you later."

Livvi quickly puts the phone down. Thinking about her unanswered call to Andrew. Vividly picturing the reason for his continuing silence.

Now her knees actually are buckling. One of them is banging against a cabinet door, and the door's wrought-iron handle is opening a gash on her kneecap. A trail of blood is snaking down the front of her leg, threatening to fall onto the floor and stain the lovely rose-colored clay tiles. She needs to reach for a towel—and stop the bleeding. Needs to intercept the damage. But she has been paralyzed. Frozen in place. By the insidiously soft sound of that sleepy female voice.

The breakfast meeting in Culver City, which has gone well, ended a little less than ten minutes ago. An oncoming car is making an abrupt left turn. David is hitting the brakes, and Livvi is sliding forward in her seat, the cut on her knee banging against the passenger side of the dashboard, making her wince.

David is maneuvering the car onto the crowded on-ramp to the eastbound Santa Monica freeway. Without taking his eyes from the road, seeming to sense Livvi's wince without having seen it, he's asking: "Are you all right?"

"I'm fine," Livvi says. "How can I not be? I've never had anyone change the course of the world for me before."

David's chuckle is self-deprecating. "I don't think the deal we just accepted from that producer can be classified as world-changing."

"The option money he gave us on the book is great. I know it wouldn't have been anywhere near that much if you hadn't been there. But what I'm blown away by is that the meeting happened at all—that you drove an hour to pick me up, and another hour and a half to get me here. And now, with traffic at a standstill like this, who knows how many more hours it will take you to get me home? I guess what I'm trying to say is you're amazing."

David holds Livvi's gaze for a long beat, then tells her: "I'm your friend. I care about you."

Livvi doesn't reply. She's gone back to thinking about Andrew. About how his response to her call for help—at dawn—didn't come until fifteen minutes ago. When the meeting was ending and the morning was already over. She's thinking about the tense, brief nature of their exchange...*Livvi, with her phone to her ear, telling Andrew there'd been an emergency but the problem had been solved—and Andrew sounding distracted, saying: "Great. Good. Anyway, I'm working a short day. Let's have lunch. Around twelve. Meet me at my place then we'll decide on a restaurant."*

While Livvi is wondering what it was that kept Andrew so silent between the hours of five and nine, she's asking: "Did I interrupt something?"

David shoots her a confused glance. "What do you mean?"

"This morning, when I called. I have the feeling maybe I interrupted something."

David seems to be thinking carefully before he answers, and tells her: "I was with someone. Someone I like."

There's an odd twinge of jealousy in Livvi—then she hears: "But at that moment taking your call was more important."

In the hush that follows David's comment neither one of them says anything more.

When Livvi finally does speak, all she says is: "When we get back into Pasadena, don't take me home. There's somewhere else I need to go."

She's nervous—her hands have begun to sweat.

Micah
Louisville, Kentucky ~ 2012

SIMPLY WALKING INTO THE PLACE HAS MADE MICAH JITTERY. Made her begin to sweat. This isn't a location she would have chosen to visit, but now that she's here there's no turning back. Which is why she's shouting above the screech of the repairman's drill—trying to make herself heard, explaining to him: "I need to see the manager. Is she around?"

The repairman, small and stoop-shouldered, is near the Laundromat's entry, squatting at the base of a dryer, installing a new motor. He's wearing a sweat-stained dress shirt and a pair of frayed brown work-pants, cinched at the waist with a wide red belt. The way he's crouched against the dryer is exposing the heels of his boots, thin and scarred—the right one almost completely worn away. He doesn't bother to look up at Micah, or to speak to her. He simply pauses the drill; jerks his thumb in the general direction of the center area, where the washers are; and then returns to his work. Running the drill at top speed. Putting an end to any further conversation.

A couple dozen people are scattered among the rows of dingy, groaning washers. Most of them female. One is black and quite young. Two of them are old and chatting to each other in Spanish. The remaining women, the objects of Micah's attention, are Caucasian. All in their late thirties or early forties.

A trickle of perspiration that has begun just under Micah's hairline is now sliding along her temple and slipping over the curve of her cheek. The air inside the Laundromat, like the air outside—in Louisville—is heavy and humid. But what's causing Micah to sweat isn't the soapy dampness of the room or the mugginess of the overcast Kentucky afternoon. She's sweating because she immediately knows which of the women she's looking at is the one she's here to see.

She's certain of the woman's identity because, after the debacle in Kansas, after mistaking a stranger for the person she was looking for, she hasn't taken any chances. She has hired a top-notch private investigator to lead her to this worn-out laundry-house.

There's not a shred of doubt that Micah is in the right place and has found the right person. The stocky, gum-chewing, stone-faced individual leaning against one of the battered washers, lazily wiping down its rust-rimmed lid, is Hayden Truitt. An individual who, many years ago when she and Micah were girls, carried a switchblade and owned a dog named Lucifer.

As Micah is walking toward Hayden—and Hayden is warily watching her—Micah can't find any alteration in Hayden's expression. Any change in the steady rhythm of her gum-chewing. Any flicker of emotion.

In Micah, however, there is absolute chaos.

It's as if a hole has opened in time and she's being sucked back into that awful moment when she first met Hayden. A meeting that ultimately led to such unimaginable mayhem.

Micah is only a few feet away from Hayden now, and she's surprised by how mannishly thick Hayden's body has become and how dead her eyes are. Hayden, her face still emotionless, is making a show of casually pressing her tongue into the wad of gum she's chewing—and pushing it to one side of her mouth.

Her voice is flat, deadpan, as she asks Micah: "You here to wash somethin'?" Without waiting for a response, she adds: "Can't be that fancy outfit you're wearin'—that little number looks right-out-of-the-dry-cleaner fresh."

Micah is so rattled she can barely speak when she tells Hayden: "I need to ask you a question."

Hayden snorts, twirls the grimy cleaning rag she's holding, and flicks it at Micah's wrist.

The hit is painfully sharp.

Hayden's eyes stay blank and unreadable. But there's a hint of a smile as she resumes her steady, lazy gum-chewing and asks: "You here for some help with stain removal? Maybe wonderin' what the trick is to getting blood off your hands?"

Hayden's question triggers a spike of guilt in Micah—Micah's voice is defensively shrill as she shouts: "Your hands are a hell of a lot bloodier than mine!"

Several of the Laundromat's patrons look in Micah's direction. She stares them down until they turn away. Then. To calm herself. She runs her hands along the sides of her silk skirt, smoothing at nonexistent wrinkles.

Hayden's gaze goes to the places on the silk where Micah's palms are leaving damp trails of sweat. "What's the matter? You look about ready to pee yourself." There's an amused, scoffing quality to the remark.

Micah waits for Hayden's eyes to meet hers. "I'm sick," she tells Hayden. "There's a good chance I'm about to die."

Hayden takes a moment to ponder this information. Then she turns her head, spits her gum into a nearby trash can, and mutters: "Holy crap." When she brings her focus back to Micah, her attitude is still essentially blank but somehow not quite as cold.

And Micah tells her: "I need to know…if a person was able to accept a punishment…one that was cruel enough and permanent enough…would it erase…" She pauses. Searching for the right word. She doesn't know what it is.

Hayden steps in close, spreading her arms wide, revealing clusters of ugly, crudely rendered, jailhouse tattoos.

She's glaring at Micah, telling her: "When you're in the middle of it, fifteen years in prison is cruel and feels pretty damn permanent."

Something in Micah recoils—and is ashamed.

A glint is appearing in Hayden's eyes. Whether it's a glimmer of hostility, or of sympathy, isn't clear.

There isn't a shred of feeling in Hayden's voice as she's saying: "After spendin' fifteen years pressed up against iron bars, whatever was sharp inside you, whatever was bad when you went in, doesn't get fixed and doesn't get better, it just gets worn down. By the time you're through, big chunks of you are gone, and the wrong you did is just somethin' you kinda remember once in a while—like a bad taste. You walk out of those prison gates pretty much who you were when you went in—only a little more tired."

Hayden leans against the washer, her head thrown back, her eyes slitted, as if she's silently laughing at Micah. "But not gettin' redeemed and all is just fine. 'Cause the truth is…what's done can't ever be undone. All that's left is to get on with things, the best you can." She pops another piece of gum into her mouth and returns to sliding the dirty rag over the rusted lid of the washer.

Micah yanks the rag away from Hayden and grabs her by the arm so that they are again face-to-face. Micah is seething as she warns Hayden: "I didn't travel all the way to goddamn Kentucky to have you bullshit me."

Hayden looks down at the place on her arm where Micah's fingers are digging into her flesh, waits for Micah to release her, and then says: "What do you want from me?"

"I need the truth. I don't believe you've never thought about wanting forgiveness, wanting to atone for what you did. You couldn't be human and not have. I need to know every single thing you've ever thought about doing that would help make it right, that would help get your soul clean. And I don't want to hear about how fifteen lousy years just washed everything away, like it never happened."

And Hayden hisses: "If I'd stayed in for twenty years. For fifty. If I'd sliced my own throat with a razor and bled to death"—Hayden's face is so close to Micah's that Micah can feel flecks of Hayden's spit landing on her cheek—"would it make things even? Would it change what happened that night?"

Micah is uncertain of the answer to Hayden's question. And unable to let go of her own guilt. Her voice is shaking as she says: "Because of things we did, someone died."

"Yeah. And me and two other people went to prison for it. One of them tried to hang himself in his cell. And none of it makes a bit of difference—'cause that poor, innocent soul is still dead. There's nothin' anybody can do about that. So I don't know what you want from me."

What I wanted, Micah is thinking, *was to hear that with the right penance I could finally be absolved for my part in what happened that night. But what you're showing me is that being punished didn't make you less guilty, didn't make you feel forgiven...it just made you hard, and old, and fat...*

Now, without intending to, Micah speaks the final bit of her thought aloud. "Maybe you're right. Maybe there's nothing I could do on this earth that would balance the scales. Maybe the

death-penalty people are telling the truth. Maybe the only real way
to pay for one life is with another."

Hayden's fingertips are surprisingly cool and delicate as they
come to rest on either side of Micah's face, and Hayden tells her:
"I don't know what idiot idea you're wrestlin' with right now. I
got no interest in it. But I'm guessin' you haven't changed a bit.
You're still the spoiled rich girl who thinks she's the star of the play
when the truth is that everybody drawin' breath is in the same play
and who's starrin' in it depends on what day it is and who's tellin'
the story. You ain't the center of the universe. You ain't got the
power to carve the future or erase the past. All you got is today,
and all you can do is try to do as good as you can till the sun goes
down. Then tomorrow get up and try and do a little better. What
you did, you did—and you're stuck with it. You dyin' isn't gonna
solve anything. All it's gonna do is let you off the hook for shit you
didn't have the time—or the balls—to stick around and face up to."

Micah jerks free of Hayden's grasp; her mind is filling with
images of tumors and scalpels and mutilation. "You have no right
to talk to me like that. You don't know what I'm facing—what
I'm going through."

Hayden slams the lid shut on the battered washer and gives
Micah a withering stare. "I'm guessin' you've led one fucked-up
life and I'm bettin' you're the one who keeps fucking it up 'cause
you're always lookin' for stuff that doesn't exist, like happiness and
forgiveness. Know how I know? 'Cause I'm cool, even after doin'
time in prison. I'm content. Right here. In this dump. Helpin'
people get their clothes clean. Married to a guy you wouldn't wipe
your shoes on."

Hayden looks in the direction of the dryers, and the little man
in the faded brown pants and the wide red belt. Then she adds:

"But you're miserable. Even after walkin' away scot-free from what happened. You're miserable and you probably live in a penthouse. You're miserable 'cause you're wasting your life eatin' your guts out over all the stuff you shouldn't have done, and can't change, and don't have, and never got—"

Micah has stopped listening. She's already walking away. Escaping to the parking lot and the taxi that's waiting there.

Hayden is calling after her, warning her: "Your problem isn't with that poor creature who died. Your problem is with somebody else and you know it."

AnnaLee
Glen Cove, Long Island ~ 1986

THE PROBLEM OF BELLA'S FEVER HAS BEEN WASHED AWAY WITH A cool bath, her fretfulness soothed with a lullaby. AnnaLee is at rest. Everything is quiet. The linen window-shades in the nursery have been drawn against the late afternoon sun. And the diffused light is making the candy-striped toddler bed, and the shelves of colorful toys, and the enormous stuffed giraffe that's propped in the corner look like illustrations in a children's book.

AnnaLee, with Bella cradled in her arms, is in a yellow rocking chair. And while she is watching her little girl sleep, she's experiencing a swell of emotion that's overwhelming. A love that's powerful, and infinitely gentle.

It is a love that has consumed AnnaLee since the moment of Bella's birth. The moment in which AnnaLee's soul fluttered, and her heart lifted away. As if it was going from her own body into her child's. The sensation was like being turned inside-out. Suddenly having her nerves and their intricately braided pathways netted on the surface of her skin. Attuned to a single mission, to keeping her baby safe.

The words AnnaLee was whispering to Bella in that incredible moment while Bella was being born are the ones AnnaLee is whispering now: "No matter how big you grow, my darling, or how old you get, or how far away from me you travel, I'll always be with you. I will always love you, and protect you. Always and forev—"

A shadow, from the doorway, has shot across the nursery floor. Ominous and quick.

Before AnnaLee can lift her gaze from her sleeping child, the shadow has vanished. Leaving in its wake the faint smell of cloves. And the malevolent stomp of thick-soled boots rapidly moving away. Toward the far end of the hall.

AnnaLee has been reminded. Things are different now.

Now, during the day, even when Jack is gone and at work, AnnaLee no longer has her house to herself.

A relentless thumping sound—muffled and hellish—has begun in the few minutes that have elapsed since AnnaLee tucked Bella into bed and began walking toward the other end of the hall.

The door to the bedroom that AnnaLee is approaching is closed. A hand-lettered sign is taped to its front—a sheet of paper ripped from a notebook and scrawled with fat red letters.

> You're not welcome here. Stay out. This is my realm.
> I am the one and only Persephone!! It's pronounced
> Per-sef-o-nee. Don't dare say it wrong!

As AnnaLee is opening the door, a black combat boot is flying through the air. Banging into the wall just above her shoulder. Leaving an ugly scuff on the apple-green paint.

Near the window, a purple-haired teenager is sitting cross-legged on the unmade bed—a sketchbook in her lap and a piece of artist's charcoal in her hand. She's stubbing out a clove cigarette: defiantly wearing nothing but skimpy, tiger-stripe panties and a pair of large headphones. The headphones are attached to an oversized boom-box. Its volume turned up so loud that the thump of heavy metal is shaking the floorboards. Not only in the room AnnaLee is in, but throughout the house.

This bedroom was once AnnaLee's girlhood sanctuary. And up until three weeks ago, it was pristine in its simple sunlit beauty. Now, the walls are plastered with images of skulls and blood and destruction. The floor is littered with piles of discarded clothes and magazines. And the air is rank with the smell of forgotten tuna sandwiches and half-eaten pizzas.

The desecration, and the sullen teenager who is creating it, are infuriating AnnaLee. But most of all, she's angry at Jack. For not having had the strength to keep his niece—this obnoxious girl—from coming here in the first place.

AnnaLee is pounding on the boombox, fumbling to find the power button.

And the purple-haired girl is leaning back against the headboard. Nibbling from a bag of Oreos.

And laughing.

Until AnnaLee manages to slam the boombox into silence.

Then the girl is roaring up off the bed in a frenzy. Tossing the bag of cookies aside and clutching at AnnaLee. Dragging her toward the door, shouting: "What's your problem? Can't you read?"

For a split second AnnaLee's outrage is as uncontrolled and furious as the girl's. AnnaLee is on the verge of slapping her.

But the girl is oblivious. Pointing to the sign on the door. Shoving her face toward AnnaLee's and screaming: "This is *my* realm and I am Persephone!"

The girl's voice is reedy. Unsteady. Pitifully childish. She's less than an inch away from AnnaLee and underneath the fragrance of cloves AnnaLee can smell the scent of bubble gum, and baby powder. She can see injury, and indescribable loneliness, in the girl's eyes.

AnnaLee is overwhelmed by an urge to hug her. To console and mother her. But the girl is shoving AnnaLee aside and heading back into the room.

"Just so we're straight on this," she's informing AnnaLee, "I think being here sucks."

"I know—"

"Wrong answer!" The girl has cut AnnaLee off and is shouting at the top of her lungs. "You don't know how I feel. You don't know anything about me. Nobody does. Why should they? Everywhere I go I'm just passing through, and that suits me fine."

She retreats to the bed and sits angrily on its edge. "Now get out!"

AnnaLee's interest has moved to the sign that's taped to the door. "Why Persephone?" she asks.

"Because I like her," the girl snarls. Then, with a haughty kind of malice, she adds: "Persephone is Queen of the Underworld."

"Did you know she was also the goddess of innocence?"

The girl's face registers a momentary uncertainty before she mutters: "That's a load of crap."

"No, it's true. Look it up."

AnnaLee is removing the sign from the door, slowly, not wanting to scar the paint. As she's disposing of the bits of tape and folding the sign into a neat square, she's asking the girl: "Is that what you'd like to be called…while you're here this summer…Persephone?"

At first the girl is surprised. Then skeptical. "You'd never do that."

In the brief standoff that's blossomed between them, AnnaLee sees the hostility in the girl's eyes being nudged aside by a trace of what looks like wistfulness, or perhaps a guarded kind of hope.

And AnnaLee says: "I tell you what. No more clove cigarettes... no more music so loud it shakes the walls...and you can be Persephone. All summer long."

"That's what you'll call me? You promise? Really?"

"Really."

The girl ponders this for several seconds, with the faintest suggestion of a smile. Then the smile vanishes.

The girl looks down. Begins methodically picking cookie crumbs out of her navel—flicking them aside, one by one—and muttering: "That stuff you were telling your kid...that stuff about how much you love her. I heard everything you said."

When the girl looks up her expression is cold. Vacant. "It made me hate you. And her."

A chill is spiraling through AnnaLee. A shiver of worry about what strangeness this summer could bring.

Livvi
Flintridge, California ~ 2012

I'M NOT COMFORTABLE WITH THIS. IT'S TOO ISOLATED. NO ONE'S here." David is in his car. At the bottom of a steep, tree-lined driveway. He's leaning out of the driver's-side window. Calling to Livvi, asking: "Are you sure you don't want me to wait with you?"

"I'm fine, go!" The words come out sounding clipped and rude—not the way Livvi intended them to.

She's at the top of the driveway, with a sprawling, shade-dappled house looming at her back, and she's nervous.

David is putting the car into reverse then immediately bringing it to a stop, leaning out the window again. There is unguarded sweetness in his voice as he's telling her: "I hate to leave you."

Livvi isn't really paying attention to what David is saying or how he's saying it; she's too distracted. She's giving him a wave she hopes will look cheery. She sincerely appreciates that David, after driving her to the meeting in Culver City this morning, was kind enough to bring her all the way out here into the hills northwest of Pasadena—to this leafy, affluent town called Flintridge. But now she desperately wants him to go away.

Until David is out of sight, until Livvi is sure she's alone, she won't be able to do what she has come here to do.

She won't have the nerve to climb the wide flagstone steps

leading to the front door. Won't have the courage to remove the spare key from its hiding place behind the potted ficus tree. And slip into Andrew's empty house. Like a thief.

It seems to take David an eternity to back out of the driveway and disappear from view. When he finally does—Livvi is suddenly afraid.

The quiet that's surrounding the house feels menacing. And it's adding to Livvi's nervousness, her gnawing uncertainty about what, or who, kept Andrew so busy that it took him five hours to answer her call, after the weather vane crashed into her car.

And now doing what she thought she wanted to do, retrieving the hidden key and turning it in the lock on Andrew's door, is only increasing Livvi's anxiety. This isn't who she is. This person who brushed off David, her best friend, without even saying good-bye so she could be left in peace to sneak into her lover's house. To rummage through his closets and drawers looking for proof that he doesn't care about her—proof that there's another woman in his life.

Livvi's reason for being here is too seedy to even think about. She's quickly reaching to grab the key out of the lock—intending to close the door, put the key back in its hiding place, and leave. But it's too late. She's seeing that the door has already begun to drift open—and her eyes are wide with apprehension.

When she turned the key in the lock she'd forgotten that Andrew's house has a security system. What if the system's armed?

Livvi doesn't know the code. She has only been here a couple of times, and never without Andrew.

Tension-filled seconds are ticking by. Leaving Livvi afraid to move, or breathe. Leaving her waiting for the blare of the alarm and the eventual wail of police sirens.

Miraculously. The stillness remains unbroken.

Without thinking, Livvi ducks inside the house. It's sleek and flat-roofed. With concrete floors and glass walls. Built on the rise of a hill, at the center of at least an acre of land. Tucked into a glade of trees and ferns. A place that's quiet and remote.

Livvi closes the door. Locking it and leaning against it. Sighing with relief. And waiting. For her heart to stop pounding.

In the few moments that it takes Livvi to catch her breath, the house remains completely still. Then the stillness is abruptly broken by three staccato notes of birdsong. Coming from somewhere outside. Rapid and shrill, like a warning. Like the sound of danger.

And Livvi is also hearing a second, more muffled noise—one that sounds like a car pulling into the driveway. Immediately she's convinced that the car is Andrew's, and she's panicked that he's home so early. The plan was for him to meet her here at noon—and it's only ten-thirty in the morning.

Livvi is glancing around Andrew's stylish living room. At the cobalt-blue sofa. The low-to-the-ground side chairs upholstered in chrome-colored silk. The glass coffee table shaped like a boomerang. And the steel desk that's as cleanly sculpted as a knife-blade. She's embarrassed to the point of tears. Even though she has changed her mind about rifling through his house, Livvi feels petty and guilty. She doesn't want Andrew to know that the reason she came here early was to spy on him.

It's July, she's thinking. *Last month was the six-month anniversary of the night we met. Maybe I could say I came early and let myself in to surprise him...to fix a celebration lunch and—*

Livvi's train of thought is interrupted—by what she's seeing in the center of the room. A recent issue of *Architectural Digest.* Open and facedown on the coffee table—she's trying to recall if she's ever seen Andrew reading *Architectural Digest*. And on the floor, beneath the coffee table, is a pair of white athletic socks—almost prissy in how immaculately new they are.

Livvi glances toward the front door and listens. Nothing but silence. No footsteps, no key in the lock. She must have only imagined that the sound she heard was Andrew's car pulling into the driveway.

She goes to the coffee table and looks down through the glass top, to the carpet below—gazing at those immaculate socks. Are they Andrew's? Someone else's? There's no way to be sure.

The possibility that the miraculous world she has found with Andrew might be coming apart is filling Livvi with a searing combination of grieving and dread—an old, familiar emotion.

When she looks up from the coffee table the first thing she sees is her own reflection, in the living room's glass wall. She's as pale as paste, except for the skin right above her cheekbones, which is blotchy red. Her eyes are full of darkness. Every muscle in her body is tight and clenched. She looks like a woman she doesn't recognize. Someone she doesn't want to be.

Seeing herself this way is putting a sick, sour taste in Livvi's mouth. She's turning toward the kitchen. Needing a drink of water. And wondering if David has gotten onto the freeway yet. Hoping it isn't too late to have him come back and take her home.

While she's walking into the open area beyond the living room, where the kitchen is, she's switching her phone on. The battery is low.

She goes to press David's number—then doesn't.

On the kitchen countertop, near the sink, are an oversized coffee cup, a half-eaten muffin, and a crumpled paper napkin. Both the coffee cup and napkin are white. Other than a few drops of coffee at the bottom of its bowl, the cup is clean. But on the napkin, there are thin streaks. Little stains. All of them pinkish-red. The color of lipstick.

Livvi's pain is instant—a knot in her chest as hard and tight as a baseball. For a minute, it immobilizes her. Then she notices, on the other side of the coffee cup, a small dish filled with strawberries. The knot in her chest eases. And she tells herself, *Andrew could have been eating a strawberry, wiping his mouth with the napkin. The red could have come from that.*

Yet the uncertainty, the torment of not knowing, is still there. And Livvi is already shredding the red-stained napkin. Stuffing it into the trash. Blindly running toward the bedroom.

In Andrew's bedroom, Livvi finds exactly what she found in his living room, and in his kitchen—a tease, ambiguity.

A scattering of change on the dresser-top, some credit card receipts. An unmade bed, the sheets lightly rumpled. A pair of boxer shorts on the floor near the bathroom door.

Was Andrew alone when he dropped them there? Livvi is wondering. *Or was someone stretched out on the bed, smiling while she was watching them fall?*

Livvi looks back at the bed—at its lightly rumpled bedding. Picturing a woman so sylphlike, so delicate, that even at the height of passion she's leaving only the slightest imprint on the sheets beneath her.

This image is sending Livvi hurrying from Andrew's side of the bed to the other. She's picking up the pillow, burying her face in it. Trying to detect the woman's scent. Envisioning Andrew's hands on the woman's skin. His lips on the side of her neck. His weight lowering onto her. Slowly. Deliciously. The way it lowered onto

Livvi, that first time in New York, in the St. Regis. When she'd felt so safe, so sure.

For what seems like endless seconds, Livvi continues to hold the pillow to her face. Her eyes closed and her mind racing.

Then. Without warning. A noise from the front of the house. Loud and insistent. Someone ringing the doorbell.

Livvi drops the pillow and steps away from the bed—inadvertently giving herself an unobstructed view of the living room. A tall, slim woman in lavender shorts and a loose-fitting sweater is outside the house. Flashing past one of the plate-glass panels near the front door.

The bell is ringing again. Louder this time. More insistently.

Livvi is convinced the woman has seen her and that she doesn't have any choice but to answer the door.

The walk from the bedroom to the living room is agony. *She's here,* Livvi is thinking. *The person Andrew is sleeping with is here and I want to die.*

When Livvi arrives at the door, she can't seem to remember how to work the lock. It takes several tries before, out of the blue, she manages to release it.

The door swings open—and Livvi is bewildered.

The person on the threshold isn't the one she was expecting. Instead of a grown woman, Livvi is looking at a young child. A little girl holding a stuffed animal, a small pink pig.

The girl is dressed in a yellow-striped T-shirt, ruffled yellow skirt, and round-toed, yellow polka-dot sneakers. Her hair, which is thick and dark brown, is in a low ponytail pulled to one side of her head, tied with a yellow ribbon.

She's studying Livvi with intense curiosity as she's asking: "Who are you?"

Livvi is too confused to respond.

How has this little girl materialized on the doorstep, out of nowhere? And what happened to the woman who was outside the house only a second ago, the one in the lavender shorts?

The child has moved closer to Livvi; she's tapping on Livvi's arm, telling her: "I'm Grace."

Livvi is still trying to figure out what's going on.

And the little girl says: "Bree brought me."

"Who's Bree?" Livvi asks.

The little girl points toward the driveway—toward an elegant BMW sedan.

A slender blond in her early twenties, wearing a loose sweater and lavender shorts, is leaning against the car, murmuring into a cell phone.

"She's my nanny," the little girl says.

"Why…?" Livvi asks.

"I don't know. She just is."

"No, I mean why did she bring you here?"

There's a hesitation. The flicker of a frown. Something that looks like worry—or perhaps doubt. Then the little girl tells Livvi: "I want my daddy."

Micah

Louisville, Kentucky ~ 2012

*B*EING DADDY IS A HARD JOB. TO DO IT GOOD I GOT TO PAY attention like crazy." The young Hispanic driver is talking to Micah while he's lifting her suitcase from the trunk of the Town Car and putting it onto the crowded curb at the Louisville airport. He has wavy hair and a dimpled grin—and is impeccably neat in his black suit and cream-colored shirt.

He's opening the car's rear passenger door, as he asks: "You got kids?"

Micah doesn't look up from the payment slip she's signing. She's thinking about the Laundromat, and Hayden Truitt. About the things she and Hayden said, and all the things they didn't.

"At first it was crazy," the driver is explaining to Micah. "Me and my wife didn't know what to do. We thought, maybe we're not the right parents for our little guy."

The driver points to a photo clipped to the visor above the steering wheel—a dimple-faced toddler with skin the color of dark caramel. A little boy no more than two; a developmentally disabled child in a surgical helmet and leg braces. "But I guess he knew what he was doing when he picked us. Now when I look at him every day I see how big his courage is, how good his heart is. It makes me humble. I am honored to be his dad."

Micah absentmindedly glances at the photo as she's holding up the payment slip, asking: "Is the tip included, or do I need to add one?"

"There is a tip included. No need for more." After he has taken the signed slip from Micah, the driver gives her his card. "Next time you are in Louisville, I will be happy to drive you where you need to go."

Micah drops the card into her purse without looking at it, wondering if she'll have time to get something to eat before her plane takes off.

The driver is helping her out of the car, flashing his dimpled grin. "I have a question I need to ask—are you a movie star?" He's extending the collapsible handle of Micah's suitcase, putting it within easy reach. "You are beautiful like a movie star."

She walks past him, taking the suitcase and wheeling it toward the terminal. "I'm not a movie star."

"Maybe you are a supermodel...?"

Micah doesn't have the will, or the energy, to look back at him. "No," she calls out. "That's not who I am."

Her thoughts are on Jason, in the coffee shop in Kansas—how happy he was, as if she'd left absolutely no mark on his life. Then she's remembering the question that came after the doctor told her about her cancer—*"Do you have anyone you can call?"*

As Micah is turning around to catch sight of the driver, she's thinking, *Who I am...is nobody.*

"What's the matter, Miss Lesser? You're breathing funny."

"I'm running to catch my damn plane." Micah is moving her phone from one ear to the other; the reception is spotty, and she's trying to keep the call connected. "Is everything okay with the galleries? No problems?"

"I need to move money to do payroll," Jillian's voice is fading in and out. "You didn't leave me the pin number on the new account."

Micah slides into an empty seat in a row of chairs along the wall and pulls a pale blue Smythson notebook out of her purse. Clinging to the cover of the Smythson is the business card she was given a few minutes ago; the card from the limo driver with the wavy hair and dimpled grin. Micah tosses the card aside and quickly flips through the Smythson.

"The new pin number is sixty-eight, seventy-one." Micah has closed the notebook. When she tries to wedge it back into her purse, it slides out of her hand.

"Six-eight, seventy-one." Jillian's voice is now coming through strong and clear. "Okay. That'll take care of payroll."

The Smythson has landed on the floor a few inches away from the limo driver's business card. While Micah is retrieving the notebook, Jillian is asking, "Is there anything else you need?" and Micah is responding, "No, I don't think so."

The Smythson is now safely in Micah's purse, but her attention is being drawn back to the floor, to the business card. "Wait," she's telling Jillian. "Hold on for a minute."

Micah has picked up the card, snapped a photo of it, and is pressing Send on her phone. "There's a driver for a car service in Louisville. I'm texting you his information. His name is Armando Rojas. Get some money to him."

"How much?"

"Ten thousand."

"Wanna tell me what's going on? That's a lot of cash."

"Make sure he knows the money is for his son...and no information on where it came from. Talk to you later."

Micah is now joining the swarm of passengers hurrying toward the departure gates. She's also opening her hand and letting the business card flutter back onto the floor.

"Don't hang up yet." Jillian is insistent. "There's something else."

Micah is intent on getting to her boarding gate; only two or three people are left in the waiting area. She's about to miss her plane. "I've got to run. I'll check in again in a couple of—"

"They called. They're ready to come and take her."

The words have struck Micah like a physical blow—staggered her. She's losing her balance.

A teenage boy, hurrying past, dragging a scuffed duffle bag, reaches out to steady her.

"What do you wanna do?" Jillian is asking.

Micah is only a few feet from the departure gate—watching the boarding agent processing the last passenger remaining in the waiting area. And all she can think about, all she can see, is the one person who has meant the world to her. The woman in the silver dress and pearl-button shoes.

Jillian, at the other end of the phone, is warning Micah: "I need to know what you want to do about her. We can't stall any longer."

Micah deliberates. Then says: "Tell them I need another week. A week—then it'll be over. One way or the other. I guarantee it."

"Why put it off? Why not decide now?"

Without thinking, Micah says: "I have a family issue I need to take care of."

Immediately there's concern in Jillian's voice. "Miss Lesser, what's going on? You always said you didn't have any fam—"

Micah has pressed the End Call button. With far more force than was needed.

She's running full speed toward her departure gate.

Three days. That's how long Micah has been locked in this hotel suite. The entire time since her flight from Louisville and her arrival in Newport, Rhode Island. It has been precious time that Micah is wasting. Because she's frightened of what she's here to deal with, and of what will still be waiting for her after this is done. Her cancer. And the woman in the pearl-button shoes.

Micah is finishing off the last of the four small bottles of tequila she took from the mini-bar less than twenty minutes ago. And she's as tense as she was when she broke the seal on the first one. Which is why she's lunging across the width of the gleaming mahogany end table. Toppling a Waterford vase filled with an extravagance of flowers. Scrambling for the phone.

She's calling the hotel spa, telling the receptionist: "I want a massage. A long one. Right now."

"Everybody on our staff is booked, but I can have one of the on-call therapists here in a half-hour."

"Fine. Half an hour."

After she hangs up the phone, Micah leaves the sofa and wanders the room—eventually stopping beside the window and gazing down onto Bellevue Avenue.

This end of the avenue, where the hotel is, is lined with tourist places; charming little shops and art galleries. At the other end of the avenue are Newport's fabled mansions; the oceanfront palaces built by the Dukes and the Astors. And somewhere in between is the spot where Micah's demons dwell.

The treatment room in the hotel spa is unlike anything Micah has ever seen—extraordinarily spacious, the size of a large bedroom. The floor is satiny-dark and the walls are wainscoted in wood paneling the color of vanilla custard. The massage table is lavishly plush, and on either side of the table are wood cabinets in the same custard color as the walls. On each cabinet top, there are bouquets of flickering candles in jewel-toned vases. At the foot of the massage table is a curtained alcove and a freestanding porcelain soaking-tub, filled with water that has been floated with a carpet of rose petals.

Micah is slipping between the sheets on the massage table. They feel weightless, spotlessly clean. The spa attendant has lowered the lights, leaving the candles as the only illumination, and has provided music that sounds like murmurs from a galaxy of distant stars.

The attendant is placing a satin mask over Micah's eyes, saying: "Unwind. Enjoy. Your therapist should be here any minute."

The attendant is very young, petite, and birdlike.

While Micah is listening to the quick, light tap of the attendant's retreating footsteps and the soft click of the closing door, it is occurring to her that one day, perhaps very soon, she'll be lying precisely as she is now—with her eyes closed, in a quiet room, stretched out on her back, on a table, naked, beneath a sheet. She's imagining the grip of the toe-tag—wondering if they still use toe tags and, if they do, which foot they'll put it on. Her right. Or her left.

Micah, drifting in the darkness created by her satin eye-mask, is hearing the noise of another soft click—the door of the dimly lit massage room being opened. She's listening to footsteps that are a little louder than the ones belonging to the spa attendant—this must be the massage therapist.

Not bothering to open her eyes, Micah simply puts the mask aside and rolls over, so that she's lying facedown.

"Any specific areas you want me to work on?" the therapist asks. Her voice is mellow and comforting.

"Nothing specific," Micah says.

"What kind of pressure do you prefer?"

"Firm."

The massage begins. The therapist's technique is faultless.

Micah drifts into sleep.

After what seems like a luxuriously long time, there's a light touch on Micah's shoulder—the therapist wants her to change positions. As Micah is coming to rest on her back, she's sleepily pulling the satin mask over her eyes.

Micah senses the therapist is very close, inches away from the top of her head.

"This is lavender oil on my hands," the therapist is saying. "I want you to inhale as deeply as you can."

Her palms are above Micah's face; Micah can feel their warmth, and that they're just shy of brushing her skin. The scent of the lavender is soothing, and the slow breath that Micah is taking is the first full one she has drawn in weeks.

She's suspended in tranquility.

The therapist is massaging Micah's neck, her thumbs resting lightly on either side, her fingers working the knotted muscles at the back.

The sensation is pure pleasure.

Then the therapist says: "I'm Christine. But I don't know what to call you...the girl at the desk didn't give me your name."

It takes Micah a few seconds to snap back into reality and tell the therapist: "Just so you're clear on how this works—I lie here, conversation-free, while you make me feel human again. If what you're asking is where the bill goes, I'm in Suite 419. Micah Lesser."

In the space of a microsecond, the time it takes to blink, the therapist's thumbs are clamping down on the sides Micah's throat. Jamming against her airway. Strangling her.

Then, as quickly as the incident begins, it ends.

And the therapist is whispering, "Ohmygod...Ohmygod." Sounding horrified.

The satin mask that was covering Micah's eyes has fallen onto the floor. And the therapist is coming around to the side of the massage table, her hand over her mouth, as if she's approaching something disastrous and incomprehensible.

"You could've killed me," Micah is rasping. "Are you fucking nuts?" She's sitting up now, leaning forward. Both she and the therapist are straining, in the massage room darkness, to get a good look at each other.

The woman sounds agitated and afraid. "Micah...? Micah Lesser? The Micah who shared the apartment in Cambridge with me?" She's taking a candle from a nearby countertop and holding it up, suddenly bathing herself, and Micah, in a glow of golden light. Her long strawberry-blond hair and the sound in her voice—the confusion, the distress—are almost identical to what they were on that morning two decades ago. When Micah last encountered her.

The shock of being with this woman again is overpowering— Micah is, briefly, on the verge of losing consciousness.

"It's me." The therapist's words are cold, clipped.

Micah knows this is the beginning of something lethal. The phrase *It's me* was the little metallic click—the sound that comes right before someone pulls a trigger.

"It's me, Christine," the therapist says.

"I know." Micah's reply is a cautious whisper.

"If I hurt you, I didn't mean to—I wasn't trying to choke you.

When you said your name—it was like I was touching somebody who was buried and dead. It startled me."

Micah is agitated. And disoriented. "What are you doing here?"

"I live across the bridge—in Jamestown. Don't you remember? This is where I grew up."

"But what are you doing *here?* What are you doing giving massages? You're a photographer, why aren't you taking pictures?"

Christine's laugh is fast and bitter—her anger, burning hot.

Micah is edging off the massage table. Taking her spa robe from a hook on the wall.

While Christine is returning the candle to the countertop and explaining: "I *was* a photographer. Until a couple of years ago. I had my own studio, up in Portsmouth, then the economy collapsed and took me with it."

She makes a sound that is halfway between a chuckle and a groan, and gestures toward the massage table. "I moved back home with my parents a year and a half ago—stomped the dream, packed up my cameras, and learned a new trade."

She pauses as if she's waiting for Micah to speak. When she doesn't, Christine tells her: "I didn't get to be you, Micah—never got to be famous. I ended up taking pictures of brides and babies. My work isn't studied in art schools—it's dangling from nails above fireplaces. In New Hampshire."

Micah's voice is so unsteady she doesn't recognize it. It sounds like it belongs to a stranger, somebody old and shattered. "You didn't have to settle for brides and babies, Christine. You were better than that."

"Really? I guess we'll never know." The statement is laced with resentment.

Micah's reply is defensive, guilty. "It wasn't the only job in the world—"

"—but it was mine. It belonged to me and you took it."

On Christine's face there is a look of insurmountable loss.

Micah recognizes it immediately. *That's the same look that was on her face the last time I saw her,* Micah is thinking. *In the apartment, that morning, back in Cambridge, when we were kids. When she was twenty-four and I was twenty-two.*

The details of that morning are crystal clear to Micah. It's as if she's watching them play out on a reel of perfectly preserved film.

...our little apartment, our one room, is chilly. It's late September but winter's already in the air...I'm just coming out of the shower, stepping around the camera bags and lighting equipment—mine, and Christine's. They're in piles, all over the floor...Morning sun is pouring through a window that's high in the wall above the kitchen area and I'm holding my fingers spread out, watching my engagement ring catching the light. I'm happy, I'm getting married this afternoon...The phone is ringing and Christine has a fork in her hand; she's trying to pry a bagel out of the toaster, before it burns...She's still jabbing at the bagel while she's picking up the phone... Then all of a sudden she's letting go of the fork, leaving it in the toaster, stuck in the bagel...I'm watching all the color go out of her face. I know what she's just heard...I'm folding over like I'm going to puke, like there's a bucket of acid sloshing around in my guts...The room is filling up with the stink of the hot fork and the toaster and the burning bagel but the only thing I can focus on is Christine—the look on her face while she's hanging up the phone—while she's asking me, "Why? Why did you do it?" And when I don't answer—can't answer—she's backing away from me; staring at me like I'm a wild animal that somebody let out of its cage... She looks like she's taken a beating and can't breathe...She's crying like she's a little kid, telling me, "Micah, they're the number-one rock band in the world. They're from Boston and they wanted a Boston photographer. Somebody young, like they were when they were starting out. And of all

the photographers who submitted photos, they chose me to do the cover shot for their final album—a cover that's going to make history. Now, just like that, they're saying I'm out and you're in. How? You didn't even enter the contest, Micah. How did you take it away from me?"...I'm listening to Christine crying, wailing like a war-widow—I'm seeing how betrayed she looks—it's making me ashamed...Stuff is coming up from my insides, pushing into my mouth, thick, like bile, while I'm explaining to her, "I got their business manager's address out of your bag. I grabbed a picture from my portfolio and took it over there on the spur of the moment, a couple of days ago. The manager went nuts for it—I guess the band did too."

For a split second, I'm losing my train of thought. I'm realizing what's just happened—my career has been launched. I'm about to be famous... And then I remember Christine—what I've done. And I'm trying to make it seem not so bad...I'm telling her, "Christine, you'll still get the money. The manager promised. Since they haven't officially announced the winner yet, he said if the band changed their mind, if they chose me, they'd pay both of us."...But she's not listening, she's backed up against the counter where the toaster is, where the bagel's on fire, where the air is stinking with the smell of hot metal and smoke...Her mouth is open, loose, like she's drunk and she keeps asking me, "Why did you do it? Why?"...and I can't tell her, I can't even look at her...

Now, seventeen years later, in this candlelit massage room where the air is sweet with the smell of lavender and rose petals, Christine is asking the same question, asking Micah: "Why? Why did you do it?"

Micah still can't answer her—still can't meet her gaze.

And it's because Micah isn't looking at Christine that the slap comes as such a surprise. Banging directly into Micah's temple. Causing her to howl with pain.

"Why?" Christine is shouting. "Why did you steal what was mine?"

When Micah can breathe again, she's furious. And she calmly says: "When you entered that contest, you asked if I was going to enter too. I promised you I wouldn't—I knew how much it meant to you. And then I changed my mind."

"Why?"

"Because as good as you were, I knew I was better. I was the one who deserved to make history."

"You went there and stole it from me, without even telling me." There is a look of soul-torn disbelief on Christine's face. "You were my best friend, my dearest friend. I loved you with all my heart."

Micah has turned away. She's gazing into a mirror across from the massage table, observing the ugly bruise that's forming on her temple.

"I've never known anybody like you, Micah. Never knew anybody as beautiful, or as talented." Christine is speaking as if what she's revealing to Micah is being said with great reluctance. "I spent years thinking about you—missing you—thinking about our friendship, the things we could've shared. Then, a long time ago, I stopped. It hurt too much."

Micah is making a point of concentrating on the mirror. Her throat is tight; her face is flushed.

"I wish you hadn't taken it from us, we had a friendship that could've lasted forever." Christine is standing directly in front of Micah. In the candlelight, she looks the way she looked when they were young, when she adored Micah and was her best, and only, friend. She looks innocent. And open.

Suddenly Micah is experiencing an anticipation that's magical. The separation between herself and Christine—the burden of the hurt Micah inflicted—feels like it's slipping away. The priceless gift of their friendship is coming back.

Christine is bringing her face close to Micah's—about to kiss her cheek.

For a moment Micah is dizzy with relief. Waiting to receive what she went searching for in Kansas. The reassurance that, among all the people she wronged in her youth, there's at least one who still loves her.

But a faint rippling is in the air. A microscopic shift in atmosphere. Then Christine's voice—low and emotionless. "Sorry. I can't do this."

She's stepping away from Micah, telling her: "I'm glad I saw you. I'll always miss you and there'll always be a hole in me that's shaped like you, but it's a burned-out place—I never want to go back there."

And Micah's relief has become misery.

While the door to the massage room is opening, and before it closes behind Christine, Micah is seeing a flash of light from the hallway. In the space of the flash, Micah is again in that life-changing September day...*in Cambridge. In the afternoon, after the awful morning with Christine. Micah is walking away from Jason, down the sun-dappled steps of the brownstone belonging to the Justice of the Peace: walking away because a handful of hours ago her future came calling. She's poised to make history, to become famous—and afraid marriage will get in the way. She's leaving Jason; knowing that he's waiting for her to come back, thinking that he will always be waiting. Convinced that she'll only be gone for a little while.*

When the flash of light from the hallway is extinguished, and the massage-room door is closed, Micah's face is impassive, her eyes dry. She is scorched, and empty.

She understands that this emptiness, the stillness, won't last. She knows this is the time to act. Now. While she is almost unable to feel. While she's less vulnerable to being seriously wounded, or doing unspeakable damage.

~∽∾~

A shadowy portico crowded with potted palms, all of them in granite urns, all of them drooping and yellowed. A set of black marble steps. On the steps, a layer of dust, and in the dust, faint lines. Cat tracks. Weaving and winding. Repeatedly looping back on themselves as if the animal who made them was lost; searching for something refusing to be found.

And there is a heavy brass knocker, vaguely shaped like a tongue, swinging toward a tarnished faceplate. Micah has let it drop from her hand and bang against the door.

This house on Bellevue Avenue is the end-point of Micah's journey to Newport. And potentially the beginning of a nightmare.

There has already been a noise, a small squeak behind a second-floor window to the left of the portico. The drapes are being opened, just a crack.

The movement is disturbingly furtive. Simply witnessing it is making Micah afraid.

She is on dangerous ground.

AnnaLee
Glen Cove, Long Island ~ 1986

"YOU'RE NOT GOING! IT'S OUT OF THE QUESTION, IT'S TOO dangerous." AnnaLee is close to losing her temper. She has run out of the house without shoes, in late July, and the gravel driveway is burning the soles of her feet like a bed of hot coals.

Persephone, in flip-flops and a leopard-print bathing suit, with a beach towel slung around her neck, is belligerently asking: "Why are you making such a big freaking deal out of this? All we're talking about is a party."

She's red-faced, indignant. "A party! Exactly like the one you're planning to go to in a couple of weeks. The only difference is, instead of putting on fancy clothes and sucking up to snobs we don't even know, we're going to the beach. Then tonight a bunch of friends will come over to Tru's house and—"

Persephone pauses. A battered pick-up truck is parked about twenty feet away, on the far side of the horseshoe-shaped driveway. She's trying to make eye contact with the truck's occupants—a tall, thickset teenage girl in a black bikini and a shirtless, rail-thin young man wearing jeans and a pair of high-topped sneakers. The young man, who has a flaming skull inked on his right bicep, is behind the wheel; the girl is lounging at the other end of the truck's bench seat, her feet propped against the open passenger door. The vehicle is ancient, at least fifteen years old, a relic from the early 1970s. Crouched in the back, in the truck's bed, panting in the heat, is an ugly, wolfish-looking dog with narrow, sharply peaked ears.

The girl in the black bikini is staring at Persephone, yawning, silently warning her, *Pick up the pace or I'm moving on.*

Persephone quickly turns back to AnnaLee. "All that's going to happen at Tru's house is people hanging out and listening to mus—"

AnnaLee cuts her off. "It will be a bunch of kids running wild." AnnaLee has sounded angry, but anger isn't what she's feeling—it's concern. "I want to keep you safe," she tells Persephone.

"Why?" The question is a mocking sneer.

The mockery, the sting it inflicts, keeps AnnaLee silent. Prevents her from telling Persephone… *"I want to protect you because in the six weeks that you've been here I've gotten to know you—to see who you are. You're lonely. And lost. You don't think anybody cares about you, and I'm starting to care deeply…"*

"Hey, lady. I asked you a question." Persephone's sneer has now become a snarl. "Are you going to answer it or not?"

She's posturing—performing for the audience in the truck.

AnnaLee understands that this isn't the time for motherly tenderness and declarations of love. She turns to the girl in the black bikini, and says: "You're Tru?"

The girl gives a bored shrug. "That's what they call me."

AnnaLee is suppressing the urge to walk over to the truck, slam the door shut, and send Tru packing. "You said your parents are away. Right?"

"Yeah. But they're cool with me havin' people over." Tru stares off into space, as if trying to comprehend the depth of AnnaLee's stupidity. "It's kinda like…y'know…they trust me?"

The shirtless young man gives an amused snort and continues to gaze straight ahead. His sinewy right arm is extended over the top of the steering wheel, his hand hanging limply from his wrist, a cigarette dangling between his index and middle fingers.

There's something about him that's making AnnaLee's skin crawl. He and Tru are people AnnaLee has never seen before—strangers Persephone met at the beach a couple of weeks ago. AnnaLee is trying make up her mind how to deal with them.

She's shifting from one foot to the other, attempting to keep the hot gravel from blistering the soles of her feet, while she's saying to Tru: "I don't know what your situation is with your parents, but my concern is Persephone. I won't allow her to be put at risk."

"Oh for Christ's sake!" Persephone is stomping around the driveway, grumbling: "It's not like you're my mother or anything— you're married to my dad's half-brother. You're barely even a relative. What's your problem?"

"The problem is you're fifteen, Persephone, and you want to go to a party where there won't be any adult supervision—"

AnnaLee is interrupted by a sharp whistle.

Tru has gotten out of the truck and is leaning against its front bumper, smirking at AnnaLee. "I'm eighteen, so technically I'm an adult. If that helps calm your nerves."

AnnaLee is striding across the hot gravel, heading back into the house, and calling over her shoulder to Tru: "Check with me when you're forty. Now get out of my driveway."

Persephone is frantically trying to intercept AnnaLee. "Please. Wait! It won't only be kids at the party." She's dragging AnnaLee to a stop, pointing to the truck. "Marco will be there. He's Tru's boyfriend. And he's an adult. He's twenty-six. He was even in the Army, I think."

That Persephone would consider this information to be a selling point is breaking AnnaLee's heart—reminding her how vulnerable and naive Persephone really is.

"I wish I could say yes. But I want too much to keep you safe." AnnaLee has instinctively wrapped her arms around Persephone and kissed her on the forehead.

Persephone has jerked away, muttering: "Screw you." She's dashing for the truck, where Tru is now inside the cab, scooting along the bench seat, to make room for her.

AnnaLee is immediately sprinting across the driveway, toward the truck.

Just as Persephone is preparing to shut the passenger door, AnnaLee is yanking it open, doing what she would do if it were Bella who was in jeopardy—she's pulling her to safety.

Persephone is tumbling off the edge of the bench seat and out of the truck. Almost knocking AnnaLee over. Spitting at her, glaring at her. Struggling to wiggle out of her grasp. AnnaLee, fighting to keep her balance, is glaring back, making it clear she has no intention of releasing her hold on Persephone.

Peals of laughter are echoing from inside the truck and its tires are being deliberately spun on the gravel—sending up a pepper spray of dirt and pebbles.

The truck is rocketing backward. Roaring down the driveway, the radio playing at ear-splitting volume. Blasting Metallica's "Master of Puppets."

While Persephone is in a cold fury, telling AnnaLee: "You're going to wish you hadn't done this."

It's almost noon. A full day since the showdown in the driveway—since Persephone rampaged into the house, pounded up the stairs into her bedroom, and slammed the door.

AnnaLee is noticing that an amended version of Persephone's hand-lettered sign has been posted. The new warning is:

This is my realm. I am the one and only Persephone. Stay the hell out. Those who defy me will pay!

The sign is increasing AnnaLee's ambivalence about the decision she has made while coming upstairs. It's true that she has begun to have a motherly fondness for Persephone. Yet there's still something worrisome about this girl. Something AnnaLee doesn't quite trust. It's why, at night, she can't keep herself from locking her bedroom door, and Bella's. It's also the reason that, when AnnaLee and Jack go out to dinner or a movie, AnnaLee doesn't leave Bella at home with a babysitter. Instead, she takes Bella to the babysitter's house, then picks her up at the end of the evening.

In light of this uneasiness, the mistrust, AnnaLee is questioning her impulse to invite Persephone to become a closer part of the family. She's wondering if it's purely an open-handed gift. Or if it is at least partially a manipulation, a move calculated to bring the potential source of danger nearer. Putting it where it can be more easily monitored.

AnnaLee is hesitant—conflicted—as she's opening the door and entering Persephone's room.

Persephone is on the bed, facing the wall—buried in a jumble of wrinkled sheets and wadded pillows. Pretending to be asleep. The bed and floor are littered with crumpled, violence-filled sketches.

The windows are closed, the shades drawn, creating a murky darkness. The air is stuffy, nearly unbreathable.

AnnaLee isn't sure how to begin. She sits on the edge of the bed, tentatively. Hoping Persephone will acknowledge her presence.

Persephone doesn't move.

After a while, AnnaLee picks up the only sketch that hasn't been wadded up and discarded—the one placed safely on top of a pillow.

The sketch has been done in vibrantly colored inks and depicts a single, powerful figure. A beautiful, and hideous, Medusa. Her torso, vined in thorns. Her arms and legs, muscled and bare. Her teeth, razor-sharp. Her face, bent toward her upraised hand, in the act of savagely biting into a blood-soaked human heart. Sprouting from the Medusa's head are masses of golden snakes. The eyes of the snakes have been so meticulously rendered that each of them is glittering—their glow crowning the Medusa with a sinister, shimmering halo.

The elegance of the piece, and its hostility, are overwhelming AnnaLee. "I've never seen anything quite like this. Did it take a long time to do?"

"Hardly any time at all," Persephone says. "I did it from memory. It's you."

AnnaLee is startled. She has to wait a while before she's calm enough to put the sketch aside and say: "Is this how you want to spend another whole day, Persephone? Lying by yourself in the dark?"

Persephone's reply is instantaneous and annoyed. "Where I want to be is with my friends, who you took away from me."

"About your friends, I think you and I need to—"

AnnaLee has been stopped in mid-sentence by the sight of Bella. Toddling into the room. Holding a Raggedy Ann by one leg and dragging it along the floor behind her.

Bella is now eighteen months old—curious and serious. Innately sweet. And, like AnnaLee, quietly pretty. Her eyes are a luminous brown and her hair is a cap of golden curls. Curls that, despite the dimness in the room, are shining as if they're lit by candlelight.

And AnnaLee is murmuring: "Bella, you make me believe in angels."

In that same moment, Persephone is sitting up and scowling at AnnaLee, muttering: "Because of you I'm trapped in this fucking house with nothing to do for the rest of the summer. I hate you."

AnnaLee has left the edge of the bed and is trying to gather Bella into her arms. Bella, with her attention on Persephone, is squirming to be free.

Persephone is now on in tears. "Tru and Marco won't ever speak to me again—they're probably still laughing their heads off. Why did you have to make me look like such a loser in front of them?"

"If they're laughing at you…" AnnaLee tells her, "…if they think you're a loser because somebody cares about you, then they're not very nice friends and they're certainly not very—"

Bella is slipping away from AnnaLee like quicksilver—running toward Persephone, with the Raggedy Ann still in tow.

"Who cares what you think?" Persephone is growling at AnnaLee. "They're the only friends I have."

Bella is now trying to find a way to boost herself, and her doll, up onto the bed. Persephone is watching—angrily.

AnnaLee, hurrying toward the bed, is calling: "Bella, no. Get down."

But by the time AnnaLee is able to reach for Bella, Persephone has already lifted Bella onto the bed. Into her lap. And while Persephone is scooping Bella's doll from the floor—handing it to Bella—she's shooting AnnaLee a look of white-hot defiance—her eyes spilling with tears. The falling tears are leaving damp tracks across the doll's face.

Bella is observing each tear as it's dropping onto the Raggedy Ann's cloth-covered smile. Then with a slow turn of her head she looks up at Persephone. After a moment or two, she slides out of Persephone's lap and stands on the bed beside her. Putting her hands on Persephone's face. Patting at the tears, gently. Trying to make them go away.

As Bella is doing this, Persephone is murmuring: "Tru and Marco—and the people they hang around with—it was all I had. Without them, I don't have anything to do."

Is Persephone saying this to Bella? Or to herself? Or to AnnaLee? All AnnaLee can be certain of is that it's giving her the opportunity to act on her decision and say: "Well, you'll definitely have plenty to do from now on."

Persephone is instantly suspicious. "Like what?"

"Starting tomorrow, and until you leave to go back to school, you will be treated exactly like every other kid in this family."

Bella is now snuggled in beside Persephone, her thumb in her mouth, contentedly playing with her rag doll.

Persephone stares at Bella, and then at AnnaLee. "Are you out of your mind?"

The question has such honest confusion in it that AnnaLee can't stop herself from laughing. "Don't worry, I'm not going to force you to watch *Sesame Street*, and eat animal crackers, and go to bed at six-thirty."

"So what exactly are you gonna try to make me do?"

"I want you to be with me. Be my girl, just like Bella is."

Persephone turns her eyes toward the ceiling, in mocking sarcasm. "Let me think...since I've been here, how many times have my mom and dad called? Oh. That's right. Never."

She leans back against the wall, wearily crossing her arms. "Lady, my own parents don't want me as their girl—why the hell would you?"

AnnaLee sits on the bed, this time, as close to Persephone as Persephone will allow. "Just take my word for it, okay? I do want you to be with me. Very much. Even though we only have till the end of the summer."

It's obvious that Persephone is ready to say something flip, but before she can get the words out, Bella has leaned toward her and wetly kissed her on the mouth.

In the span of that innocent kiss, to AnnaLee's surprise, she's seeing the suspicion and the anger in Persephone begin to recede. Just the tiniest bit.

The morning trip from AnnaLee's driveway in Glen Cove to a parking space on Main Street, in the neighboring town of Oyster Bay, has taken only a few minutes.

In that short time, AnnaLee has observed Persephone's mood ricocheting between grudging teenage surliness and cautious, child-like anticipation.

Now the three of them—AnnaLee, Persephone, and Bella—are on their way into Mrs. Wang's store. Bella is in her stroller and AnnaLee is wheeling it toward the store's entryway, which is recessed between a pair of wide, multipaned windows. The wood frames of the windows are painted gleaming white; the front door of the store is finished in glossy, dark-green enamel. This building, and all of Main Street, is an idyllic representation of American colonial charm. Scrubbed and pretty, and welcoming.

Persephone, leaning past AnnaLee to hold the door open, is asking: "So exactly what is it that's supposed to happen today?"

"You and Bella and I are about to do what families do—run some errands—and later, because this is our first time officially being together, we're going to celebrate. With a very nice lunch."

AnnaLee sees the hint of skepticism in Persephone. The expression in her eyes suggesting that Persephone is wondering if today really will be something special, or if it will turn out to be a situation she's better acquainted with. Simply another empty promise.

"Where's lunch gonna be?" Persephone asks. "In some little kid pizza place with Cheerios and sippy-cups all over the floor?"

"It's going to be right over there." AnnaLee is indicating a cozy brick-fronted restaurant across the street. Snowy tablecloths, glowing candles, and wreaths of sparkling pin lights can be seen through the large front window. On the surface of the window, painted in a fanciful gold script, is the name of this lovely place—Delice.

"It's my favorite restaurant," AnnaLee explains. "It's wonderful. In every way possible. I save it for special occasions."

Persephone is smiling. The smile is open. Uncomplicated.

And AnnaLee is giddily happy.

Then without any explanation Persephone's smile has evaporated and she's frowning, focusing on something farther down the block.

AnnaLee turns and sees Tru, the girl from the pick-up truck. The arrogant girl that was in the driveway, the day before yesterday.

Tru, who's lounging against a lamppost, is muttering something to the two young men she's with—her boyfriend Marco and a taller, tougher-looking character whose spiked hair is dyed in various shades of bright, Kool-Aid orange. The three of them are gesturing in Persephone's direction and snickering.

Persephone is cringing. Uncertain. Looking from AnnaLee to Tru, and back again.

Without saying a word, Persephone has darted around Bella's stroller—and is dashing for the lamppost. The needy, begging way that Persephone is running toward Tru is almost too painful for AnnaLee to watch.

Persephone's response to rejection is as automatic, AnnaLee is realizing, as a dog's response to a whistle at dinnertime. Somewhere along the line, groveling for acceptance in the face of coldness and ridicule seems to have been programmed into her.

AnnaLee is doing her best to hear the conversation between Persephone and Tru, but engine noise from a delivery van idling at the curb is making it impossible. What AnnaLee can see is that Persephone's appeals to Tru are being met with a series of dismissive eye-rolls.

Tru is turning to walk away. Persephone is refusing to let her go. There's a quick verbal exchange—the mood between them seems to shift.

This takes place while the delivery van is pulling away, moving down the block. AnnaLee can hear Tru muttering, "Okay. If that's what would happen, how would it get done?"—and Persephone answering, "Maybe an open door? And nobody around…?"

Tru frowns and says: "Yeah, maybe."

The two girls are ambling along the sidewalk, approaching AnnaLee. Marco and the young man with the Kool-Aid orange hair are behind them. As the group comes closer, AnnaLee notices there's a bruise on one of Tru's cheeks, and that her eyes seem glassy and dilated. Just as they reach AnnaLee, Tru and her entourage abruptly cross the street, abandoning Persephone without saying good-bye. Leaving a waft of pungently stale body odor in their wake.

"What were you talking about?" AnnaLee asks.

"Nothing. Tru's been trying to think up an idea for a horror movie. I was helping her." Persephone is moving toward the entry to Mrs. Wang's shop. "Why didn't you go in? You didn't have to wait for me." Persephone is holding the door wide, making way for AnnaLee; and for Bella, in her stroller.

As soon as the door is opened, Mrs. Wang is calling out from the middle of the store—energetically hurrying toward AnnaLee, announcing: "What a big surprise! Why you not tell me you coming? Long time since I see you! Welcome!"

The store, like Mrs. Wang, is chic—and Asian. Fragrant with the scents of musk, mandarin oranges, and peaches. The art and the porcelains and the lamps and the rugs that are for sale are an eclectic mix of styles and periods; yet the mood of the store, its essence, is quintessentially Chinese. The walls are lacquered in cinnabar red and edged in black. Throughout the room, scattered like exuberant flowers, are trails of large, colorful, silk umbrellas. Near the door is a miniature waterfall, made of crystal-clear glass. And at the center of the room is a majestic Buddha carved from a stone that has the translucence of a pale green sea. At the base of the Buddha is a brass offering-bowl containing a single, creamy-petaled lotus blossom.

When Mrs. Wang arrives at AnnaLee's side, she murmurs: "Good. You here right on time." Then she slips her arm through AnnaLee's and loudly proclaims: "I just think of something! My customer over there, Mrs. Jahn. She new to the neighborhood. You should meet her."

Now Mrs. Wang is motioning to the stocky, heavily jeweled woman, who is on the other side of the store examining a large tapestry. "Mrs. Jahn! Come! Let me introduce you to my good customer and good friend AnnaLee!"

The woman waves and says: "Be with you in a minute."

Mrs. Wang hurriedly whispers to AnnaLee: "Lot of money. She buy big estate I told you about. Now what she want is to know people. Also want to start nonprofit foundation to help children who are sick. She looking for somebody to run it. Your husband is doctor, and lawyer. That make him perfect for job of running good works organization for sick children. All you need to do is make sure she find out about him—make sure she meet him, and she like him."

Bella has begun to fuss, and Persephone is lifting her out of her stroller, saying: "Okay, short stuff, I'll set you free but watch yourself. This looks like a 'you break it, you buy it' kind of place."

"This the girl you tell me about?" Mrs. Wang asks AnnaLee.

Persephone's expression promptly becomes closed and defensive.

Mrs. Wang is giving Persephone a knowing smile. "You the one good at sketching? You the big creative talent?"

Persephone, holding Bella close, is incredulous, asking AnnaLee: "It that what you really said about me?"

"She say she think your subject matter crazy, but she also think maybe you turn out to be some kind of artistic genius." Mrs. Wang steps back, studying Persephone. "I think same thing about my granddaughter. Except she genius with design—with decorating. She doing design for Mrs. Jahn's party. You want to meet fellow genius?"

"Yeah, I guess..." Persephone's shrug is uncertain.

AnnaLee takes Bella from Persephone—and Mrs. Wang calls to a slender, stylish girl who is arranging a display in one of the store's windows. "Rebecca! I want you say hello to somebody who is great artist, like you."

As soon as Mrs. Wang has started Persephone toward the window with a brisk push, she turns to AnnaLee, and in a low whisper, asks: "I told you when party is, right?"

AnnaLee nods. "Yes. It's all I can think about. I've had it on my calendar for weeks but—"

"Don't worry. Don't worry." Mrs. Wang has noticed that the heavily jeweled woman, Mrs. Jahn, is walking toward them. Mrs. Wang quickly drops her voice even lower as she tells AnnaLee: "I take care of everything. After I introduce you, if she doesn't think of it herself, I make sure she invite you."

Now that the woman has come closer, AnnaLee sees that she is probably in her late sixties and has had skillfully done plastic surgery. Her face is as seamless as the shell of a freshly laid egg; the only spark of life is in her eyes. They're trusting and kind.

"I'm Amelia Jahn. My husband and I recently bought the old Evans estate on Bricklane Road and we—" She stops and leans in toward Bella, marveling at her. "What a precious little girl." Then she asks AnnaLee: "Have you and your family lived here long?"

"I was born here, in the next town over, in Glen Cove. I went away to college, and after that to Manhattan—I was a dancer. Then for a while, when my husband got his first job after law school, we lived in New Jersey. I came back here just after my daughter was born and we moved into the house where I was raised."

"Oh, how wonderful for you! This is such a lovely area."

"You should see her house where she live with her husband," Mrs. Wang says. "Home of very old family. Many antiques. Very beautiful."

AnnaLee is blushing, embarrassed by this shell game she's playing.

"You grew up here." There is excitement in Mrs. Jahn's voice. "You must know quite a few people."

"Oh, she know all the important families," Mrs. Wang says.

"I would love to get acquainted with some of my neighbors." Mrs. Jahn is addressing this to AnnaLee with deference, and eagerness.

"I'd be happy to introduce you," AnnaLee tells her. "I can only imagine how difficult it must be to make friends in a place where you don't know anyone at all."

Mrs. Jahn's face lights with sudden inspiration, and she says: "I'm having an end-of-summer gala in two weeks. The guests are mostly business associates of my husband's. All Manhattan people. No one from around here. It's a costume party—a Gatsby theme."

"*Great Gatsby*. Famous book from long time ago about Roaring Twenties," Mrs. Wang says. "Very good theme for party."

"I'd be honored if you'd come." Mrs. Jahn extends her hand to AnnaLee. "You seem so nice, I want us to know each other."

AnnaLee has to reposition her hold on Bella before she can accept Mrs. Jahn's offer of a handshake. And she finds that Mrs. Jahn's grip is warm and steady, as if the two of them are already old friends.

"Lucky you came in at same time as Mrs. Jahn have her appointment with me today," Mrs. Wang tells AnnaLee. Then she beams at Mrs. Jahn and adds: "Lucky thing you meet each other. Lucky because…"

AnnaLee's attention has shifted from Mrs. Wang to the shop's open front door. Through it AnnaLee is seeing Jack. And it makes her think of the timeworn phrase "speak of the devil."

Jack is strolling along, on the other side of the street. Contentedly reading from an open book he's holding in his hand.

AnnaLee instinctively knows that he has just gotten off the train. She knows that, even though it's only a few minutes before one o'clock, he has already put an end to his workday. Because he has found it intolerable.

And the sensation in AnnaLee is as if she's choking. Like she's swallowing a mouthful of lead.

She is counting the days until Mrs. Jahn's party—praying for a miracle.

Livvi
Flintridge, California ~ 2012

THE SENSATION OF SWALLOWING LEAD. THIS IS WHAT LIVVI IS experiencing while trying to make sense of what she's seeing. The blond in Andrew's driveway, leaning against a sleek BMW, murmuring into a cell phone. And the dark-haired child resolutely standing on Andrew's doorstep.

The child who is claiming her name is Grace and that the young blond is Bree, her nanny. The fancifully dressed little girl in a ruffled yellow skirt and polka-dot sneakers, who has seemingly appeared out of nowhere, clutching a stuffed pink pig and announcing: "I want my daddy."

It has to be a mistake, Livvi is telling herself. *She's at the wrong house. Please let it be that she's at the wrong house.*

But there's something in the child's eyes, in her body language, that says she knows this place; she belongs here.

Against all hope, already knowing the answer, Livvi asks: "What's your daddy's name?"

"Andrew."

Livvi is heartsick.

The little girl cocks her head and looks at Livvi as if she's mildly confused by her. Then she simply steps around Livvi and walks into the house.

Trying desperately to understand all of this, Livvi is following Grace into the living room—listening to Grace say: "I told Bree to bring me. For a surprise. I have something special to show Daddy."

Grace is eagerly looking toward the kitchen area, then toward the open bedroom door. "If nobody was here, Bree said we'd go home and have ice cream."

Livvi is barely able to speak. "Home? Where do you live?"

"Palos Verdes." Grace is scrutinizing Livvi. Intently.

"But Palos Verdes is forty-five miles from here." Livvi is bewildered. Grace's story doesn't make sense. "Why would your nanny drive all that way without finding out, first, if your...your daddy was going to be home..."

Livvi's voice has trailed away. She's struggling to comprehend the news of Andrew being a father. Yet it's as if she has already absorbed the blow. Accepted it with a kind of blank resignation. On some level, from her earliest days, Livvi has been shown that being truly loved was something meant for other people, not for her.

"We didn't drive for long, we were here already," Grace is explaining. "Bree's mommy lives in a town...I don't know the name...but it's close to here. We were at her house, visiting. She has bunnies. She lets me play with them." Grace is now at the other end of the room, putting the stuffed pig onto the floor and tugging at the sliding doors that lead to the rear yard.

Livvi is still lost in thought, blinded with pain, as she asks Grace: "Where are you going?"

"To the pool," Grace explains. "Sometimes when my daddy isn't inside, that's where he is."

For a fraction of a second the look on Grace's face is utterly solemn, then she gives Livvi a smile that's radiant and hopeful.

Absolutely enchanting. So tentative and vulnerable—it's almost heart-rending.

It creates a shock of recognition in Livvi—and instantly she's determined not to bring any hurt, any disappointment, to this strangely endearing little girl.

Livvi gently takes Grace's hand and leads her back toward the center of the room. "Your...your daddy...isn't here right now, he's at work."

"Will you let me stay till he comes?" Grace asks. "I really want to show him my surprise. It's special."

And again there is that solemn, earnest look followed, after a brief hesitation, by the bright smile. It's as if Grace has learned to be guarded, a little cautious, before fully revealing herself.

Seeing that small wound in Grace, and knowing that Andrew may have had a hand in putting it there, is tearing Livvi apart. It's a wound that has been in Livvi for as long as she can remember.

She's barely able to speak. She has to clear her throat several times before she can say: "Grace, I have to leave now. So...I'm going to go outside, and ask your nanny to come in and take care of you until your daddy gets home."

Livvi has picked up her purse. And walked to the door. But as she's opening it, she's seeing that the driveway is empty. The BMW is gone—along with Bree, the blond nanny.

Livvi is alone with Andrew's child. And she has no way to deal with her. Livvi doesn't even have a car. When Livvi came here, David had dropped her off, after the meeting in Culver City. An hour ago.

During that hour it's as if her world has been ripped off its axis and sent hurtling into space—Livvi is utterly and completely at a loss. All she can think about is getting out of this house.

"What's Bree's number?" she's asking. "We need to call your nanny and tell her to come back." Livvi has managed to pull her phone from her pocket, but her grip is shaky; the icons on the screen are jittering and floating.

There's something strangely sympathetic in Grace's expression as she reaches up and takes the phone from Livvi. With a small frown of concentration, she begins to enter a number. Then she stops and hands the phone back to Livvi. "The light went out."

Livvi presses the phone's power button. Nothing. The screen stays dark. The battery has died. Livvi glances up, scanning the room.

"What are you looking for?" Grace asks.

"A land line. The kind of phone that plugs into a wall."

"Oh. Daddy doesn't have a phone like that—just his cell phone."

A mild panic is rippling through Livvi. Time is slipping by—the nanny, Bree, is getting farther and farther away. Livvi doesn't want to be here when Andrew arrives. She doesn't want an awkward confrontation. Not in front of Grace.

"Do you work for my daddy?" Grace is asking.

It takes Livvi a beat or two before she can think clearly. "No, honey, I don't work for your daddy. I'm...I'm a friend of his. We're friends."

Grace seems nervous. "Are you special friends?"

While Livvi is trying to decide on the appropriate thing to say, Grace tells her: "Mommy doesn't like it when Daddy has special friends who are ladies."

Grace has delivered this news with a sense of apprehension, and a hint of concern, as if, in spite of whatever her own worries might be, she wants to keep Livvi away from harm.

The word *Mommy* has hit Livvi with brutal force.

Does Andrew have a wife? Getting the answer to that would be as easy as saying to Grace, *Are your mommy and daddy married to each other?*

Livvi's not sure she wants to ask, not certain she wants to hear the answer. The only thing she is sure of is that she doesn't want to hurt Grace in any way. So instead of asking questions, Livvi is sliding her phone back into her pocket and suggesting: "Let's go to the neighbors' house and use their phone to call Bree."

Grace's distress is instantaneous. "I don't want to. I don't like the old man next door. He's mean. He scares me."

Livvi can see that Grace is genuinely afraid, and wants to take the fear away. "What if we don't go to the old man's house? What if we go to one of the other houses?"

Grace shakes her head no. She's clutching her little stuffed pig, and pleading: "I don't want to go anywhere. I only want to wait for my daddy."

Livvi glances across the living room to the clock on the steel desk. It's just before noon. Andrew should be arriving any minute now.

Without intending to, Livvi has already put her purse down at the end of the sofa. She's realizing that, as much as she wants to leave and avoid dealing with Andrew, she wants, even more, to stay and comfort Grace. She wants to soothe whatever it is in this little girl that's making her so anxious. "It's okay," she's telling Grace. "You don't have to go anywhere you don't want to. We'll stay right here, together, and wait for your dad."

Grace is reluctant, guarded. "You promise...?"

Livvi nods.

"Pinky promise?"

Livvi nods again.

After a long pause—Grace smiles.

A radiant smile that goes straight to Livvi's heart.

What Livvi assumed would be a wait lasting only a few minutes has spanned more than four hours. It's now shortly before five o'clock. And there's still no sign of Andrew. Yet Livvi hasn't made any effort to find a way out of Andrew's house.

Every time she has checked her watch or looked toward the door, thinking she should go to one of the neighbors and ask to use the phone, she has deliberately postponed doing it.

Livvi is staying marooned in Andrew's house because she doesn't want to end her connection with Grace.

There has been an innate warmth—an instinctive trust—between Livvi and Grace.

It has stirred an emotion in Livvi that she can't quite name. One that is incredibly gentle and fiercely determined. Something that feels precious and powerful. A critically important piece of knowledge she once had and has now forgotten. And she's determined not to leave until she can remember exactly what it is.

Livvi is on the sofa, paging through a magazine—Grace is nearby, sitting cross-legged on the floor in front of the coffee table. There is an open, jumbo-size box of crayons on the tabletop, along with a large sheet of paper.

Grace, deep in thought, is concentrating on the picture she's drawing. Her back is resting lightly against Livvi's leg.

Livvi isn't moving a muscle. She doesn't want to lose the feathery weight, the gentle warmth, of Grace's body against her skin. This is an intimacy she has never experienced before—this wordless closeness with a child.

"What are you drawing?" Livvi asks.

"Just something," Grace murmurs.

Earlier, Livvi and Grace listened to, and sang along with, every children's album in Andrew's music collection, and Livvi is asking: "Is it something from one of your songs?"

Grace shakes her head no.

"Is it a picture of your pig?" (After the sing-along, they played hide-and-seek—Grace's pink pig was the hidden object Livvi was assigned to find.)

Grace gives another negative shake of her head and this time Livvi asks: "Is it a picture from one of your stories?" (After hide-and-seek, Grace brought Livvi a stack of storybooks from a cabinet in the hall and settled herself in Livvi's lap; and Livvi read each book aloud from beginning to end until there were no more books to read.)

It was following the story session that Grace took the crayons and the paper from a drawer in Andrew's steel desk, and with her back resting against Livvi's leg, began work on the drawing that she has now completed.

Grace is scooting forward, sliding the crayoned paper across the coffee table.

Livvi's first shock is the sudden coolness on her skin where Grace's warmth has been. The second shock is the bizarre parade of images that Grace has created.

On one side of the paper is a childish rendering of a house. Erupting from the house, exploding through its roof like a wild-eyed Godzilla, is the stick-figure of a woman with billowing silvery hair, emerald eyes, and a grim, harsh-looking mouth. The woman and the house are surrounded by a blizzard of jagged scribbles—a torrent of black lightning.

At the center of the drawing is the stick-figure of a man. His eyes are round and dark, and the line of his mouth is vague. A smile? A grimace? It's hard to tell. One of his arms is reaching toward the house, the other toward a thicket of huge, rainbow-colored flowers. The arm nearest the house is being splintered by the black lightning. In each of the man's hands is a gift box. The box in the hand directed toward the house is significantly larger than the box directed toward the flowers.

Hiding in the midst of the flowers is the stick figure of a little girl wearing a ruffled skirt the color of a ripe summer lemon. Her eyes, like the male stick figure's, are round and dark. But where her mouth should be—nothing—a blank.

As Livvi is looking up from the drawing, her eyes are meeting Grace's. Livvi knows that Grace has told her a secret. An awful secret. A secret that neither she, nor Grace, knows how to discuss. They are suspended in a puzzling limbo, neither of them knowing what to do.

Grace, eventually, takes the picture from Livvi and puts it into a bottom drawer in Andrew's desk. Then she asks: "Want to see my surprise for Daddy?"

"Yes," Livvi says.

Grace positions herself beside one of the low, silk-covered chairs near the sofa—putting her hand on top of the chair back, bringing her legs close together. She rotates her toes outward, with her heels touching. And does a perfectly executed ballerina's plié.

Livvi sits forward, ready to applaud.

"Not yet," Grace tells her. "That wasn't the surprise."

Grace lifts her hand from the chair back, ever so slightly. Leaving a tiny space between her palm and the top of the chair. She focuses her gaze in mid-distance, and with unblinking determination does a second, flawless plié. She then shifts her gaze to Livvi. After a momentary pause, she smiles and says: "I can do it without holding on. That's my surprise for Daddy."

Daddy. Andrew.

How did he keep his daughter such a perfect secret? And why? Livvi is thinking. *What kind of person could deny his own child? And what does it say about me that I fell in love with him?*

"You look sad, Livvi." Grace is whispering this into Livvi's ear, as if she doesn't want to startle her. After she has said it, Grace sits on the sofa, a slight distance away from Livvi. Her ankles crossed. Her hands neatly folded in her lap.

And Livvi wonders, *Is there only you? Or do you have brothers and sisters? And who is your mother? Is that where you've been hiding? With her? In Palos Verdes? How could you have been less than fifty miles down the road, all this time, without me having any clue that you existed?*

Livvi's instinct is to somehow apologize to Grace. But Livvi knows it wouldn't make any sense. All she can manage to say is: "You're being really, really quiet. Is everything okay?"

"Yes," Grace tells her. "Except…"

"Except what?"

The reply is very small. Very faint. "I'm hungry."

The only things Livvi finds in Andrew's refrigerator are a pack of batteries, two bottles of champagne, and a square of eye-wateringly pungent Bleu cheese. (The freezer contained nothing but ice cubes and a large bottle of vodka.)

Grace is watching Livvi with an air of trusting curiosity. The ribbon that has been holding Grace's hair to one side of her head, in a ponytail, has come loose, and her hair is hanging free. She looks tired—and very, very hungry.

Livvi has no idea how she is going feed her. "Are you still sure you don't want us to walk to one of the neighbors and use the phone? We could call your father. Then we could order a pizza."

"I don't want pizza. I want to stay here. With you. And wait for Daddy."

Livvi is searching every cabinet in the immaculately empty kitchen, keenly aware of how much Grace is in need of food, and concerned she'll have to stay that way.

As if sensing Livvi's anxiety, Grace tells her: "Don't worry. I know you'll make something nice."

In turning to look at Grace, Livvi is noticing the dish of strawberries that she'd seen earlier, when she first arrived at the house. And she's discovering that behind the strawberries, farther back on the counter, is something she hadn't noticed. A bakery box. Inside the box, Livvi finds a banana muffin. And at the other end of the counter, there's an unopened bottle of water.

While Livvi is inventing this makeshift meal, arranging the strawberries and the muffin on a plate, Grace has gone to sit at the table, and Livvi is explaining: "We don't have any milk. Only water."

"I like water," Grace says. "I like it the best." It's clear she wants to put Livvi at ease.

Grace's generosity and her intrinsic goodness are touching Livvi's heart, stirring, again, the emotion that she can't quite name.

"Are you okay?" Grace asks.

Livvi nods and puts the plate with the strawberries and the muffin onto the table—along with a napkin and the bottle of water.

"I'm glad you're okay," Grace says. "Because I think you're nice."

Livvi is slipping into a chair, across the table from Grace.

And just as Livvi sits down, Grace gets up.

She goes to the kitchen counter and begins bringing things to the table. A napkin. A second plate. And an empty glass. After she arranges them, with great care, on a placemat in front of Livvi, she says: "If Daddy doesn't come, can we go before it gets dark? I don't like it here when it's night."

Grace seems to be deciding whether or not to reveal something more, something very personal. Then with her head slightly bowed she tells Livvi: "When it's night, this house is scary. You can see the trees through the walls because they're glass. The trees make scary shadows and I have bad dreams." She raises her head, searching out Livvi's gaze, asking in a voice full of curiosity: "Did you ever have bad dreams?"

Livvi's thoughts go to the haunting image of the woman in the pearl-button shoes and she tells Grace: "Sometimes I still do."

After considering this, Grace gives a pensive nod. "I like it," she says. "That you have bad dreams."

Livvi is surprised. "Why?"

With a shy smile, Grace tells her: "Because it makes us the same." And without segue or another word on the subject of bad dreams, Grace returns to her chair, bows her head, folds her hands, and whispers: "Bless us, O Lord, for these thy gifts we are about to receive. Amen."

Then Grace, with her stomach grumbling loudly, pushes the plate containing the muffin and the strawberries into the center of the table, along with the bottle of water.

"If you're hungry too," she murmurs to Livvi, "we can share."

Livvi reaches across the table and runs her fingers through the silk of Grace's hair.

There's nothing more to say. There are no words.

It is the beginning of a love affair.

In the early evening Livvi and Grace are being driven away from Andrew's house in a gleaming, gray Audi R8. A sports car so refined that its interior contains only a driver's seat, a passenger's seat, and behind them, a boxlike space designed to hold nothing much larger than a medium-size suitcase.

Grace has just popped up from the interior of the boxlike space.

And Sierra, who is at the wheel of the car, is saying: "Get back down! The last thing I need is a ticket for hauling a kid around without a seat belt."

"Or a seat," Livvi chuckles.

"Beggars can't be choosers, honey, and this car's full of nothing but beggars. Your ride has a weather vane through its roof and my Jag's still in the damn shop. We're lucky I could get hold of this platinum-plated joy ride. It wasn't easy. The rightful owner and I were halfway out the door heading for an X-rated sleepover in Malibu when you called." Sierra pauses. "Wait a minute. You said your phone's dead, how the hell were you able to call me?"

"A FedEx guy rang the doorbell—making a delivery. He let me use his phone," Livvi says.

"And in your hour of need, your landlady was the first person you tapped to get you off the desert island? Interesting. I didn't know you and I were that close."

Sierra has said this jokingly. But Livvi knows Sierra is aware that Livvi must have tried to contact other people and is asking for details. Livvi's reluctant to give them, worried about the impact they might have on Grace. Livvi wants to protect Grace—the calls to both her nanny and her father went unanswered, directly to voice mail. Livvi doesn't want Grace to hear that Sierra, a stranger, was the first person available to come to her rescue.

So Livvi tells Sierra: "I promise I'll fill you in later. But right now I have another favor to ask. Grace hasn't had very much to eat today. We need to stop and pick up some dinner."

Grace, who is still peeking over the back of Livvi's seat, whispers: "Can we have McDonald's?"

"I've met your dad—" Sierra stops and shoots a quick look in Livvi's direction that says *"he's a shit,"* before glancing over her shoulder at Grace and telling her: "Your old man is a pricey-organic, high-end restaurant type. You're sure he lets you eat at McDonald's?"

Grace slowly, solemnly, shakes her head from side to side. Then, after a brief hesitation, as she's sliding down out of sight, there's the hint of an irresistibly hopeful smile.

Whatever lightness was in Grace during the drive to Livvi's guest-house, and the stop at McDonald's, has given way to a fidgeting, sleepy fretfulness.

Livvi is taking off Grace's shoes and socks, helping Grace to get ready for a bath. They are in Livvi's bedroom, sitting on Livvi's high, white bed. Sierra is in the bathroom, filling the tub with water. And Grace, so tired that her eyes are half-closed, is, for the third time in as many minutes, asking: "Is my daddy coming soon?"

It's close to seven and Livvi still has no idea where Andrew is. Ever since leaving the house in Flintridge, she has been consumed by anxiety about what the explanation could be for Andrew's continuing absence. Now she's trying to deflect Grace's worry by saying: "You know what? I bet if we go see what Sierra's doing, we'll find out she's making a big, giant bubble bath for you."

Grace is restless, yawning. Looking around the room—noticing the brightly painted thrift-shop table Livvi uses as a desk, and the laptop that's there. "While we wait for Daddy, can we play a game on your computer?"

"I'm sorry, baby. I don't have any games on my computer."

Grace seems bewildered. "Then why do you have one?"

"It's, um...not for fun...I use it for my job. I'm a writer." Livvi goes to the table, picks up a copy of her novel, and brings it back to the bed, showing it to Grace and explaining: "I write books. This is the first one I wrote. I started writing it a long time ago, but this is what it looks like now. It's called *The Book of Someday*—"

"—and so many people liked it," Sierra says, "that those who published it want her to write another book." Sierra is coming out of the bathroom, drying her hands on a washcloth.

Grace points to the computer. "Is your other book in there now?"

"Not yet," Livvi says.

"Will it be there soon?"

Sierra sits on the bed beside Livvi and laughs. "I think the kid has a future as a New York editor."

And Livvi tells Grace: "It will be there as soon as I know what the story is."

Grace, cuddling her little pink pig, leans sleepily against Livvi's side. "Can you make it be like *Winnie the Pooh*? That's a good story because Piglet's in it."

"I'll do my best." Livvi gathers Grace up, intending to carry her into the bathroom, and Grace immediately says: "I don't need help. I take baths by myself."

Livvi releases her hold on Grace; Grace quickly disappears through the bathroom door; and Sierra says: "That kid is what...? Five, maybe six? It's weird how calm she is. It's like she's totally used to being left on her own—with strangers. What sort of a twisted shit of a father could that guy be?"

The feeling Livvi experienced earlier, when she saw the lipstick-colored stains on the napkin in Andrew's kitchen—that feeling of being hit in the chest with a baseball—is hitting her again. "I've been with him for seven months…and I honest to God didn't have any idea he had a child."

Sierra gives a cynical snort. "Bullshit. You knew there was something about him that wasn't kosher."

Livvi is riding out a wave of nausea. "I can't believe how stupid this sounds…I didn't think that whatever it was I didn't know about him could be something this big."

"Well, I did. Starting with Valentine's Day," Sierra says. "You guys were supposed to be all hot and heavy in love—and he's not around? And his story was that he's in Europe, on business? I didn't buy it for a minute."

Livvi goes to her desk, sits, and puts her head in her hands. She feels like a fool. Worse than a fool. Like an idiot.

"Hey. Don't beat yourself up. You had the love goggles on. There isn't a female in the world who hasn't been blinded by those things at least once. Hell, there's probably a woman somewhere right this minute hooked up with a guy sitting on death row for murdering a carload of preschoolers, and that goggle-eyed girl is saying, 'Gosh, I never saw it coming—he was always nothing but sweet to me.'"

Livvi's response is an embarrassed laugh.

"Besides," Sierra says, "your goggles came equipped with those special green lenses."

"What do you mean…?"

"All the cash your boy likes to throw around," Sierra explains.

"The hot-air balloons and the sailboats. The fancy restaurants. All that champagne and caviar—"

"Money had nothing to do with it," Livvi insists. "Money doesn't make any difference to me."

Sierra is leaving, going into the living room. Her tone has a take-no-prisoners honesty to it. "Money makes a difference to everybody, kiddo. All I'm saying is…he was able to turn life into such a thrill ride it didn't give you a chance, or the desire, to do a lot of thinking."

For the second time today, Livvi is experiencing the sensation that she's swallowing lead. As much as she doesn't want to admit it, there's an element of truth in what Sierra has just said. Not about the money. But about wearing the goggles, being willingly blind. Before Andrew, Livvi's life had been so closed in that, without giving it a second thought, she'd let the freedom and the excitement that Andrew gave her overshadow all the questions he brought with him.

It takes a while before the sickened feeling passes. As soon as it does, Livvi's first thought is of Grace; Livvi quickly goes to the open bathroom door, to check on her. "Ready to come out?" she asks.

"Not yet," Grace says. She's scalloping the side of the tub with mounds of bath bubbles.

Livvi walks back into the bedroom—to the bedside table—where her phone is in its charger. In the less than ten minutes since she's been home, Livvi has been intentionally avoiding this moment. Knowing that the instant she reconnects with reality she'll open the door to staggering hurt. But she can't put it off any longer. She has to face the pain and somehow survive it. Livvi touches the phone. The screen instantly displays a text. From Andrew. Sent today, at 11:32 a.m. The message reads:

> Can't make lunch. Surprise visit from out of town clients.
> Stuck in meetings through dinner. Will call later. If too late,
> tomorrow.

Following Andrew's message is a second text. Also sent today. From David:

> I'm at the airport. Glad the weather vane crashed your car.
> Glad about Culver City. Glad I got to see you.

David's message barely registers. Livvi is preoccupied with Andrew and his monumental, unspoken lie—she's preoccupied with Grace.

Livvi's eyes shift to a scrap of paper lying on the bed. It contains the telephone number belonging to Grace's mother. Livvi asked Grace for the number as soon as they came in the door. But she has been unable to use it. Too afraid.

Livvi picks up the paper. Looks at the number. Then puts the phone on speaker and presses Andrew's number instead. No answer. Straight to voice mail. Livvi sends a text:

> Grace came to your house while I was there. She's with me.
> Call ASAP.

Livvi's hand, the one she's holding the paper scrap in, is damp with sweat. She has run out of options: she doesn't have a choice. Grace can't spend the night here without anyone knowing where she is. Livvi knows she has to call Grace's mother. But still, she's reluctant. Thinking about the grim-faced stick figure in Grace's drawing—and the torrent of black lightning raining down from the sky.

When Livvi finally enters the numbers from the paper scrap into her phone, she leaves the phone on speaker—unwilling to hold it to her ear. Nervous about being in too close a proximity to the dangerous-looking creature in the drawing.

On the second ring, the call is answered by a melodious female voice that sounds like it was polished in a finishing school.

"Is this Grace's mother?" Livvi asks.

"Yes, who's this?"

Livvi is tense; she can hardly breathe. "I'm a friend of Andrew's. I'm calling because—"

Instantaneously Livvi is cut off by a sarcastic snarl: "Just for the record, 'Friend of Andrew's,' you are speaking to Grace's mother… but more importantly, you're speaking to Andrew's *wife*!" The finishing school purr has become a dockworker's roar. Livvi is backing away from the phone.

And the woman is screaming: "Don't ever dare call me again, you slut. You bitch."

After that the phone at the other end of the call is abruptly switched off.

In the brief silence that follows, Livvi hears a small gasp. Grace is in the room. Dripping wet. Clutching a towel. Her eyes wide. Her face ghostly pale. And in a frightened whisper, she's asking: "Mommy's mad, isn't she?"

Livvi recognizes the look on Grace's face. It's the emotion that ruled Livvi's childhood—the terror of not knowing how to navigate the dangers, and madness, of the world into which you've been born.

Grace darts back into the bathroom. Livvi quickly crosses the bedroom, to follow her. When Livvi arrives in the bathroom, Grace is at the window, shivering, facing away from Livvi.

"I want my daddy." Grace's arms are wrapped around her chest, her hands visible on either side of her back. She's cradling herself in a sorrowfully lonely embrace.

Livvi kneels and wraps a dry towel around Grace, turning her so that they're facing each other. "Why are you holding yourself like this?"

"Bree taught me. So I always have a hug if I need it." Grace's eyes are filling with tears.

Livvi is again experiencing the sensation that came over her earlier while she and Grace were waiting for Andrew, that feeling of gentleness with its undercurrent of fierce determination. Livvi intuitively knows that whatever this is, it's important. Information that she once had, and somehow lost track of.

As she's looking at Grace, Livvi is slowly remembering the thing that she had forgotten—a key piece of knowledge about herself.

She's realizing that buried underneath her pain there has always been a wellspring of love. The kind of love she had glimpsed through a telescope. The love she had always wanted to receive. Love flowing between a mother and child. A pure, unshakable love she'd instinctively known she was born for—and would someday be able to give.

And that day has come.

Livvi is opening her arms to Grace—inviting her in. "Would you like me to rock you to sleep, baby?"

Grace nods, and folds into Livvi's embrace.

Livvi carries Grace into the bedroom. To the high, white bed. And dresses her in a fresh cotton T-shirt that Livvi hasn't worn yet. On Grace, it looks like the calf-length robes of a cherub.

Livvi holds Grace, rocking her gently. And wondering how, now that she has found her, she will ever be able to let her go.

When Grace has drifted into sleep, when Livvi is tucking her in, drawing the covers up around her shoulders, there is the sound of the doorbell in the living room—and Andrew's frantic voice asking, "Is Grace okay?"

Before Sierra has finished saying, "Of course she is," Livvi is already in the living room—pulling the bedroom door closed behind her.

Sierra is glaring at Andrew as she adds: "Livvi's been watching over that kid like Grace belongs to her—what a shitty deal that the same can't be said about Grace's parents."

Andrew appears to be in anguish.

Sierra, picking up her purse and keys, is murmuring to Livvi: "I made you some coffee. It's in the kitchen. Call me if you need anything." Sierra gives Andrew a disgusted stare. "When my goddamn phone rings, I answer it."

After Sierra has gone, Livvi and Andrew are riveted in place.

Livvi is burning with questions. Choking with disappointment, and anger.

Andrew is the one who speaks first. His voice is hoarse, tense. "I was going to tell you about Grace. I was going to tell you everything."

"Everything?" Livvi is steeling herself—asking and at the same time not wanting to know: "How much more is there?"

Andrew, as if he hasn't heard her, is saying: "Things got out of hand. It took awhile before I knew I was in love with you and by then I'd let too much time go by and I—"

"How did you erase her so completely, Andrew?" Livvi is thinking of Grace, at the window, in the bathroom, holding herself in that lonely embrace. The sadness of it is making Livvi furious. "Do you ever spend any time at all with her?"

He seems shocked. Indignant. "Of course I do."

A small, heavy, stone statue—a woman holding a basket of fruit—is on the table near the sofa. Livvi's hand is closing around the woman's neck. For the first time in her life Livvi is being moved to violence. Tempted to smash the statue into the side of Andrew's head. To somehow avenge the wrongs that have been done to Grace.

Livvi, with the statue clutched in her hand, is rapidly moving toward Andrew. "I don't believe you do spend time with Grace. I've been with you for seven months. I would have known if she was part of your life."

There's a sudden flare of anger in Andrew. It's white-hot and stops Livvi in her tracks.

"Grace has been here from the beginning, Olivia. She's the reason I walked out on you. That first night, at the fundraiser. I got a text from the nanny. Grace had a fever. They couldn't get it down, and they were thinking about taking her to the emergency room."

Livvi's mind is going to the stick-figure drawing. The torrent of black lightning and the little girl in the lemon-colored skirt. All alone. Hiding in a forest of flowers. It's as if Livvi is talking to herself, not Andrew, as she asks: "When were you ever together? When was she actually with you? And how did I never know?"

The anger in Andrew has been replaced by what seems like overwhelming weariness. "You didn't know because I saw her on weeknights when I wasn't with you. When I said I was working, or tired. And on weekends. When you were out of town at book signings. A lot of times we go to the park, the zoo, we go to lunch. I have Bree bring Grace to my office during the day."

Bree. The girl with the lavender shorts and the BMW.

The memory of her sets off a flare of jealousy in Livvi. "Is she really Grace's nanny?"

Andrew seems offended by the sarcasm in Livvi's voice. "What the hell are you implying?"

"Most nannies don't drive brand-new BMWs."

Andrew flinches. Closes his eyes. Turns away.

He goes to the sofa and sits. His head dropped between his shoulders, his elbows on his knees. In a dull monotone, he says: "The car is Kayla's. It belongs to my wife."

Hearing Andrew say those words: *My wife.* It's as if Livvi's heart is taking a flurry of cuts from a freshly sharpened razor.

After a short pause, Andrew tells Livvi: "I'm not sleeping around."

And Livvi, reeling from the burn of those cuts to the heart, asks him: "Is that the same story you tell your wife?"

Andrew looks up, annoyed. "Hold it right there, Olivia. You've got no idea what you're talking about. Kayla and I have been married for eight years." He raises his voice, stopping Livvi before she can interrupt. "And we've been separated for close to three. Long before I ever met you."

His tone is quieter as he says: "There are a lot of reasons we haven't gotten a divorce. The situation with Kayla is difficult. She's emotionally frail. An innocent. Old-school Catholic. My first marriage, the one I told you about when you and I were in Canada, it lasted a couple of months and was annulled—in Kayla's mind, this is the only marriage for either one of us. She's also very close with my parents. Me pushing for a divorce would've put incredible stress on her, and on my folks. And the truth is, until I met you, I didn't have any reason to want a divorce."

The weight of the stone statue is heavy in Livvi's hand. She wants to put it down, but can't. The anger—the blistering sense of betrayal—is holding it too tightly.

Andrew seems to be terribly upset as he's saying: "Kayla wasn't the one who wanted our marriage to end. When I left, it almost killed her—I felt like I was clubbing a baby seal. Every time I see her, I still do."

A dry, involuntary laugh comes out of Livvi. She's dying inside as she's explaining. "I spoke to your wife, Andrew. She doesn't come off as an innocent, or a baby. I called her—to try to let her know where Grace was. She screamed that I was a bitch and hung up on me."

In the midst of her desolation, and her fury, Livvi is experiencing an irrational need to have Andrew hold her, console her. But he's staying where he is, on the sofa, informing her: "First of all, Kayla wasn't being callous about our daughter. When she got that call from you, she thought you just wanted to rub her nose in the fact that I was seeing someone—she had no idea you were calling to let her know where Grace was. Bree had told her Grace was fine. When Bree left Grace at my place this afternoon, she saw Grace go inside after somebody opened the door—she assumed it was me."

Andrew has gotten up from the sofa and is restlessly pacing the room. Repeatedly circling past Livvi. Without looking at her.

And Livvi, left alone, listening to him defending his wife, is slowly filling with an aching need for mercy.

While Andrew is insisting: "I want you to understand…it's hard for Kayla…the idea of me being involved with anyone else. It tears her apart." He deliberates, then quietly says: "That's why I didn't tell you about Grace. If I'd told you, you would've wanted to meet her and I couldn't allow that to happen."

Again there is the sensation of dying inside as Livvi asks: "Why?"

"Because if Grace knew about you—Kayla would've known, and she would have lost her mind. I didn't want to expose Grace to that kind of drama. She's already been through enough."

Livvi wonders if this explanation was meant to make things better, to lessen the ache: it hasn't. "I was never really part of you," she says. "I was excluded. Disposable."

"It wasn't about exclusion, Olivia. It was about protection." Andrew waits until he and Livvi are looking directly into each other's eyes before he tells her: "I hid Grace from you to protect her. There's no other reason."

Livvi desperately wants to believe him. She wants, with everything that's in her, not to go back to being alone. While she's asking: "How do I know you're not lying?"

"All the things I've ever said to you are the truth, Olivia. I've never spoken one lying word to you. I love you. I want to be with you. That's the truth. It's what's important."

He reaches out to put his arms around her. Livvi pulls away, feeling like she's in a maze of mirrors, searching for a doorway. "The fact that you have a wife is important. You lied about that…and you lied about Grace…"

"I didn't lie," Andrew tells her. "All I did was not spell out every syllable of the truth."

Livvi thinks about this, then says: "Hiding the truth is the same as telling a lie." And as she's finishing her thought, a hard edge of accusation is creeping into her voice. "The lie you told me—hiding Grace, making it seem like she didn't exist—that was despicable."

Andrew is no longer trying to hold Livvi in his arms. But he has stepped very close to her, close enough for her to feel the anger in the beat of his heart. "Before you say anything you'll be sorry for," he's warning. "Don't forget, you play the same game with me. You have plenty of blank spaces you haven't bothered to fill in. How about the phone calls? The ones that come every once in a while in the middle of the night and leave you rattled for days? Ever talk to me about them? Ever told me who they're from?"

Livvi looks away, her anger blending with a vague sense of guilt.

"And what about the nightmares?" Andrew is asking. "When you wake up shaking and crying? What's that about? Maybe your life before you met me? There's got to be more to your backstory than that you grew up with a single father you haven't spoken to in years."

Livvi takes several steps backward, trying to put distance between her secrets and Andrew's. But he's quickly closing the gap, telling her: "You never really open up about what's down deep inside you—you toss me the Cliff Notes. I'm not an idiot, Olivia. Don't you think I know there're things in your life you haven't figured out how to handle? It was obvious from the first night in that butler's pantry, when I asked you to tell me about yourself and I saw the terror in your eyes. That's why I let you off the hook—did the fortune-telling act and turned it into a game."

Andrew is breathing hard, his words coming out in a rasp: "For me, it didn't make you despicable, it just made you human."

Livvi's response is quiet, nearly inaudible—she's not sure she's right about what she's saying. "This is different. What you did is different."

"The only difference is I'm forty-two and you're twenty-seven. I've had more time—bigger things—to fuck up."

Still lost in the maze of mirrors, and still searching for the doorway, Livvi tells Andrew: "I called you this morning at five-twenty, when the sun wasn't even up. After the weather vane crashed into my car." Her voice is rising now, not with anger, but with uneasiness. Her grip on the stone statue is inadvertently tightening as she says: "You didn't call back till after ten. Where were you for all that time?"

Andrew is grabbing the statue from Livvi's hand. Throwing it across the room, smashing it against the wall. Shouting: "I was in goddamn Palos Verdes!"

He draws a deep breath, and then says: "I went down there to try to talk to Kayla—for the first time ever—about a divorce. Grace was spending the night with my parents, it seemed like a perfect chance to explain things. I told Kayla we needed to get a divorce because there was someone special in my life, someone I love. And she completely fell apart."

Andrew is refusing to take his eyes off Livvi's. "She tried to kill herself, Olivia. I had to stay with her."

Before Livvi can speak, Andrew clamps his hand over her mouth. "I stayed because I didn't have a choice. The mother of my child needed me." He gently lifts his palm away from Livvi's mouth, and says: "Yes, my phone was off. It was necessary. Me taking calls and sending texts would only have pushed Kayla over the edge. As it was, it took her until midmorning to calm down enough to fall asleep—and when she did, my first call was to you."

Andrew looks at Livvi tenderly, for a long moment. "If you were my wife, wouldn't you want me to take care of you…the best way I could?"

He seems to be begging for Livvi's compassion. "I feel responsible for what's happened to Kayla. I'm the one who walked away, the one who broke the promise. I owe her a soft landing. Please tell me you understand."

Without waiting for an answer Andrew pulls Livvi toward him. His kiss is as possessive and full of desire as it was on that first night—the first time he ever touched her. And for an instant, there is that spellbinding chemistry—that feeling in Livvi of ascending into paradise.

She's melting. Forgetting. Wanting to forgive.

But then she thinks of Grace. At the bathroom window. Shivering and alone. Waiting for her daddy.

And Livvi is stepping away from Andrew. She's saying: "You need to leave. You need to get Grace and take her home."

Andrew seems ready to insist that they stay where they are and work things out—but then he appears to change his mind, and lets Livvi lead him toward the bedroom.

As he's following her through the bedroom door, Andrew says: "You and I love each other. Nothing is going to change that."

Livvi stays silent. She doesn't want to lie to him. And can't tell him the truth. She doesn't know what it is.

When they arrive at the bed, where Grace is sleeping, Livvi positions herself in front of Andrew—momentarily blocking his access to his little girl.

Livvi passionately wants to stay with Grace. To protect her. Hold on to her; never let her out of her sight. But Grace is Andrew's child, not hers. Livvi understands she has no power to do anything but step away.

When she does, it's as if her heart is being ripped out.

While Andrew is taking his place at Grace's side, Livvi hands him the lightly woven woolen throw that's at the foot of the bed. She watches as he wraps Grace in it, reverently—and carries her toward the living room.

Grace and Andrew are slowly disappearing from sight. Grace, in a half-sleep, is murmuring "Daddy!" in the same awestruck way she might whisper the word "Magic!"

In hearing that murmur Livvi is being drawn back into the place where she is Olivia—hungering to feel the beat of her father's heart, and the warmth of his embrace.

It takes several long moments before Livvi returns to the present. Before she realizes that her phone is ringing.

When she picks the phone up and puts it to her ear, a whispery voice is asking: "Olivia, is that you?"

And there is the sensation of fire and snakes and knives in Livvi.

While the whispery voice is telling her: "If you don't listen to what I have to say, you will regret it until the day you die."

Micah
Newport, Rhode Island ~ 2012

A LIGHT WIND IS WHISPERING AMONG THE SHADOWS. IN THE portico. Rustling through the sea of potted palms. Traveling across the black marble steps. And over the tongue-shaped brass knocker that Micah, only seconds ago, let drop—and bang—against the door of this crumbling, subdivided mansion in Newport.

A sudden squeak has come from behind a second-floor window. The drapes have been opened, stealthily. For a half-second, Micah is genuinely frightened.

A crackle is sputtering from the intercom speaker near the door. It's being followed by a hush—a void in which someone is listening, hovering. Deciding.

Micah is suddenly exhausted. She rests her forehead on the intercom's rusted, mesh-covered mouth. It has a stale, musty smell. She breathes it in, like a punishment.

After several long beats, she asks: "Do I have to beg you to open the door?"

The hush continues. And continues. Until a woman's voice, an arrestingly rich contralto, announces: "I don't receive visitors anymore. Go away."

Micah steps back from the intercom and looks toward the second-floor window—arms raised, face upturned. Waiting to be seen, to be acknowledged. The hush remains unbroken. The impact of this is like being stripped naked and rolled through broken glass. And Micah wails: "Do you really not recognize me?"

A pause. Followed by an indistinct noise at the other end of the intercom. "Are you someone I knew well?" the woman asks.

"No," Micah tells her. "I'm your daughter."

"Cry Me a River." That's the song that's playing—the lyrics that are being sung. "Cry me a river, 'cause I've cried a river over you." The singer's voice is enthralling. Luxuriantly rich and limber in its power and sensuality.

Micah, frustrated with trying to be heard over the volume of the music, is searching for the sound system's remote control. Her mother's ornate second-floor sitting room is cluttered with a lifetime's worth of knickknacks and memorabilia.

After a while, Micah discovers the remote on an enormous tabletop crowded with crystal figurines and dominated by a large, framed portrait. The photo, circa 1970, is of a voluptuous brunette onstage at the London Palladium—her low-cut dress displaying her figure to eye-catching advantage as she's bowing to the crowd, receiving a riotous standing ovation.

Micah clicks the remote. The music fades. And her mother says: "I thought you were one of my fans—it's why I didn't recognize you right away." She's stroking the fur of the large, smoke-colored cat that's curled in her lap. With each pass of her hand, she's watching the light from the window dance across the jewels on her ringed fingers. "My fans are incredibly loyal," she's telling Micah. "There are always emails, letters…and, quite often, visits."

Her mother's face, an older version of the one in the framed photograph, is serene as she's watching Micah. But her tone has an undercurrent of accusation. "I couldn't have survived without the love and concern of my fans. They are the only thing that sustains me. Without them, I think by now my heart would be completely broken."

This is meant as an insult, a well-placed barb. Micah sidesteps it. Determined not to take the bait—not to open the floodgates and let the demons loose. Determined that this time, things will be different. Because this time things *are* different. Micah may be dying. And before it's too late, she needs to find someone: someone who knows her, who is willing to give her comfort. And reconciliation.

Her mother has turned toward the window, and Micah is wondering if she's looking at her own reflection—taking an impromptu inventory of her ongoing battle against time. Assessing whether or not, beneath what is now soft and fleshy, she can still find some trace of what was once firm and ripe.

Her mother's voice is a sigh as she transfers her gaze from the window to the cat and quietly says: "I looked forward to my motherhood with such excitement and it turned into such disappointment." Then she sits up very straight and speaks directly to Micah. "I expected it to be absolutely miraculous, and you took all the joy out of it."

She's shaking her head, puzzled, as she adds: "When you were a baby, you worshipped me and that was sublime, but then when you were a little girl for some reason you changed. You became outrageously selfish. No matter how much I gave you, nothing was good enough. You always wanted something else." A tremulous, wounded quality is creeping into her voice. "You were horrible to me. You were a horrible, horrible little thing."

This barb has hit its target—the floodgates are open. The demons are loose. And Micah tells her mother: "They should've ripped your uterus out the day you were born."

"How dare you…? I was a magnificent parent. My god, you celebrated your sixth birthday in Paris and your tenth at the Sydney Opera House."

"I was backstage on a cot at the fucking Sydney Opera House. With an ear infection." Micah's need for comfort is being overwhelmed by a furious desire for justice. She's slamming the remote against the tabletop, again and again, sending waves of crystal figurines smashing to the floor. "I saw you for maybe five minutes in Australia—during a costume change. And Paris was being alone in a hotel suite with a boxed birthday cake and a rented babysitter. You were across town, launching your ten-millionth concert tour."

Her mother cuts her off with a shout. "Your goddamn birthday present was a ruby and gold bracelet specially made for you by a jeweler who worked for Cartier. Do you know how excited I was about that present…and how much you hurt me when you weren't?"

"I was six. I wanted a dollhouse!"

"See? See what I mean? Nothing was ever enough for you. Not the presents, not the trips. Not even my getting you into Harvard."

"I got into goddamned Harvard on my own!"

"You can't be simpleminded enough to think once they found out you were my daughter…which I'm sure they must have…that it didn't help."

And through gritted teeth, her mother adds: "What did you do in return? You threw it in my face and dropped out."

"How in hell did my time at Harvard have anything to do with you?"

"That you could even ask…shows how blind and ungrateful you are." Her mother is now cuddling the smoke-colored cat to her chest, like a child soothing herself with a favorite toy. "Everything you had, everywhere you were able to go, was because of me, because I lived my life as a sacrifice."

Her mother lowers the cat into her lap and glares at Micah. "Do you give any thought to that—to how much I sacrificed for you? I worked three-hundred sixty-five days a year. Never missing a concert or a recording session. Never refusing an interview, an autograph. Always providing you with the best. The best clothes. The best schools. The finest tutors. You weren't raised by some drab, faceless little housewife. I gave you the gift of being the child of a music icon—"

"You didn't give me shit."

"—and all I ever expected in return was that you would love me in the way I'd always imagined—that you would appreciate me and want to make me happy. I gave so much and asked for something so simple—a child who cared enough to reward me with her devotion. I was an extraordinary mother while you, Micah, were a disaster of a daughter who has never done a single thing to make me proud."

Micah's rage—her hurt—is volcanic.

She's lunging at her mother, dragging her to her feet: the smoke-colored cat shrieking and darting away while Micah is screaming: "What was my favorite bedtime story? How old was I when I got my first period? Who did I go to my senior prom with? How much of your coke did I snort when I was twelve? Where do I live? What do I do for a living? Come on, Mother, pick one! Take your best shot!"

Micah is shaking her mother with such force that she can hear her mother's teeth chattering—it's spurring a fleeting desire in Micah to reach in and pull them out by their roots. Shove them down her mother's throat. And kill her.

Her mother is defiantly observing Micah through narrowed eyes, as if reading her mind—warning Micah: "It won't do you any good. You're not in the will."

Micah's laugh is spontaneous and bitter. "Fuck you," she tells her mother. "I'm rich."

Her mother has pulled away and dropped back into the wing chair near the window. There's a feisty combativeness in the tilt of her chin. "I haven't seen or heard from you since you were in your twenties, Micah. Other than to badger me into leaving you my money…what reason could you possibly have for being here? Tell me."

And now it's Micah who's the one being shaken—the one experiencing the sensation of having her teeth rattled.

"Well," her mother says, "what do you want? Whatever it is must be something big—you once swore you'd go to your grave without ever setting foot in this house again."

Her mother's words are draining all the fight, and fury, out of Micah. She's dropping into a sitting position beside the wing chair—and letting her head come to rest against her mother's thigh.

It has been more than two decades since Micah has touched her mother's body. Touching it now is like unexpectedly touching heaven, while brushing against hell.

Micah is picturing the future. What it will hold if she decides to fight her cancer. She's picturing the surgery and the things that will come with it. Chemo. Nausea. Hot putrid vomit. Skull-splitting headaches. The drying-out of her skin and eyes. The steady loosening and falling-away of every hair, every eyelash, every trace of her eyebrows, until her face, which has always been so lovely, is bald and waxy. Nothing but a skull pushing against lard-colored flesh. And there will be searing pain in her legs and arms and feet that will leave her weak. She'll be robbed of her strength, her beauty. Her breasts. And in the end, there'll be no guarantee that the cancer won't win. The toll seems incomprehensible.

And Micah says: "There's a fight I'm supposed to take on—and I'm not even sure I have a right to be in it. The price of walking away is death, but the end result of staying and fighting might simply be death postponed. I have no idea what to do.

"I need you," Micah tells her mother. "I'm very, very sick. They might not be able to make me better. I have breast cancer."

Her mother's hands flutter up like startled birds. Then slowly come to rest on the crown of Micah's head.

For the briefest of moments it's as if Micah is being bathed in the warmth of a fragrant, healing oil.

She is infinitely grateful.

And, for a while, she is where she has always dreamed of being.

Then when her mother moves her hands away, gathering the smoke-colored cat into her lap, she tells Micah: "You didn't get it from me. I've never grown any sort of cancer. No one in my family has."

And Micah feels as if she is already dead.

After a long beat of emptiness, nothingness, Micah gets up from the floor, goes to the table where the shards of broken crystal are, retrieves the remote for the sound system, and hands it to her mother.

Her mother fidgets with the remote. Sets it aside. Picks it up again and says: "Your father is at the house in Maine."

"Thank you," Micah tells her. "That's good to know."

"Well. If you're interested…"

"Right. Okay."

"Okay then." Her mother gives Micah a bright, celebrity smile. Holds it for the length of a camera-flash. Then turns her interest to the remote, and to turning up the volume on the music.

Micah—in the midst of her desolation—is understanding how ridiculous it was to make this trip to Newport. She should have known, even before getting on the plane, that to seek comfort from her mother would be as foolish as licking battery acid hoping for a taste of honey.

While she's descending the stairs of her mother's house the rooms above are filling with the sounds of lush orchestration. With her mother's seductively powerful voice singing, "There's a somebody I'm longing to see…hope they'll turn out to be…someone to watch over me."

Through the tears welling in her eyes, Micah is seeing the face of the only person who has ever, truly, watched over her. The one person who loved her in the way she'd always wanted to be loved. The woman in the silver dress and pearl-button shoes. The best and kindest human being Micah has ever known.

AnnaLee
Glen Cove, Long Island ~ 1986

*I*NNOCENCE, ANNALEE IS THINKING. *IT'S SOMETHING I NEVER dreamed I'd associate with Persephone, but unbelievably here it is. Innocent is the only way to describe how she looks right now.*

Persephone is in the garden, sitting beside AnnaLee. In the old wooden swing. On a late August afternoon. Her head is bent low over a piece of copper wire that she's shaping and reshaping as easily as if it were embroidery silk. The slant of the sun is washing the copper with a fiery glow, turning it into a trail of liquid light.

Bella is hovering at Persephone's knee, watching with fascination.

While AnnaLee is asking: "What's it going to be?"

"I don't know yet, but isn't this wire cool?" Persephone says. "I found a bunch of it when I was with Rebecca Wang, helping get everything ready for the party at Mrs. Jahn's estate. Rebecca came up with the idea that the dance floor should be inside a really pretty gazebo and the carpenter that's working on it—or maybe it was the electrician—left pieces of this stuff all over the place. You should see the gorgeous decorations Rebecca has come up with. Mrs. Wang was right, her granddaughter really is a genius."

Persephone is glowing with enthusiasm. "The party's going to be incredible. And Rebecca is like out-of-this-world nice. I'm not just one of the people helping her anymore—she made me her assistant.

And guess what? She said I'm the most creative visual thinker she's ever met. Can you believe that?"

"Yes," AnnaLee says. "I believed it the first time I saw one of your sketches."

"Really, that's what you think? You really think I'm good at being creative?"

"Yes. You're tremendously talented."

Persephone returns to working with the copper wire. "I used to really like doing sketches and I still do, but—"

Bella, fascinated by the sunlit wire, is doing her best to tug it out of Persephone's hand.

AnnaLee lifts Bella's rag doll from the seat of the swing and Bella immediately loses interest in the copper wire, happily taking the Raggedy Ann instead.

Persephone is now sitting cross-legged in the swing, facing AnnaLee, leaning toward her, confiding: "I'm really good at sketching, but after working with Rebecca on Mrs. Jahn's gala, I'm starting to think there might be other things I could be even better at. AnnaLee, it's like for the past few weeks I've been finding out I'm good at all kinds of different stuff. Like sewing. I mean, who knew? I never really sewed anything before Rebecca taught me how."

She seems both bashful and proud as she's explaining to AnnaLee: "There're going to be these mannequins around the pool dressed like characters from the Gatsby book. Rebecca let me design some of the costumes and she showed me how to sew them. I had to work like a maniac to get it right, but they turned out great." Persephone's voice drops into an amazed whisper. "Rebecca said the geometry of the designs was outstanding, so did Mrs. Jahn. They said the way I see shape and pattern is unique."

AnnaLee is seeing the darkness that has been in Persephone since her arrival in Glen Cove being eclipsed by the elation of self-discovery. In celebration, AnnaLee is drawing Persephone into a warm hug.

When they move apart, AnnaLee brushes Persephone's forehead with a kiss; Persephone seems startled. "You do that with Bella sometimes," she says. Then with poignant uncertainty, she asks: "Why do you do it with me?"

AnnaLee sighs and smiles. "Believe that I love you...won't you please?"

Persephone ducks her head—delighted and tongue-tied. She picks up the copper wire again, giving it her full concentration, braiding it into a series of intricate loops and knots.

"I heard Mrs. Jahn wants you and Rebecca to come to the party as invited guests," AnnaLee says. "Have you decided what to wear?"

"Rebecca and I are making our costumes from fabric remnants, stuff from Mrs. Wang's shop." Persephone's expression changes; she's worried. "But, AnnaLee, what about you? The stuff the adults will be wearing is really expensive. A lot of the women are having their outfits custom-made by big-time designers who do Broadway shows."

It's as if AnnaLee is being doused with ice water. She never guessed that Persephone, in the short time she's been here, has already noticed the money problems.

"I'm planning to dress up as a Ziegfeld girl," Persephone is saying. "Have you ever seen how cool their costumes were? I found some fabric in the back room at Mrs. Wang's that's perfect. It's sort of the same shade as those flowers over there." Persephone is pointing toward a bank of coral-colored day-lilies at the edge of the lawn.

"A Ziegfeld girl?" AnnaLee asks. "Are you sure? Some of the things they wore were pretty skimpy."

"Yeah, but it's not like I'm going to be in real clothes. It'll be a costume, from like a million years ago, in the 1920s. And anyway since the sixties everybody and their granny walks around in miniskirts. So basically it doesn't make any difference if I'm in something skimpy."

Bella, clutching her Raggedy Ann, is climbing into Persephone's lap as Persephone adds: "It's the eighties, AnnaLee—skimpy isn't what it used to be."

There's a chuckle of laughter from the terrace. AnnaLee looks up. She sees Jack walking down the steps, coming toward the swing, carrying two brown grocery bags. She reflexively checks her watch.

"It's five-thirty," he says. In spite of its lightness, his tone has a hint of irritation. "I thought I'd put in a little overtime."

Then Jack smiles and holds up the grocery bags. "Lobsters, fresh corn, and two quarts of handmade peach ice cream. No kitchen duty for you tonight, Lee. I'm taking care of dinner."

"Wow, Uncle Jack. It's really easy to tell that you and my dad are only half-brothers. You two are like totally opposite. For my dad, midnight is knocking off early. It's cool how different you are from him." Persephone, with Bella at her side, is taking the grocery bags from Jack and heading toward the house.

"See?" Jack says, as he's kissing AnnaLee. "I'm cool."

And AnnaLee smiles. Because, in many ways, he is very cool.

Jack loosens his tie, stretches out on the grass in front of the swing, and begins to gently massage AnnaLee's bare feet. Then he asks: "So what's this about skimpy not being what it used to be?"

"It's nothing really. We were just talking about outfits for Mrs. Jahn's party."

AnnaLee is tense—the party is an issue she and Jack have been tap-dancing around for days. "You'll need to figure out a costume," she tells him. "So will I."

He grins and says: "We won't need to come up with costumes if we don't go."

"We have to go," she snaps.

"Why?"

"Because—" AnnaLee is frustrated by how difficult Jack is making this. "We have to go because working on this party has transformed Persephone, made her happy. Changed her whole world. She's looking forward to going. We can't disappoint her."

"Then I think she should go. We'll drive her there, come back and pick her up, and let her tell us all about it on the way home."

AnnaLee is desperate for Mrs. Jahn to meet Jack as soon as possible; she's sounding more strident than she intends to as she says: "We were invited, Jack. We don't have a choice. We need to be there."

He's quietly observing her, mystified by her intensity.

AnnaLee hasn't told Jack that their attendance at the party is a setup and that she's hoping it will be a first step toward finding him a job that he'll work at for eight hours a day—a job where he might finally make a dependable living.

She's attempting to keep things light by suggesting: "Maybe all you'll need is to slick your hair down and wear your old tuxedo. Nothing says 'Gatsby at a Gala' better than a side-part and a tux, right?"

AnnaLee had hoped to sound breezy and carefree—she knows she wasn't even close.

Jack is sitting up now. On guard. And watchful. As if it's occurring to him that they're talking about something much bigger, more significant, than a party, and he's trying to come to a decision about what he wants to say—about how much blame he wants to accept.

A complicated series of emotions is playing across his face. "I'm no good at parties, Lee. I'm no good at a lot of things. Too many things. And I know I make you unhappy."

"You don't make me unhappy, Jack. It's—"

"I know, I know. It's the money thing."

If you understand the problem, why don't you ever do anything to fix it? AnnaLee wonders.

And Jack is saying: "Lee, I'm trying my best to give you what you want. That's why I've been putting in more hours at work lately. For you. I'll do whatever it takes to make you happy."

AnnaLee understands that Jack means every word he has just said—that he loves her beyond measure. *But this is the same conversation we've had, the same breaking-point we've come to a million times before,* she's thinking. *It's where we always end up. With me pushed to the brink. And you acting like it's the first time I've been there. You scramble around trying to reassure me, save me, by throwing yourself into a whirlwind of longer hours and fatter paychecks. Then once the crisis has passed, you slide back...little by little...into being slow and quiet and dreamy. You go back to being Jack. Then when the bills start piling up again, I go back to being afraid. And angry. Scared I won't have the strength to keep going...*

"What're you thinking?" Jack is asking.

The only thing AnnaLee can do is to give him a weak smile. Because she loves him and can't bear the thought of hurting him.

"Don't stop believing in me, Lee, please, please don't." Jack's words are chaotic, rapid—like a frantic prayer.

"Jack, I just need you to—"

He is immediately interrupting her. "I'm sorry, Lee. I apologize. I'm no good at my profession. I'm lousy at being a lawyer, no good at truth-bending and backstabbing. We both know I'd be out on my ass if my brother wasn't a client and his legal work didn't bring the firm a steady income. I'm a failure at the law for the same reason I was a washout as a doctor. I can't stand the bloodletting. I don't have big enough balls."

"Jack. Please. We're only talking about a party, a couple of hours."

"You're wrong. We're talking about me, Lee. About me letting you down one more time. Because not only am I lousy at my job— I'm lousy at socializing. I'm not good at bullshit and small talk."

Jack's expression is painfully defenseless as he's explaining: "The things I am good at, nobody cares about. Not in a man anyway. I'm good at thinking, Lee. And learning, and reading. I love peace, and books. I crave being at home with my family. I'm good at loving my wife and my daughter. The truth is I would never leave you, or Bella, or this place, if I didn't have to."

He seems heartbroken. "Whether or not we want to admit it, Lee, the things that make me who I am are what make me a sorry excuse for a husband."

AnnaLee has left the swing to sit on the grass, beside Jack. Her arms have gone around him and her lips are pressed close to his ear. She's whispering: "You're not a sorry excuse for a husband. You're a man who hasn't found his place, that's all. You graduated from medical school—and from law school—with honors. You're brilliant. I believe in you. I just need you to believe too."

Jack's sobs are wrenching. "I want to be the man you need, Lee. I don't want to let you down."

"Then don't. Keep looking. Keep searching. Find where you're supposed to be. That's all I need."

AnnaLee can feel Jack holding on to her with every ounce of love and strength he possesses. "I'll take care of you, Lee," he's promising. "I'll kill and die for you. I swear."

 ⁓

As AnnaLee is entering the darkened living room and switching on the lights, the hope that Jack might finally find a way to earn a decent living is tantalizing her to the point of torment. It's eleven-thirty and she's roaming the house. Wide awake, too unsettled to sleep.

She's thinking about Mrs. Jahn's gala; worried that Jack, at the last minute, will retreat into his shell and refuse to attend.

While she's trying to come up with a way to keep Jack on track, AnnaLee is crossing the room, and going to the fireplace. Where the only thing on the mantle is the blue-and-white porcelain. The vase that, in its singleness, is the symbol of her difficulty with Jack. She needs to put it away—somewhere where she doesn't have to look at it.

As she's taking the porcelain from the mantle, she is recalling the heart-wrenching day when she sold its mate. She's remembering Mrs. Wang saying, *"No honor in a man who look at a woman for his support."*

Hearing that comment had made AnnaLee hideously embarrassed. For herself, and for Jack. And later that day when the full loss of the vase, her mother's wedding present, finally hit—AnnaLee had briefly wished she'd never met Jack.

And now, in remembering that, she's letting herself wonder, *What would a life without Jack have been like? Would it have been better? What if some other doctor had been on duty that night in Brooklyn? And*

Jack and I never even saw each other? How would my life have turned out? If I'd come home, here, to Glen Cove to recuperate instead of—

She is suddenly thinking of Bella.

Without Jack there would be no Bella.

AnnaLee knows that her musings are pointless. She has nothing, really, to wonder about. Bella is AnnaLee's life. Jack, with all his flaws, is AnnaLee's love. Her story has been written; there is no alternate version.

After putting the porcelain vase into a cabinet beside the fireplace, and just before turning off the light, AnnaLee pauses to straighten a painting near the wall switch.

When she leaves the darkened living room, she's worrying about the party, about it being a costume affair; worrying about finding a way to get Jack to willingly attend; worrying about money, and the fact that property taxes will soon be due.

It isn't until she's halfway down the hall, fretfully wandering through the house again, that AnnaLee is recalling what she did just before she left the living room—her absentminded straightening of a painting. The portrait of a beautiful young woman in a silver dress and pearl-button shoes.

The straightening of that portrait was a small, seemingly insignificant gesture. And yet, in thinking about it now, AnnaLee is finding an unexpected glimmer of inspiration.

Livvi

Rolling Hills Estates, California ~ 2012

THE AMOUNT OF TIME THAT HAS PASSED SINCE ANDREW LIFTED Grace from Livvi's bed and carried her out of Livvi's house has been short and profoundly significant. Two months. In which Livvi has discovered how conflicted her feelings about Andrew are—and how essential and all-encompassing her love for Grace is.

There have been moments in the past eight weeks when Livvi was convinced she never wanted to see Andrew again. There have been other moments when she desired him so much she was on fire. And there hasn't been an instant when she wasn't missing Grace. When she wasn't loving her, and concerned about her— longing to be with her.

Now, after several days of phone calls, and late-into-the-afternoon lunches, and sweet lovemaking, and promises that there will be no more lies—no more secrets—Livvi is in Andrew's sil-ver Mercedes. Entering the countrified splendor of a community tucked between the Pacific Coast Highway and the Pacific Ocean. A green and glorious place called Rolling Hills Estates.

The road Livvi and Andrew are traveling—the entire length of it—is bordered by a whitewashed, split-rail fence. Inside the fence is a bridle path lined with a colonnade of pepper trees. The leaves on the trees are slender, light green: the branches are willowy, slowly lifting and falling on the ebb and flow of the breeze. Beneath the trees, soft earth is being turned under the cantering hooves of passing horses. Making the bridle path look like a ribbon of brown velvet.

"It's beautiful here," Livvi murmurs.

"Yeah. It was a great spot to grow up in." Andrew's right hand is resting, lightly, on Livvi's thigh. He has been in physical contact with Livvi, caressing her, touching her, for the entirety of their drive, as if he's trying to keep this fragile new beginning from slipping out of his grasp.

"And Palos Verdes is only a couple of intersections away—isn't that right?" Livvi asks. Palos Verdes is the neighboring town, the home of Andrew's wife. The allegedly frail creature who has threatened suicide if Andrew leaves her. The woman Livvi is so curious about—and jealous of—and unsettled by.

At Livvi's mention of Palos Verdes, Andrew shoots her a wary, questioning glance.

She looks away—turns her attention to watching a girl and boy galloping a pair of perfectly matched Palominos along the bridle path.

Livvi is rattled. Worried about her complicated relationship with Andrew and the volatile situation with Andrew's wife. Nervous about meeting Andrew's mother and father for the first time. And wildly anxious to be reunited with Grace, who is with Andrew's parents, waiting for Andrew and Livvi to pick her up.

Andrew has slowed the car to a stop, preparing to make a turn onto a side street. "You're sure you're okay with this?" he's asking.

Livvi's heart is pounding—shaking her in her seat. She's terrified. But she will do whatever it takes to see Grace, to hold Grace in her arms again. Which is why Livvi's response is: "Of course I'm okay."

She's having a hard time keeping her voice steady. "This is what we agreed to. The new 'us.' No more secrets. Everybody knows everybody. I'm ready to know, and be known."

Andrew has completed the turn, and his hand, the hand that has been on Livvi's thigh, is now restlessly moving from the steering wheel to his knee, then to the car's control panel. Roaming the buttons: agitated. Shuffling the music, jumping from one song to another.

"We won't stay long," he says. "I told them we're planning to say hello—pick up Grace—and leave."

Andrew has angled the car onto the apron of an iron-gated driveway paved in fawn-colored bricks. He's leaning out of the driver's-side window, entering a code into a keypad embedded in a stone pillar.

Livvi's attention is riveted on the house, which is at the far end of the winding driveway, on the other side of the gates.

She is looking at a home with towering windows set into pale stone walls. A palace. Its massive roof gleaming in the sun—like a work of art tiled in blue-gray slate. A magnificent French chateau that should be crowning a hilltop in Provence.

Livvi's pounding heart—is pounding harder. She isn't ready for this. She has never flown first class. Or shopped at Neiman Marcus. Or been to a spa. Before going away to college, she'd never ever been inside a restaurant.

She feels so insignificant. So inadequate. It's actually making her dizzy, and sick.

The towering iron gates are swinging open, while Andrew is telling her: "We're going to make this work."

"It's okay," she's saying. "I'm fine." Her voice is thin and small.

"I'm not talking just about today, just about meeting my parents. I'm talking about us. You and me. We're going to make it work."

Livvi lowers the car's passenger-side window. She's quietly gasping for air.

After Andrew has parked the car not far from the mansion's front doors, he reaches for Livvi and turns her toward him, very tenderly. "Olivia, listen to me. The way I handled the situation with Grace—not letting you know about her—was stupid. I've apologized for it. I've learned from it. I'll never do anything like that to you again. From now on my life will be an open book. You have my word on that."

"Andrew, I..." Livvi can't finish her thought. She is clattering with anxiety.

He kisses her. Then says: "I love you. I don't want to be without you."

While Andrew is opening his door and coming around the car to open Livvi's, her attention has gone back to the house. She's picturing the people who live here. Imagining that Andrew's parents will be like their home—imposing and regal, larger than life. She's also recalling what Andrew has said about their relationship with his wife—that they're deeply fond of her, extremely protective.

And as Andrew opens the passenger door—Livvi says: "Maybe I'll wait in the car."

The look in Andrew's eyes is impossible for Livvi to decipher. It could be disappointment or, perhaps, relief. All he says is: "I won't be gone long."

While she's watching Andrew walk away and head toward the mansion—the extraordinary place that was his boyhood home—she's seeing how seamlessly he fits here. How beautiful he is; how at ease with his world. Every movement directed and purposeful.

Andrew is at the door of the mansion now, pausing to look over his shoulder at Livvi, mouthing the words, "I love you."

It's making Livvi want, just for a little while, to push away all the nagging doubts; all the places Andrew has taken her where there are gaps and unanswered questions.

And with the soft ocean breeze flowing into the car, and the late September sun warming her shoulders, Livvi is closing her eyes. Willing her thoughts into the other places—the lovely places she has gone with Andrew.

...she's in Canada. Waking up to singing waiters and a Paddington Bear. To a birthday that Andrew has filled with wonder.

...she's in San Francisco, the night before Easter. Laughing uncontrollably. At Andrew. He's wearing rabbit-patterned boxer shorts and a bow-tie while he's dancing alongside a pair of music-box bunnies, to a silly version of "Tiptoe through the Tulips."

...she's in Flintridge on a June morning. Hand-in-hand with Andrew. They're flying off the diving board of his pool. Cannonballing into the water. Shouting and giggling like teenagers.

...she's in bed, early this morning. In her little guesthouse in Pasadena. Cradled in Andrew's arms. She and Andrew are talking, and telling jokes, and making love. Easily. Endlessly. Until the sun is pushing its way into the noontime sky. Their conversation is about how winter will soon be here; she's whispering to Andrew, "I've always wanted to be in a real winter, in the mountains, with snow and hot chocolate and a fireplace."

Andrew is announcing, "We'll do a winter trip. In December. We'll go to Colorado. Aspen. I'll teach you how to ski."

Then she's saying, "David is lining up a December speaking engagement for me at a literary luncheon in New York." And she knows, even as she's mentioning it, that if it conflicts with Andrew's plans, she'll decline the invitation.

She's laying her head against Andrew's chest, murmuring, "I'm going to Aspen. I'm going to learn to ski, that's amazing."

While Andrew is promising, "Amazing is how it will always be for us. And more than that, it'll be—"

A war zone.

A war zone is what Livvi has been dropped into—surrounded, suddenly, by earsplitting noise. The grating din of an engine being raced and tires squealing.

A car—which seems to have come out of nowhere—is rocketing up the driveway. Like a bullet. Aiming directly for Andrew's Mercedes.

Livvi is staring into the rearview mirror, bracing for the collision, certain that she's going to die. Then the car, a brand-new BMW, slams to a stop—inches away from the Mercedes' back bumper.

Livvi screams. With relief. And fright. The BMW's horn is blaring. Being held in a prolonged, piercing assault.

In the rearview mirror, Livvi is seeing the driver of the BMW. A woman whose platinum hair is framing her features like a silvery cloud. There are tears pouring down her face, which is contorted with rage.

The woman is shrieking—the sounds of her shrieks lost in the blare of the horn. Her mouth is shaping the word "whore." She is alternately backing up and then revving the BMW. As if getting ready to plow full-speed into the Mercedes—and into Livvi.

Livvi is afraid of staying in the car and being hit—and she's afraid to get out and risk being run down. She has turned away from the rearview mirror and is looking over her shoulder at the woman in the BMW. Realizing that it's Andrew's wife—the vengeful, black lightning stick-figure that was in Grace's drawing.

Out of the corner of her eye Livvi is catching sight of rapid movement—two people running past the Mercedes, hurrying toward the BMW. Andrew. And a tall, slim woman: older, dressed entirely in red.

The blare of the BMW's horn is inexplicably getting louder. The door beside Livvi, the passenger door of Andrew's Mercedes, has been yanked open. Someone is taking hold of Livvi's arm, saying: "Let me get you out of here."

While Livvi is scrambling out of the Mercedes, the BMW is careening backward down the driveway, swerving madly, barely missing a collision with the gate pillars—shooting out into the street, skidding to a stop.

The tall, older woman in red is shouting at Andrew: "Go after her, goddammit! You're the cause of all this unhappiness. You're the only one who can fix it."

Livvi is being hustled along a brick path at the side of the house, by a man in his midthirties, wearing a long-sleeved plaid shirt and khaki pants. He's slightly pigeon-toed, a little pudgy, and has Andrew's marvelous dark hair and steel-gray eyes.

As they're rounding the corner of the house, he's glancing back toward the driveway. "I'll show you some of the sights, keep you out of the line of fire," he's telling Livvi. "It may be a while before things calm down. This is the family that put the 'psycho' in psycho-drama."

He stops and gives a comically courteous little bow. "I'm James. I'm in town visiting the lord and lady of the manor, they're my parents. I teach math in a high school in Long Beach, and I'm Andrew's kid brother."

Livvi is aware of who James is, Andrew has mentioned him, but she's too shaken up to say anything more than: "I'm Livvi. I'm—"

"You're the reason for all the fireworks." James says. "Trust me, everybody here knows who you are. You've been the sole topic of my mother's conversation for weeks—by the way, you just met her back there in the driveway—she was the one in red. Anyway, you've been the source of much agita."

The path they are on is sloping sharply downward. Livvi is struggling to keep her footing—and struggling to understand what's happening. She's not sure where she's going, or why Andrew's brother has offered her his protection.

"I'm figuring you can probably guess what agita means." James's tone is apologetic. "It's Italian slang for heartburn, misery. Andrew and I grew up with it. My mother is Bronx Italian."

In the midst of her confusion, Livvi is gasping in surprise. Not at what James has said, but at the scene that has just come into view: a spectacular, European-style horse barn with tan and gray stone walls. It has a steeply pitched slate roof and a wide, arched entry. And beyond the barn is a paddock where the grass is emerald green. Beyond the paddock is an astounding, panoramic view of the Pacific Ocean.

"As you can see, my mother married money," James says. "Dad's loaded. Used to be the go-to guy for cardiac surgery on the west coast."

Livvi is trying to come to terms with of all of this. The opulence. The craziness in the driveway. And the dawning realization of what James has just told her. About the agita. About being actively disliked by Andrew's mother. A woman who hasn't even waited to meet Livvi before deciding she doesn't like her.

"Am I a source of agita for your father too?" she asks.

"Maybe. Probably. I don't know. He isn't easy to read."

Livvi is in a whirl of confusion.

"What about you?" she asks. "Why are you being so nice to me?" The words have come out sounding vaguely snippy. For an instant Livvi doesn't understand why—then realizes that, in addition to being hurt, she's angry. And jealous. Angry that it's a stranger, not Andrew, who's at her side in the midst of this mayhem. And jealous because Andrew is at his mother's side—and quite possibly his wife's.

And Livvi tells James: "I'm sorry. I didn't mean to be rude. It's just that I don't know any of you and I don't know, really, what any of you know about me. I don't know what Andrew has told you. All I do know is that your parents don't like me—and I'm not welcome here. I guess, based on that information, it seems a little odd that you're trying so hard to be nice to me."

A blush is sweeping across James's face, as if he's been insulted or embarrassed.

"I better go," he says. "There's something I need to take care of."

Livvi suspects she has hurt him—that wasn't her intention.

While she's watching James disappear into the interior of the barn, Livvi is trying to think of how to apologize. She's also experiencing a sudden sense of being terribly vulnerable—exposed to view from every one of the mansion's rear windows.

Within seconds Livvi is running toward the barn's entryway.

What she finds on the other side of that entry is wondrous. A set of wide-planked, pale gray walkways arranged in the shape of an enormous cross. Lining the walkways are horse stalls. Spotlessly clean. Paneled in varnished wood the color of toffee, and fitted with gleaming black hinges and grates. The barn's support pillars and roof beams, and its vaulted ceiling, have been recently painted. They're the color of fresh milk.

In the open area in the center of the barn, a Latino man who's short and muscular is saddling a skittish horse that's enormous and mahogany brown.

James is calling to the man, saying: "You can put him back in his stall, Carlos. I think my mother's riding plans just got cancelled."

The massive horse is snorting and shuddering—rearing up,

scissoring the air with its hooves, pulling hard on the ropes tethering it to the barn wall. Livvi is nervously backing away.

"He's just showing off," James says. "Offer him a carrot and he's as docile as a puppy. All bark and no bite."

"Really?" Livvi asks.

"No. But he can't get loose, can't hurt you." James gives Livvi a smile. "I just wanted you to know you were safe."

Livvi returns the smile, appreciating the kindness he's showing her. She feels a little calmer now, less frantic.

James indicates a bench beside the entry, near a display case filled with championship ribbons and riding trophies. "You can wait there if you want, and I can go see if the coast is clear...but I don't think we've given it enough time yet. What do you say we stay down here for a few more minutes?"

Livvi nods.

"Excellent choice," James says. "Let's take a stroll."

While James is walking her out of the barn, toward the paddock and the spectacular view of the ocean, Livvi, wondering if it was Andrew, asks: "Who won all the ribbons and the trophies?"

"They belonged to Katherine."

A shiver flits down Livvi's spine—she's back on that rainy day in Chicago, hearing Andrew say: "...*that girl looks exactly like Katherine...somebody I loved.*"

There's a terrible sense of foreboding in Livvi; she can barely speak. "Tell me about Katherine."

"Andrew didn't tell you?"

"No," Livvi whispers. She can sense that what's coming isn't going to be good.

"He didn't tell you that he...and Katherine...and our other brother, Mark...were triplets?"

"No, Andrew never mentioned that."

Livvi has the gut-wrenching feeling that, in listening to whatever James is about say, she'll be taking a plunge into darkness.

His words are slow, and quiet. "Katherine and Mark were killed. When they were fifteen."

"What happened?"

James looks out toward the ocean. "I guess I'm not surprised Andrew hasn't mentioned it. It's a difficult thing for our family to talk about."

After a space of several seconds, James tells Livvi: "We always go away for a couple of weeks between Thanksgiving and Christmas. We were up at a vacation home we used to have in Lake Arrowhead and my parents were out at dinner one night…I was with them, I'd just turned eight. Katherine and Mark and Andrew didn't come with us, because earlier that afternoon my dad caught the three of them underage-drunk, on beer, out at the end of our boat dock, and they were grounded."

James seems to be having trouble keeping his voice steady. "Mark and Katherine were in the house. Upstairs, asleep. There was a problem with an oil heater and the place burned to the ground. They died in the fire."

Before Livvi can say anything, James tells her: "I'll save you the trouble of asking how come Andrew is still with us. He wasn't in the house…he was down at the lake. He'd sneaked out. To be with a girl."

What James has just revealed has dropped Livvi to the ground—left her in a sitting position on the grass, with her back against one of the paddock's fence-posts.

James sits beside her and quietly adds: "As far as my parents are concerned, I think that night split Andrew right down the middle for them. Half of him, a pariah—the horny brother who slipped out and left his siblings to die. And the other half, a treasure—their firstborn and the only one of their picture-perfect triplets still walking the earth."

"It's horrible," Livvi murmurs. "All of it…"

She's overwhelmed by the monumental nature of Andrew's secrets—and wondering how many others he might still be keeping.

"My brother is a decent guy who's had a lot of indecent things happen to him." James is tilting his head in the direction of the house. "You crossed paths with two of them in the driveway a few minutes ago."

In response to Livvi's look of surprise, he tells her: "Andrew's wife is a vindictive former homecoming queen who's out of her mind, and my mother is my mother—and I love her—but she can turn life into a living hell when she puts her mind to it."

Livvi isn't sure what to make of James. "Why are you telling me all these things?"

"Because I think you should know what you're getting into. And because I want you to be kind to my brother. He's dragging a heavy load."

Livvi doesn't respond. And James says: "He's screwed up a lot of things—more than he should have. But he has a good heart. You need to understand that, need to believe it."

Livvi isn't sure what she understands, or believes, about Andrew.

After a while, she asks: "How long have Andrew and his wife been separated?"

"I don't know…two, maybe three years."

"And why did he leave her?"

"It's not exactly as clear-cut as that. Technically Andrew didn't leave Kayla, she left him. But in another way he did leave her—by not going with her."

"What happened?" Livvi is almost reluctant to hear the answer.

"The house in Flintridge was where they lived until a few years ago—when Kayla decided she wanted to relocate down here, to have a bigger place and be closer to her parents, and mine. Andrew didn't want to move."

Livvi indicates the lush lawns and the ocean view. "Why? This area is like something you'd see in a movie."

"I don't think he particularly wanted to be that close to my folks, or to hers. And it would've made his work commute a nightmare—at the height of traffic it would've been a couple of hours each way. Kayla told Andrew he'd get used to it. She went ahead and bought the place in Palos Verdes, moved in, and waited for him to show up. He never did. I think he was relieved that she came down here. I think he was looking for a way out."

And the question in Livvi's mind is, *If he really wanted out, why didn't he ever ask for a divorce...?* But before she can ask it, James has already gotten to his feet and started toward the house, announcing: "It's time to go back now."

Livvi is scrambling after him. While James is pointing to one of the mansion's terraces, where a handsome old man is standing beside the woman in red. "That's my father, he's eighty-two. There's a major age difference—my mother is his trophy wife. He's a little deaf, when you talk to him you have to speak up."

As soon as Livvi and James have completed their journey across the lawn and have stepped onto the terrace, the woman in red, James and Andrew's mother, who has been looking directly at Livvi, deliberately turns away and goes into the house.

The old man, Andrew's father, tells Livvi: "While we were watching you walk up here, my wife was saying she couldn't understand what Andrew sees in you. It might be time for her to have her eyes checked. You're a gorgeous young woman."

Livvi is thunderstruck by how much this man, even in the frailty of old age, looks like Andrew.

"I hope you weren't unduly upset by the family drama," the old man is saying. "I think I can assure you it's over, at least for the moment. Andrew has driven Kayla home and he's upstairs—getting Grace ready for her weekend with the two of you."

The old man sits down onto a cushioned teak bench, with effort and a small grunt, muttering to James: "Inform Andrew that Livvi will be waiting for him in the car."

After James has gone, the old man tells Livvi: "There isn't any need to subject you to my wife's wrath—and inviting you into the house would only serve to do that. My wife is very fond of Kayla—she considers her a daughter. Kayla is the woman my wife personally selected for Andrew. Unfortunately, vengeance is visited on anyone who dares to interfere with my wife's choices."

The old man gestures for Livvi to sit beside him. And in a light, amiable tone, he tells her: "I'm a man who understands right from wrong and I recognize that you're being treated badly—but I'm at a place in my life where I'm unwilling to rock my own boat in order to steady someone else's."

He is looking out over the rolling lawns, letting his gaze linger on the ocean view. "When I was middle-aged and at the top of my game I discarded a family—and a wife who was as middle-aged as I was and who was comfortable with me. I married a woman who was young and bedazzled by me. Now that I'm ancient of days, and at the tail-end of my game, I need her to stick around and be happy with me."

His voice has the faintest hint of a tremor as he adds: "I've seen what happens to old men when they're discarded and alone." After a long moment, Andrew's father puts his hand on Livvi's, then briskly says: "Good-bye. And good luck."

His touch makes Livvi shiver. Makes her want to leave the teak bench and run as fast, and as far, as she can.

The old man's hand, which is almost identical in shape to Andrew's, is weightless. Like the carcass of a small bird. Nothing more than a clutch of hollow bones wrapped in skin as thin, and as dry, as a sheet of parchment.

Livvi is walking quickly across Andrew's parents' driveway. Listening for a shout, a scream, the roar of an approaching car. Wishing she could vanish into some other place, some other time, where this diabolical afternoon never happened.

She's in tears—wiping at them with the back of her hand.

The mansion's front doors are flying open. And Grace, clutching her little pink pig, is running out of the house. Her eyes lit with joy and fastened on Livvi.

Instantly, Livvi is dropping to her knees—with her arms outstretched.

Grace is hurling herself at Livvi. Burrowing into their mutual hug like a rootless drifter suddenly finding home. "Livvi!" is the only thing she says. And in that single word there is absolute euphoria.

"I've missed you so much," Livvi tells her. The sweetness of holding Grace again—the contentment, the rightness of it—is perfect.

"Don't ever go away. Ever. Ever." Grace's arms are around Livvi's neck, her face buried against Livvi's shoulder.

For the tiniest breath of time Livvi is in complete bliss.

But then Grace is suddenly stiffening—pulling away—putting distance between them.

Andrew's mother, the woman in red, has appeared on the doorstep of the mansion. Holding a phone. Her eyes focused on Livvi, and icy cold. As she's telling Grace: "Go back in the house. You forgot to give your grandpa a kiss good-bye."

Grace puts her toy pig into Livvi's care and whispers: "Hold Piglet for me and don't go away. I'll be right back."

As always, Grace's solemn, earnest look is followed, after a brief uncertainty, by a hopeful smile.

Seeing that look, and that smile—understanding the depth of its vulnerability—is bruising Livvi's heart.

Grace has left Livvi now and is dashing past Andrew's mother, into the house. Bree, the blond nanny, is on the other side of the open door.

When both Bree and Grace are out of sight, Andrew's mother turns toward Livvi—Livvi is surprised by how youthful she is. Her shoulder-length hair is thick, dark; only the slightest hint of gray. Her skin is smooth, except for a netting of fine lines around her mouth. Her eyes are large, olive green. And as they are coming to rest on Livvi, the look in them is murderous.

Andrew's car is only a few feet away—Livvi is wanting to get to it as quickly as possible and lock herself inside.

But Andrew's mother freezes her with a withering stare, and says: "I was hoping it was my son who was out here. He's wanted on the—"

She is being interrupted by the sound of footsteps. Andrew coming around the side of the house, carrying a pink-and-white blanket and a small pink suitcase.

He seems beaten-up, depleted. Like a worn-out copy of himself. The look he gives Livvi is one of exhaustion, and heartbreak.

Livvi's first impulse is to go to him, but she's not quite sure what's happening. Today has already held too many unpleasant surprises—she doesn't want to walk, head-on, into another one.

Andrew's mother has come down the steps of the house and placed herself directly between Andrew and Livvi.

Andrew moves past his mother without a word and opens the trunk of the Mercedes. She follows him to the car, her voice low and sarcastic. "Ducking out the back? Creeping along the side of the house? Were you planning to sneak off without saying good-bye?"

"I think we've said enough for today." Andrew drops the blanket and the pink suitcase into the trunk, closing the trunk-lid with a slam.

He's coming around to open the passenger door for Livvi; his mother is once again blocking his way. This time, she hands Andrew the phone that she has been holding.

She's staring daggers at him as she says: "Kayla needs to talk to you."

"About what?" Andrew growls. "It's been all of fifteen minutes since I drove her home."

There's a strangled wildness, a trapped animal look in Andrew that Livvi has never seen before—a caged tiger dreaming of sinking its teeth into a sadistic trainer.

"Answer the damn phone," Andrew's mother tells him. "It's about Grace."

Andrew puts the phone to his ear and looks at Livvi. Mutely telling her he's sorry. Then he turns away, with his shoulders slightly hunched. As if trying to create some form of isolation. And Livvi wonders, is he trying to shield her from his wife?—or trying to shield his wife from her?

After a brief exchange in which Andrew's voice is little more than a murmur, he hands the phone back to his mother and says: "Kayla wanted to confirm what time Grace will be home on Sunday night. I told her it would be the same time I agreed it would be when I saw her fifteen minutes ago."

"Speaking of Grace, you need to take her shopping for new bathing suits. I'm still working on dates…but for the family winter trip this year, I'm thinking in terms of Bermuda."

"We'll talk about it later." Andrew is attempting to maneuver around his mother, making it clear he wants to head in the direction of the car, and Livvi.

His mother says: "Try to have a nice weekend." She gives him a pat on the cheek. It starts out quick and mean. Then turns slow and tender. A vicious slap—wrapped in a tender caress.

And in that spiteful gesture, Livvi is seeing what James had described when he talked about Andrew sneaking out of the house where his brother and sister were burned to death—*"As far as my parents are concerned…that night split Andrew right down the middle for them. Half of him, a pariah—the brother who slipped out and left his siblings to die. And the other half, a treasure—their firstborn and the only one of their picture-perfect triplets still walking the earth."*

The delivery of that caressing slap—the reminder to Andrew that his mother loves him just as much as she hates him—is showing Livvi why James said, *"…be kind to my brother, he's dragging a heavy load."*

Andrew's mother is passing Livvi now, on her way back into the house; and she's saying: "I want you to know…the circumstances that pushed Kayla to behave as she did today are disgusting. I have a son who is treating his wife, and his marriage vows, like garbage."

The way this statement has been delivered makes Livvi feel like she's just been spit on.

Almost instantly, Andrew is wrapping his arms around Livvi, kissing her, cradling her. "Don't pay any attention. I'm sorry, I shouldn't have brought you here. I had no idea she'd be so rude—"

Livvi isn't listening.

She's saying: "You have a dead sister, and a dead brother, you never told me about. There's no point to this. I don't know you, Andrew. I don't know who you are."

Andrew has lifted Livvi from the ground, holding her to his chest, turning her in a circle, pleading. "You do know me. You do."

"I didn't know about Grace. I didn't know about your wife, or your sister, or your brother…"

Livvi is in torment.

"You do know who I am," he's insisting. "You know the man I am now. You know that I love you."

Wanting to escape from Andrew, and terrified at the thought of living without him—Livvi is being ripped to shreds.

"None of what happened here today has anything to do with us," he's saying. "I'm getting a divorce. I swear." Andrew releases his hold on Livvi—gently letting her feet touch the ground again.

"What good will it do?" Livvi is exhausted, defeated. "Your mother won't care if you're divorced, neither will your wife. They'll never set you free."

"That doesn't make any difference." Andrew is trying to kiss her tears away. "No matter what happens, no matter what, you'll always be my first choice."

And Livvi, with a sinking heart, is thinking, *But I'll never be your only choice.*

Micah
Wiscasset, Maine ~ 2012

You always chose her over me. Why?"

Micah has asked this softly and suspects her father will answer it softly. For the last few minutes the sound of their footsteps crunching on the leaf-covered path has been louder than either one of their voices. This meeting with her father, uncharacteristically civil. The shocks and losses in Kansas, and Louisville, and Newport, have taken the fire out of Micah.

"I never pushed you aside to choose her." Micah's father's tone is patient, gentle. "I simply went where I was needed." He has inadvertently walked through a spider's web and is brushing at the sleeve of his shirt, a pale-blue chambray. An old work shirt beginning to fray at the collar and cuffs, but freshly starched and perfectly pressed.

Micah's father has always been meticulous about his clothes and his grooming. He's a small, dapper man with white hair and clean fingernails, and breath that smells like peppermint. "Do you think we should go back to the house?" he's asking. "Or walk down to the water?"

They are in the woods behind the well-kept farmhouse that he and Micah's mother own in Maine. The air is bracing and won-derfully fresh. Breathing it during the course of the walk has made

Micah feel stronger—less hopeless, less sick. It has made her cancer seem less real.

Her father, finished with the removal of the spider's web, is bending to admire a tangle of wildflowers growing at the base of one of the trees. And he's saying, cheerfully: "Back to the house or onward to the water—which will it be, my girl?"

"I was never your girl. She was." Micah's words are muted. Jealous.

Her father has heard the jealousy, and there's defensiveness in his voice. "Your mother had a million invisible fractures running through her."

"What does that mean," Micah asks, "a million invisible fractures?"

Her father isn't bending over the wildflowers any longer; he's standing up now, holding one of the blossoms. He walks the few steps to where Micah is, and with a gallant flourish, tucks the flower behind her ear.

"Your mother was damaged, Micah. You never were. From the time you were barely more than a baby, you were headstrong and self-directed. Boldly walking your own path. Anyone trying to guide you seemed to just get in your way."

Her father is looking directly into Micah's eyes; she's seeing how proud he is of who she is. It's making Micah wish that over the years she'd been kinder to him, gentler with him.

In spite of this, there are still things about her father she resents. Unresolved issues she's determined to make him explain. It's why Micah has come here, to Maine, after visiting her mother in Newport.

She's pulling the delicate wildflower from behind her ear and turning it in her fingers, watching it beginning to wilt under the heat of her touch, as she's telling her father: "When I was growing up you were hardly ever around, you were always off with her."

Her father takes the flower from Micah and drops it onto the ground. "What can I tell you that you don't already know?"

A childlike frustration is in Micah as she says: "I know the 'what'…what I want to know is the 'why.'"

"They're the same, Micah. The situation was the explanation. Your mother was a big star and I was her agent and producer. More than that, I was her confidante. Her moral support—"

"But what about me? What about what I needed from you? The whole time I was in high school I saw you maybe three times a year—four if I was lucky. Why did you just forget about me like that?"

"I never forgot about you. I was giving you room. Without it, I thought you'd run so far—and so wild—I'd lose you forever."

Micah slams her hand against the trunk of the tree. Making her father jump. Feeling as if she's being blamed for his failures. "What the hell are you talking about?" she whispers.

"You remember how you were as an adolescent. I truly believed if I didn't back off, you'd self-destruct." Her father is changing direction and walking away, heading deeper into the woods.

And Micah is running after him, insisting: "That's such a fucking cop-out." It's as if Micah is sixteen again—cut to the quick with adolescent injury. And she's asking: "Isn't it a parent's job to stick by their kid? Support them? No matter what?"

Her father has stopped—waiting for her to catch up. When they are again side-by-side, his response is subdued. "You were on a path to destruction. Does a loving parent support his child in that? Or does he do whatever it takes to get his child onto a safer path?"

To Micah it sounds as if he's simply offering excuses, and it's tearing at her. Making her wish she had the strength to scream.

"What goddamn path did you think you were putting me on by walking away?" she asks.

If her father is as tense or as upset as Micah, he isn't showing it. There is calm, and what sounds like caring, in his voice. "If you're referring to that summer when you and I had no contact at all, you're wrong to describe it as me having walked away from you. I didn't. I stepped back and waited in the wings. And never took my eyes off you. You were always my girl."

The storm of emotion in Micah is getting stronger and more chaotic. But the crushing blows she has already taken (from Jason, and Hayden Truitt, and her mother) have left her too weak to do anything more than murmur: "That's not true."

While her father is telling her: "Dealing with you during your adolescence was like trying to juggle dynamite, Micah."

She shakes her head and turns away. "Dealing with me was your job...I was your fucking daughter."

And now her father sounds annoyed, as he's asking: "Don't you remember how you were? How mercurial? How out of control? If I came too close...if I showed interest in your friends or your studies...you said it made you feel smothered. When you were in boarding school, if I came alone to see you...you were furious because your mother didn't come with me...it proved to you she didn't love you. If I brought your mother to see you... you wanted her to go away because people were taking her picture and asking for autographs. You said you felt pushed aside by her celebrity—"

"I did feel pushed aside."

"—and then there were the drugs, and the acting-out. The wild friends. I brought you counselors, and mentors, and tutors, and changes of scenery. And finally—that summer, when you'd left me no place else to go—I stepped away. Tell me, Micah, what else was I to do?"

"I don't know," Micah tells him. "But you could've done better."

This comment seems to knock the breath out of her father. It takes him a long time before he says: "That isn't a judgment you're qualified to make, Micah. You have never for as much as a day been anyone's spouse. Or anyone's parent."

Although he is keeping his voice low, it's evident he is upset. "You dealt with two of life's most demanding challenges by avoiding them. You shirked the hard work of marriage—the labor of dedicating yourself for a lifetime to another human being. And you turned your back on the demands and sacrifices of being a parent."

Her father's voice sounds as if it's about to break. "To my knowledge, you've never even had a pet, or a house-plant. You've never taken responsibility for the welfare of a single, living thing other than yourself. You have no right to criticize me, Micah. I was fighting with all that was in me to do my best as a husband. And a parent. I was battling, head-on, with trials and obligations you've never had the courage to go anywhere near."

Micah is watching her father struggle to keep his composure while he's explaining: "I was married to someone I greatly loved, who happened to be terribly gifted and terribly flawed. A woman that sang like a siren-goddess and had the soul of a needy little girl. I was the father of a daughter bursting with talent and consumed with arrogance, and anger. A young woman who refused to blossom until she'd succeeded in forcing me to let go of her."

He's brushing at his sleeve—at the place where earlier he had broken the spider's web. "Perhaps I did everything wrong, but I did the best I could."

Her father has shown Micah a version of their story—truths about his life, and hers—that she has never acknowledged before.

She wants to say she's sorry. And can't. She has let too much time pass. She isn't capable of forming the words.

"I don't think it's me you're really angry with, Micah. I think the problem is that you keep using people up and wondering why they don't love you." Her father hesitates, as if sorting through his thoughts as he's speaking them aloud. "You wanted to be famous, to prove to everyone around you that you were the best. It became your life's work. And you let it blot out everything else."

He pauses. When he speaks again, his voice is soft with pity. "I don't think you understood that being revered isn't the same as being loved." Her father sighs and says: "Awe is reserved for gods and film stars. Creatures that keep themselves separate from the rest of us. Out of our reach. Behind stained-glass windows and cinema screens.

"Micah, you were the one who separated yourself from me. I never for a moment wanted to leave you." Her father is standing perfectly still, seeming as if he's struggling to know what to do next. "I'm here," he says. "I've always been here. And you've always been my girl."

His head is bent. The breeze is ruffling his hair. It's thinning, and as white as snow. And there is space, all around, between the frayed collar of his neatly pressed work-shirt and the sallow, ropy muscles of his neck.

Micah is seeing that her father is old. That he is full of regret.

When she drives away. In the late afternoon. Micah kisses her father good-bye.

Wanting to tell him, I love you.

Saying nothing about her cancer.

On the third floor of Micah's Boston brownstone, there is a large, carefully arranged room. The room is cool, dark, and spare. Much of the time it's silent—except for the occasional rustle of ghosts.

This is the last stop on Micah's journey. The final person she needs to settle things with. Before she decides whether to battle her cancer, or surrender to it.

Micah is holding on to the doorknob. Has been holding on for several minutes. And still—she can't turn it.

She's too afraid.

She's not ready.

Not yet.

AnnaLee
Glen Cove, Long Island ~ 1986

A NNALEE! ARE YOU READY YET?" THERE IS EXCITEMENT AND happiness in Persephone's shout.

AnnaLee is thrilled by the sound of that happiness. She's hurrying down the hall. Seeing that the door to Persephone's room is open, and that the latest version of the hand-lettered sign simply says "Persephone's Realm."

The hostile teenager who arrived at the beginning of the summer is now entirely gone, replaced by a new Persephone—a vibrant, caring girl who has captured AnnaLee's heart. Completely.

"How come you're still in your robe? AnnaLee, you need to get dressed. You're my creation tonight. I want to see how you look!"—is the excited greeting AnnaLee is receiving as she's entering the room.

Persephone, perched on the edge of the bed with Bella in her lap and an open makeup case at her side, is putting on a headdress, a towering arc of rhinestones and apricot-colored feathers. As soon as the headdress is in place, Persephone quickly slides Bella out of her lap and onto the bed.

"What do you think?" she asks AnnaLee.

Persephone is standing up now. Showing off her costume—a snug bodice of glittering beads in hues of gold and apricot, and a shimmering diaphanous skirt, shaped like an inverted, exquisitely petaled flower. Each ruffled petal is flawless—each one a different, muted shade of coral-colored chiffon.

"What do you think? Do you like it? Do I look like a Ziegfeld girl?" Persephone asks.

"You look like a dream," AnnaLee says. "I want to complain about the skirt being too see-through. But it's too lovely…I can't."

"Great! Now get your costume on, we're running out of time. Rebecca will be here to pick me up in a few minutes." Persephone is hurriedly tossing a tube of lip gloss into her purse. "We're going to Mrs. Jahn's early, in case there's any last-minute stuff to do on the decorations or—"

She looks around, suddenly frantic. "The camera. Where did I leave Rebecca's camera? She's putting together a scrapbook—to get new clients. It was my job to photograph the work while we were doing it and tonight I'm supposed to take pictures at the party, with everything all perfect and finished—and now I don't know where the camera is. Shit, oh shit, oh *shit*!"

Bella, who's still on the bed exploring the contents of Persephone's makeup case, looks up, interested.

AnnaLee shoots Persephone a warning glance.

Persephone winces. "Sorry, Bella. I didn't mean to say shit."

AnnaLee does her best not to smile.

She's sorting through a pile of clothes on the floor near the bed. Unearthing the missing camera, handing it to Persephone and saying: "I think what you need to do right now is calm down."

"But what about your costume, AnnaLee? I want to see how it fits."

"It's fine, and besides, it doesn't sound like you'll have time to make any alterations."

"I will. Really. Rebecca's coming early but we're having sand-wiches here, before we go. Because we'll be crazy-busy at the party and won't have a chance to eat anything once we get there."

Persephone is excitedly pushing AnnaLee into the hallway. "I can chew and baste at the same time, I swear. And I really, really need to get a look at your outfit before I leave."

"Don't worry, you'll see it at the party." Her costume is the least of AnnaLee's concerns at this particular moment. She's worrying that Jack isn't dressed yet and wondering if he has told the babysit-ter what time they'll be dropping Bella off.

Persephone is tugging at the sleeve of AnnaLee's bathrobe, explaining: "I had tons of help from Rebecca when I made my outfit. But I did all the work on your costume by myself. Yours is my first ever, start to finish, totally on my own sewing creation."

There's an earnest seriousness in Persephone as she says: "I didn't make that costume for just anybody. I made it for you. I want to be sure it's totally perfect. Don't you understand?"

AnnaLee is overwhelmed with affection, and pride. "I'll meet you downstairs in five minutes."

As AnnaLee is brushing Persephone's forehead with a kiss, Persephone is pointing to the bed. "Maybe you ought to give your-self more like ten minutes."

What AnnaLee sees makes her laugh.

Bella. Gazing into Persephone's makeup mirror. Studiously coat-ing her face with bright red lipstick.

AnnaLee, with Bella perched on the bathroom countertop, is using a fresh washcloth to wipe away the last traces of the lipstick. The ones she has already used are in a pile nearby, all of them stained with blotches of brilliant, fire-engine red.

Bella is squirming. Turning her head from side to side, making a game of trying to avoid the swipe of the washcloth. And AnnaLee—still concerned about Jack, and about being late for the party—is telling Bella: "Not now, sweetie, we'll play later. We'll play tomorrow. Tonight we have to get Daddy where he needs to go—"

AnnaLee has stopped short—struck by a thought she has been avoiding for weeks. There is nothing set in stone about this evening. There's no guarantee that Mrs. Jahn will hire Jack. No guarantee that tonight AnnaLee's life will change—that it will ever change.

There is a sensation in AnnaLee like she has just stepped out of an airplane. Parachuteless. Into midair.

Without realizing it, she has dropped the washcloth she's been using to wipe Bella's face. Bella is picking it up and trying to hand it back to her.

AnnaLee, adrift, has forgotten about the washcloth. She's staring at herself in the bathroom mirror, but talking to Bella. "Love isn't enough, Bella. Promise me, when it's time, you'll find someone who is strong—who can stand beside you in holding up the roof over your head. Promise me you'll choose somebody who knows how to help you fight the battles your life will bring."

She rests her cheek against Bella's and whispers: "No matter how much in love you are, or how pure his soul is, don't choose a man like your daddy. His helplessness will hurt you—it'll hurt so much you'll think you're going to die."

AnnaLee straightens up—abruptly aware that she and Bella aren't alone anymore. Someone else is in the room.

Even before she has turned to see who it is, AnnaLee knows it's Jack.

He's dressed in his old tuxedo, with his hair slicked down. A reddening flush is spreading high across the tops of his cheekbones, leaving the rest of his face as white as his shirtfront. He has the lonely, startled look of someone who has just been murdered.

AnnaLee is devastated.

"I can't survive without you, Lee," he says.

"You won't have to," AnnaLee promises him.

His reply comes slowly, as if he's distracted, as if he's being shown some ominous part of his future. "If you leave, how will I stay alive?"

"I love you, Jack. I'll never leave."

The sadness in Jack's smile is excruciating. "Never is an awfully long time, Lee."

While Jack is gone, driving Bella to the babysitter, AnnaLee is leaning in close to the mirror. Applying the finishing touches to her makeup. Following Persephone's scribbled instructions to the letter.

She's brushing her lashes with a coat of shiny black mascara. Dabbing a hint of color onto her cheeks. Lighting up her mouth with a swipe of fire-engine-red lipstick. And—as the final touch— she's tucking her hair up, concealing it under the thrift-shop wig that Persephone has shaped into a sporty, 1920s bob.

As AnnaLee is looking into the mirror she's seeing an altered, boldly rendered version of herself—one that's fascinating and dramatic. Undeniably beautiful.

This person in the mirror—this woman that Persephone has created—is spectacular.

Simply looking at her is lifting AnnaLee's spirits, making her think, *Maybe tonight really will be something extraordinary. It's not impossible that everything could go perfectly—that Mrs. Jahn could see the potential in Jack and give us the chance to begin a new life. And—*

A clattering noise is coming from the kitchen. Followed by shouts of laughter—Persephone and someone else. Probably Rebecca Wang.

It's time to go downstairs and see the girls off to the party.

But AnnaLee, reluctant to turn away from the mirror, is double-checking her makeup and mascara. Delaying her departure from this enchanted place where she's someone so different. So glamorous and full of possibility.

When AnnaLee arrives downstairs, Persephone is at the kitchen table sharing a turkey sandwich with Rebecca Wang. Both girls are wearing aprons to protect their Gatsby-era costumes from any accidental spills.

AnnaLee is met with a smile from Rebecca and an outraged howl from Persephone. "You're still in your bathrobe! Why aren't you in your costume?"

"I am. Under the bathrobe." The admission has caused AnnaLee to blush.

"And you're doing the bathrobe thing because…?"

"Because I'm used to being in 'mom clothes,' Persephone, and this dress is shorter and a lot slinkier than I'm comfortable with. I feel a little awkward."

Persephone is immediately upset. "You're not going to wear it to the party? You're not even going to let me see you in it?"

"No, sweetheart, of course I am. Just give me a minute to get my courage up."

"What do you need courage for? You look fantastic." Persephone is insistent. "The 1920s hair, and your makeup—it's like totally off-the-charts great."

AnnaLee is buying time by taking a glass from one of the kitchen cabinets. While she's filling the glass with water, she's noticing Rebecca Wang's expression. It's evident Rebecca has an opinion about what's being discussed but is maintaining a well-mannered silence.

AnnaLee is fascinated by Rebecca Wang. The girl has a self-possession that's unusual in someone her age. A Zen-like quality that makes her appear to be perfectly calm, perfectly centered.

Which, perhaps, is why AnnaLee feels the need to explain herself to Rebecca. "I know it sounds like I'm being silly. But Persephone has done almost too good a job on my costume. I'm in a dress that belongs on a Hollywood sex symbol, not a Long Island housewife."

Rebecca's response is enthusiastic and genuine. "I've seen the sketches. Honestly, you don't have any reason to be nervous about your outfit. It's perfect for you."

Persephone immediately adds: "Rebecca knows what she's talking about. She's graduating from the Rhode Island School of Design next year. She's like the most gifted person they've ever had."

Rebecca Wang is leaving the table, taking off the apron she has been wearing, giving an embarrassed laugh while she's telling AnnaLee: "Persephone's just saying those nice things about me because we're friends."

Persephone's mood abruptly shifts. She pushes away from the

table, hurrying out of her chair, muttering: "I need to go upstairs. I have to make a phone call."

Rebecca is looking at her watch, saying to Persephone: "If we don't leave now, we'll be late."

And AnnaLee is asking: "Why waste time going all the way upstairs? Use the phone in here."

Persephone seems to be unable to decide whether to stay or to go. Almost as if she's in a mild state of shock. Then all at once she's running to the phone that's on the wall near the refrigerator.

While she's lifting the receiver and dialing, she's calling out in a self-conscious chirp: "Rebecca, tell AnnaLee about the master of ceremonies Mrs. Jahn hired...the guy Johnny Carson keeps inviting back as a guest on the *Tonight Show*."

"He's terrific," Rebecca says. "He's insanely funny..."

As Rebecca launches into her story, AnnaLee sees that Persephone is putting her mouth close to the receiver. As if she doesn't want to be overheard while she's whispering: "Forget what we talked about. When I said I'd do it, I was still making up my mind, but things are different now so—"

"There's this one routine involving the audience where he..." Rebecca Wang is continuing her story about the comedian who's such a favorite on *The Tonight Show*.

The next thing AnnaLee hears is Persephone saying: "Call me as soon as you get this message. Bye."

"Is everything all right?" AnnaLee asks. "Are you okay?"

"Yeah, I'm fine," Persephone says.

And she seems fine. Seems relieved, like a great weight has been lifted from her. She's taking off her apron, picking up her purse and Rebecca's camera.

While Persephone is following Rebecca out the door, Rebecca

says: "There's only one exposure left, we should put fresh film in the camera before we get to the party."

Persephone stops short, whirling around to AnnaLee. "The party. Your costume! I can't go without seeing your costume."

"I...I don't want you to be disappointed."

"AnnaLee, I won't be. And besides you have to lose the bathrobe to go to the party. An hour from now, two hundred people will be seeing you in that dress." The vulnerability in Persephone is sweetly childlike as she's telling AnnaLee: "I just want to be the first."

Persephone is asking AnnaLee for a gift; asking for her trust and approval.

AnnaLee can't say no.

She's reluctantly shedding the bathrobe, letting it drop to the floor.

Persephone's reaction is a startled gasp.

It flusters AnnaLee—embarrasses her.

She takes a quick step backward. Retreating into the shadow of the dining room doorway.

There is the sudden whirr of a camera.

And Persephone—saying in a murmur no louder than a breath: "Oh my god."

Livvi

Pasadena, California ~ 2012

LIVVI AND ANDREW HAVE JUST FINISHED A TURNING, GLIDING dance. Which began as a slow ballet. Led by Andrew. Deftly piloting Livvi. Bringing her, first, to the thrill of small tingles. Tingles he then subtly transformed into cascades of tiny shudders. Shudders that, under his expert touch, began to blossom. Individually. One by one. Each of them, rapidly expanding. All of them diamond-bright. Effervescent and luminous. Exploding low and deep in Livvi. Sparkling, erotic bursts of sexual gratification. Each and every one skillfully delivered—by Andrew—as a separate, glittering pleasure. Pleasure that coursed through Livvi like torrents of liquid electricity.

And now Andrew and Livvi are lying absolutely still. While he's saying: "This is how I want to fall asleep every Saturday night for the rest of my life." He is spooned against Livvi's back, his breath warm on the nape of her neck.

The sweetness. The closeness. The murmured conversation. Andrew never fails to share these small gifts with Livvi after they've had sex. It's an aspect of him she cherishes, a lovely place of intimacy.

Andrew's voice is mellow with contentment as he's telling Livvi: "This is perfection. You and me in your nice cozy bed. Grace sleeping in the other room, spending the weekend. The three of us leaving for Aspen the day after tomorrow." His sigh is long and lazy. "I'm a happy man, Olivia."

Livvi is inhaling the scent of their lovemaking and the clean, fresh smell of Andrew's skin. It has been almost ten weeks since the chaotic afternoon in Rolling Hills—the confrontation in Andrew's parents' driveway with his wife, and his mother.

Livvi is aware that since that day Andrew has been devoting himself to making her happy. Lavishing her with time and attention. And love letters written in cocoa-brown ink on buff-colored stationery. Notes tucked into the pockets of her clothes and the corners of her dresser drawers. Little hidden treasures designed to calm and reassure her.

In each of these letters, above Andrew's signature, there is the same phrase—the thought he's expressing to Livvi now: "I adore you."

And Livvi is replying: "I adore you too."

But she hasn't turned to look at him while she's saying it. Livvi's love for Andrew has changed, lost some of its intensity and purity. Lately, there has been a thread of mistrust in it. The suspicion that, as soon as some fresh hell breaks loose, Andrew will disappear. Into the drama of Palos Verdes and Rolling Hills.

"By the way," Andrew is informing Livvi, "the feeling is mutual."

Livvi gives him a questioning frown; she isn't sure what he's talking about.

"Haven't you been listening? I'm telling you I'm not the only one who adores you. I have major competition from Grace. She thinks you're wonderful."

Just hearing Grace's name lights Livvi with happiness. "And I'm crazy about her."

"Believe me, she knows. The idea of the three of us going on this trip to Aspen has put her over the moon."

Livvi props herself on one elbow, worried a little. "Do you think it'll be a problem for her to miss a whole week of school?"

Andrew slides Livvi's elbow toward him and pulls her near. "It's the middle of November, and Grace is in kindergarten. She's five. The biggest thing she'll miss out on is making Pilgrim hats out of construction paper. And my guess is…not knowing how to turn cardboard into headgear won't hurt her chances of getting into a decent college." Andrew is yawning, switching off the light.

After a while. When Andrew is asleep. Livvi quietly gets out of bed—she's thirsty and wants a glass of water.

On her way to the kitchen, she passes the sofa in the living room, where Grace is sleeping. The little pink pig is nestled on Grace's pillow. And on Grace's hands are a pair of brand-new, pink-striped, woolen mittens—a present from Livvi, for Grace to wear on their Aspen ski trip.

At the sight of Grace's hands in those mittens, Livvi whispers: "I love you too, Gracie."

For a long time Livvi simply watches Grace sleep. In complete, peaceful silence.

And then, unexpectedly, jarring noise is coming from a few feet away. In the kitchen. Loud, buzzing sounds. Livvi, worried that they'll disturb Grace, hurries to put a stop to them.

Livvi's phone—the source of the noise—is on the kitchen counter where she left it when she, Andrew, and Grace came home from dinner. While she's taking her phone from the counter, she's checking the caller ID.

It's a number Livvi recognizes; one that she has seen more and more often, over the past few weeks.

Every time it appears it brings stomach-churning dread.

Yet she has no choice other than to answer. The person who's calling refuses to interact with voice mail. If Livvi doesn't allow this individual to connect with her, in person, even for a microsecond, the calls will continue. Relentlessly—throughout the night. Until Livvi surrenders and picks up the phone.

The pattern has become for Livvi to say hello and then quickly disconnect, before the whispery-voiced caller can get out more than a word or two.

Now, as she's putting the phone to her ear, Livvi is thinking of Grace, and their trip—not wanting their time in Aspen to be shadowed by this stubborn intruder.

Determined to prevent the person from coming, even in the form of a phone call, anywhere near Grace, Livvi is insisting: "Don't call here again. And don't even think of contacting me in person. I won't speak to you. I will not deal with you. Now. Or ever."

Livvi is for a brief moment triumphant. But her bravado is rapidly turning into fear. Fear that she's just jeopardized everything she was trying to keep safe.

The whispery voice has become an angry hiss. Warning her: "You're wrong, Olivia. You will deal with me. Much sooner than you think."

It has been a perfect Sunday morning for the three of them: Livvi, Andrew, and Grace. Silly games and laughter. Pancakes for breakfast. And a rush of last-minute packing for tomorrow's trip to Aspen—to sleigh rides and fresh-fallen snow.

The exuberance of this morning and the beautiful California

November weather, the clear skies and warm sunshine, are calming some of Livvi's uneasiness about last night's phone call. Making the threat it carried seem less meaningful.

With Grace's hand snug in hers as they're hurrying across the lawn that separates Livvi's guesthouse from the main house, Sierra's house, Livvi is trying to believe she's being irrational in thinking the whispery-voiced caller actually has the power, or the desire, to reach beyond the confines of the phone. After all, the person who's calling is someone from another place and time. And that's where—Livvi is convincing herself—they'll probably stay.

Grace is pulling at Livvi's hand as she's skipping up the steps of Sierra's back patio where Sierra, in a rhinestone-studded warm-up suit and oversize sunglasses, is stretched out on a lounge chair.

"Livvi," Grace is saying. "I bet I know what you're thinking about."

She pauses on the top step and gives Livvi a conspiratorial grin. "You're thinking about chocolate chips."

"Really?" Livvi has no idea how Grace has come to this conclusion.

Grace, running ahead, eager to greet Sierra, is calling over her shoulder to Livvi: "I know you're thinking about chocolate chips 'cause that's what I'm thinking about too."

While Livvi is coming up the steps and onto the patio, Grace is telling Sierra: "After Livvi's finished talking to you, we're going back to her house to make cookies and that's the kind I think we should make, chocolate chip. They're for us to take on our trip tomorrow."

Sierra lowers her sunglasses and announces to Grace: "Just for the record, honey-bun, when it comes to chocolate chip, I'm a purist. No nuts. And I demand a cut on any cookies baked on my property. Got it?"

Grace nods, slowly, looking from Sierra to Livvi, not sure of what she has just agreed to.

"Sierra wants to share our cookies," Livvi explains.

Grace's uncertainty is replaced by a bright smile. "Okay. Then hurry up with the talking so we can go home and bake some for her."

Livvi is about to respond, but Grace's interest has been captured by a large bird fluttering onto a tree limb at the edge of the patio.

While Sierra, pointing to the file folder Livvi is holding, is asking: "Is that the bimonthly reckoning?"

"Yup. As soon as you've looked over the bills and signed the checks, I'll get everything in the mail."

"You know, if I wasn't giving you cut-rate rent in return for you balancing my books I could be saving a lot of time, not to mention a shitload of trees, by doing all of this online. Like the rest of the world."

Livvi laughs. "You'd have to start by figuring out how to get online."

They have this same lighthearted exchange on the first and fifteenth of every month.

Livvi sits in a chair across from Sierra's, putting the file folder and her phone on the ground nearby. "I can't tell you how grateful I am that you're a computer illiterate. I get down on my knees regularly and thank God for it."

"You're a smart girl," Sierra tells her. Then she cocks her head in Grace's direction and says: "You two seem to be spending a lot of time together."

Livvi's smile is instantaneous. "She's got me wrapped around her little finger. And I love it."

"I hope you understand the minefield you're walking into. Grace is a great kid, but she's not exactly a blank slate—she comes with a lot of baggage. The insanity with her mother won't ever go away.

And even if by some miracle it did, Grace'll always be somebody else's kid, not yours."

"I'm aware of that, I am. But…" Livvi is trying to figure out how to make Sierra understand her bond with Grace and knows she can't. "The only thing I can tell you is…the way I love her… it's like she is my own."

"Maybe so. But depending on how her mother wants to play it, the cost you end up paying on your love affair with that kid could be pretty steep."

The thought of not being with Grace is too painful for Livvi to bear. She picks up the file folder containing the bookkeeping information and hands it to Sierra—making it clear she doesn't want to discuss what the price tag might be for loving Grace.

Sierra puts the file folder aside, tilts her head in Grace's direction, and says: "So…according to the little one, you're taking a trip. Where to?"

"Aspen," Livvi tells her. "Skiing. For a week."

Grace, her attention still on the preening bird, is calling to Sierra from the edge of the patio. "Daddy's coming with us! And we're going on a plane."

Sierra shoots Livvi a knowing look. "A private one, no doubt."

Livvi blushes.

Sierra laughs. "The man's got a pile of cash, nothing to be embarrassed about. And speaking of the man, where is he? Back at your place…sleeping in?"

"He's at his office. He needed to take care of some things before we leave tomorrow."

Sierra checks to be sure Grace isn't listening. "What about his divorce…has he taken care of that?"

"He's working on it," Livvi says. "It's a difficult situation." She reaches for the file folder again—wanting to head off any discussion about Andrew's wife.

Sierra studies Livvi for a moment. "I'm not saying this to rattle your cage. I'm saying it because I don't give a shit about your boyfriend, and I care a hell of a lot about you." She pauses, satisfies herself that Grace is occupied with the bird, then adds: "This bind he claims he's in—the need to be so careful and take everything at a snail's pace—how much of it is really about protecting the kid? And how much is about him still being in business with her mother?"

"I don't know." Livvi's response is fast and flustered: Sierra has hit a raw nerve.

Livvi's thoughts have gone to that afternoon in Rolling Hills: *Andrew holding a phone to his ear. Taking his wife's call. And looking at Livvi—mutely telling her he's sorry. While he's turning away with his shoulders hunched. Making Livvi wonder, "Is he trying to shield me from his wife? Or shield his wife from me...?"*

And Sierra is warning Livvi: "I don't know what's going on with your boy and his crazy wife, but I can give you the bottom line—he's in no hurry to shut the door on her."

Sierra levels a gaze at Livvi that says *"Go ahead. Try to tell me I'm wrong."*

Livvi puts down the file folder, glances in Grace's direction, and signals to Sierra to walk with her to the other side of the patio.

Livvi is attempting to convince both herself and Sierra, as she's saying: "I've seen Andrew's wife. The only logical reason for the way he caters to her has to be that he's protecting Grace. His wife is a mess. She's horrible. There's no way he could be in love with her."

"It doesn't mean he isn't in love with her drama," Sierra says. "Depending on where your kinks are...having somebody tell you you're the center of their universe, and they'll die without you, can be a real ego-stroke. Even if it's coming from somebody who's fucked up beyond belief."

Livvi, wanting to think only about Grace and Aspen, is trying to push this idea as far away as possible. "What's keeping Andrew stuck isn't love," she's insisting. "It's guilt."

Sierra gives Livvi a steady, unblinking stare. "As long as he's staying stuck, does it really make any difference what kind of fucking glue he's using?"

Livvi flinches.

Sierra's attitude immediately softens. "Honey, all I'm asking is how much of his not getting a divorce is about taking care of Grace...how much is about taking care of the wife...and how much of it is about taking real good care of Andrew. Because I don't see where any of it is about taking care of you."

Livvi doesn't respond. She doesn't know how to explain that none of this makes any difference—because, in her own way, she's just as stuck as Andrew is.

As if she's recognizing Livvi's dilemma, and determined not to ignore it, Sierra asks: "So what keeps you from kicking him to the curb, kiddo?"

"A lot of things." Livvi hopes Sierra is ready to let the discussion end.

Instead, Sierra puts her hands on Livvi's shoulders, looks her straight in the eye, and after a long pause says: "Who was the first boy you had a crush on in elementary school?"

"Nobody." Livvi ducks her head, embarrassed. "I didn't go to elementary school, or high school. I didn't know any boys."

Sierra spends a long time looking at Livvi. Searching her eyes, and her face. Slowly connecting the dots of a story that Livvi has never told her.

"Holy shit," Sierra murmurs. "No wonder you don't know how to let go of him—Andrew was your first."

"Not technically." Livvi glances down, embarrassed. "There was an old man, a professor. When I was in college. It was only that one time. And—"

"—and then nothing till Andrew?"

"A few dates, here and there. But..." Livvi's voice has trailed off. She's being overwhelmed by shuddering sense memories. The passion. The intense physical pleasure. The sexual wonderland she's been introduced to. By Andrew.

"It's like before him, I'd never been alive," she murmurs.

"Oh honey, that's what everybody says when they get righteously laid for the first time."

"I know...but for me it really is true. And the sex isn't even the biggest part of it." Livvi glances away, self-conscious. "Before Andrew, I'd spent my entire life in a box. Eighteen years, locked away in my father's house. Then in college, locked up in my own prison. Too scared to even talk to anybody. And after college—for most of these last four years—I spent my workdays sealed in a research library, and my nights locked in my bedroom, pouring misery onto paper, writing *The Book of Someday*."

Livvi looks at Sierra and tells her: "Before Andrew, I honest to God had never known what excited, spontaneous happiness was. All I knew about happiness...or fun...was what I imagined it might be. And then there was Andrew—and he made those things real."

Sierra winces. Then gives Livvi's hand an awkward, affectionate squeeze. "You're making this guy sound like God. 'In the beginning, Andrew created the heavens and the earth.'"

Sierra's tone is light—Livvi knows that she's being teased.

"It almost feels that way," Livvi says.

Then she adds: "I had never been anywhere. I'd never done any-thing. And I'd certainly never done anything just for fun. Sierra... Andrew showed me what joy was. He's taken me places, taught me things I didn't even know how to dream of."

"Kiddo. The world, the fun, the joy, the great sex—it's all out there. Open to the public. Andrew being the first one to show it to you doesn't make him Master of the Universe—it just makes him a guy with a sense of adventure and a credit card."

"Maybe. But I've never before known anybody even remotely like him...and I don't think I could ever find anyone like him again."

Sierra wraps her arms around Livvi, holds her tight, then steps back and says: "Oh baby, you have so much to learn."

Livvi glances across the lawn toward her little guesthouse where she and Andrew, before they went to sleep last night, shared such intense, and spectacular, pleasure.

"He loves me," Livvi says. "He's the only man who ever has."

"It doesn't mean he's the only one who ever will. You can do better, kiddo. While he's playing around with you—having all that fun—he's staying married to his wife. That makes him a jerk."

Sierra has gently put her arm around Livvi's shoulder.

And in the shelter of that gentleness, Livvi is admitting: "Sometimes I think, no matter what he does, I'm just lucky he wants me. There're things about the weird way I grew up—the people who raised me. I'm not like everybody else. I'm different. A misfit. Sort of second-rate..."

Several minutes pass in silence.

Then Sierra says: "There's a famous episode from an old TV show called *The Twilight Zone*. It's about this woman who's hideously ugly. Can't even go out in public. Which is why she volunteers for this risky surgery, it's her one chance to not look like a freak anymore. Her face is covered the whole time and all you see of the surgeons are their hands and arms. Then in the last scene, after the surgery, she's lying there—miserable—because they're telling her nothing's changed, she's still ugly. The camera tilts up to show the surgeons, and they're all completely grotesque. Then the camera tilts down, to show the woman. She's gorgeous—looks like she could be on the cover of *Vogue*."

Livvi gives Sierra an uncertain glance.

And Sierra tells her: "What I'm saying is, you're the beauty…and whoever raised you, they were the freaks."

Livvi doesn't have time to respond—her phone has begun to ring. It's still on the ground near the spot where she and Sierra were sitting earlier. And Grace is dashing across the patio, calling out: "I'll answer, I'll answer!"

Before Livvi can stop her, Grace is picking up the phone and saying: "Hello?" After a quick beat, she's frowning, insisting: "No. This is Livvi's phone."

Then she's holding the phone out to Livvi, puzzled. "They want to talk to Olivia."

Livvi takes the phone—her heart is hammering.

Something has gone unbelievably wrong. These calls always come late in the night. Never, ever, in the daytime.

Livvi is aware that all the color must be draining from her face. She can see the look of alarm in Grace, and in Sierra.

The voice at the other end of the phone is calmly informing her: "You've left me no choice. I'm here, Olivia."

Livvi is shaking. "Where…?"

"I'm in your house."

And Livvi's skin begins to crawl—as if she has just brushed against a snake.

Her voice is strained and tight. "I have to go," she tells Sierra. "I need for Grace to stay here with you for a while."

"Is it about Mommy? Is Mommy mad at you?" Grace is full of apprehension.

Livvi can barely speak. "No," she says. "It isn't your mommy. It's somebody else."

The air in the room feels poisonous and stale. There's a chill—a deadness—that has never been here before.

But, to her surprise, Livvi isn't afraid. She's defiant, ready for battle. The uppermost thing in her heart and mind is Grace. Livvi is prepared to do whatever it takes to keep Grace separated from this evil.

"How dare you come into my house?" she's asking.

The answer is toneless, unapologetic. "Your door was unlocked."

"How did you find out where I lived?"

A thin smile accompanies the reply. "I was brought here by the Lord, Olivia. He led me to a young man at my church who knows how to use the Internet."

Livvi's unwelcome visitor has been looking around the room, taking in every detail. Now the visitor's flat, black gaze is coming to rest on Livvi. The same flat gaze that was in that other house, where the air was stale with the sour odor of boiled cabbage and the wintry funk of unwashed blankets. Where the nights were shattered by the rampage of demons.

"Get out," Livvi tells Calista. "Or I'll call the police."

Calista is gazing down at her shoes, slowly shaking her head, as if she has been terribly wounded. "You always had a nasty disposition, Olivia."

Calista, with her ink-black eyes and soap-white face, is fleshier than she was. Slightly wider and slower. She's wearing a bulky, shapeless coat and rubbery, thick-soled shoes. While she's crossing to the sofa, the soles of her shoes are squeaking on the rose-colored floor tiles. "I've been very afraid of coming here. And I was right to be afraid. May God forgive me for saying it, but you were an unpleasant, frightening girl, Olivia. And you've grown into a heartless and frightening woman."

Now she's sitting, stiffly—crowded against the arm of the sofa. Her hand going to her coat collar, meekly holding it closed over the base of her throat. As if she's defenseless and this is her feeble attempt to protect herself.

The gesture—its stagey timidity—infuriates Livvi.

Calista's hand remains on her coat collar. But her attention has been drawn to the pink pig and the little, pink-striped mittens lying on one of the sofa cushions.

"You have a child...?" For a moment, Calista's mouth is slack, her eyes vacant. As if she's being faced with something unnatural—beyond comprehension. Her tone is hushed, offended, as she says: "You? You have been blessed with a child?"

Calista is reaching for Grace's pink-striped mittens.

Before she can pick them up—Livvi has hit her. Hard enough to snap Calista's head back against the sofa. And send her eyes rolling in their sockets.

"Don't touch anything belonging to people I love," Livvi hisses. "Don't bring your wickedness anywhere near them—or me."

Calista, reeling from Livvi's blow, is shrieking: "When I married your father, he told me your mother ran away and he never explained why. But now I think I understand. Her leaving had nothing to with him. It was because of you. The minute she laid eyes on you, your mother must have sensed what a dreadful creature she'd brought into the world."

For a moment the hurt of that statement paralyzes Livvi, crushes her. And her only thought is to plead with Calista to leave.

But then Livvi sees Grace's pink pig and is reminded of how little Grace is. How innocent and vulnerable. Livvi is thinking about the tender feelings of protectiveness she has toward Grace. And she is wondering how, when she was just a little girl, innocent and vulnerable, Calista could have done such unspeakable things to her.

Livvi is remembering…*a time when she is barely eight years old. Being "taught a lesson" because she's afraid of the huge, lunging German Shepherd that Calista has brought home as a pet, from the pound. She's locked in the toolshed with the dog. Its roaring barks, shaking the walls. Her terror so intense that her nose is starting to bleed. Her dress and socks are soaked with sweat and Calista is outside the door telling her, "Dogs can smell fear—that's when they attack. The sooner you decide to stop being afraid, the better." And the fear is surging. Spurting a trail of pee down her leg. While everything around her is swimming. And going black.*

In thinking about it now, Livvi is wondering where her father was during the countless times she was terrorized by Calista. She's realizing that he must have been where he so often was. Off, by himself. Roaming the hills. Mute and blank-faced.

When Livvi turns her attention back to Calista, she's baffled. "Why?" she's asking. "I was just a little girl. How could you have been so cruel to me?"

Calista stares Livvi down and tells her: "I was never cruel. I gave you discipline. Spare the rod, spoil the child. And God knows, in the years you had been alone with your father, you'd been spared the rod long enough."

For the first time, Livvi is seeing the staggering depth of Calista's arrogance. Seeing how nastily, boneheadedly stupid she is. And it's wiping away Livvi's fear of her. It's altering Livvi's pain. Turning it into outrage.

Livvi is seething as she's telling Calista: "My father had spared me from a lot more than the rod, and you knew it." Her voice is a growl as she adds: "I was a motherless little girl who'd been spared from ever having a storybook read to me. Or ever being hugged. Or tucked into bed...even once...with a good night kiss." Livvi's voice is a furious whisper as she says: "And your answer to that was *discipline*...? You were a pair of monsters. You. And my father."

"For so long, I prayed. I begged the Lord not to let me die an old maid," Calista says. "I begged him to give me a husband and a home."

Calista seems to be talking to herself, not to Livvi, as she murmurs: "The Lord refused me. He left me wandering in the desert. Then one morning, at work, while I was cleaning the church office, I looked up and your father was in the entryway. You were outside waiting by the edge of the road. That was the one and only time your father ever darkened the door of a church. He said he wanted to talk to the pastor because he needed to find a good woman willing to take on the raising of a little girl—he was alone and he needed a wife. It was the answer to my prayer. I told your father I was who he was looking for. A week later, we were married."

Calista is staring into mid-distance. Lost in thought. "I was ready to give myself to him in every way, but he hardly ever touched me. Only at night. Sometimes. And he would never look at me, never call my name. Do you know that in all these years, he hasn't kissed me? Not once."

It's as if Calista is gazing into the past—seeing a detail she hadn't noticed before. "I was an innocent bride in a house where you took up all the space. Your father's thoughts…his few words…his every waking moment. They must've all belonged to you. But I accepted it, accepted you, as the cross that the Lord—for some reason—was asking me to bear." Her tone is sticky with self-pity.

And Livvi, finished with Calista's spite and stupidity, tells her: "Get out of here, before I hit you again."

Calista jumps up from the sofa. Edging around behind it—making a show of attempting to shield herself from Livvi. While she's whining: "I never wanted to come here in the first place. You forced me to. I could've told you on the phone what I'm here to tell you now, but every time I called, you wouldn't listen."

Livvi is worried that this conversation is going on too long, and that Grace will come back before it's over. She wants Calista gone, quickly. "What is it you're here to talk about?"

"Your father."

"I'm not going to discuss my father with you."

"For whatever your hateful reasons, you haven't spoken to him since the day you went away to college. You've left that man abandoned for nine years, Olivia. You've broken his heart."

Livvi's reply comes from a place of loss and grief. "I wish he'd had a heart to break."

"He gave you life, Olivia. He's the only father you will ever have."

Livvi is recalling that turning-point morning in Santa Ynez. Her father's fingers digging into her hair as he is lifting her off the ground. Letting the full weight of her body hang from her scalp.

"Your father wants to see you," Calista is saying.

"I don't care." The sound of heartbreak is in Livvi's voice.

And in Calista's there is smugness, a bitter sort of triumph. As if she's finding pleasure in the pain she's inflicting. As she announces: "Your father is dying."

Livvi's response is guttural—an almost inaudible moan.

"This is what I was calling to tell you, all those nights, when you were hanging up on me…"

The rest of Calista's rant is garbled. Muffled. Like it's coming from miles away. Livvi is trying to picture herself at her father's side—one last time. Trying to picture what it might be like. But all she can see is a little girl hiding, in a faded nightgown. Waiting. On that cold winter morning. For the love that never came.

And Calista is telling her: "Your father is in New Jersey, where you were born, and where his home was when he was young. He'd been in Santa Ynez since you were a baby, since just after the two of you were deserted by your mother. And when the doctors told him the end was near he wanted to go back to where he, and you, began."

Calista is moving out from behind the sofa. A torrent of words rolling out of her—loud and dramatic—like a hell-fire sermon from a backwoods preacher. "Your father is a proud, proud man, Olivia. He knows how you've hardened your heart against him. It would destroy him to have to beg you to come. That's why I was forced to wait until the nighttime to call. Why I had to keep my voice as quiet as I could—why I whispered. We live in a small apartment. I didn't want him to hear, didn't want him to know, that even when a soul in need is crying out to you, you don't care enough to listen."

"Save your breath," Livvi tells her. "My mother abandoned me to my father, who was an overeducated, uncaring madman. My father abandoned me to you, a Bible-thumping witch. And you—when I was just a little girl and you thought you were going to have a baby—you threw me away with a single sentence. You told me, 'From now on, Olivia, you'll be on your own.'"

Livvi has walked to the front door and opened it wide. "I feel the same way about you and my father as you used to feel about me—I don't have time for you."

As Calista is walking past Livvi, on her way to the door, she's glancing back at Grace's little pink-striped mittens. And she's reminding Livvi: "You were his child, his blood." Then she mutters: "No matter what you remember about him—what you believe about him—he loved you."

All Livvi says is: "Go away."

"He doesn't have much time, Olivia. I am on an eleven o'clock flight. I'm asking if you'll come with me. Tonight."

Livvi shakes her head. She can't speak. She's throttled with tears, and mourning.

"If not tonight, then when?" Calista asks.

"I'm not sure. I don't know."

Livvi is revisiting a list of dreams and promises written in a child's careful cursive…*Someday I'll have a birthday party with people and singing…someday I'll wear pink ballet shoes and have a friend who thinks I'm nice…and when I'm grown, I won't hit, especially with a wooden hairbrush, because the hurt never stops, even after the bruises go.*

And Livvi says: "I still remember my father too well—I remember the things that he let happen in his house. I'm not ready to see him. If I ever am, it'll be a long, long time from now."

The look that Calista gives Livvi is as dark as the floor of an open grave.

"In a matter of weeks, Olivia, your father may no longer exist."

Micah

Boston, Massachusetts ~ 2012

IT WASN'T UNTIL THE MOMENT AT THE TOP OF THE STAIRS, ON THE third floor of her house, when she was gripping the handle of the closed door, that Micah realized she still wasn't ready. The opening of that door would, in essence, be the opening of a grave. And it required a courage she still hadn't found.

This is why Micah walked away. Down the stairs and out of the house. Without thinking. Without remembering to take a coat. With no plan other than to buy time—find enough strength to face the woman waiting behind the closed door.

After almost two hours Micah is still walking, still roaming the streets of Boston. Thinking about the woman, the crimes of the past. And about what punishments the future might hold.

Micah is halfway down a historic Beacon Hill side street, a cobblestone lane only a few feet wide. Lined with red-bricked, black-shuttered houses and streetlights that look like old-fashioned gas lamps. An early afternoon November wind has begun to blow, causing the temperature (which is probably in the mid-fifties) to feel more like forty. Micah has been steadily picking up her pace—intent on trying to keep warm and get home as soon as possible. But she's coming to an abrupt stop. Surprised at where she is. Wondering if this is an accident, or if she has brought herself here as the result of an unconscious plan.

This place has profound significance for Micah.

Once, a long time ago, she spent an hour in the house that's directly across the street. An hour that throughout her life, every time she has thought of it, has troubled her.

Although Micah is uncomfortably cold, she's continuing to stand in the blowing November wind. Looking at the house. Remembering what happened there—the brief conversation that permanently altered the course of her life.

While Micah is recalling the details of that conversation, she's also hearing the sounds of echoing footsteps. A man, casually well-dressed and carrying a stylish canvas shopping bag, is rounding the corner at the top of the block.

He and Micah are on opposite sides of the street. But the street is so narrow that they're only a few feet apart as he's stopping and staring at her.

He's in his early thirties and astonishingly handsome. His eyes are golden brown—the same lustrous color as his hair. His body, which is in perfect proportion to his height, is strong and lean. Everything about him, from the way he's dressed to the way he's holding the canvas bag, seems artless and unassuming.

"Are you lost?" he's asking.

Micah shakes her head no. In spite of how cold she is, and how preoccupied, she's keenly aware of what an incredibly attractive man he is.

He looks up and down the empty street. "Then you must be a tourist."

"Why a tourist?"

"This is Acorn Street, the picture on millions of postcards. It's the most photographed street in Boston."

Micah gives an ironic grin. "I'm aware of that." She has crossed her arms and hunched her shoulders. Her teeth are chattering a little.

"Are you in some kind of trouble? Do you need help?"

"I'm okay," Micah tells him. "A long time ago I knew someone who lived in the house you're standing in front of. He managed a rock band. His name was Miles Gidney. I was just—"

"You knew my father?" The man is surprised, clearly intrigued. "I'm Eric," he says. "My dad hasn't lived here since the nineties. He went to Italy and bought a villa."

The way this man, Eric, is scrutinizing her is something Micah's accustomed to. It's the standard male reaction to her face and figure.

"You look…" He seems to be searching for the right word.

There's no question in Micah's mind that it will be something like "beautiful" or "sexy" or "unbelievable."

It comes as a shock when she hears "…cold and alone."

He's unlocking the door to the house, observing Micah's lack of a coat (and her shivering) with concern and sympathy, holding up the canvas shopping bag, saying: "I have a good Pinot Noir, fresh bread, and a couple of interesting cheeses. Come in for a few minutes. Have something to eat, get warm."

Micah can see that what he's offering her isn't sex. It's simple, unencumbered hospitality. Something she has almost forgotten the existence of.

The wine bottle is nearly full. The bread and the cheese are untouched. And the room—Micah is thinking, as she's gathering up her underwear and bra—is unchanged. The black walls and the framed gold records. The plush carpet and staggeringly expensive furniture. All of it precisely as it was when she was here twenty years ago. When she thought she knew exactly what the future would bring. When she believed she was invincible. And didn't understand that she could ever be old, or sick.

Eric, who has stepped back into his trousers and is buckling his belt, is apologizing—explaining to Micah: "I didn't mean for this to happen."

"I didn't either," Micah says.

"It's not why I invited you in." He sounds disappointed in himself. "I didn't do it to take advantage of you. You looked so cold and lost. I wanted to help."

Micah is thinking that he did help. What happened between them was extraordinary. An unanticipated and grace-filled exchange.

Micah is now in her sweater and jeans, pulling on her socks and her boots. "My last name is Lesser," she says. "I'm Micah Lesser. Google it."

There's a glimmer of confusion in Eric's expression.

"It's important," she tells him. "Google it."

He goes to a laptop on a small stand near the window. After a moment, he looks up, stunned. "You took the photo for that last album cover? My god, you're famous. That cover made history, there isn't anybody over thirty who doesn't recognize it on sight. It was the ultimate punctuation to the band's legacy, and my dad's."

He takes a deep breath, overwhelmed. "Wow. That album and the cover was all anybody talked about. I remember I was thirteen when it came out and it blew me away."

Hearing the ten-year age difference between them makes Micah wince.

Eric, as if recognizing her discomfort, says: "Now I'm thirty-three.

It doesn't matter how old I was then." He has gone back to looking at the computer screen—scrolling through information on Micah's connection to the album cover. "You were selected from a field of a thousand hopefuls…what a rush that must've been."

Micah is apprehensive as she's asking: "Did your father ever mention how he chose the winner?"

"I remember him saying the photographer was a young girl who didn't submit a portfolio. Who just turned up at the last minute. And showed him a single photograph that became sort of a legend. He talked about that photo in all the press conferences but nobody ever saw it, because she…you…would never allow the picture to be displayed publicly."

"The subject matter was very personal," Micah says.

"But not too personal to show to a total stranger? In order to win a contest?" he asks.

There's a taste, acid, like sulfur, in Micah's mouth. "I was betraying something sacred when I handed your father that photograph. I was so greedy I was evil. I knew how extraordinary the picture was and I didn't want to wait my turn—I wanted my career to take off." Micah's voice is softening, trailing away. "Being famous was all I was thinking about…"

The room is slowly filling with an awkward silence. And with shadows. Outside the window, the pale light of afternoon is surrendering to the pearl-gray of evening.

Micah is recalling how, after she let Eric's father see that life-changing photograph, she had also let him undo her blouse. And jam his hand up under her skirt. And shove his fleshy tongue into her open mouth.

And in remembering this, she's needing to know the truth about what actually launched her career.

"When your father talked about the girl who did the album cover, about me," Micah says. "Did he ever mention why I got the job? Was it based purely on how good I was at taking pictures? Or was there something else in the mix?"

"That final album and your part in it is something Dad still talks about," Eric tells her. "And it's always the same story. The job was yours the minute you walked in the door. When he saw the one, single photograph you'd brought."

Micah makes a sound that's somewhere between a laugh and a sob—between relief and anguish.

"I know what kind of guy my dad used to be. There were a lot of women, back in the day. A lot of girls. But he never hired anybody because they were pretty. You got the job because you were a creative powerhouse."

"Thank you for telling me. I've never been sure."

He kisses her lightly. Then says: "No problem."

It's clear now that Eric knows exactly what he and Micah have been talking about. Her questions have told him there was something physical between Micah and his father. There isn't any hostility in his attitude, but he's distant. Somber. In a way that he wasn't a few minutes ago.

"I would've loved to ask you out. To have bought you flowers and invited you to dinner," he tells her.

Micah is thinking that she, too, would have loved it—the innocence of a first date and flowers.

As he's walking her to the door, he's saying: "It's getting dark, will you be warm enough? Will you be all right?"

The only answer Micah gives him is a wave.

When his door closes behind her, Micah is experiencing sorrow. And a sense of strength. She has—quite by accident—faced down the ghosts on Acorn Street: the betrayals she committed there, and the mistakes she made.

And now, she's saying to herself, *it's time to go home.*

∾⦿∾

Micah has climbed the stairs to the room on the third floor of her brownstone. The room that's cool and dark. And spare.

This is the last stop on her journey—the dwelling-place of the person she ultimately needs to settle things with.

Micah is opening the door and turning on the light.

Waiting for her, at the other end of the room, is the woman in the silver dress and pearl-button shoes.

AnnaLee
Glen Cove, Long Island ~ 1986

A WONDERLAND IS WAITING FOR ANNALEE AS SHE AND JACK ARE walking out onto the rolling lawns of Mrs. Jahn's estate—into the splendor of Mrs. Jahn's party.

Tiny pinpoints of light are everywhere. In massive clusters. Netted in the tress and scattered across the grass. Like silvery stars.

And there are pairs of masked harlequins. Dancing through the night, side-by-side. Juggling flurries of slender, golden hoops. While unicyclists in sequined tuxedos are gliding in and out of the crowd. Twirling enormous, glittering batons.

At the edge of the swimming pool—his reflection rippling across its surface like a genie rippling out of a bottle—is a bare-chested man in white satin pants. A fire-eater. Maneuvering a flaming torch into his mouth with a flourish, and a wink.

And there is music. Bright and infectious. Coming from the lantern-lit gazebo in the center of the lawn. A brassy jazz band—playing Cole Porter and the Charleston.

AnnaLee is bewitched—she feels as if she's strolling through a fabulously beautiful fantasy. And, at the same time, she's terribly uncomfortable.

As she and Jack are moving through the sea of guests, all of them costumed in Gatsby-style elegance, AnnaLee is worried that she's too scantily dressed. Too exposed by her outfit. By the plunge of its neckline and the shortness of the skirt.

She's holding tight to Jack's arm, asking: "How silly do I look...?...like Betty Crocker trying to pass as Marilyn Monroe? I look foolish, don't I?"

Jack lifts AnnaLee's fingers from where they're resting on the sleeve of his tuxedo and kisses them, one by one. "Lee, you look like a woman beautiful to the point of being dangerous." Then he adds: "You also look a little green around the gills."

"I have a bad case of nerves. I keep forgetting to breathe," she says. "We have so much riding on tonight."

A ripple of tension moves along Jack's jaw.

He sounds as if he's being coerced as he asks: "Where do we start?"

AnnaLee stiffens. "By mingling."

She knows she has sounded like a general giving an order to an obstinate soldier—but this is a battle she can't let Jack back away from.

It's apparent that Jack is annoyed by her tone. He's looking at the partygoers rather than at AnnaLee, as he's announcing: "I'm a coward. Not a traitor. I won't let you down." Then he mutters: "But first, I need a drink." And he walks away.

Having him march off, without even a backward glance, is worrying AnnaLee. She made it clear, explained it to him in the car—this is a night that requires charm and diplomacy. Jack knows exactly why they've come to this party.

After she told him about the job at Mrs. Jahn's foundation, and about this evening being a greased-wheel audition for that job, Jack had nodded and said: "As much as I hate being treated like a dimwit who can't handle things on his own, I understand why you're doing this, and I know I've brought the situation on myself. Tonight I'll give you what you want, Lee, or die trying."

But now while she is watching Jack (who isn't a drinker) walk toward the bar—defeated and angry, head down and hands in his pockets—the frayed thread that has been connecting AnnaLee to hope is finally breaking. She's seeing how slim the chances are that this evening will work out well.

And she's numb with disappointment.

It takes a long time before AnnaLee moves—and begins, slowly, to maneuver through the crowd.

She's working her way toward the bar. Where Jack is. To tell him she has given up. The battle is over. They're going home.

In this same instant, a silver-haired man and a woman in fuchsia silk have just walked past AnnaLee—she barely notices them; her focus is on Jack. But the woman is suddenly whirling around in surprise, saying: "AnnaLee? Is that you?"

The woman, Mrs. Jahn, the party's hostess and the person AnnaLee had hoped would transform Jack's future, is now giving AnnaLee an enthusiastic hug, telling her: "Oh my goodness! You look completely different. I honestly didn't recognize you."

"It's the wig Persephone found for me, and the makeup. I'm having a hard time recognizing myself."

"And that dress..." Mrs. Jahn's eyes are wide with admiration. "It's outstanding—exceptionally dramatic."

"You're a vision," the silver-haired man at Mrs. Jahn's side tells AnnaLee.

"This is my husband Carl," Mrs. Jahn says. "Carl, this is Persephone's mother AnnaLee."

"Persephone?" Mrs. Jahn's husband asks. "The girl who helped with the decorating?" His admiring gaze is sweeping AnnaLee from head to foot. "You seem far too young to be the mother of a teenager."

"Actually I'm not her mother, I'm her aunt. Persephone is my husband's niece," AnnaLee explains.

"I don't believe it. I could have sworn you were mother and daughter," Mrs. Jahn says.

AnnaLee is mystified. "Really, why?"

"—the way she talks about you. With such sweetness, such love."

For a blink of time the problem of Jack, and the plans for the outcome of this party, don't seem to matter as much—this news about Persephone is making AnnaLee unbelievably happy.

"As a matter of fact," Mrs. Jahn is saying, "Persephone was singing your praises when I was talking with her just a moment ago. She was asking permission to use one of the phones in the house. It sounded like there was an important call she needed to ma—"

Mrs. Jahn has been interrupted by the arrival of an effusive woman in a dress composed entirely of peacock feathers. And over Mrs. Jahn's shoulder, AnnaLee is catching sight of Persephone running across the lawn, in her audacious coral-colored costume.

Persephone is heading in the direction of the Jahn's floodlit, music-filled mansion. And there's something in her body language—a tension—that seems out of place.

AnnaLee is about to leave and go to Persephone—but Mrs. Jahn is intercepting her. Talking about Jack, saying: "I've heard such nice things about your husband from Mrs. Wang. I'd love to meet him, where is he?"

Jack is still at the bar. AnnaLee can see him from where she's standing. He is turned away from her. His shoulders tense, his eyes downcast. "I'm not sure where he is," she tells Mrs. Jahn. "I'll do my best to find him."

AnnaLee is simply being polite—she doesn't have any intention of introducing Jack to Mrs. Jahn. She has abandoned any hope of making this evening a success.

Jack's sullen look and the slumped way he's bent over his drink are showing AnnaLee what a disaster it would be to try to force him to perform for Mrs. Jahn, to charm her. Small talk and hidden agendas are things completely foreign to Jack, not in his nature. The end result would be awkwardness and embarrassment for everyone.

Mr. and Mrs. Jahn have already moved away to visit with other guests—leaving AnnaLee to cross the lawn and walk toward Jack. She isn't accustomed to wearing high heels. And a stabbing, intermittent pain in her left ankle is forcing her to move slowly.

She is utterly and completely disheartened. The strength to continue lifting Jack up is evaporating. She's tired of trying to propel him into being somebody he doesn't know how to be.

When AnnaLee finally reaches Jack's side it's obvious he knows she's there. But he stays hunched over the bar, continuing to sip at his drink. His third. There are two empty glasses at his elbow.

"I want to go home now," AnnaLee tells him.

"Me too," he says.

Everything in AnnaLee is heavy. Worn out.

Jack puts down his half-empty glass and turns around, looking out at the party. "The woman in the purplish-red dress, is that who I was supposed to impress? Is that the magnificent Mrs. Jahn?"

AnnaLee nods. She wants to burst into tears, and fall apart.

He turns back to the bar with a wry smile, and slowly finishes his drink. Then, before AnnaLee fully comprehends what he's doing, Jack is slamming his empty glass onto the bartop. He's leaving— and heading in Mrs. Jahn's direction.

When he's several feet away from AnnaLee he loops back toward her. Holding his hand out, telling her: "Come with me, Lee. I'm always better when you're with me."

AnnaLee is almost afraid to believe what's happening. "Jack, you don't have to do this."

"Come with me, Lee," he's saying. "I want to make you proud."

Just after ten o'clock, AnnaLee is in the car, outside the babysitter's house. Jack is silently bundling a sleeping Bella into AnnaLee's arms. The silence remains unbroken as Jack closes the passenger door and AnnaLee settles Bella onto her lap.

When Jack has come around to the driver's side of the car, he slips behind the wheel and closes the door—turns the key in the ignition, but doesn't put the car into gear.

Jack and AnnaLee haven't spoken, or looked at each other, since they drove away from Mrs. Jahn's estate. It's as if what eventually happened to them there was something so incomprehensible, so far from their norm, it has left them unable to speak.

And they continue to stay that way for a little while longer.

Then AnnaLee asks: "Was it hard?"

And Jack says: "It was like being marched out in front of a firing squad."

Bella stirs, whimpering in her sleep. AnnaLee soothes her, then tells Jack: "I'm sorry it was awful for you."

When Jack responds his voice is rimmed with wonder. "I did it, Lee. I stepped up. I did right by you."

"Tell me again what she said."

Jack laughs. "Lee, I talked to the woman for an hour and a half. You were there, you heard everything."

Somewhere in the region of AnnaLee's heart is the sensation of an expanding shaft of sunlight. Ascending happiness. "Tell me what she said—at the very end."

"She said 'I suspect I've found the perfect person to head the Louella Jahn Foundation and I want to meet with you next week.'" Jack is slowly shaking his head, as if he can't believe what he's saying. "It looks like we're finally on our way, Lee."

In the long-held breath that AnnaLee is releasing, there's an unspoken prayer—*Thank you, God, for this miracle.*

Jack meanwhile is putting the car into gear. And speaking so softly AnnaLee is having trouble making out the words, as he's asking: "Should I be ashamed that I needed three drinks in me before I had the courage to finally be a man?"

AnnaLee and Jack are home now—they've been here for about ten minutes.

AnnaLee is upstairs, tucking Bella into bed.

She is kneeling at Bella's bedside. Her head resting on the pillow beside Bella's. She's being lulled by the buttery scent of Bella's skin, the clean sweetness of her breath.

The room is quiet and perfectly calm.

Bella's eyes flutter open—she seems momentarily startled.

AnnaLee is still in her costume from the party. The wig and the makeup are probably making her look unfamiliar. "Shhh," AnnaLee whispers. "It's me, it's Mommy. Go to sleep, baby. Sleep in heavenly peace. I'm here, watching over y—"

AnnaLee pauses. And listens.

A sound. Very faint. Is coming from outside. The crunch of tires on gravel. As if a car has pulled into the driveway. And stopped.

AnnaLee glances at her watch. She and Jack left the gala early. It's not quite eleven. Too soon for the party to be over and for Rebecca Wang to be bringing Persephone home. AnnaLee goes to the window, raises the linen shade, and looks out. No one. Nothing. Only darkness.

In the time it takes her to lower the shade, AnnaLee's thoughts have already gone back to the conversation with Mrs. Jahn, and to Jack's triumph, and to the brightness that may soon be in their future. Jack is downstairs in the living room. Reading. And AnnaLee is eager to tell him, for a second time, how proud she is of him.

As she's exiting Bella's room, AnnaLee is leaving the door slightly ajar. She wants to be able to hear Bella, if she wakes up.

AnnaLee is moving into the hall—approaching the window at the top of the stairs—a window, like the one in Bella's room, that also overlooks the driveway. As she's passing the window, just about to go down the stairs, AnnaLee is certain she has heard another noise come from outside the house. This one, slightly louder. Faintly more distinct. A sound like a car door being closed.

From this window, AnnaLee has a clear view of the section of driveway that's directly below it. Again, she's encountering exactly what she saw when she looked out of Bella's window—the empty dark of night. But the counterpoint between the muffled sounds and the motionless darkness is making her uncomfortable.

She looks again, more closely. Sees nothing. Wonders if she's imagining things and leaves the window.

AnnaLee is halfway down the stairs when she hears the crash. Coming from the kitchen—from somewhere near the back door.

The sudden noise of breaking glass.

The chilling sound of a window being smashed.

Livvi
Pasadena, California ~ 2012

IN THE WAKE OF THE DISTURBING VISIT FROM CALISTA EARLIER IN the day and the news it brought about Livvi's father being on the brink of death, old wounds have been reopened.

And Livvi is doing her best to hide her pain. Behind a mask of giggles and smiles. She doesn't want to visit any of it on Grace.

For the past two hours Livvi and Grace have been in Livvi's kitchen, baking cookies. Surrounded by flour and vanilla and drifts of sugar. Tomorrow morning, the three of them—Livvi, Grace, and Andrew—are leaving on their trip to Aspen. And Grace is excited about taking the cookies with them because they are Andrew's favorite. Chocolate chip.

Grace is at the counter, standing on a low stepstool, carefully dropping spoonfuls of dough onto a baking sheet.

Livvi has just answered the phone. The call is from David; he's telling her: "You never got back to me about the Manhattan Literary Luncheon. I pulled every string I could think of to make sure you were one of the invited authors. It's next month, December 20, and—"

"David, I know we talked about it and I'm so sorry I forgot to call you." Livvi is wiping sugar from the countertop—her mind on her father. On the fact that he might soon be dead. And that he wants to see her. After all these years. When she thought he didn't even remember she existed.

"This luncheon is important," David is reminding her. "It gets serious press coverage, generates major book club chat on the Internet, which is valuable for you right now. You need to keep people talking, interested. We want to keep your name out there, especially since you still haven't gotten your second book off the ground."

The mention of her inability to get started on a second book is an embarrassment to Livvi. While David has been relentless in work-ing to promote her writing career, Livvi has been doing nothing to help. Her every waking moment has been consumed by the drama with Andrew. And his wife, and his parents.

Livvi knows she's letting David down—letting herself down. But she doesn't know how to fix it. The truth is that she's lost in Andrew's maze of secrets. And delights. And promises.

A part of her is wondering if she is already too far into the maze to ever find her way out.

"Livvi, you should make your travel arrangements right away." There's a subtle persistence in David's voice. "The luncheon is—"

"Can you wait for a minute?" Livvi is asking.

Grace is holding up the baking sheet, showing off wobbly balls of cookie dough, excited for Livvi's approval. Livvi's tucking the phone between her shoulder and her ear. Giving Grace a round of silent applause. And in return, receiving one of Grace's irresistibly enchanting smiles.

"Livvi, this is important. You need to start making plans," David is insisting. "The luncheon is on the twentieth. Right before Christmas. When lots of people will be looking for hotel rooms in New York."

Livvi's thinking that during the week before Christmas Grace will be with Andrew—and with her—and that she promised Grace they would spend every single day together, either at Andrew's house or at Livvi's.

She's hating how ungrateful she seems as she's explaining to David: "I won't be at the luncheon. I can't come to New York next month."

"Oh" is all David says. A single syllable in which there is surprise and irritation—and what sounds like profound disappointment.

After Livvi has ended the call and dropped the phone back into her pocket, she takes the baking sheet from Grace and carries it to the oven.

Grace climbs down from the step stool, following Livvi across the kitchen. "When you were my size, who baked cookies with you?" she asks.

Beneath the surface of lightness in her response there's a cavernous sense of emptiness in Livvi, as she says: "Nobody baked cookies with me, Gracie."

"Then who showed you how?"

"I showed myself." Livvi is back at the kitchen counter now. Gathering the mixing bowls and measuring spoons. "I learned from a book, after I was all grown-up."

Grace observes Livvi for a moment, then climbs onto the step stool and wraps her arms around Livvi's waist.

"This is an extra-special hug," Grace says.

"What for?"

"Because your face looks so sad."

Determined not to feel sorry for herself, Livvi dips her finger into one of the measuring cups and rapidly freckles her cheeks with flour, while she's crossing her eyes and breaking into a goofy grin. Chirping in a cartoon voice: "Me not sad. Me hungry. For cookies!"

Grace bursts out laughing and dots her own face with flour, mimicking Livvi's silly tone. "Me too. I'm hungry for cookies too. I'm—"

Grace's eyes suddenly light with surprise. "Daddy," she calls out. "You're back!"

Andrew has come into the kitchen—Grace is running to him.

And Livvi is seeing that he looks the same as he did on that afternoon in Rolling Hills, in his parents' driveway. He looks beaten up. Depleted.

Livvi is immediately bracing for whatever axe is about to fall. "How come you're back so soon, Andrew? You said you'd be stuck at the office until dinnertime."

Andrew turns to Grace and asks: "Where's Piglet, and your games?"

"In Livvi's bedroom," she says.

"Go in there and play for a while, honey. I need to talk to Livvi."

Grace's eyes dart from Andrew to Livvi—full of alarm. "I want to stay. You can talk. I'll be quiet."

Andrew points Grace toward the door. "Go," he says softly. "I'll be in to get you in a few minutes."

Livvi watches as Grace gives Andrew one last beseeching look. Then circles around him and walks away. Heartbreakingly small and defenseless.

"What's going on?" Livvi asks.

Andrew seems emotionally ravaged. He gestures toward the living room, where their suitcases are stacked beside their skis and poles. And says: "The trip's off."

Instantly. For Livvi. The sensation of falling into the bottomless hole.

While Andrew is saying: "Kayla's not comfortable with the idea of you, me, and Grace going off on what's essentially a family vacation. It's tearing her up."

Livvi's stomach has heaved. She's trying not to choke.

"Olivia, I don't have a choice," Andrew insists. "I've just gotten Kayla to the place where she's agreed to meet with a divorce lawyer. The last thing I want to do right now is make the situation any harder on her than it has to be."

Livvi, for the briefest instant, is thinking of grabbing a knife from the kitchen counter. And...

...and what?

And nothing. Grace is in the next room. Livvi doesn't want to make a scene. She goes back to the sink and begins washing cookie dough out of a glass mixing bowl.

"You have to understand." Andrew's voice is shaking with emotion. "Kayla is my wife, Grace's mother. I can't just trash her life and then turn my back on her. I can't inflict that kind of hurt."

And the hurt in Livvi is crushing her. Bending her over the sink. Pushing down on her like a brick wall.

While Andrew is explaining: "I've spent too much time damaging people I love. What I'm trying to do is make up for that."

He moves closer to Livvi, as if he wants her to look at him. She can't—she doesn't have the strength.

"Olivia, I've run up debts that I'll never come close to being able to repay. I owe a big one to Kayla. I bailed out on her. What I did destroyed her. It's me, it's what I've done, that's made her so bitter and crazy. Which means I also owe a gigantic, unpayable debt to Grace. For putting her in the crosshairs of all of that."

Livvi is barely able to listen to him, as he's saying: "Grace and Kayla aren't the only ones...I owe my sister and my brother too.

Because I wasn't there when they needed me. My mother has every right to keep on making me pay for that. I've taken things from her that are irreplaceable."

Andrew sounds sick with guilt. And shame. "I sneaked away. To have sex. While Katherine and Matthew burned to death. I wasn't anywhere near as drunk as they were that night. If I'd been there, maybe my mother wouldn't have had to bury her only daughter. Along with her first-born son." Andrew pauses, then says: "I'll never be able to get out from under that. I'll owe her until the day I die."

For several moments there is unbroken quiet in the kitchen.

Then Andrew puts his hands on Livvi's shoulders and quickly removes them. As if he isn't sure he has the right to touch her.

"Won't you please talk to me?" he asks.

Livvi shakes her head. Not looking at him. She has no words, no thoughts—only the sensation of the bottomless hole.

"Olivia, listen…this Aspen news, it isn't as bad as it sounds. Kayla understands how excited Grace is about going, and the last thing she wants to do is disappoint her. The trip isn't canceled. Everything is the same. Except for one little detail. Instead of us taking Grace to Aspen, Kayla wants to be the one to take her."

In Livvi's head, a pair of echoes—Calista saying, *"It wasn't cruelty, it was discipline"*…Andrew saying, *"Everything is the same, except for one little detail."*

And Livvi is shouting: "Liar!"

While she's smashing the glass mixing bowl into the sink. While she's whirling around and slamming Andrew with her full weight. Sending him stumbling backward. Into the wall.

"It isn't Aspen that Grace is looking forward to," Livvi is telling him. "What Grace is excited about is the three of us being there together. And you know that!"

Andrew takes a deep breath—walks a short distance away. His voice is full of apology when he says: "I'm flying up with them in the morning, to get them settled. I'll make sure Grace is okay and then come straight home. I'll be back by tomorrow night."

Livvi is looking at Andrew—seeing his unhappiness—hearing James say, *"…be kind to my brother. He's a decent guy who's had a lot of indecent things happen to him."*

There is decency in Andrew. But the decency is crowded in with guilt and weakness. And now Livvi knows that to stay with Andrew is to spend the rest of her life being shuffled aside. Waiting. While he's making room for the women who came before her.

It'll be like going back to Santa Ynez, she's thinking, *always wondering, "Do you see me?" "Do you remember me?" "Do you love me enough to keep me safe?"*

Livvi is turning toward Andrew. Preparing to tell him *"I need to leave you."* But as she's opening her mouth, she's seeing that Grace is in the room.

It's as if Grace has read Livvi's mind. "Don't go away," she's begging. "Be here when I get back."

And Livvi is remembering the little book of dreams and promises wrapped in a white paper cover. She's remembering the promise that said, *Someday when I'm a mommy I'll never run away because I'm selfish and bad. I'll stay and I'll say I love you.*

It was a promise Livvi vowed she would never break—when she became a mother.

But Livvi isn't Grace's mother. Grace already has a mother.

And that—is Livvi's dilemma.

Silver bells. Department store Santas. Early December. The shine of Christmas has arrived in Pasadena. Elves and tinsel. People brimming with holiday cheer. A month has passed since the aborted trip to Aspen.

Livvi and Grace are in a bustling, family-friendly restaurant on Colorado Boulevard. They have just ordered lunch.

Livvi is a little less raw, less wounded. Andrew has done everything in his power to make amends. He has been loving and devoted. And like Livvi, he is also tentative, and shaken. They're both aware that, if it hadn't been for Grace, they might not have found a way to hold on to each other.

Most mornings Livvi and Andrew wake up in the same bed. Most evenings they eat at the same table. Most nights they make fervent love. The chemistry, the attraction, the caring they share is undeniable. What is equally undeniable is that there are now places in Livvi's heart where she's so separate from Andrew that at times he seems to disappear. Places where Andrew is overshadowed. By the demands of his wife and the dictates of his parents. And by Livvi's father. And the fact that he's dying and wants to see her.

Livvi is watching Grace happily exploring *Green Eggs and Ham*, the new book that Livvi has just bought for her. And Livvi is thinking of her father—remembering that it was because of him that she first discovered the charms of Dr. Seuss. And the drama of Dickens. The sly wit of Jane Austen. And the magical realms of Narnia.

It was her father who taught Livvi to read. And in his rows and stacks and piles and shelves of books she found poetry. And history. And the power of ideas.

"I can't wait for you and me to read this story together, Livvi." Grace is glowing with excitement. "I love it when I have a new book!"

"Me too," Livvi says.

Her thoughts are returning to her father, to when she was a child and his books were her lifelines, the magic carpets on which she sailed away to worlds that were clean and sane and full of hope.

And now that I'm an adult, Livvi is thinking, *it's my father's gifts—words and books—that have given me my career.*

For a brief, burning instant Livvi is desperate to see her father. But then she's remembering his silences, and rages. And even though—except for that soul-shredding morning when he lifted her by her hair and threw her across the room—his physical violence was never directed at her, Livvi can't forget the hurt of the emotional wounds he inflicted. She can't forget that her father has never once told her he loved her.

"Okay, guys, time to chow down." The waiter, a skinny man with a nose ring and shaggy haircut, has appeared at the table.

While he's laying out their lunch order, he's saying to Grace: "Tell me if I got everything…two of our grass-fed, organic beef burgers and an order of sweet-potato fries. Right?"

Grace nods enthusiastically.

"And we're splitting a fruit salad," Livvi says.

The waiter hurries away. "Sorry, totally slipped my mind, I'll be right back."

Grace takes only a single bite of her hamburger before reaching for the crayons and drawing paper piled in the middle of the table. Smiling brightly, she announces: "I'm going to make you a picture of the Christmas presents I asked Santa to bring."

"Gracie, we can't do that right now." Livvi apologetically slides the sheet of drawing paper out of the way and replaces it with Grace's lunch plate. "We sort of lost track of time in the bookstore and now we're late. You'll have to draw the picture when you get home. Bree will be here any minute to pick you up."

At the mention of going home, Grace's smile disappears, and her hand instantly travels to her face—her thumb and index finger nervously pinching at the skin just above her eyebrow. It was shortly after the rearranged trip to Aspen that Grace developed this habit.

Livvi's heart aches every time she sees it. She's leaning across the table, wrapping her hand around Grace's. Gently slowing and then stopping the frantic motion of Grace's fingers. "Don't," Livvi murmurs. "There's nothing to worry about. I promise."

Grace seems both hopeful and vaguely troubled. "Daddy says he's getting you something special for Christmas so you won't be mad at him."

Then, in a worried afterthought, as she's pointing toward the front of the restaurant, alerting Livvi to the fact that Bree has arrived, Grace whispers: "I think Daddy's getting you diamonds. Mommy doesn't know. Only me. And Daddy. So don't tell, okay?"

Livvi isn't sure how she feels about this news of Christmas diamonds. An engagement ring, a request from Andrew to become his wife, would be slightly insulting—Andrew currently has a wife. And the gift of earrings, or a necklace, would seem like Andrew was trying to use their glitter to obscure the truth—the fact that Livvi is never quite on solid ground, that at any given moment she can be exiled by the whims of Palos Verdes and Rolling Hills.

And as Livvi is in the midst of thinking these things—

—Bree is saying: "Wow. This truly sucks."

She's slipping into a chair at the table, commenting on the untouched food on Grace's plate. "You guys just got here, huh?"

"Ask for a hamburger too." Grace pushes a menu toward Bree. "And we can stay here for a while and not go home till later. Please?"

Bree checks her watch. There's sincere regret as she's telling

Grace: "No way, doodle-bug. We gotta roll." Bree then looks at Livvi and says: "Sorry."

"Not even a couple more minutes?" Livvi asks.

"I wish," Bree replies. "But I'll be in huge trouble if I get her home late."

As Livvi is calling to the waiter, asking for the check and a carryout box for Grace's lunch, she's being torn apart by Grace's pleading gaze.

While Bree is explaining: "I have to get Grace back in time for the Christmas family portrait. It's this afternoon, at her grandmother's house."

Grace has gone back to her drawing—moving a crayon over the paper in a rapid blur. "Wait, wait," she's begging. "I need to finish this.

"It's for you," Grace tells Livvi. "It's special. For Christmas." She's frantically snatching up one crayon after another. Working as fast as she can.

"It's all right, Grace," Livvi says. "We'll be together on Christmas Eve. You and Daddy and I are going to see *The Nutcracker*, remember? You can give it to me then."

Grace remains intent on her drawing. She doesn't see Bree looking at Livvi, silently saying no. Grace doesn't see what Livvi sees—Bree taking one of the crayons and scribbling something on a napkin.

Bree slides the napkin toward Livvi, showing her the message:

Annual family winter vacation—Bermuda.

Bree's tone is subdued, sympathetic: "He hasn't told you, has he?"

It's as if Livvi is being hit by a speeding train. Everything seems to be happening at once. The news about Bermuda. The waiter handing her the carryout box containing Grace's lunch. Grace insisting she doesn't want to leave, begging Bree to let her stay. Bree producing an iPod from her purse and tucking the ear buds into Grace's ears, saying: "Hey, look what I've got. Muppet songs."

As soon as Grace is distracted by the music, Bree turns to Livvi. "I'm gonna get my Christmas spirit on, and give Andrew the benefit of the doubt. Maybe he didn't tell you about the family trek to Bermuda because he hasn't found out about it yet. I just got the info this morning—from Grace's other parent."

Bree checks to be certain Grace isn't listening, then tells Livvi: "That woman doesn't give a darn about Grace, all she's interested in is hanging on to Andrew." Bree glances at Grace again, then says: "The truth is I'm not a big fan of Andrew's either, but I know how much crap he gets. This time Mommy Dearest is threatening to 'treat' Grace to a trip to Europe—like right this minute—and stay there until after New Year's Eve—if Andrew doesn't agree to be part of the family Christmas in Bermuda."

Bree leans close to Livvi, keeping her voice low. "If Andrew doesn't show up in Bermuda, he won't see Grace for the holidays. And if he fights it, he'll not only get world-class crap from his parents, but he runs the risk of Kayla going all psycho-meltdown and scaring the shit out of Gracie. The whole thing is a monster circle-jerk. I don't get why he doesn't just dump that nut-job and be done with her."

"I don't either," Livvi murmurs.

Bree is instantly apologetic. "I'm sorry I hurt your feelings. I shouldn't have said all that." She stands up, quickly disconnects Grace from the iPod, and lifts her out of her chair. "Come on, doodle-bug, you can finish your drawing in the car."

"But if we leave now, how will Livvi get it? I want her to have it today," Grace frets.

"I'll scan it on the computer, and we'll e-mail it to her. Come on, Gracie, be a good girl. We're gonna be late, we're gonna get in trouble."

Grace runs to Livvi, throwing her arms around her. "I love you." Grace's breath is warm against Livvi's ear.

Then Grace is gone.

Livvi leans forward and rests her head on the cool metal of the tabletop—consumed by the emptiness left by Grace's departure. And by the devastating news that she won't be with Grace, or with Andrew, at Christmas.

It isn't until hours later when Livvi has gone home and is working on Sierra's year-end bills that the feeling of emptiness lifts—and is suddenly replaced by an impulse to break free.

While checking a date on her December calendar, Livvi has discovered a note in the calendar's margin. And it's causing her to recognize something about herself she hasn't clearly seen before. When it comes to Andrew, she's been living her life as if she's still locked in her father's house, as if she's a powerless little girl, with no choice other than to endure whatever new misery is being delivered to her.

Livvi is seeing that her sense of being optionless and trapped doesn't have anything to do with reality—it's completely self-imposed. And this realization is bringing her to an entirely new point of view. *I can't do anything to erase the hurt of being discarded at Christmas,* she's thinking. *But I can definitely do something to make it hurt less.*

The calendar note that Livvi is looking at was jotted down several months ago, when she assumed she'd be with Andrew for the holidays and was postponing any other plans until she knew his exact schedule. It's a penciled, question-marked reference to the Manhattan Literary Luncheon.

When Livvi picks up the phone and calls David to ask if it's too late to change her mind about attending the luncheon, his answer is: "I'll move heaven and earth to make sure you're put back on the list."

"Thank you," Livvi tells him. "I'll book a cheap flight then get to work finding a hotel I can afford."

For the first time in months, she has a direction. A goal. Livvi is putting herself on track to go someplace where she's wanted. And valued. She feels excited. She feels strong.

"You'll be arriving at the height of the Christmas season," David says. "It may be tricky finding a decent place to stay at a reasonable price. But no worries. My grandmother read your book and was crazy about it. She has a big wonderful old house. She'll be thrilled to have you as a guest."

"Thank you doesn't seem like enough, David. But it's all I have. Thank you for everything. I can't wait."

There's a microscopic pause. Then David says: "I'm glad you're coming. What changed your mind?"

"I'll explain when I see you," she tells him.

Livvi suspects that whatever explanation she comes up with won't be the whole truth. Because it's too complicated. Because part of it is about getting away from the past. And part of it is about changing the present—making today something stronger and better than yesterday was. And part of it is about the future. About who Livvi will be after she goes to New Jersey and stands in front of her father. For the final time.

Micah

Boston, Massachusetts ~ 2012

Micah has opened the door to the dimly lit room at the top of the stairs and is in pain. She is finally, at last, in the presence of the woman in the silver dress and pearl-button shoes.

The woman has been in this room—year after year—waiting for Micah to come and to face her. Being with her again after all this time is taking Micah's breath away.

The woman, even though she is Micah's creation, is far more compelling—more vivid and disturbingly enigmatic—than Micah had remembered.

While Micah is crossing the room, there is only the faraway sound of the night wind. Like the murmuring of a distant ghost.

When Micah arrived at a stop in front of the woman—in front of the artist's easel and the photograph it holds. The wind is dying down. The ghostly murmurs, fading away.

Over the course of the past two decades this woman, this picture, has taken on mythological importance to Micah. And to the art world. "The Woman in the Pearl-Button Shoes" is the only existing photograph by the famous Micah Lesser that contains the likeness of a human being.

With a single exception, no one other than Micah has ever laid eyes on this unforgettable image.

It has become an invisible icon. Etched into the world's consciousness by the explosion of publicity that surrounded Micah's cover shot for the history-making rock album. And by the fantastic tale told by Miles Gidney. About the heart-stopping photograph that convinced him Micah was worthy of the job. A work of art he described as "Astounding!"

After Micah, in her ambitious heat, had impulsively showed this photo to Gidney in his house on Acorn Street, she immediately regretted what she had done. Immediately wanted to repent. And knew it was too late.

Which is why, when she returned to her little apartment in Cambridge, she locked the photograph in a closet. And wailed. The way she imagined Judas must have wailed. Feeling the dead weight of those thirty pieces of silver, falling onto his grasping, guilt-stained palm.

And now Micah is wailing again. For the unforgivable wrong she has committed.

The entire scope of Micah's sin is captured in the details of this single, transcendent, and disturbing photograph. It is in the image of the quietly beautiful woman. And in the matrix of dissonance and contradiction that surrounds her. It's in the darkness of the half-shadow into which the woman seems to be retreating. It's in the hope and brightness that are shining in her eyes. It's in the daring, blatantly sexual way in which the woman is dressed—and in how guileless she is. It's in the plunging neckline and provocative gleam of her silvery gown. In the explicit, tantalizing embrace of the fabric as it cups the curve of her hip. It is in the delicacy of her pearl-button shoes. And in the purity of the small detail on the floor, the outline of a child's toy—indistinct but recognizable, hidden in the shadow at her feet. It's in the innocent way the woman is facing the camera—the unquestioning trust she has in the photographer.

Micah is in agony.

While she's gazing at the woman in the photograph, asking: "What was it like for you? At the end, when the terror came? What did you see? Did you know what was happening?"

The thud of her own heart is all that Micah can hear. As she's wondering, *Did you know what I had done?*

AnnaLee
Glen Cove, Long Island ~ 1986

ANNALEE IS HALFWAY DOWN THE STAIRS. FROZEN IN PLACE. Listening to a thud coming from the kitchen, from the area of the back door. Hearing the sudden noise of breaking glass. The chilling sound of a window being smashed.

Now there's muffled commotion. Scuffling footsteps, muttered conversation. Someone—more than one someone—inside the house. Coming nearer.

AnnaLee is suddenly in motion. Racing up the stairs, into the dark of Bella's room.

She's opening the closet door. Pulling Bella's winter blankets from the shelf and piling them onto the floor, in the closet's farthest corner. Making a small nest.

Then AnnaLee is lifting Bella from her bed and carrying her into the closet—laying her on top of the blankets and closing the door. Fervently praying that Bella stays quiet and asleep.

Surely Jack must be aware of what's happening downstairs. He's in the living room. But the only movement, the only sound, that AnnaLee can hear is emanating from the back of the house. From the kitchen.

She quickly leaves Bella's room and hurries down the hall to her own bedroom—the one room upstairs that has a phone. She's trembling, prickling with fear.

When AnnaLee puts the phone's receiver to her ear, the fear spikes. And becomes fever.

There's no dial tone.

Faint sounds are echoing through the earpiece. Footsteps. Low voices. Someone—a man—muttering the word *fuck.*

One of the downstairs phones (either the one in the kitchen or the one in the living room) must have been taken off the hook. AnnaLee has no way to call for help.

She's looking around the bedroom. Searching for something she can use as a weapon.

It's as if she's surrounded by objects in a trivia museum.

A hairbrush on the dresser. A nightgown at the end of the bed. Framed photographs on the nightstand. A leather-bound calendar on the arm of a chair, open to today's date, August 30. Nothing of substance. Nothing she can use to defend herself.

And with every passing second the noise from downstairs—the threat beneath her feet—is getting louder and closer.

Where's Jack? Why haven't I heard his voice in all of this? AnnaLee is frantic. *What will happen if Bella doesn't stay asleep and out of sight... in her hiding place?*

AnnaLee has left her bedroom and is heading for the stairs. Her only option is to go down into the kitchen. And face whatever is there. Do whatever it takes to keep Bella from being found.

She comes down the staircase quickly. When she reaches the bottom step, the hallway in front of her is in semi-darkness. The door leading to the kitchen is to her left—slightly ajar. Allowing only the faintest bit of light to escape. The entry to the living room is on her right. Dark and soundless.

It seems to AnnaLee that someone is lurking at the other end of the hall. The danger doesn't stop her. She's being propelled by the rapid, rhythmic beating of her heart…*Keep Bella safe. Keep Bella safe. Keep Bella safe.*

AnnaLee is stepping off the last stair. Into the darkened hallway. And a woman is rushing at her. Out of the gloom. Panicking her. Causing AnnaLee's eyes to widen and her mouth to fly open.

Within a microsecond, AnnaLee is understanding that what she's seeing is her own reflection. In a mirror. At the far end of the hall. A reflection she didn't recognize because she's still dressed in her glittering costume from the gala.

But this realization has come too late.

At the first glimpse of the woman in the mirror, AnnaLee has screamed.

And that scream is why someone is opening the kitchen door, flooding the hallway with light.

AnnaLee, her back pressed to the wall, is moving as rapidly as she can toward the living room. Toward her only hope of safety. Toward Jack.

And she's thinking as she continues to move that her chances of getting away, of survival, are nonexistent.

AnnaLee is watching the person in the kitchen doorway raise a gun. And aim it at her.

The brute solidity of the gun, the matte-black of its squat barrel, the darkness inside the neat circular opening at its tip, are terrifying.

But even more frightening is what AnnaLee is seeing out of the corner of her eye.

The thing that's taking shape in the shadows.

At the bottom of the stairs.

Livvi

East Norwich, New York ~ 2012

*I*T IS CHRISTMAS EVE—CHILLY IN THE ATTIC. IN SPITE OF THAT, Livvi is being slow in descending the attic ladder, taking as long as possible before arriving at the second floor landing. She wants to delay the moment that will reveal what's waiting for her on the ground floor of this house. At the bottom of the stairs.

Savoring the moment just before discovering a surprise, and being certain that the surprise will be something delightful, chosen especially for her, is new to Livvi. And yet, like so much else that has happened to her in this house, the sensation seems faintly familiar. Like something she once experienced. Long ago. In a dream.

There is stability here, and serenity. Livvi has been welcomed with open arms. It's as if after all these years she is in the home—in the peace and joy—that was Olivia's heart's desire.

Every morning since coming to this lovely old house on Long Island where David's grandmother lives, around nine o'clock Livvi has found a gift waiting at the bottom of the stairs. On the first morning, the day Livvi attended the Manhattan Literary Luncheon, the gift was an antique book of poetry. A slender volume holding the faded scent of cigar smoke and gardenias. It had as its bookmark a flattened length of gold braid—a delicate artifact that might have once graced a debutante's gown or the uniform of a dashing young naval officer. On another morning, the surprise had been a nosegay of holly and pepper berries, tied with a red ribbon. Yesterday, it was a glossy brown paper bag no larger than a drinking glass. Filled to the brim with hand-made caramels. Rich and mellow with sugar and butter, and sparkling with the taste of sea salt.

The gifts are from David. All of them small and thoughtful. And, each in its own way, perfect. He has never mentioned that he is their giver. And Livvi, although she has expressed how charmed she is by them, has never directly acknowledged that she knows who they're from. The giving and the receiving has become a sort of innocent flirtation. And the whimsical manner in which the gifts arrive, seeming to appear out of nowhere, at the bottom of the stairs, like magic, has created a wonderful anticipation in Livvi. An enticing sense of possibility.

Which is why, now, as she's seeing that there's absolutely nothing waiting for her, she's feeling a twinge of disappointment. She wasn't ready—just yet—to lose the pleasure of those small surprises.

Livvi is holding a heavy lace tablecloth that she has just taken out of the attic. As she's starting down the stairs, she's wishing that David's delightful gifts and her fun in discovering them could have gone on a little longer. And she's wondering if there's some particular reason that David chose today as the end-point for their lighthearted version of hide-and-seek.

Several moments pass before Livvi comes back to reality and realizes she isn't alone anymore.

David has just appeared at the foot of the stairs. Holding a little white dog in his arms.

The dog is young and bright-eyed, wearing a garland of miniature silver bells around its neck. And David is telling Livvi: "This is your Christmas present."

David seems to immediately understand the wonderment in Livvi. The unspoken question that's asking, *"How did you know?"*

And he's saying: "One day, right after we'd closed the publishing deal on your book, we were at lunch and you mentioned that when you were a little girl you'd always dreamed of having a dog. A small white one, with a curly tail."

Livvi has now reached the bottom of the stairs—David is putting the dog into her arms. "This one doesn't have a curly tail but—"

"She's exactly what I wanted."

Livvi is overcome with happiness. Amazed by this gift—and its simple perfection.

It takes Livvi a moment before she can find her voice and ask: "What's her name?"

"She belonged to a guy in our office who just found out he landed a job in France. He only had her for a couple of days. She doesn't have a name yet."

"I think I'll call her Granger," Livvi says. "It's the name of someone...something...that was very special to me."

"A man?" David asks.

"No, a woman," Livvi explains. "A woman I didn't know, but dearly loved."

Livvi is looking into David's eyes. And at first, what she's seeing is fascination, as if he's intrigued by the things she's just said. Then she sees something else—centered exclusively on her. Something steady and pure. Like the glow from a sea of freshly lit candles.

It's as if she's being shown a beautiful piece of heaven.

Livvi's voice is soft, incredulous. "That lunch...when I told you about wanting a dog...that was more than two years ago. How could you have remembered? For all this time...?"

David's tone is as soft as Livvi's, and as full of wonder. "There was no way I could forget. I spend every day thinking about you."

All there is in Livvi is awed stillness. As if she is waking up in the dawn of an unexpected new world.

David seems worried by her silence—nervous that he's said too much.

Livvi has no words—only sensation—the sudden desire to be kissed by David. And to touch him.

But the moment is passing; the silence is going on too long. David is filling it with small talk. "It's almost nine, you're dressed like you're headed out for a run. I thought you always ran first thing in the morning."

The shift in the mood is both a relief and a letdown. Livvi's not sure where they should go from here—isn't sure where she wants to go. She's trying to figure out what it was that just happened between them. Was the expression in David's eyes, and her reaction to it, something real? Or something she simply imagined?

While she's working to put the pieces of this puzzle together, she's telling David: "I was out the door and running before dawn, I just haven't had time to change. I've been busy helping your grandmother get ready for tonight."

"Tonight will be unforgettable. Grandma's Christmas Eve dinner is always the best part of the holidays." David seems perfectly content to keep things light and conversational. He's picking up the lace tablecloth from the spot on the floor where Livvi dropped it in her excitement over the dog. "So the old girl has you bringing the lace tablecloth down from the attic, huh? Has she put you to work polishing her great-grandmother's silver too?"

"I did that right before I went up to the attic…" Livvi's voice has trailed off. She's wondering if, in what happened between them a few seconds ago, David really was offering her more than simple friendship. And she's being startled by the discovery that some part of her may be open to that offer.

"Fetching the tablecloth and polishing great-great-grandmother's silver…that's quite an honor. Grandma is obviously crazy about you. Those are chores she usually reserves for family."

The reference to family shifts Livvi's thoughts to Andrew. And to the awful afternoon in his parents' driveway. To his wife, and the way in which Andrew is shackled to her. It's making Livvi think about how sweet it would be. Being with a man available to love and be loved—without guilt or shame. A man who would truly include her as part of his family.

And in thinking about family, Livvi is thinking about the only relative she has. Her father. She's thinking about the fact that he's dying, that she'll soon be an orphan.

And in this same moment, David is saying: "Arrange the place cards at dinner tonight so you're sitting next to me."

The kitchen of David's grandmother's house is bathed in a clear winter's light, fragrant with the scent of rosemary and red wine. David has been gone for an hour or so. And Livvi is helping his grandmother, Evelyn, prepare for tonight's Christmas Eve dinner.

Evelyn is at the old-fashioned stove—adding the rosemary and the wine to a beef bourguignon already savory with pearl onions, and mushrooms, and fresh garlic.

Evelyn's eyes are a pale blue-gray. Her smile is radiant. Her skin, lined and thinning, pearly with age. She is tiny, barely five feet tall. Her hair is silver-white—and she is beautiful. And in the time that

Livvi has been in her house, she has made Livvi feel beautiful too. Because she has made Livvi feel loved.

Evelyn is glancing up at Livvi, asking: "How are you doing, sweet girl?"

"I'm getting there," Livvi tells her. "But I don't understand why it's taking so long." She's methodically chopping carrots into inch-long pieces, each one diagonally cut at the top and bottom—doing her best to match the sample Evelyn has left on the cutting board.

"Well, I'd say you're doing just fine." Evelyn is at Livvi's side now, her hand closing over Livvi's, adjusting Livvi's grasp on the knife. Guiding it in a flowing motion that's sectioning the carrot into picture-perfect pieces. Evelyn's touch is warm—filled with affection.

And Livvi is imagining, just for a minute, that she belongs here. At Evelyn's side. Resting in her kindness. Wrapped in her caring.

For an instant, Livvi is able to capture the sublime feeling of being the daughter of a wise and loving mother.

But she can't hold onto it. There's too much going on. The puppy, Granger, is bounding in circles around Livvi's legs—and darting across the room to nuzzle Evelyn's fingertips. While Evelyn is saying: "It's nice to have new life in the house, especially at this time of year."

Then she's telling Livvi: "I'm glad you decided to stay with us for Christmas."

"Are you sure I haven't worn out my welcome?" Livvi asks. "I honestly thought I'd only be here for a couple of days, only as long as it took to go to the Literary Luncheon and have a quick meeting with my editor, but—"

"—but every day, either David or I have managed to find a way to keep you from leaving." Evelyn has slipped her arm around

Livvi and is giving her a quick hug. "I've loved having you here with me."

There's a hint of wistfulness in Evelyn's voice when she adds: "That's one of the downsides of old age, it can get a little bit lonely."

Livvi is surprised by this. "But David is in and out of here all day. He has coffee with you every morning."

Evelyn's laugh is merry, spontaneous. "He's here because you're here, Livvi. David is a devoted grandson but his life is in the city. The only reason he's twenty minutes away, suddenly busy fixing up that old beach cottage, is because he wants to be near you. He inherited that place from a miserable old aunt who passed away years ago—this is the first time he's set foot in it since her funeral."

Evelyn is moving away from Livvi, as if she wants to observe Livvi's reaction while she's saying: "David is in love with you. You do know that, don't you?"

There's a flutter in Livvi. For a moment she isn't in the kitchen anymore. She's at the bottom of the stairs hearing David's voice—*"I spend my life thinking about you."* And she's feeling that unexpected stir of desire. The desire to be kissed by him, and to touch him.

"Livvi? Did you hear what I said?" Evelyn asks.

Livvi nods. She has gone to sit at the kitchen table and is running her hand over its surface—wood worn smooth by the generations who have gathered around it to rejoice. And to grieve. To grow up and to grow old.

The knowledge that she may one day be invited into this house as part of this family and the feeling that she has no right to that invitation are making Livvi heartsick. As she's explaining to Evelyn: "There's someone else."

Evelyn takes the chair beside Livvi's and says: "Earlier this week when you asked if it was all right to have a package delivered to you at this address, did that have anything to do with the someone else?"

"In a way. He has a little girl, Grace. Her nanny sent me a text that Grace wanted to mail me a Christmas present."

The thought of Grace, and of how much Livvi loves her, and of how far away she is, is bringing tears to Livvi's eyes.

"This man, Grace's father," Evelyn says. "Do you love him?"

"I'm not sure. I used to. Without question. But I haven't loved him that way for a while. The way I love him now is different. It's complicated."

"Why are the two of you not together at Christmas?"

"He's in Bermuda with his family. He's still married, and his wife is very upset. He doesn't live with her but..."

Livvi isn't sure how to finish—there seems to be no way to tell the story and have it make any sense.

"I've heard you at night, crying out in your sleep," Evelyn says. "Is he the reason?"

Livvi shakes her head. "No, it's a nightmare I have sometimes. I see a woman with a silver gown and dark hair. And red, red lipstick. There's something horrifying about her and I don't know what it is."

Granger, the little dog, has jumped into Livvi's lap and is laying his head on Livvi's arm while Evelyn is saying: "I can only guess the nightmares you must have lived through."

Evelyn sees Livvi's surprised look and tells her: "I read your book. I'm eighty-nine, and I've figured out some things along the way. The pain, the level of loss in that book, was too raw. Too clear. It couldn't have simply been imagined, you had to have lived it."

Evelyn takes Livvi's hands in hers and holds them tightly. "It's such a terrible thing. No one deserves such a beginning."

"And I can't get away from it," Livvi says. "I feel like there's a part of me that's broken, and ugly, because of where I came from. Because of the things I learned there."

Livvi is aching as she's asking: "Evelyn, how does God decide? How does he choose who to bless and who to punish? Why did he say to your children, 'I want you to be born into light and love,' and say to me, 'For you, I want darkness. I want your mother to run away and never look back. For you, I want pain you'll never forget.'"

Evelyn puts her arms around Livvi and holds her. "No one knows the answer to that question. But I suspect that God, and the lives we're born into, are far more complicated than we can understand. Perhaps this life isn't what we think it is. Maybe it doesn't begin with our birth and end with our death. Maybe it's only a fraction of some larger story. And it doesn't contain enough information for us to really know, for sure, about God's love, or God's fairness."

Evelyn again takes Livvi's hand. "Deciding what sort of story is being told by our time on earth might be like looking at a few seconds of an intricately made movie. And assuming we know all there is to know from having glimpsed only that tiny snippet. It's entirely possible we were somewhere else before we were born, and we'll be somewhere else after we die. And what appears to be senseless and unfair to us now may, in a larger context, take on quite a different meaning."

Evelyn stops and wipes away Livvi's tears. "No matter how painful your life has been, you have the choice to learn from your past and then leave it. You have the choice. Every day. To love and be loved. To find your purpose. To work and to give. And to shape your world into something that's quite remarkable."

The kiss that Evelyn places on Livvi's cheek is light and quick. "I've been watching you carefully in the time you've been here—and

I know the person you are. You didn't come away from your beginnings broken, or ugly. Miraculously…you've come away strong and
filled with love. Find your purpose, Livvi. Use the power of your
love to fulfill it."

After a while, when there doesn't seem to be anything more to
say, Evelyn leaves and goes into the dining room to arrange the
place cards for Christmas Eve dinner. Livvi stays at the kitchen
table. Thinking about the things that Evelyn has told her. Thinking
about loving and being loved. About Andrew. And Grace. She's
thinking about the past, and about the future. And she's thinking
about David.

Being a part of David's family Christmas Eve dinner has been like
stepping into a fantasy for Livvi. Every moment of it could have
been taken from a greeting card. The long dining room table with
its white lace cloth and shining silver. The centerpiece of scarlet
roses. The heirloom wine glasses, artfully mismatched, sparkling
in the light of ivory-colored candles. The dinner—Evelyn's beef
bourguignon and a butter lettuce salad scattered with candied
walnuts and pomegranate seeds. The dessert—little, sugar-frosted
ginger cakes.

All night long—the laughter of a big, close-knit family. Countless
bits of conversation beginning with the phrase "Remember the fun
we had when…" And the members of this same lovely family raising their glasses in a toast: "To Livvi, welcome!"

And as dinner was ending, there was Livvi catching sight of
David's smile—and experiencing a happiness that could hardly
be contained.

It's the same happiness that Livvi is experiencing now, when dinner is over, and she and David and his family are in Evelyn's living room, decorating the Christmas tree that's just been brought in from the outside. A tree that is snow-dusted and cold—filling the air with the smell of fresh pine.

David's mother, a woman with violet-colored eyes and a charming openness, is layering the tree with garlands of golden ribbon while she's saying: "Having you with us tonight is a treat. I hope you come back often."

David's sister, a pretty, young wife and mother, is calling out: "If you're in the city next week, Livvi, and in the mood to go shopping, let me know. I'll show you where all the good sales are."

David's father, affable and ruddy-faced, is near the fireplace with two of David's uncles—in a lively discussion about politics and sports. Several of David's aunts are nearby, exchanging pictures of children and grandchildren.

David is in a circle of cousins playing a boisterous game of Trivial Pursuit, talking about getting together in Manhattan tomorrow for their long-standing Christmas tradition, brunch at the Plaza and then ice skating in Central Park.

Evelyn, as she's passing Livvi, is whispering: "Merry Christmas, sweet girl."

I'm in a dream, Livvi is thinking. *And I don't ever want to wake up.*

But someone is tapping on her shoulder. Calling her away from the dream and back to reality. One of David's nephews, a bashful middle-schooler, is informing Livvi: "There's a person at the front door asking for you."

While she's walking toward the door, Livvi is assuming this must be a mistake. She doesn't know anyone on Long Island other than the people in this house, and no one outside of this house knows her.

But then.

Livvi sees who it is that's waiting for her. And she is flabbergasted.

It's Bree, Grace's nanny. Saying: "I wanted to make sure this was the right place."

Livvi has no idea what Bree is talking about—but she's noticing that a cab is idling in the driveway.

"I wanted to make sure this was the right address." Bree glances at the cab then back at Livvi. "It's been hell. Andrew brought up the divorce the minute we got to Bermuda. Kayla has been screaming at him ever since."

Bree glances at the cab again. "This is my Christmas present to Grace."

Livvi's heart leaps. "Grace is here?"

"Yeah. We hopped a ride on the family plane. I'm kind of dating the pilot. It was like a two-hour flight. No big deal."

"And all of this was okay with Andrew? And Grace's mother?"

"Actually, I didn't tell anybody we were coming."

Livvi can't believe what she's hearing.

"It's okay. I left a note." Bree is shrugging, making an exasperated palms-up gesture. "When he finds it, Andrew will be glad Gracie's with you. The grandparents'll huff and puff—for like half an hour. And Kayla will say all the right 'concerned mommy' things and basically not give a shit. She'll probably do a little secret dance. Like I told you, all she really cares about is being with Andrew. And now she gets to have him all to herself for Christmas Day. She'll love it."

"Bree, are you sure...?"

"Hey. Other than Andrew, the only person raising Grace for the last three years has been me. It's why her mother hired a full-time, live-in nanny. She's too busy being rich and crazy to worry about where her kid is." There is a triumphant defiance in Bree as she adds: "Even if I get fired for this, it'll be worth it. Because tomorrow morning Gracie's gonna have exactly what she wanted for Christmas. She'll be waking up someplace happy, with you."

Livvi is already running to the cab.

She's opening the rear door, eagerly reaching for Grace, who's curled up on the backseat, fast asleep.

David is in the entryway of the house. Calling to Livvi, asking: "What's going on? What is it...?"

Livvi is gathering Grace into her arms—telling him: "It's a Christmas miracle."

After taking Grace from the backseat of the cab the rest of the night passes in a blur, events flashing by like falling dominos.

...Livvi tucking Grace, half-asleep, into the four-poster bed in Evelyn's guest room. The small, cozy place where Livvi has been staying for the past week.

...Grace's eyes fluttering open, and, for the briefest of moments, that solemn, earnest look of worry and concern. Then—as Grace understands that it's Livvi who is there—the dreamy smile. And Grace's slow drift back into sleep.

...The call from Andrew. The sound of his voice, hoarse and distraught. His words a rushed tumble of emotion. "Olivia, I've been worried out of my mind. Since you went to New York, you haven't returned a single phone call. I'm glad Grace is with you. She needs you. I need you. I love you like I've never loved anyone before. I'll make all of this up to you. I give you my word. Don't throw me away. Just don't throw me away."

...The sense of safety in that four-poster bed—lying with Grace snuggled close. Listening to the tick and sigh of the fire that David has laid in the little fireplace in the corner. Hearing him say, "Sweet dreams, Livvi," as he's preparing to drive away into the winter night.

...The sound of Evelyn's murmur at the door. Just before dawn. Asking, "Livvi, are you awake?" Evelyn in the glow of the firelight. Looking like a Christmas sprite with her white hair and holly-green bathrobe. Holding a pair of gossamer butterfly wings that are shimmering and pale-pink. Telling Livvi, "These are for Grace, from Santa." And then, with a twinkle in her eye, saying, "I have glitter and glue and know how to use them. But I promise you, these are straight from the North Pole."

...Evelyn wanting to know if Livvi has slept. Livvi looking down at Grace, nestled at her side. Saying, "I'm too happy to sleep." Evelyn gently advising Livvi, "You have a lot to sort out." Livvi murmuring, "I don't know where to begin." Evelyn saying, "A nice, long walk is where I always used to begin."

...Evelyn pulling a chair close to the bed. Taking Grace's hand with a carefully light touch. Ensuring that Grace's sleep will be undisturbed. And whispering, "I'll watch over her, you go..."

These are the images flowing through Livvi's mind as she's jogging the quiet streets that are leading her away from the serenity and safety of Evelyn's home.

Dawn has broken and Livvi is moving briskly toward the rising sun, the light of the new day, a silver-white gleam. Her face is tingling with the Christmas cold. Her breath leaving puffs of fog in the morning air.

She's entering the town's business district. Slowing her pace to a walk as she's coming onto Main Street.

The storefronts are charming. Each one scrubbed and pretty. Dressed in pine boughs and plaid ribbons. Livvi is passing a drugstore and a real estate office. And a brick-fronted restaurant decorated with wreaths of sparkling pin-lights.

Farther down the street is a store that appears to belong to a decorator. A shop with a dark green door recessed between a pair of wide, multi-paned windows. While Livvi is walking toward the store she's noticing, in one of the windows, an Aubusson carpet draped over a stately Federalist sideboard.

In the other window, there is a delicate Venetian-glass vase filled with out-of-season peonies. And just behind the vase—there's a painting. A full-length portrait. The style and colors are clearly from another era. A card tucked into the frame identifies the subject of the painting as a young heiress named Miriam Moran and the year of the painting's completion as 1922.

As Livvi is coming closer to the window.

And to the painting.

She's horrified.

Everything is there. The dress shimmering like a column of star-light. The high-heeled shoes fastened with a strap at the instep, each strap, anchored by a single pearl button. The glittering bracelets. The chestnut brown hair styled with a C-shaped curl on each of the woman's cheeks. And the lips that are fiery red.

Livvi is experiencing an upheaval that's racing from the soles of her feet to the crown of her head.

The woman in the pearl-button shoes is no longer an apparition haunting the dark of Livvi's nights. She is a reality. Existing in the cold clear light of Christmas day.

Micah

Boston, Massachusetts ~ 2012

THE COLD REALITY OF WHAT SHE'S DOING IS HITTING MICAH LIKE a blast of Arctic air. She wants to be rid of this man hovering at the foot of her bed, in his dark-rimmed glasses and black Savile Row suit. The bed is draped in layers of orange-hued cashmere and snowy Egyptian cotton. He looks like a vulture in a flower garden.

His voice is sharp with irritation as he's reminding Micah: "My clients made it clear there was a deadline on this." He glances at Micah's assistant Jillian, who's sitting in a chair near the head of the bed. "There have been countless telephone conversations. Countless emails."

He returns his full focus to Micah. "It's unfortunate you've delayed things to the point where we have run out of time and I've been forced to come here on Christmas morning—to take possession on a delivery that should have been made months ago."

Even though Micah knows the purpose of this meeting, even though she reconfirmed its terms late last night, even though up until this very moment she fully intended to give the man what he has come to take, Micah is now deciding she can't do it.

To go through with this transaction would be a self-serving sin.

"You can't have her." Micah's voice is faint. She's weak; so ill she can barely speak.

"Her…?" the man asks.

Jillian gives Micah a pain pill and a sip of water, then tells the man: "In the contract, the print is called 'Photo Number 101' but Miss Lesser refers to the piece as 'The Woman'…'The Woman in the Pearl-Button Shoes.'"

The man is ignoring Jillian—looking at Micah as if she's out of her mind. "Miss Lesser, this new museum will house the world's premiere collection of photographic images. The main gallery will bear your name and have your finest work on permanent display. For generations, people will come to the Micah Lesser Pavilion to see Micah Lesser's art—art made by a master photographer. And the centerpiece of that, the Holy Grail, will be 'Photograph Number 101.' An image that has become a legend. Without that photograph we will not honor our contract with you."

He fixes Micah with an icy stare. "If you refuse to relinquish this photograph, you will be turning your back on immortality."

Micah's thoughts are traveling to the spa in Newport—to Christine. The first person Micah betrayed on her clawing journey to immortality. Micah is hearing herself say to Christine, *"As good as you were, I was better. I'm the one who deserved to make history."*

Now Micah's memory is returning her to the house on Acorn Street…*and she is twenty-three. The photograph propped up on Miles Gidney's desk is the photo of the woman in the pearl-button shoes. With one hand Gidney is pulling Micah's blouse open to reveal her breasts. He's shoving his other hand under her skirt and plunging his tongue into her open mouth. While Micah is staring into space. With a smile in her eyes. She's picturing her name in headlines—right beside the word "Famous."*

Then Micah is remembering herself, again, in that same house. A short time ago. Telling Gidney's son Eric, *"I was betraying something sacred when I showed your father that photograph. But I did it anyway. Because I was so greedy I was evil."*

And the man in the black Savile Row suit is asking: "What's it going to be? Do I leave here with the photograph or not?"

Micah isn't answering him. She's returning to the moment in which the photograph was created...*she's feeling the weight of the camera in her hands and the brush of her eyelashes against the viewfinder. The camera shutter is clicking, and the words "Oh my God" are coming out of her mouth. Because she's startled. Overwhelmed by the indescribable, haunting beauty of the image she has just captured—and by how passionately she loves the woman on the other side of the lens.*

And the man in the Savile Row suit is announcing: "Without 'Photograph Number 101,' there will be no Micah Lesser Pavilion. By not allowing us to have that photograph, you are walking away from the pinnacle of your creative fame."

Micah—who has always hungered, who will always hunger, to have her talent held higher than anyone else's—is struggling to sit up straight. Grappling for strength. As she's telling the man hovering at the foot of her bed: "Go away. It's over. You can't have her."

Jack

Glen Cove, Long Island ~ 1986

Jack is fighting to keep from falling facedown onto the freshly mounded earth of AnnaLee's grave.

The sun is at the edge of the cemetery. Fading and golden-low. Jack is alone. The only remaining mourner. A late summer wind is beginning to scatter flowers from the bouquets that were laid only a few hours ago—at the conclusion of AnnaLee's funeral. When Jack was watching her coffin being delivered into the ground.

Jack is staggered with grief, snatching at wind-blown petals and blossoms that are sailing beyond his reach. He's losing his footing, his balance. And as he is being brought to his knees, he's noticing something he hadn't seen before—two uniquely different objects that have been left on AnnaLee's grave. Tucked in among the flowers.

The object closest to Jack is a sheet of lavishly thick paper containing a set of brush-stroked Chinese characters: each of the strokes precise and flawless. The other item is near the foot of the grave, glinting like a jewel in the setting sun. A delicate, copper-wire cross.

The attendance at AnnaLee's funeral was sizeable—large numbers of people crowded the church and the graveside. Jack has no clue as to where these two offerings have come from. But he knows he somehow needs to find a way to take them home and keep them safe.

It will be dark before he'll be able to succeed in grasping each of the items and maneuvering it into a coat pocket.

His shoulder is broken—his hands, clumsy with bandages.

The drapes are tightly closed. The only intrusions into the almost total darkness are three slim fingers of moonlight. Coming from the spot where a drapery panel has been torn away from a terrace door—and there are narrow gaps in the pieces of plywood covering the door's shattered glass.

In a corner of the darkened room, a male voice is announcing: "Arrests have been made in connection with the murder of a young mother who died at her Glen Cove home during a burglary last week."

Jack is huddled in an old leather chair. Staring blankly into the bluish glow of the television. While the man on the screen is saying: "This is the news for September 3, 1986. I'm Anthony Sasso."

Jack's bandaged hands are limp in his lap. His feet are about eight inches apart, planted flat on the floor. He is in the same rumpled suit he wore to AnnaLee's funeral. Dirt from her grave is dusting the tips of his shoes and caught in the cuffs of his pants. His hair is uncombed. He has the deadened look of a refugee waiting to be taken to a prison camp.

The reporter's face has disappeared from the television screen, replaced by footage of three handcuffed individuals being hustled into a police station—a thin, heavily tattooed man in his mid-twenties, a slightly younger man with spiked orange-colored hair, and a cold-eyed teenage girl. The reporter's dispassionate monotone continues to drone on. "Being held in connection with the murder is twenty-five-year-old Marco Brigante...twenty-two-year-old Sean Thomas...and eighteen-year-old—"

At the sight of these people, Jack, with his feet still flat on the floor, moving only his upper body, has leaned over the arm of the leather chair and vomited. The vomit has landed in a bucket—the slowly filling receptacle into which he has been vomiting for hours.

Now there's footage of Jack's neighbor, a beefy middle-aged dentist, a former football player, looking into the television camera and explaining: "My wife and I were out back having a glass of wine. We heard shots coming from next door." The man pauses, flushed with emotion. "Jack's a hero. The first thing I saw when he was coming toward me—asking us to call for help—was that his face and both of his hands were bleeding. He was banged up like you wouldn't believe. He put up one hell of a fight trying to keep those punks from murdering his wife. AnnaLee. Her name was AnnaLee..."

"...her name was AnnaLee," Jack murmurs.

He is imagining—in ghastly staccato flashes—what must have happened in the last few seconds of her life.

...AnnaLee coming down the stairs in her dazzling, shimmering dress, the costume from the gala.

...Someone—the man with the tattoos or the fellow with the orange hair or perhaps the girl—in the kitchen doorway. Raising that matte-black gun. Aiming it at AnnaLee's heart.

...AnnaLee in terror. Inching along the wall. Trying to make her way to safety. To the living room. To the place where Jack is.

...The BANG. The fired bullet.

...AnnaLee's flesh tearing open—a steel bolt exploding in her chest.

...AnnaLee sliding down the wall, helplessly watching a shape emerge from the shadows at the bottom of the stairs—the shape of something she thought was safely tucked away.

...Then AnnaLee's lips—her beautiful, beautiful lips—slowly parting. Preparing for a scream she won't live long enough to utter.

The shape emerging from the shadows is Bella.

Jack believes that what he is imagining is exactly what happened. Because he knows Bella was upstairs, asleep, when the trouble began. And he also knows that when he came back into the house with the police, after AnnaLee was dead, the first thing he saw was Bella. Crouched at the bottom of the stairs.

And while these horrific visions of Bella—and AnnaLee, and AnnaLee's death—are flashing through his mind, whatever in Jack that was clean is turning to rot. Whatever was whole is breaking. Whatever was honest is being forever corrupted. Whatever was alive is dying.

Livvi

East Norwich, New York ~ 2012

*I*MAGES OF THE SHIMMERING DRESS AND FIERY-RED LIPS ARE STILL flashing through her mind, transforming whatever certainty there was in Livvi into chaos.

It happened over twelve hours ago—plenty of time for the shock to subside. And for Livvi to have calmed down. After seeing the woman's portrait in that store window, in Oyster Bay. But the shock is steadily growing stronger.

A fantasy in a nightmare has become reality.

And the eeriness of it, the fright of both the nightmare and the reality, have taken Livvi's thoughts into the past. Into those nights when she would wake up screaming. And her father would already be on the other side of her doorway. In the dark. With a look that was soft like sadness then harsh like the sharp edge of a stone.

The memory of that look—the sorrow and the stone in her father's eyes—is the thing that has now compelled Livvi to find him. And confront him, before it's too late.

The cell connection is bad. Calista's voice sounds thready and distant. She's asking: "Do you need me to repeat the address?"

"I have it," Livvi says. She's looking at the note she's just made. The numbers and letters seem to be swimming on the page.

Livvi is afraid. Afraid of the woman she sees in her nightmare—and of the woman she saw in the portrait—and of what the explanation for their existence could possibly be.

She's tightening her grip on the phone to steady herself as she's ending the call—saying to Calista: "Tell my father I'm coming to see him."

When Livvi puts the phone down, she's turning toward David's grandmother. "I need to ask you a question, Evelyn. How do I—" Livvi stops, takes a deep breath. She doesn't want Grace to see how upset she is.

Grace, in this moment, is happily content. She's wearing the pink butterfly wings sent by Santa, and delivered by Evelyn, early this morning; and she has Granger, Livvi's little dog, snuggled in her lap. Grace is at Evelyn's kitchen table, with David. Eating ginger cake and playing checkers. Using a red felt-tipped marker to keep score—on the back of a Christmas card.

And while Livvi is watching the two of them she's struck by how accepting David is of Grace's presence in his grandmother's house, how unquestioning and welcoming he has been.

As if he senses Livvi's gaze, David looks up and smiles at her. Grace's attention remains on the checkerboard—focused on her next move.

Livvi glances in Grace's direction and quietly tells David: "You're a remarkable man…being able to be so nice. To a perfect stranger."

David studies Grace for a second, then says: "It's funny you should use the term 'perfect stranger.' For a while, when I was a kid, I thought perfect stranger meant something entirely different. I thought it was the name for an earthbound angel…one who was a little shy. And absolutely terrific."

"Where did you get that idea?"

"From books. From the kind of story where a boy on his bike

is hit by a car, and somebody steps out of the crowd and holds his hand until help comes…or a poor family wakes up hungry on Thanksgiving morning and finds a feast waiting on their doorstep. The people who brought those little, quiet, unanticipated gifts— they were always described as being perfect strangers."

David sends Livvi another smile, then turns his attention to Grace and the checkers. Livvi is realizing that David is extraordinary beyond measure. A man whose goodness—whose love—knows no bounds.

Livvi is about to tell David how much she treasures him—but Evelyn is saying: "Finish your question, dear. What were you wanting to ask me?"

And immediately, the anxiety is back.

Livvi quickly crosses to the kitchen counter, where Evelyn is putting away leftovers from the Christmas dinner of baked ham and roasted green beans that she, Livvi, and Grace shared earlier in the evening—before David returned from celebrating with his cousins in the city and joined them for dessert.

"Evelyn, I need to go to New Jersey—right now," Livvi says. "How do I get there from here?" Livvi asks the question very softly. She doesn't want Grace to hear.

A flicker of worry crosses Evelyn's face. "It's getting late. Are you sure this is the best time to go?"

"I can't just sit here not doing anything—the shop where I saw the portrait is closed for Christmas and won't be open until noon tomorrow. If I have to wait that long to start looking for answers, I'll go crazy."

Simply talking about the painting, and the woman from her nightmare, has Livvi in a cold sweat.

Evelyn leads Livvi to a chair at the table where Grace and David are, while she's telling her: "My mother used to say life is mostly a game of hide-and-seek. All of us looking for something. All of us hiding something."

When Livvi has settled in at the table, Evelyn adds: "Some people are defined by what they're looking for. Others by what they're hiding."

"I'm not quite sure what you're trying to tell me," Livvi says.

"It's been my experience that the people who define themselves by what they're hiding are in greater pain than the rest of us. And they can be a little dangerous—without meaning to. On this trip to New Jersey tonight, you should be careful. Take care of yourself."

David looks up from the checkerboard, surprised. "You're going to New Jersey? Tonight?"

In a flash, Grace has rushed out of her chair, upset. "You're going away, Livvi? Don't go away. Don't go!"

Livvi is taking Grace into her lap, assuring her: "I'll only be gone for a little while. I'll be right back."

But Grace is insistent. "No. I need you. I need you to stay. Always."

Livvi is holding Grace, telling her—"I will, Grace, I'll stay, I promise"—and having no idea how to keep that promise.

David is pushing the checkerboard aside, asking: "What's in New Jersey that's so important you have to go right now?"

"My father," Livvi says. "He's dying. I need to see him before it's too late."

Grace is clinging to Livvi so tightly that it's making it difficult for Livvi to breathe as she's explaining to David: "I have to go. I have to go there tonight." She's gazing down at Grace while she's adding: "And I don't know how to do it."

During this exchange between Livvi and David, Evelyn has

reached across the table and picked up the red felt-tipped marker lying beside the checkerboard.

Evelyn is leaning close to Grace's ear—her voice infinitely gentle as she's whispering: "Do you remember I told you that Santa and I are old friends? And that's why he asked me to be the one to make sure your butterfly wings were waiting for you, right in the middle of your bed, when you woke up this morning?"

Grace nods—but doesn't look at Evelyn.

"Well, I'd like to show you something. It's magic. The same as Santa is. I learned how to do it a long time ago when someone I loved needed to go away for a while to fight in a war, and I was afraid to be apart from him. Do you want to see the magic?"

Grace buries her face against the side of Livvi's neck and shrugs. "Maybe…"

"I need you to open your hand wide and hold it out to me."

Grace does as Evelyn asks.

Evelyn then moves the red felt-tipped marker in slow, sure strokes. When she is finished, she says: "Look, Grace. Look at the magic."

Grace hesitates. Leans away from Livvi just the slightest bit and turns her head. Curious to see what has happened.

In the cup of Grace's hand is a rounded, delicately shaded heart. One that is absolutely magnificent—so skillfully executed it seems almost three-dimensional.

Grace is gazing up at Evelyn. Evelyn's silver hair is shining in the soft light of the kitchen—she's wearing a red-and-white striped apron over a Christmas sweater patterned in snowflakes. And Grace is asking, in a voice full of wonder: "Are you Santa's sister?"

Evelyn is folding Grace's fingers so that the heart is hidden within Grace's grasp. And she's telling Grace: "This isn't any ordinary heart. It's the magical part of Livvi where she keeps all her love for you. And now you're holding it right in your hand."

There's an awed excitement in Grace. "Really?"

"Yes," Evelyn says. "And that's why it's all right to let Livvi go away for a little while tonight. Because she'll come back to you, Grace. She'll always come back because you have her heart. You're where her love is."

Grace is fascinated—gazing down at her palm—murmuring: "Don't worry, Livvi. While you're gone I'll take very good care of your heart."

And David is asking: "Where in New Jersey do you need to go?"

Livvi's father's apartment is nothing more than three narrow rooms on the top floor of a sagging, wood-sided house. A house at the dead end of a bleak street in Passaic.

Livvi is loosening the top button of her coat, trying not to inhale too deeply. The air is overheated, stale with the smell of fried eggs and sickness.

A man in a baggy sweater and cantaloupe-colored corduroy pants is leading Livvi through a maze of clutter—piles and towers of mildewed, dust-covered books. He has introduced himself as Albert and is scarecrow thin: an assemblage of skin-covered bones. Livvi is following him along a path that winds across the living area, and spans the short distance between the front door and the apartment's bedroom.

Calista is nearby in a shallow alcove that contains a pitted sink and small refrigerator. And, incongruously, a brightly lit aluminum Christmas tree. She's hunched over an electric griddle that's caked with grime, scraping up bits of burned food, and informing Livvi: "You might as well leave. You're too late. You waited too long."

Albert shoots Livvi a sympathetic glance and says: "Your father'll be happy you're here. He was happy when he heard you were coming. I know he was—I know the signs."

It's obvious that Livvi is confused, and Albert explains: "I'm your father's hospice worker."

Hospice. The cushioned good-bye. Before the final breath.

Livvi is stumbling against a stack of books. They're banging onto the floor like crumbling stones falling out of a fortress wall—raising puffs of dust and the odor of decay.

David is waiting outside in the clean, cold air. Ready to take Livvi back to Grace—to a house where the rooms smell of fresh pine and ginger cake. Livvi wants to turn and run.

But Albert has already ushered Livvi to her father's bedside and discreetly left them alone.

The room is not much bigger than a closet. And has only a single dim lamp, on the floor, near the bed. When Livvi's eyes adjust to the gloom, she discovers that the walls are stacked with books. And with old cardboard boxes sealed with yellowed strapping tape, brittle with age. And wedged into a corner, among the books and boxes, is the little pine table that was her desk in Santa Ynez.

In the bed, lying on the hammock-shaped mattress, under a colorless blanket, is Livvi's father. His hair is thin; Livvi can see that his scalp is mottled and flaking. His eyes and mouth are closed. His arms are at his sides, on top of the blanket, motionless. He is slender and fine-boned.

Livvi is astonished.

She had remembered her father as being so intimidating. So dangerous. So much larger than life. For all these years she has been remembering and fearing a lion—and now she's looking at the remains of what, must always have been, a gazelle.

"Can you hear me?" she asks.

Her father says nothing.

Livvi is about to repeat the question but changes her mind and looks away. She sees that on the other side of the bed there's an open door. Beyond the door is a miniscule bathroom. A sink, a toilet, and a cramped shower stall. Above the sink is a glass shelf neatly stocked with bandages and cotton balls and a pair of needle-nosed, stainless-steel scissors.

Livvi is recalling the skill and attention with which her father handled her cuts and scrapes when she was a child. The bandages always pristine. Snug and precise. The touch of his hands was light and sure.

The memory of this is making Livvi's voice gentler as she asks him again: "Can you hear me?"

No response.

"It's Livvi," she tells him. "Olivia."

He doesn't move. The tempo of his breathing doesn't change. He remains uncannily still.

And there's a flash of fury in Livvi.

She knows that her father knows she's there. She understands he's choosing—deliberately—to die. Without giving her answers to the questions she has been asking for a lifetime.

Her tone is matter-of-fact when she tells him: "I think I hate you." But then without warning, she's strangling on the words she has just spoken.

Livvi leaves the bed and walks to the little pine table. It is stacked and crowded with her old schoolbooks and papers. All these years, her father has kept them—and Livvi wants this to make a difference.

She wants the idea that he might have remembered her, and cared about her, to change everything. She wants to be overflowing with daughterly love.

But there is only the raging desire to be finished with him.

Livvi leans toward the pine table. And in a rapid series of swift, strong sweeps, she begins.

When she is finished. She has sent every dusty book. Every warped, moldering story from her childhood. Every relic of Olivia. Slamming onto the floor.

And when she straightens up and steps away—the tabletop has been wiped clean.

For a fleeting moment Livvi is bereaved.

And then she is set free.

She tells her father: "I hope you can hear me. I want you to know that you are a horrible, horrible man. And even if it's true that there's something more than just what happens in this life…if it turns out that even people like you can be redeemed in the end…I don't care. That's God's business, not mine."

Livvi walks back to her father's bed and stands beside him. "I want you to understand that I hate you. I hate all the mean, cold-hearted things you did to me. And the hate is making me tired. There's no point to it. There's no point to carrying the burden of you around with me anymore. I need to let you go."

Livvi has lifted her father's arm from its resting place on the sheet. She is pressing her lips to the delicate flesh on the inside of his wrist. His skin is wet with her tears.

She's heartbroken.

"It's over," she's telling him. "You're on your own now."

And then within seconds Livvi is outside. In the cold night air. With the sagging, wood-framed house, and her father, behind her.

She's running across the patch of frozen, scrubby ground that separates the house from the curb. Where David is waiting—with open arms.

His beach cottage is weathered and small—the wood-lath walls of the little front room have been sanded to a pearly beige, but not yet painted. The furniture is draped in white sheets. And on the floor, David has spread a thick, soft, heather-blue blanket.

Moonlight is streaming through the open door—shimmering and silvery bright.

Livvi and David are sitting, in their coats and gloves, side-by-side. On the heather-blue blanket. Looking out at the water. Listening to the waves rush toward the beach then pull away again.

In the time that has passed since Livvi left her father's apartment, she and David have spoken only a few words: David asking, as they were driving away from New Jersey, "Do you need to go somewhere and just be quiet for a little while?" and Livvi answering, "Yes. Please."

For the better part of an hour they have been here, shoulder to shoulder. Gazing out at the moonlit ocean. David—gently, steadfastly, holding Livvi's hand. Livvi—silently, slowly, coming to terms with what has happened tonight. The finality of the loss she suffered. And the powerful sense of freedom she found.

Now Livvi has told David: "I'm okay. We can go."

Together they have gathered up the heather-blue blanket. They've folded it and put it onto a tabletop.

Moonglow is glimmering on the pearly walls and white-sheeted furniture.

The only sound is the rush of the ocean.

Livvi and David are in their own private dreamscape.

And Livvi is being swept into David's embrace. Being wrapped in his honesty, and his unwavering devotion.

"I love you," he's telling her. "Do you think you could ever love me?"

And Livvi's answer is: "Yes. Yes, I do."

David's sigh is a combination of elation and relief.

Livvi gives an involuntary shiver. The night air coming in from the beach is growing colder.

"It's getting chilly," David says. "Do you want me to take you home?"

Livvi nods—there is nothing she wants more.

Yet she doesn't move out of his embrace.

The boards beneath the soles of her shoes are numbing her feet with cold. An icy night wind is beginning to slip over her coat collar and bite at the back of her neck.

And Livvi is continuing to hold on to David.

Deliberately postponing—for as long as possible—the moment of letting go.

On this second night spent tucked in the four-poster bed, with Grace beside her, the hours have passed slowly for Livvi.

There were long spaces in which she wanted to linger forever in the quiet of Evelyn's sleeping house—and the newfound bliss of David's love. There were other places in the night where she was frantic for daylight to come. For noon to arrive. For the door to the shop in Oyster Bay to open, and solve the riddle of the woman in the pearl-button shoes.

Now the hands of the clock in front of the real estate office on Main Street are clicking together—right beneath the twelve.

And Andrew is on the phone, saying: "I'll be at the airport when you and Grace get back. I can't wait to see you. Can't wait to hold you."

Livvi is walking toward the store window where the portrait is—her pulse racing.

While at the other end of the phone Andrew is insisting: "I need you. You're my life, Olivia."

Livvi can't take her eyes off the painting, the image from her nightmare. And as she's looking at it, Livvi is also seeing the image of the cluttered tabletop she swept clean last night, in her father's New Jersey apartment.

She switches her phone from one ear to the other and tells Andrew: "Don't do it again—ever."

"What are you talking about?"

Livvi's gaze is still on the portrait. "Don't call me Olivia. Olivia is from a place that's gone. I don't live there anymore."

"What's going on with you?" Andrew asks. "For Christ's sake, talk to me, Olivia."

Livvi is seeing that the Closed sign has disappeared from the door of the shop. "Andrew, I need to go."

"I'm sorry, Olivia. It was a slip. I meant to call you Livvi. From now on I'll try to remember. It'll just take some time—"

"Andrew, I need to go."

"No, wait. Listen to me." His tone is insistent, determined. "I love you. I intend to do whatever it takes. Stand up to whoever I need to. I will put an end to the craziness."

Livvi knows how far the distance between Andrew's intentions and his accomplishments can be—she knows, in spite of how much he wants to, that he probably won't be able to keep the promise he just made.

She also knows that, no matter what happens, or where she goes from here, there are places in her heart that will belong always, and exclusively, to Andrew. The "first" places. Places that will never exist again.

The series of places where only Andrew went.

Where, piece by piece, he opened the world to Livvi.

The place where Livvi received the gift of her first birthday party. The place where she was first shown the power and beauty of sex. The place where, while sailing skyward in a hot-air balloon, she was introduced to unbridled excitement for the first time.

And most important of all—the sacred shining place where she first found Grace.

"Livvi, talk to me," Andrew is demanding. "Tell me what's going on."

Her heart is too full—her nerves too raw. All she can tell him is: "I have to go now."

Livvi has opened the shop's wide, green door. And she is stepping inside.

The store's interior is chic, with walls lacquered in cinnabar red and edged in black. In the center of the room, there's a Buddha carved from translucent green stone. And the Asian woman who is coming toward Livvi is slim. In her mid-forties, ethereally beautiful. She's saying: "I'm Rebecca Wang. How can I help you?"

Livvi's mouth is dry and the pulse in her temple is pounding as she answers: "I need to know about the painting in the window."

"Oh, a lot of people come in and ask about it. The woman in the picture was the daughter of a wealthy family in the Hamptons. Her name was Miriam Moran and the painting was done in 1922, shortly before her twenty-first birthday. But I'm sorry, it isn't for sale."

"I don't want to buy it," Livvi explains. "I need to know where it came from."

Rebecca Wang smiles apologetically. "All I can tell you is that it belonged to a friend of my grandmother's—I don't recall the woman's name—but my grandmother acquired the painting when her friend's house was being sold. I keep the portrait in the window because my grandmother loved it and this store used to be hers."

Livvi feels like Alice cartwheeling down the rabbit hole. "Please. There must be somebody who knows."

Rebecca Wang stays silent—for several long, agonizing moments. Then says: "Wait. Yes. There is someone."

And Livvi can breathe again.

Rebecca Wang is pulling a faded address book from a desk drawer, quickly paging through it, then using an ebony pen to enter information onto one of her store's small note cards.

Livvi is shaking as Rebecca Wang hands her the card and says: "If the person is still at this address, you should be able to find out everything you need to know."

Micah

Boston, Massachusetts ~ 2012

M ICAH IS DRIFTING IN AND OUT OF CONSCIOUSNESS. GLIDING through a parade of flickering images:

A wonderful summer garden. Surrounded by soft green grass and a sea of coral-colored lilies.

Her mother. Stroking the fur of a smoke-colored cat while the light from a window is dancing across the rings on her fingers.

Jason. On the office steps of the Justice of the Peace. Mutely begging Micah, who is walking away, to stop. And come back.

A slant of sunlight. Painting a piece of copper wire with a fiery glow. Turning it into a trail of liquid light. While it's moving in Micah's hands. Smoothly and easily. Like embroidery silk.

A warm embrace. And AnnaLee's voice, sounding like music. Saying, "Believe that I love you...won't you please?"

Now the music of AnnaLee's voice is becoming the South Boston cadences of Micah's assistant Jillian, and Micah is opening her eyes.

Jillian is in the bedroom with Micah, leaning over Micah's chair. And Micah, for the first time, is noticing that Jillian is pretty— younger than Micah had always assumed.

Jillian is telling her: "Miss Lesser, there's someone—"

"Wait," Micah says. Now she's noticing the concern Jillian has for her, realizing that it has always been there, and she has never taken the time to see it.

"Miss Lesser, I need you to listen."

Micah is remembering the doctor's question, *"Is there someone we can call, someone you're close to?"* And she's begging Jillian, "Please. No more Miss Lesser. It's time that we—"

"Miss Lesser!" Jillian is startled, overcome with emotion. "You've never said 'please' to me before."

It takes Jillian a moment to pull herself together. Then she says: "There's someone here to see you."

Pain medication has Micah in a haze and she's confused by this other voice, not Jillian's, telling her: "Rebecca Wang sent me."

The mention of Rebecca Wang's name is carrying Micah back to that summer with AnnaLee. The image in Micah's mind is the image of a grave—and a length of copper wire being formed into the shape of a cross.

In the split second that it takes Micah to pull her thoughts away from the cross and the grave, Jillian is stepping aside. And a stranger—a quietly pretty young woman with luminous brown eyes and a cap of golden curls—is coming closer.

She seems tense, painfully nervous, as she's telling Micah: "My name is Livvi Gray and I need your help with this." She's holding out a cell phone.

There's a picture on the phone's screen but Micah isn't looking at it. She's staring at the young woman; trying to remember where she has seen her before.

The young woman is pointing to the cell phone—her voice trembling with emotion. "For as long as I can remember, I've had nightmares about the person in this painting. Her name is Miriam Moran. She lived in the Hamptons and the painting was done in 1922. I have to know how I could've grown up in California dreaming about somebody who lived on the opposite side of the country, and existed almost a century before I was born."

She holds the phone out to Micah, pleading: "Help me. Please. Rebecca Wang said you could tell me what this means."

When Micah looks at the phone, she sees that the photograph on the screen is of a portrait, in a store window. Micah recognizes it immediately. It's a painting that was in AnnaLee's house—the portrait that inspired AnnaLee's costume, the one she wore to Mrs. Jahn's gala.

And now Micah understands why the young woman's luminous eyes and golden curls were so instantly recognizable.

Micah is dizzy with guilt. And surprise. She can't take her eyes off that sweet face and those golden curls.

And with both trepidation and remembered fondness, Micah says: "Bella...?"

The young woman appears to be mystified—gives no response.

"Bella. That was your nickname when you were a baby," Micah tells her. "When you were born, your mother thought you looked like a fairy princess. They started out calling you Tinkerbelle, then Belle, then Bella."

"You're mistaken. I don't know you, we've never met." The young woman takes a cautious step backward, away from Micah—but continues to hold the phone so that Micah can see the screen. "Please, all I need is for you to tell me what you know about this painting. And then I'll go."

"No, don't go." Micah is leaning forward, reaching for the young woman, wanting her to understand. "You and I do know each other. Your father and mine are half-brothers, Bella. And one summer, when I was a teenager I lived in your house. In Glen Cove. On Long Island."

The young woman is glancing at the array of medications on the little table beside Micah's chair. "My name is Livvi. You have me confused with someone else."

"No," Micah insists. "You and I spent that summer together. When you were little. When you were Bella…"

Micah's voice has trailed away and, for an instant, she is in a late August afternoon…*sitting beside AnnaLee in the garden swing. With her head bent low over the piece of copper wire that she's shaping and reshaping. And Bella, a toddler with a rag doll, is hovering at Micah's knee, fascinated.*

Micah's voice is blurring with tears as she's trying to explain the past to this beautiful golden-haired girl. "It was the most wonderful summer of my life. Your mother let me be who I wanted to be… she let me be Persephone…and to her I was somebody special. She showed me I had talent, and loved me in a way I'd never been loved before."

Now Micah's visitor is glancing at Jillian: asking an unspoken question—is Micah insane?

"I'm not crazy. I know you," Micah says. "Your given name is Olivia. Your middle name is Lee. Your mother's name was AnnaLee. Your father's name is Jack. And your parents were devoted to you."

Micah is watching, helplessly. As this girl, Livvi, is going deathly pale. And falling. Like she has been body-slammed by a ghost.

Jillian is intercepting Livvi's fall—helping her into a chair.

While Livvi is murmuring: "How can it be possible…?"

And Micah is realizing this is the moment of truth.

The moment she was searching for. And couldn't find—in Kansas. Or the Laundromat in Louisville. Or her mother's house in Newport.

Which is why Micah is slowly opening the collar of her silk

robe. Exposing the flesh just above her breast and just below her shoulder. Revealing the ghoulish snake tattoo—directing Livvi's attention to it. And telling her: "It's a picture of who I was at the beginning of that summer."

This is the moment in which Micah will discover if she has any hope of absolution. Livvi—Bella—is the person who holds the greatest debt on Micah's sin. She's the one who has the right to decide what should become of Micah.

As she begins to tell her story, to describe the events that led to the disaster, Micah is laying it out so that Livvi can see everything clearly. Everything that happened in those few, unforgettable weeks. When Micah was Persephone.

…In the first week of the summer, Persephone has purple hair and is exploding with anger. Saying to AnnaLee, "That stuff you were telling your kid—that stuff about how much you love her. It made me hate you. And her."

…In midsummer, Persephone is on Main Street in Oyster Bay. In the company of Hayden Truitt. Hungry for her approval. Plotting a crime. Then telling AnnaLee, "It's nothing. I'm just helping Tru think up an idea for a horror movie."

…At the end of August, Persephone is in AnnaLee's kitchen. And she fiercely loves AnnaLee. She's rushing to make a phone call. She's wearing a Ziegfeld costume the same coral color as the lilies in AnnaLee's garden. Persephone is working at keeping her voice low so AnnaLee won't hear. While she's whispering about the crime, and about AnnaLee. She's nervously leaving a message. Saying, "Forget the plan we decided on. When I told you I'd do it, I was still making up my mind. Things are different now…"

"But it was too late," Micah is explaining. "The plan was already in motion." Micah gazes down at her snake tattoo—momentarily lost in thought. Then she says: "Hayden and her boyfriend Marco were always needing money. For drugs."

Micah's visitor, Livvi, seems utterly confounded. "But how do those people have any connection to me?"

"You'll understand. Just let me finish." Micah tells her. "That day when I said I was thinking up an idea for a horror movie, what I was really doing was letting Hayden know about your parents going to Mrs. Jahn's party. I promised Hayden I'd leave the back door unlocked so she and Marco could come in and rob the place—"

"But I still don't see why you're telling me all of this." Livvi is leaning forward. Her eyes full of apprehension. "What you're say-ing doesn't—"

"Wait, just listen. I need to tell you everything exactly the way it took place; otherwise, it won't make any sense." Micah is plunging ahead, not wanting Livvi to stop her. "At first I hated AnnaLee, but by the time the party happened, everything was different. I loved her. It wasn't until I was walking out the door, with my new friend Rebecca, that the plan I'd made with Hayden came back into my head. I called Hayden a dozen times but she never answered. I kept leaving messages. Hayden and Marco…and the guy who was with them…all of them were high when they got to your parents' house. They were angry about the back door not being unlocked. They had a gun. And—"

"And what?" The mention of a gun has brought Livvi to the edge of her chair.

"They shot your mother. They murdered her. She was still in her costume from the party, the costume I copied from the portrait— the silver dress and the pearl-button shoes."

Livvi sways. Ever so slightly. As if she's about to faint.

Micah feels dirty. Coated with shame. As she tells Livvi: "I killed your mother...I killed AnnaLee. She died because of what I did."

Micah's throat is tightening and closing—while she waits for Livvi's wrath.

But Livvi seems completely unaware of Micah. Doesn't appear to even realize she's in the room. To Micah it looks as if Livvi has lost contact with reality. As if she's mentally traveling into some strangely distant world.

A minute clicks by. Then another. And another.

As each moment is passing, the sense of dread in Micah is building. Showing her she won't be able to survive the fury that Livvi is preparing to unleash.

Micah is at her breaking point. "Don't you have anything you want to say to me?" she asks.

The lost look in Livvi's eyes is slowly beginning to clear—it's being replaced by an odd combination of injury and elation.

"My mother died?" Livvi says.

"Yes," Micah tells her.

"My mother didn't run away? She died?"

Micah is thunderstruck. "How could you think your mother ran away?"

"It's what I've always been told...she was a party girl who wanted to have a good time."

"It's a lie. Who told you that?" Micah is annoyed—instinctively wanting to defend AnnaLee.

"My father told me..." Livvi says, "...and my stepmother."

"That's ridiculous. Your father was devoted to AnnaLee. The night she was killed, he almost died trying to save her. He came to the funeral with a broken shoulder and his hands in bandages. Your father is one of the sweetest, kindest men I ever met."

And Livvi tells Micah: "Now you're the one being ridiculous. My father was an uncaring monster."

This bizarre statement leaves Micah's head spinning. It makes no sense.

Livvi has gotten up from her chair. And is pacing the room. Rapidly. Erratically. As if she's sorting through a frantic tangle of thoughts and emotions.

Then she stops and turns to look at Micah. "I don't understand. How did my father get to Santa Ynez? When did he leave Long Island?"

Micah tries to remember. "I'm not sure. I guess it was a couple of months after AnnaLee died. At some point the two of you just disappeared. My father tried searching for you, for years. But nobody could find you. Nobody knew where you went."

Livvi is leaning against the wall. Bent forward, her hands clamped against her breastbone—like she's in terrible pain. "All the things you've said...this story you've told me...is it really the truth?"

Micah—hating that there's no comfort she can offer Livvi—simply nods.

Livvi sounds as if she still can't quite believe what she has just heard. "And that's all you know? About my parents? About me?"

"Yes," Micah says. "I was only there for those few weeks, that one summer, but—"

There's a feeling in Micah. Like being caught in a vise. It's crushing her. Squeezing the life out of her. As she adds: "—but there's something else I need to tell you."

Livvi's tone is quiet, fearful. "What more could there possibly be?"

A chill is building in Micah.

And she's saying: "In payment for your mother's murder, Hayden and Marco, and Marco's friend, went to jail. For a long time. I went to Harvard. Then I went on with my life." Crippling shivers are running through her as she tells Livvi: "Now I need to pay for that. The universe has already handed me the bill, I just don't know how big the payment should be. You need to help me decide."

"What exactly are you asking…?"

Livvi glances from Micah to the little table containing the medications—then she looks up at Jillian.

Jillian appears to have tears in her eyes. She mouths the word *cancer*.

"My breasts were removed last week," Micah explains. "Treatment is set to begin the day after tomorrow—a clinical trial. It's a long shot, but I need to know if I have the right to take it."

Livvi is continuing to lean against the wall, for support. As she says: "And you want me to decide?"

"I took your mother's life. You're entitled to ask for mine in return."

Livvi slowly pushes away from the wall and begins to pace again. Wandering. Distracted. Circling the room.

While Micah is waiting. Waiting—and terrified.

After a while, Livvi comes to a stop in the center of the room. Her gaze moving from the white plastered walls—to the spotless floors—and then to the polished, mostly empty, tables and shelves.

She appears to be searching for something. When she can't seem to find it, she asks Micah: "Are you married?"

Micah gives a negative shake of her head.

"A family? Children?" Livvi asks.

It is as if Livvi is stripping Micah's soul and laying it bare. Micah is aching with regret as she says: "I thought I would have all of that. Someday. But…"

"Are you in love?"

"I was. Once. A long time ago." The sense of loss is almost intolerable. "I loved a man that I left, and thought I was coming back for."

"Miss Lesser is a legend," Jillian tells Livvi. "Why don't you ask her about her career?"

"I don't want to talk about my career," Micah snaps.

Then she looks at Livvi. Micah is riddled with guilt as she tells her: "I bought my career by stealing pieces of other people's lives—starting with that picture I took of your mother."

Micah's body is wet with a sticky, sour sweat. "Your mother died because of me. I want to know if, in order to make that up to you, you need me to die too."

When Livvi doesn't respond, Micah tells her: "It isn't fair that I get away without paying for what happened."

The expression on Livvi's face is tender, full of sadness. "I don't think you did get away without paying for it."

Livvi is looking around the room again as if she's taking note of the things that aren't there. The personal touches. The tokens of love. "I have the feeling you've paid, one way or another, all the way along the line."

There is a quality in Livvi's voice that seems to suggest that finally, all of this is beginning to make sense. "Miss Lesser... Micah...I can't tell you whether you deserve to live or you deserve to die for what you did wrong in the past. But I can tell you that what you did today was a blessing. You gave me somebody I've been yearning for all my life. You gave me my mother."

Livvi has crossed the room and is standing beside Micah now, telling her softly: "You gave me a priceless gift—you let me know I was loved."

Livvi's touch on Micah's shoulder is bringing Micah a sensation of being lifted up into the light. And being cleansed. It is the feeling of absolution: the miracle of forgiveness.

Micah is gazing at Livvi—seeing Bella. Bella with her luminous brown eyes and cap of golden curls.

After a long, quiet moment, Micah tells her: "You make me believe in angels."

A little while later, when Livvi is leaving, she's pausing in the doorway of Micah's room—with a hopeful, hesitant smile—asking: "What was my mother like?"

"She was like you," Micah says. "She was exactly like you."

Livvi

Kennedy Airport, New York ~ 2012

L IVVI IS IN THE PASSENGER SEAT OF DAVID'S VOLVO. GRACE IS IN
the back—eagerly undoing her seat belt and chatting to
Granger, who's in a travel crate on the floor of the car.

David is opening the trunk, unloading Livvi's large, black suitcase and
Grace's small, pink one. The air outside is cold. Shrill with the whistles
of traffic officers. Pungent with the smell of jet fuel and car exhaust.

Livvi's hand is poised over her phone. The conversation she had
yesterday in Boston, with Micah Lesser, has given her so much
important information. Yet it left so many issues unresolved—a
catalogue of loose ends that's making Livvi wonder, *When, and why,
did my father disappear from Glen Cove and from everyone who'd been in
his life? And why was the person Micah described…the person she called
sweet and kind…why was he so different from the cold, distant man who
raised me in Santa Ynez? And the woman I saw in my nightmares…the
woman with the dark hair and the fiery-red lips…was she the person in the
portrait, or was she my mother? And if it was my mother, how did that
image of her find its way into my consciousness?*

Livvi is entering Micah's number into the phone. But then she's
changing her mind and dropping the phone into her lap. Frustrated.
Realizing the call is pointless. Micah would have no way of knowing any of these things.

And Grace is asking: "Are we going on a big plane or on our own plane, like Grandpa does?"

"On a big plane," Livvi tells her.

"Grandpa says when people travel around, the time changes. Will it be today or yesterday when we get there? And if it's yesterday, can we do everything we did today all over again?"

"Wherever you go, sweetheart, it's today. It's the day you're in," Livvi says. "Yesterday's always over and gone."

In having this conversation with Grace, Livvi is being reminded that the past and the unknowable answers to its questions are out of her reach. She's being shown that, as maddening as the prospect is, the healthiest thing to do with the burden of those questions is what she did with the suffocating weight of her father. Release them. Let them go. And give herself to the future.

"Are you ready?" David is asking.

He has opened the driver's door and is leaning into the car. Looking at Livvi with love, and hope.

A draft from outside is sending what appears to be a tiny golden bird fluttering from under the driver's seat and into the air.

Livvi is leaning forward and catching it. It's Japanese: Origami. A square of gold foil that has been intricately folded into the shape of a crane.

"I was wondering where that went," David says.

"Did you do this?" Livvi is marveling at how beautiful it is.

"I asked a friend to do it for me," he tells her. "I needed a pattern." David has slipped into the driver's seat and closed the car door.

An airport security officer is tapping on the Volvo's hood, indicating that the car can't stay parked at the curb much longer.

David quickly tells Livvi: "There's a Japanese legend that says the making of a thousand cranes will bring you your heart's desire."

"What a lovely myth," Livvi says.

David seems both confident and heartbroken. "It's how I'm going to spend my time—while I'm waiting for you to find a way to come back to me."

Livvi is thinking how fragile the little bird is. "How many have you made so far?"

"Three. I started my first one that night—the night we got back from New Jersey."

That night. For an instant, Livvi has returned to it. And to the memory of the patch of frozen ground separating her father's house from the sidewalk. His house, and its coldness, were behind her while she was running toward the warmth of David's arms. Then, later, in David's beach cottage, she was being held with such devotion. Such honesty. When he said, "I love you. Do you think you could ever love me?" and she told him, "Yes. Yes, I do."

And now, as she's sitting beside David, recalling his question and the joy that was in her answer, there are tears in Livvi's eyes. *I'll never forget that night,* she's thinking. *It was when I closed the door on my past. And when I opened my heart to David.*

It was when everything changed. That night was both the beginning, and the end.

Jack

Passaic, New Jersey ~ 2012

IT'S BEGINNING. THE END.

In almost imperceptible increments, Jack's body is becoming lighter. And there's another sensation too. Like the tug and sway of a train pulling away from the platform.

It's dark where Jack is. Not midnight dark. Closer to end-of-twilight dark. There's just enough illumination for Jack to see AnnaLee. She is walking away from him. He's trying to tell her, *"Bella came. She came all the way to New Jersey—to see me,"* but he has no voice. So of course AnnaLee doesn't hear, doesn't turn around. And Jack is relieved. How could he face her if she did? She would look into his eyes and know that he had, again, been a coward. That he hadn't had the courage to speak to Bella. He'd only had the cringing need to know she was there and standing at his side, one last time.

Jack had been unable to open his eyes, engage his child. Frightened that, if he did, he would draw her closer to him. And if she came too close, she would smell his awful scent—the rot that had begun in him on the night AnnaLee died.

His fear of exposing that lingering odor held Jack prisoner for most of Bella's life. And made him afraid to give himself to her. Afraid that if she caught even a waft of it, she would understand its source and know the truth about him.

His need for self-protection—for distance—is the reason that, in all the years of her growing up, Jack never once called his daughter by the pet name her mother gave her on the day she was born. He never called her Bella. He always called her Olivia.

The decay that began in Jack with AnnaLee's death, and the stain it left on his soul, were the reasons that less than two months after AnnaLee's funeral he ran to Santa Ynez and locked himself away. And locked Bella away. He did it so no one could come near him and his motherless child, and somehow recognize what he had done.

The swaying, trainlike motion is picking up speed now. The end of twilight is becoming the beginning of darkness for Jack. At the edge of the darkness he's in the house in Santa Ynez. Sitting on the top step of the porch. The sun is warm on his skin (which at the moment of AnnaLee's death went cold, and stayed that way). Bella is three years old. She's in a little blue dress. The sun is making the curls in her hair glitter like gold. She's playing with a pair of dolls, one large and one small—and she's asking, *"Where did my mommy go?"* Jack is saying the first thing that's coming into his head—because it's a sliver of the truth—and a sliver is as much as he can risk. He's telling Bella, *"Your mother was all dressed up and she went to a wonderful party."* And when Bella asks, *"Is she coming back?"* the scent of decay in Jack is so strong it sends him scuttling to the bottom of the porch steps. While he's saying, *"No, she's never coming back."*

And now Jack is remembering how he had continued to hide himself from Bella—for the rest of their days together. Relentlessly keeping her at arm's length. With the exception of that one awful morning—when he had lifted her up by her hair.

That morning was an aberration. He thought Bella was gone—the way AnnaLee was gone. He'd been wild with guilt and grief.

When he looked down and saw his little girl in that rectangular space, folded into that topless box where she was hiding, it was like looking into a coffin. He was in a frenzy. He had to reach in and pull her out and throw her free of it.

For the briefest instant, he had felt heroic. Like a rescuer. Then he realized he had touched her, let her come too close. And as Bella stood there in her faded nightgown, gazing up at him, needing things he couldn't give, he was thinking of AnnaLee's coffin—and of what he'd said about AnnaLee, to Bella. *"...She went to a wonderful party."*

Now, as Jack is moving into the mouth of what seems to be a velvet-black tunnel, he's wondering, *When did it happen? When did the story change and AnnaLee become a brassy party girl who ran away? Was it when Calista began to tell it? Yes. It was. And I let her tell it that way. Because it gave the story an ending that kept me safe.*

Jack wants to scream. Like a lunatic. Again, he has no voice. But the need for this scream is reminding him that he is—in actuality—a lunatic. It's reminding him that after AnnaLee's funeral he lost his mind. Eaten alive by what he'd done on the night she died. Spending the rest of his years raging through the house in Santa Ynez. Crying out in pain. Smashing windows. Driving his fists into walls. Never stopping until his body failed and he began to die—and was too weak for lunatic screams and a madman's violence.

A pool of wavering light on the wall of the velvet-black tunnel has gradually widened and encompassed Jack. He is gone from the tunnel. He's in Glen Cove. In his old leather chair in the living room, reading.

The house is quiet. Then there's the sudden noise of breaking glass. The sound of a window being shattered. Muffled commotion. Scuffling footsteps, muttered conversation. Someone, more than one someone, inside the house, and coming nearer. Jack's heart is racing. AnnaLee and Bella are alone upstairs.

Jack is terrified. He switches off the reading lamp and listens. A loud thump from the kitchen sends a scare through him. He's scrambling out of his chair, stumbling toward the phone—it's on a table across the room, near the entry to the hall. He needs to call the police. To call 911. He's dragging the phone toward the hall, his hands like rubber, fumbling with the dial, his attention on the noise in the kitchen.

He's about to press the first number, the nine—and there's a crashing sound. Whoever is in the house is coming toward the hall. While Jack is ducking back into the safety of the living room, he still has the phone's receiver to his ear. It seems as if there's someone else on the line. As if, on one of the other phones in the house, someone is listening.

And from the kitchen—scuffling sounds. Low voices. A man muttering the word *fuck*. Then, a few seconds later, the noise of a woman's high-heeled shoes coming down the stairs. Stepping onto the hallway floor.

Jack is dropping the phone, glancing toward the hall. Seeing semi-darkness. And AnnaLee. Still dressed for the gala in her glittering gown. She's letting out a spine-chilling scream.

And Jack is running. Dashing across the living room. Blindly pushing open one of the glass-paned terrace doors. It's swinging shut behind him. He's outside the house.

Frantically gulping the night air.

Realizing what he has just done.

He's turning around, racing back to the door. But can't get it open. It's jammed. He's smashing the glass with his hands, reaching through—trying to grab the handle on the inside. His hands are running with blood; he can't get a grip. He's terrified, convulsing, like he's having a seizure.

From somewhere inside the house—a single, horrendously loud gun shot.

Jack is losing control of his bowels, shitting himself. Trying to run for help. Water from the lawn sprinklers has pooled on the terrace, and he's slipping. Falling onto the flagstones—his shoulder breaking—pain radiating down his arm. But he can still hear the echoing sound of the gunshot. And he's up and running. Across the wet grass. Slamming into the untrimmed limb of a tree—opening a gash on his forehead. His lungs are on fire.

The noise of a second gunshot is booming inside the house.

He's halfway across the yard. Soaked in blood and excrement. His neighbor, a broad-shouldered dentist, is coming toward him. The blood is pouring from Jack's face and hands. He's strangling on his own stench, the smell of his cowardice. Desperate to hide his awful smell from this man, he's shouting, "Go back. Call 911!"

The neighbor is galloping away. Jack is hearing the squeal of tires on the road in front of the house—he knows the intruders have fled.

What Jack does not know is that later, when the television cameras arrive, his wounds will be interpreted as the marks of his courageous fight to save his family—and he will be called a hero.

The pool of light in the velvet-black tunnel is shrinking then flaring wide again. And Jack is seeing himself—with his ruined trousers and bleeding face—going back into the house. Where AnnaLee is on the hallway floor.

She is in the dress that's shimmering like a column of starlight and she's wearing pale-colored high-heeled shoes fastened with a strap at the instep, each strap anchored by a single pearl button.

Her arms are outstretched, bracelets glittering at her wrists. A thin silver band encircles her head, and in the band there's a plumed white feather. Her hair is hidden beneath a caplike, chestnut brown wig. Her face is in shadow. Only her lips are visible. They are bright with the fiery-red lipstick she wore to the gala. And they're parted. As if making way for a scream, which, when it comes, will be the sound of unadulterated horror. She is looking toward the foot of the stairs. Toward the last thing she must have seen before she died. Bella. Moving out of the shadows. And into the sights of the gunman.

The pool of light on the tunnel wall is vanishing. Jack is going into darkness now. Traveling swiftly toward a narrow, unlit portal. He's not sure if it's the door to heaven, the entry to hell, or the gateway to oblivion. In spite of knowing which destination he deserves, he's curious, and the tiniest bit hopeful.

A cold draft is passing over Jack. And as his spirit is leaving his body, he's seeing AnnaLee. In the garden swing. Surrounded by coral-colored lilies. One of her legs bears a neat line of surgical scars—the marks made by Jack—when AnnaLee had been a broken ballerina and he was a doctor, a healer.

Jack's heart is shattering as he's calling out to AnnaLee, knowing he has no voice, no way for her to hear him say, "*I was a coward and a failure. But oh how I loved you. How I wish we could do it over again. How I wish that instead of simply making it possible for you to walk, instead of giving you a life that kept you chained to the ground, I could have—just once—seen you dance.*"

Epilogue...Livvi

LIVVI IS IN THE AISLE SEAT OF THE PLANE THAT IS CARRYING HER back to California—and wondering how long it will take to fold a thousand squares of golden foil into the shapes of a thousand cranes. Wondering if at some point along the way David will abandon the effort and open his arms to someone else—and ask what he asked Livvi in the shimmering moonlight, *"Are you ready for me to take you home?"*

As New York, and David, are dropping away beneath the wings of the swiftly moving plane Livvi is closing her eyes. And imagining:

...She's with David, and their children...children who have Livvi's passion for books and David's graceful, generous spirit. They're living in a house that's traditional and lovingly furnished, unpretentious—very much like Evelyn's house. Which is so much like Mrs. Granger's—the house of Livvi's dreams. It's Christmas and the air outside is brisk East Coast air, and the air inside smells like fresh pine, and cinnamon. Livvi and David and their children are surrounded by family—by Evelyn, and David's open-hearted parents and his pretty sister, and his dozens of cousins. The house is noisy. Happy. Lit with love. Livvi is gathering her children around the Christmas tree but she's seeing the lights on the tree dimming, the happiness in the house fading—Grace isn't there. The loss, the emptiness, is unbearable.

That feeling of emptiness is jolting Livvi out of her daydream and bringing her back to the present.

Bringing her back to Grace.

Grace's hand is resting in Livvi's. Warm and gentle. The red-inked symbol of Livvi's heart is in Grace's open palm.

And Grace is asking: "What are you thinking about?"

"I'm thinking about a long time from now—someday when you're all grown-up and have gone off to conquer the world."

Livvi is picturing the future...*her hair is the slightest bit gray, and she has gained a few pounds. But she's still trim and in good shape—at fifty. She's in New York. Andrew is probably waiting for her in a nearby hotel. She's on Madison Avenue. In a store called Bauman's—a genteel showplace for rare and beautiful old books. She's holding a first edition of Salinger's* Catcher in the Rye *and wondering what it must have been like to possess that kind of talent. Now she's glancing up from the book—seeing David walking past the window, outside, on the sidewalk. There are lines in his face. He's wearing glasses. But he is essentially unchanged. He is still—in every aspect—sweet, perfect, David. Livvi is straining to see if there's a wedding ring, but he has an umbrella in his hand, and she can't. She's running toward the door. Pushing it open. Calling to him. Wanting to tell him where life has taken her—wanting to know where he has traveled. But he's already disappearing into the crowd of people on the sidewalk. He's already vanishing.*

And a woman's voice is telling Livvi: "Your little girl is adorable." It's the flight attendant—handing Livvi a cup of coffee and glancing toward Grace.

While Grace is saying: "Livvi, how do you spell Evelyn and gether?" Grace is busily working on a drawing. A thank-you to Santa for her Christmas present, the glittering butterfly wings. "I want to write 'it was nice being two gether with Evelyn.' I know how to spell two, but I don't know how to spell gether. Or Evelyn."

Livvi gives Grace the spelling of the words—and hears Evelyn's voice saying, *"You didn't come away from your beginnings broken and ugly. Miraculously…you've come away strong, and filled with love. Find your purpose, Livvi. Use the power of that love to fulfill it."*

And Livvi tells Grace: "We'll have a beautiful life, you and I. Everything's going to be fine."

"How do you know?"

"I just do…"

Livvi is murmuring this while thinking, *Everything will be fine because I was wrong about having my back to a cliff. We're not alone, Gracie. The world is full of people like Evelyn, and Sierra, and Bree, and your Uncle James. And David. And hundreds of others we haven't even had the chance to meet yet. People who are strong and willing to help. We have a safety net, Grace. All around us.*

Grace is glancing up at Livvi with that familiar cautious expression. "You'll never leave?" she asks.

"I'll never leave. No matter what. No matter who tries to make me."

Grace's caution has been replaced by a smile that's wide and bright. Radiantly happy.

Livvi is at peace.

Grace goes back to her drawing.

After a few minutes, Livvi opens her laptop and begins to type.

Grace is curious. "Are you doing work?"

"Yes."

"What kind of work?"

"I'm starting the first chapter of a new book."

While Livvi is slowly running her fingers through the silk of Grace's hair, Grace asks: "What kind of story is it?"

And Livvi says: "It's a love story."

Reading Group Guide

1. *The Book of Someday* opens with a quote from poet Antonio Machado: "Traveller there is no road, the way is made by walking." How does this quote relate to what takes place in the novel? Why do you think the author chose it for the opening page?

2. When she's a little girl, Olivia makes a list that contains dreams and wishes for her future. Some of the wishes on her list come true in very unexpected ways. Of the dreams for your life that you had when you were younger, what was the one that came true in a way that surprised you the most and changed your life the most?

3. As the story unfolds, Livvi finds herself faced with incredibly difficult decisions. Choices that are life changing—for her and for other people. Do you think Livvi's commitments to the promises she made as a child are helping her in the choices she makes as an adult? Or are they hurting her?

4. Do you see Livvi as a woman who is strong and self-directed? Or a woman who's allowing her past to have too much influence on her future?

5. When Grace first appeared in the novel, what was your reaction to her? In Livvi's place, what decision would you make about Grace?

6. When Sierra is talking about Livvi's connection to Grace, she says Livvi is just beginning her life and that Livvi's responsibility is to herself and her own happiness. Do you agree?

7. At the end of the book, as Livvi is being offered the chance to make her sweetest dreams come true, should she let anything, even her feelings for Grace, stop her from claiming those dreams?

8. Do you think that someday Livvi might regret the choices she makes during the course of this novel?

9. At one point, Livvi asks Evelyn: "How does God decide who to bless and who to punish?" Would your answer to that question be different from the one Evelyn gives?

10. Among Livvi, Micah, and AnnaLee, who did you relate to the most, and why?

11. If you were single, and David and Andrew were both available to you, which one would you choose? And what do you think your choice would say about you?

12. Do you think Andrew is a man doing his best to honor all of his commitments? Or is he a man who has found an intriguing way to avoid fully honoring any of them?

13. Does Andrew's story suggest that there are times when it's actually impossible to do the right thing?

14. Do you feel empathy or anger toward Andrew?

15. What are your feelings about David?

16. If you were to run into David five years after *The Book of Someday* ends, where do you think he would be in his life?

17. What do you think about Sierra's theory of the "love goggles"? Do you agree that, at one time or another, every woman in the world has worn them?

18. Micah is described by one of the other characters as someone who gets off on making her own rules, going over the top, and being hell on wheels. How do these qualities affect your feelings about her? Do they make you want to put her in her place or go out and have a cup of coffee with her?

19. Why do you think Micah gave away that anonymous $10,000 dollar gift? Was it openhearted generosity? Or a selfish attempt to buy a little bit of cosmic forgiveness?

20. Does knowing Micah's background give you any sympathy for the way she lived her life and the person she turned out to be?

21. If life offered you what it offered Micah, the opportunity to be rich and famous, what would you be willing to sacrifice for that?

22.   Some readers have said that they see quiet, shy AnnaLee as the strongest and most heroic of the women whose stories are told in this book. Do you agree or disagree...and why?

23.   In your opinion, who was most responsible for what ultimately happened to AnnaLee?

24.   If there were a way to bring Jack to trial for his failures, and you were on the jury, what would you convict him of? And what would you want his punishment to be?

25.   At the heart of this novel is a mystery, a web of secrets. Secrets that ultimately cause the people keeping them to make incredible mistakes as they try to protect, and unwittingly betray, themselves and the people they love. Which secret in this book startled you the most? Was there one you thought was unforgivable?

A Conversation
with the Author

1. What do you love most about writing?

I love the thrill of telling stories about ordinary people caught up in extraordinary circumstances. I love exploring the mysteries of the human condition. And I love the poetry of words.

2. What inspires you the most as a writer?

Life. How hard we all try to get it right. How easy it is to get it wrong. The intriguing unpredictability that's always lurking in that balance point between right and wrong.

3. When do you know the story is finished?

Wow. That's a good question. The truth is…it's weird. Even before I begin writing, I know exactly what the ending of the book will be, exactly what the words in the final sentence will be. Maybe it's because the stories I tell have very specific plots and I know, going in, precisely how the plot needs to unfold.

4.   What is one thing you know now that you wish you knew when you started your writing career?

I think if I'd known how lovely and generous the readers are I would have started writing novels much sooner. The readers… their comments, their support, their enthusiasm…it's wonderful!

5.   Did you always want to be a writer, or did you start off in a different career?

Always. Always. A writer. That's what I wanted to be.

6.   What is the most challenging part of being a writer?

The discipline it takes. And how solitary it is.

7.   What research or preparation did you engage in before writing *The Book of Someday*?

I traveled to the locations where the various sections of the book play out—I think it would be difficult to clearly depict a place you've never experienced—landscapes you've never seen, wind you've never felt, air you've never smelled. And I also did extensive interviews with breast cancer survivors. I needed to hear from them exactly what it was like to make the journey through chemotherapy.

8.   Are any of your characters inspired by the people around you?

Not specifically. But aspects of certain people in my life did find their way into the characters in *The Book of Someday*. And now that we're talking about this, I'm realizing that one of the most complicated characters in the book is very much like someone I was close to, a very long time ago.

9. ***The Book of Someday* starts out with a dramatic opening scene; did you always know that the novel would open with Livvi hiding from her father, or did you add this in later?**

    No, the structure was what it was and never changed. Luckily for me, because I realize how much easier it made the writing process, the book was in my head, pretty much full-blown, even before I sat down to write it.

10. **Which character do you share the most in common with—Livvi, AnnaLee, or Micah? Which character are you least like?**

    I guess I can see bits and pieces of all three of them in me— parts that are good, and not so good—but it's Micah that I'm the least like. I'm not as bold as she is. Not even close.

11. **The ending is a little bit ambiguous; did you always know that it would end this way, or did you have alternate endings?**

    For me, the book was always exactly what it ended up being on the page. There was never an alternate ending. Writing this novel was an interesting experience. The story found me and presented itself in its entirety. I feel very lucky. I never had to go looking for any missing pieces. The sequences always seemed to be flowing, from beginning to end, without needing to take any detours.

12.   Did you (or do you) have your own Book of Someday like Livvi? What would you want to put at the top of your Book of Someday list?

What would I put at the top of my Book of Someday list? That's a great question. I guess if we're talking about real life, I'd want, someday, to know that I'd made a difference, had in some way made the world a better place. But if we're talking about fantasy, then someday I definitely want to be taller, at least five-eight. And I kind of like the idea of being able to write a country song. A really good one.

13.   You beautifully describe the woman in the silver dress with the pearl button shoes; where did you get the inspiration for this painting?

Now you've hit the heart of where this book came from. The woman in the pearl button shoes is someone I used to dream about when I was a child. But to this day, I still have no idea who she is. I always wanted to tell her story but could never figure out how to do it. When I came up with the plot for *The Book of Someday*, I realized I'd finally found a way to have her make sense. Whoever she is, wherever she is, I hope she approves of the context I gave her.

14.   Livvi fields some pretty interesting questions and comments during her book signing; what is the most

interesting question that you have ever answered about your writing?

Oh, that would have to be when a man at a book signing for my first novel *The Language of Secrets* wanted to know how, as a female writer, I'd managed to make Justin Fisher, the main character in the book, so completely real. He then asked me if I'd actually been a man at some point in my life. I laughed. But after a split-second of awkward silence, I realized he wasn't kidding. It was a truly bizarre moment.

15. Can you talk about Jack and why you think he has such a hard time deciding what he wants to do with his life?

There were times while I was writing Jack's chapters that my heart broke for him. His situation seemed so sad to me—a man who dreams of something he's incapable of being. What Jack desperately wants is to be a hero, but he doesn't have a hero's heart or a hero's strength. And over the years, his weakness has shredded him, made him a lost soul.

16. If you had the opportunity to go to dinner with David or Andrew, which one would you choose and why?

Well, I guess if I were in the mood for an evening of excess and excitement, I'd choose Andrew. But if what I needed was something sweeter and more meaningful, I would want to be with David.

Acknowledgments

With boundless gratitude to Alice Tasman for her patience and guidance as this book was being written—and to Shana Drehs for her brilliantly skillful editing of the completed manuscript.

With heartfelt thanks to Chrissy Blumenthal for her smart, careful notes—and to Barbara Hutchins for her invaluable research.

With deepest affection and appreciation to George Woodward, Ed Bacon, and Jon & Mary Bruno—friends whose faith in me made the writing of this book a joy.

With hugs to Julie Campoy for the scones and the cookies and the laughter.

And with love, always, to Dan—and to my extraordinary, amazing, wonderful family!

About the Author

Dianne Dixon is a screenwriter who has been nominated twice for an Emmy and is the recipient of the prestigious Humanitas Prize for outstanding work done in television. She was appointed to the position of Visiting Professor of Creative Writing at Pitzer College in Claremont, California, and has taught screenwriting at the Dodge College of Film & Media at Chapman University in Orange, California. *The Book of Someday* is her second novel.